MIAMI

Also by Pat Booth

Sparklers

Big Apple

Master Photographers

Palm Beach

The Sisters

Beverly Hills

Malibu

MIAMI

PAT BOOTH

CROWN PUBLISHERS, INC.
NEW YORK

Published by Crown Publishers, Inc., 201 East 50th Street,
New York, New York 10022.
Member of the Crown Publishing Group.

Manufactured in the United States of America

Library of Congress Cataloging-in-Publication Data
Booth, Pat.
Miami / Pat Booth. —1st ed.
p. cm.
I. Title.
PS3552.0646M5 1992 91-23490
813'.54—dc20 CIP

ISBN 0-517-58415-8

10 9 8 7 6 5 4 3 2 1

First Edition

In loving memory of Dede.
Wishing you were somehow here again.

MIAMI

1

November 1991 Miami

Christa was an animal. She looked like one. She felt like one. Backstage, wrapped tight in the cloak of heavy rock music, she paced the small space as if testing the limits of a cage. Soon she would be free, free to terrify, free to ravage, free to thrill. But now, as the awesome feeling built within her, there was nothing but the excitement, the anticipation, and the laser power of her focus. Out there, in the audience, were the men with the megabucks . . . the mountains of money that she was about to force them to make over to her. She shivered in the eighty-degree heat. Then she arched her back and pushed out her hips, sending muscle ripples down her stomach as she yawned away the tension in the moments before the appearance she already knew would be a triumph.

"Two," said the technician, mouthing the words in the tempest of sound. He held up two fingers. Christa took a deep breath. She shook her lion's mane of hair from side to side, testing the way it would swing on the catwalk. She braced her legs, feeling the delicious stretch in her taut quadriceps, the tension in the gluteals, the stirrings of an energy that was sexual. She looked into the mirror at her side and checked the visuals. Green eyes flashed back at her, a wild animal's eyes, darting, daunting, dangerous. She threw back her head and growled a laugh as she let inhibition go. Hands on the upper outer quadrants of drum-tight buttocks, her breasts pushed forward to prick the eyes of the men who would want her. Her lips were parted in a snarl of sensual hunger, and she flashed her tongue over them to make them shine brighter in the spotlights that would so soon be the fires of her forest.

"One," said the finger of the technician.

Christa was panting now, like a lioness close to the kill. She was hyperventilating on purpose, washing the carbon dioxide from her blood to increase the feeling of tension that she would transform in seconds into straight-up visual excitement. Her chest rose and fell as she fought to hang on to the feelings. Her concentration was total. She must continue to feel like this, like a goddess, the power coursing through the body that would drive men mad and women crazed with jungle-green jealousy. The sizzling, searing memories of Christa Kenwood would steam up their dull lives until they would have no choice but to bid for the part of her that was for sale. Only then would they discover that they had competition, and there would be no mercy, no prisoners in the auction that would follow.

The technician's hand was in the air. The music stopped. In the crashing silence, the excitement built. Christa braced for takeoff. Her weight was on her toes. She could feel the eagerness of the audience. There were four hundred people out there in the Star Room of the Miami Intercontinental Hotel, and nobody wanted to move, to cough, to breathe.

Down went the hand, and Christa shot forward like an arrow into a quivering, universal heart.

* * *

Peter Stein never did what crowds did. It was an article of personal faith. Now he betrayed it.

Everyone in the room took a single short sharp breath at Christa's entrance. So did the Pulitzer Prize–winning author. But already his mind was doing what it did best, analyzing, sifting, making sense of experience . . . putting feelings into words. He sat back in his chair, and he tried to remember if he had ever seen anyone as interesting. It wasn't just the startling face; the dramatic cheekbones emphasized by makeup to mimic the look of a cat, the lips bared back from milk-white teeth, the fiery green of her eyes. It wasn't the lithe feline grace of her body as it stalked the stage, flowing with the rhythm of her wild-side walk, the sinews steel-strut strong, the sunburnished skin honey-brown against the black of the diamanté-studded Lycra dress/leotard. It wasn't even her breasts, pouting and ambitious, as they thrust against the sheer material. It was her animal magnetism. This girl could hypnotize.

Peter Stein smiled. He knew a thing or two about ambition, but he had never seen it so naked and unadorned. For the last three years Christa Kenwood had been the number-one model. Almost single-handedly, she had taken the pain from the process of standing at supermarket checkout counters. Oh, there were other great models, but Christa was in a class by herself. A few years back, she had made a movie that had done gangbuster business, and then she had infuriated Hollywood by refusing to do another. Now she was here in Miami to sell a book at the book fair. The book, called simply *Christa*, was a beauty book with a difference. It encapsulated everything that the girl had learned on her climb to the top of the modeling tree. There was the Kenwood philosophy, beauty tips, Christa's diet, Christa Kenwood's new line of diamanté exercise gear that doubled as evening wear, how to turn dross into gold in terms of good looks, how to get accepted by a model agency, how to trump Trump in a deal. The gossip was that Christa was her own agent. She had apparently set up this presentation through a hotshot New York P.R. firm, and anyone who was anybody, including Mr. Peter Stein, literary hero, had turned up for her one-woman show on the strength of her name and reputation. She had shown them a little bit of everything——before and after makeup, a funny, upbeat, and curiously wise dissertation on life and how to live it, and now, as the hormone-revealing finale, she was demonstrating both her exercise gear and how to model it. Over the next few days, the book would be auctioned to the publishers who had gathered for the Miami Book Fair, one of the most important in the country. The excitement Christa had generated was immense. Peter felt certain that she would walk away with the book deal of the decade. For once in his life, the making of mere money had acquired a glamorous connotation. Was that what she wanted? Was money the open-sesame to the Kenwood heart? She for sure wanted something. From the top of her shining, backcombed hair to the red-tipped toes of her bare feet, she was a lush, voluptuous parcel of ambition. But what exactly was her dream? Why did she want so hard, when she clearly had so much? Again he smiled, because he realized that he needed to know, he, Peter Stein, whose interest in his fellow human beings was at its height when he was fast asleep.

Christa twirled in a tight pirouette as she hit the halfway stage on the catwalk and her eyes searched the spotlit audience for a face to focus on. It was an old trick of hers. She would target a single person in the crowd and then do the show entirely for them. She would read the feedback on their fascinated faces and vibe off on it, lifting both her own spirits and theirs until there was only positive reinforcement in a whirligig ride to the peak experience. Someone close was best. It didn't even have to be a man. Sometimes women were better.

There he was. He was sitting in the front row, and his smile said she had gotten him going. There was time, despite the intensity of the moment, to think about him. His eyes were big, but deep, and Christa was drawn into them. She knew instinctively that the craggy good looks, the aquiline features, the sensuous mouth, the jutting angle of a certain jaw, were not the main point of this man. His mind was, and the way to the mind was through the eyes. In the second it took to size him up, she had already started to work on him. First she targeted him, sweeping past but continuing to gaze at him, her head swiveling to the side and then behind her to hold his eyes with hers. His smile was fixing itself to his face in a way that said it was no longer his to control. He seemed to be sitting farther back in his seat to escape the beam of her interest, and yet at the same time his attention was grid-locked onto her. His attitude defined ambivalence. Hah! She had reached the end of the runway. She turned away from him, losing him on purpose.

Beneath the layers of fevered fantasy, Christa knew that this wasn't her. This was image, the persona she wore like a mask. If she was lucky and worked hard enough, it could be switched on, like now. Then it could be used to unleash the dreams that delivered the goods. Nobody wanted to know the truth about her. Nobody was interested in reality. Oh, they paid lip service to that desire. Will the real Madonna stand up? Can the genuine Marilyn please be counted? But they would never forgive you if you bored them, and showed them for a single moment that there were bits of you that were just like them. So she forced truth from the runway and cranked up illusion on the four-foot catwalk, as she searched the audience for the man to vamp.

Boom! She shot herself into him, from twenty, fifteen, ten feet. Her personality exploded around him in phosphorus starbursts. She stopped when she reached him, standing on the stage, close to him, and swaying closer. She bent at the knee. Her eyes hooked onto him, a smile of liquid sex playing around the edges of her delectable mouth. She tossed her lioness's hair, and she scratched at the air in front of his face as if her hand was a paw and her fingertips the claws of the cat she had become. All the time the green eyes transfixed him, as her body canopied over him, threatening to devour its prey in a feast of lustful longing. But, at the very moment he was supposed to squirm with both embarrassment and desire, Peter Stein's eyes closed down on her.

Christa lost him. At the beginning he had vibrated in tune to her body like a fine wineglass. Then, as if sensing the danger of her attraction, he had retreated to some safe place in his head, and blocked her out. It was not a trick that many were able to perform, and it left her out on a limb, up on the stage shining down at someone who to all intents and purposes was no longer there. She stood up, still swaying to the rhythm of the music, and she was impressed and disappointed all at the same time. She would have to move on, and she did, but his face was still clear in her mind as she retreated. The applause surged around her but Christa was no longer thinking of megabuck book deals, the triumph of her appearance, and the thrill of the ride to success . . . She was thinking of the stranger in the front row.

2

Christa stood in line, carefully incognito. She wore blue jeans, a plain white T-shirt, a pair of battered Topsiders, and no makeup. In fact, she was the real Christa Kenwood, and, a few paces ahead of her, sitting at a table piled high with books, was the real Peter Stein. It hadn't taken long for Christa to find the name of the stranger in her crowd. It had taken less time to discover that the famous author was scheduled for a book signing, and later a speech, at the Miami-Dade Community College where the major book fair events were held. It had been a shock to find out who he was, because he was someone she already admired. She had read his book, *Eclipse of the Heart,* and had enjoyed it in the way that one enjoyed cold showers, brisk walks, and programs that were good for you on public TV. Immediately she had decided to meet him face to face, and she was completely unfazed by the fact that she had all but made love to him, in public, the day before at her show. Such doubts were for lesser mortals. She hadn't even bothered to dredge up a mutual acquaintance to introduce them formally. Instead, she had simply decided to join the line at his book signing and have him sign a book for her. Full-frontal assault had always been the Christa Kenwood preferred campaign plan.

She was about fifteen feet from him now. His face made her think of Jesus, but a cross Christ rather than Christ on the cross. It was obvious that signing his books and small-talking his awestruck readers was not a job Peter Stein relished. A man had arrived at the table. He scooped up a title from the pile of books and placed it reverently before the author. Christa was near enough to hear bits of the conversation.

"To whom shall I dedicate it?" Stein's voice was modulated, tightly controlled. It was clear that even this straightforward question was a reach for the Pulitzer winner. His voice was locked behind bars of self-control. The impression lingered that Peter Stein would rather throw the book than autograph it. Christa felt the butterflies take off in her stomach. Tension clung to Stein like an aura. It was exciting ten feet from him.

"To Laura . . ." said the man.

Stein's felt pen raced across the page.

"No . . . yes . . . I mean 'to *John* and Laura,' " said the man, changing his mind.

"Can't it be 'to Laura and John?' " The Stein lips were pursed.

"John and Laura would be better. I'm a bit old-fashioned." The man laughed apologetically.

"But I've already written 'to Laura' . . . " Irritation dripped from his words.

Silence.

"Are you old-fashioned enough to buy another book?" asked the iced voice of Peter Stein.

The man shifted nervously. Christa smiled. Peter Stein looked physically fit for an author. And healthy, or at least brown, which, in Miami, were the same thing. His whole upper body was taut like the string of a bow. Broad shoulders formed the platform for a long neck, which in turn supported a fiercely intelligent face. His brown eyes darted beneath unruly, curly hair, and his features twisted that way and this in a fascinating outward demonstration of his inner emotions.

"Well?" he said.

" 'Laura and John' will be fine," said the man uncertainly.

"Laura . . . and John," said Peter Stein finally, as he scrawled the message. "Ladies first," he muttered to himself. His addendum was short, but as she heard him, Christa suddenly understood volumes about Peter Stein. For him, ladies *would* come first. He would be far from a womanizer, but he would be a man who loved women, who loved their company, their softness, their common sense. He looked tough and rangy, the very opposite of effeminate, yet there was nothing macho about him. Here was a man for whom the locker room would be a torture chamber; the Saturday ball game a monumental bore; the hairy, horny, back-slapping camaraderie of male bonding a hideous charade. Good! Excellent! Christa took a step forward. There were four or five people ahead of her.

She watched him as she waited. It was fun to watch a famous, brilliant man who could be seen, but could not see. The moment their eyes met, the rules would change. He would recognize her instantly, despite the dramatic difference in her appearance. He would remember their catwalk "meeting" and a new and far more complex game would begin.

"I detect the influence of Joyce in *Lonely Moments,*" said the next man to arrive at the Stein table.

Peter winced. It was clear he hated pretension. Then, suddenly, his lips were mischievous. They curled at the corners in an almost-smile.

"Joyce who?" he said.

Christa laughed out loud. Immediately, his eyes swiveled. They zeroed in on her. She was in his sights. His features softened the moment he saw her. Across the short distance that separated them, her laughing face melted his hard one. She saw it happen. She felt it happen. Her beauty flowed over him like surf on a beach, washing away his irritation. He smiled at her, as they both enjoyed the joke. Then he turned back to the business at hand. One thing was crystal clear. He knew she was a beautiful woman, but he had no idea she was Christa Kenwood. Her mind stopped in shock. It had never occurred to Christa that he wouldn't recognize her. Shit, she recognized *him.* She tried to rationalize it. After all, she had been in stage makeup, and in a diamanté leotard. She had been hidden behind the mask of her fame, playing the part of her public personality. Now, she was herself, and the difference was as vast as she had always intended it to be. But still she couldn't suppress the disappointment. She had given the guy her best shot, and it had obviously missed him. She smiled a rueful smile as she learned two lessons. One, the only thing worse than being universally recognized was to be ignored. Two, Mr. Peter Stein, brain box, prickly joker, and lover of women, would be no stage-door Johnny pushover.

Once more she was listening to him.

"The question of influence is so difficult, isn't it?" he said, in softer tones. "I've read Joyce, of course. Never liked him much. But then dislike is influence, isn't it? Nearly everything is."

"That's very well put," said the man, much mollified.

"Thank you," said Peter, allowing a touch of irony into his voice.

He looked up. Again he caught Christa's eyes. His brown ones sparkled. Her green ones sparkled right back.

Christa was nearly there and she knew Peter Stein was aware of it. He might not know exactly who she was, but he had been deeply touched by her beauty. Christa was sure of that. He was going through the motions of talking to his readers, but inside that tall, bright forehead, his brilliant brain would be full of her. Christa's heart quickened. She took a deep breath. The woman in front of her was gushing over Stein like a Roman fountain.

"Oh, Mr. Stein, you can't imagine what an honor it is to meet you, and I can't wait for your speech. I've read everything you've ever written, and my favorite is . . ."

He didn't cut her off. He was gentle with her, in a way that he hadn't been with the men. He thanked her graciously, and said that writers led lonely lives and lacked feedback from their readers, and how kind it was of her to take time to tell him she had enjoyed his work. He meant it, too. Christa could tell. Another angle of Peter Stein took shape . . . the lonely artist, wracked by uncertainty as he cranked out pearls for the swine; the sensitive creator who was grateful that someone had bothered to say thank you.

Christa stood by the table. He looked up. A smile lit his face.

"Why do I feel as if I know you already?" he said. His teeth were alabaster white against his mahogany suntan. She could see a little patch of hairs high up near his ear where he had forgotten to shave. One luminous eye was quite distinctly larger than the other.

"I read *Eclipse of the Heart,* so I feel I know you, too," said Christa without missing a beat. She looked right at him, not letting his eyes go. He fought to hold her gaze, but it was he who blinked. He looked down, and then back at her again. Now his smile was a little worried.

"Can one know writers by what they write?" he said. It was hardly a question.

"Whatever. I loved it." Christa wasn't going to be drawn into a debate. Something was happening here that wasn't English Literature 101.

"Is that the one you'd like me to sign?" said Peter, reaching for *Eclipse of the Heart.*

"No, I want another one. Tell me which."

She was taking control. Damn it! Why did she automatically do that with men? The strong ones didn't like it. Or rather the ones who cared about being *thought* strong didn't like it. There was a difference.

His hand hovered over the pile. It landed on one book, moved to another, went back to the original one.

He peered up at her, his head cocked to one side.

"It's not easy to know what someone else will like," he said.

"Don't worry," she laughed. "If I don't like your recommendation, I won't sue."

"*What* a relief!" He picked up *Death of a Friendship* and flicked it open. "To . . . ?"

"Christa Kenwood."

She threw down her name like a gauntlet. It was a punishment for his failure to know her. But even as she did so, there was time to wonder about her feelings. She had hardly met the guy and she wanted to *punish* him?!

His eyes narrowed. He peered at her closely.

"Good God," he said. "You're Christa Kenwood? You look . . ."

"Younger," said Christa quickly. "Models always do without makeup."

He smiled quickly. It was Christa's turn to wait. The ball was in his court.

"I was at your show yesterday," he said. It was the bare minimum reply. Was there the hint of red high up on his cheeks?

"I know. You were in the front row. I sort of picked you out. I hope you didn't mind. It makes it easier to communicate with one person, rather than the entire audience." She smiled at him. Hard. This was his punishment. She was swamping him with her up-front personality and yet at the same time she was downplaying the importance of the fashion-show "meeting."

"I'm glad to have been of some small assistance," said Peter Stein with a dry smile.

"Actually, I asked someone who you were."

"Ah!" said Peter Stein.

His smile was no longer dry.

"And then you read *Total Eclipse.*"

"No, I read that last year. So I sort of knew who you were."

She threw a leg forward, setting the angle of her butt, and pushing out her chest. Her hand flicked through her hair. It was a totally unselfconscious gesture, but it never failed. It didn't now.

"I thought your show was terrific," said Peter Stein, trying not to look at her body. "Make sure you hold out for a tip-top offer on the book."

"Thanks," she said, with a laugh and a shake of her head. God, he was attractive. He was totally in control, and yet weirdly vulnerable all at the same time.

He held his head to one side, as if debating whether or not to say something.

"Well, I never thought I'd have Christa Kenwood standing in line at one of my book signings, although in a way it makes us equals. I stood in line once to see your movie. It was excellent."

"One monkey don't stop no show," said Christa.

"You're far too young to remember Joe Tex," said Peter with a laugh.

"Harrumph!" The woman in the line behind Christa cleared her throat impatiently.

Peter and Christa exchanged glances. This couldn't be prolonged.

Peter pulled the book toward him. He wrote fast.

"To Christa Kenwood, who could stop any show, any time, anywhere . . . and who ain't no monkey. Warmest regards. Peter Stein." He pushed the book across the table to Christa.

"Are you staying for my talk?"

"For sure."

He paused. Indecision hovered across his face. Then he took the plunge.

"Listen, there's some sort of party afterward . . . that the Miami people are giving . . ."

"I know. I've been invited. I'll see you there," said Christa.

He looked surprised, then pleased, then confused again. The man who lived by words was clearly about to run out of them. "Oh, good," he said. Christa unleashed her most dazzling smile, picked up her book, and walked away from the table. She didn't even know which title it was, and she didn't care. All she knew was that the adrenaline was roaring through her body, and that she was gripped by a feeling of total unreality. What on earth was happening? Her palms were sweaty. Her heart was racing. Hell, her mouth was dry. She tried to get a bead on it. Men were never her problem. She was theirs. It had been that way from the beginning. But here she was, walking on air across a crowded room on an enchanted evening, and if her stomach hadn't been full of fluttering insects, it would have been churning on the clichés. She took a deep breath, well aware of his eyes on her back. Deep down, she knew what was going on, of course. Brilliance turned her on. An intellectual artist was just the right stuff for Christa Kenwood. She had been accepted by Brown, but she had decided against college at the last moment. It had seemed crazy to spend time and money on an education when she was being offered modeling contracts worth hundreds of thousands of dollars. So she had traded books for bucks, and had ended up with a superb brain computer but a deficiency in programming. Somehow, no amount of self-education had bridged the gap. Hence her fascination with men like Peter Stein. But that was all rationalization. The interesting question was what should she do about it? The voice over the intercom preempted her.

"Welcome to the Mitchell Wolfson campus of Miami-Dade Community College. Please take your seats in the auditorium for the address by Mr. Peter Stein. Thank you, ladies and gentlemen."

Christa merged with the throng. She felt the beads of sweat between her shoulder blades, a damp patch between her breasts. Thank God for the air-conditioning, and the low lighting in the darkened auditorium. She needed some anonymity to collect her thoughts. She settled into her seat. All around her the audience hummed with anticipation. Peter Stein was the star attraction of this, the biggest Miami Book Fair so far. Not many writers could draw this crowd—Mailer, Michener, maybe a handful of others—and all around the heavy hitters of the publishing world rubbed shoulders with the handful of locals who had been lucky enough to get tickets for the main event. Now, the auditorium quieted as a man walked onto the stage.

"Ladies and gentlemen, it is very seldom in real life that somebody needs no introduction. Such a man is Peter Stein. He has thrilled us with his words. He has held us spellbound by the brilliance of his imagination. He has touched us all with the exquisite delicacy of his compassion. Today, many of us have had a chance to meet him in person, and to experience firsthand the man who has done so much to enrich our lives. We are grateful to him for allowing us inside his mind tonight, and we are proud that he lives among us in Florida, in Key West, as a permanent reminder that great literature can and does flourish here in the Sunshine State. Ladies and gentlemen . . . Mr. Peter Stein."

Christa joined in the applause. The man on the stage looked to the wings. He held out one hand in greeting, his face wreathed in a smile of welcome. The applause roared on. But there was no Peter Stein. Christa's clapping lost its initial momentum. The smile on the face of the announcer began to freeze. His welcoming hand began to wilt. Where was the author? Several people had stopped clapping. The applause was dying. Anxiety was rising. Christa felt the tension. At any minute now, the auditorium would be plunged into an anticipatory silence. The announcer would have to fill in. Phrases would have to be dug up from somewhere. Seconds before, Peter Stein had needed no introduction. Now it looked as if he might require a very long introduction indeed.

"Mr. Peter Stein," said the announcer loudly, a second time. It was no longer a ringing welcome. It sounded instead like a desperate request. Every eye in the room was focused on stage entrance right. And every eye in the room was wrong.

Peter Stein came in from the left. He walked fast, head down, as if intent on avoiding an acquaintance in the street. He headed for the back of the announcer, who stood by the central lectern. Christa caught sight of him out of the corner of her eye. Peter Stein reached the announcer, who had no idea he was there, and he tapped the unsuspecting man on the shoulder. The announcer spun around, his face registering shock, confusion, relief.

"Oh, there you are," said the announcer.

"Here I am," said Peter Stein.

Christa clapped a hand to her mouth. It was pure music hall. It was so funny she could hardly believe that it hadn't been done on purpose. One or two people joined in her laughter, and those not brave enough to laugh openly, smiled broadly. But Peter Stein did not laugh. Nor did he smile. He placed a single sheet of paper on the lectern and said to the announcer, "Thank you."

Christa could have sworn that he had said "good-bye." The announcer had been dismissed. He hurried offstage, visibly relieved that his ordeal was over.

"Perhaps the most important thing that a novel can do," said Peter Stein in a loud, clear voice, "is to surprise."

He had them. All of them. He didn't spell out what he had done. He didn't need to. His delayed entrance had been a demonstration of his opening remark. His novels had surprised them. So had the novelist. It was brilliant. Christa could hardly believe it. She looked around her. In his absence, he had been playing his audience like a fish on a line. Mild anticipation of a pleasurable learning experience had merged into anxiety. Anxiety had been replaced by humor. Humor had hovered briefly on the borders of superior patronization. Then, at the crack of the lion tamer's whip, the literati had jumped collectively through the fiery hoop. Now he had them where he wanted them, listening in total awe to the sound of their artistic master's voice.

"Wow!" muttered Christa to herself. She dissected him with her eyes. He stood bolt upright, as if at attention, and he stared into the bowels of the room at some fixed point that instinctively she knew was not a face. He was there, but he wasn't really there, in the way, perhaps, that Moses had not really been there when he had brought the tablets down from the mountain. He appeared like a messenger from God, a channeler speaking from some distant and superior civilization. The impression gave an enormous authority to his words, coating them in a liquid charisma that made them absolutely unforgettable.

"We are frightened of surprises in life, but also we want what we fear, so we look for surprise in books."

Christa nodded. It didn't matter whether or not his remark was true. What mattered was that she knew she would remember it. And that was a function, not of his words, but of the personality of the man who spoke them. He was inside her head. It was the supreme art of the teacher. Peter Stein cared. Peter Stein believed. Peter Stein's concentration on what he was saying was total. Christa quivered with excitement in her seat as she listened to him.

"And surprise takes many forms. The unexpected. The unexperienced. The out-of-context. Surprise may be the familiar when the exotic was anticipated. It may be the quiet, when you were braced for the storm. And surprises come in different sizes, the shock of the axe's blade on the nape of a neck, the gentle jar of an unusual word . . ."

He was looking for her. Somehow, in the vast audience he had found her. She was absolutely sure of it, and yet she knew it was impossible. It was too dark. There were too many people. But his eyes were shining into hers. He was speaking to *her* about surprise, and to nobody else. Had he turned the tables on her as revenge for her treatment of him at *her* show? Then she turned sideways. The woman next to her was leaning forward in rapt attention. So was the girl on her other side. Christa took a deep breath. It was obvious they were feeling the same things she was feeling. Mmmmm! Peter Stein could speak to everyone at once. The path to his affections would not be a road less traveled.

"Surprises can be as cheap and as stupid as the cry of 'fire' in a crowded auditorium. They can be as valuable and as uplifting as the sudden realization that you yourself are worthy and wonderful . . ."

"I want to know you," said the voice in Christa's mind. "I want to know you and be with you so that you can surprise me and I can surprise you. I want to lie down beside you and drown in your thoughts, and your ideas, and your creation."

She took a deep breath, but her internal voice hadn't finished. "Watch out, Christa," it said. "You're falling in love."

3

The wall of sound slapped Christa in the face as she stepped from the corridor onto the rooftop terrace of the Park Central Hotel. She stood beneath the arbor of flowers, which served as the entrance to the party, and she breathed in the warm air, heavy with the smell of night-blooming jasmine. It seemed God had forgotten it was November. Here was a preview of summer, and all around her the crazy, over-the-top colors of the partygoers howled in harmony with the blood orange of the sun as it set behind the shimmering skyscrapers of downtown Miami.

Her practiced eye took in the scene. She had been down here for three months now, and she was getting used to the uninhibited energy of South Beach parties, but this one looked like a Louis Canales/Tony Goldman special. Music was by Vesper Sparrow. The raunchy all-girl rock band was blasting it out from a raised dais in the center of the room and the sound waves threaded into the heat wave, raising the temperature, and hiking expectations as the young warriors of SoBe slipped into top party gear. Christa took a bead on the crowd. It was the usual suspects, but with topspin. Languid artists lounged by pony-tailed publicists. Frenetic nightery entrepreneurs talked double-time into the faces of sweating journalists. Owl-faced New York publishers wandered bemused and excited among the muscled males and the tanned, super-fit girls of the Miami modeling scene. Earth tones were forbidden. Color ruled. Nothing succeeded like excess. Skirts were belts, boys were topless, and the dancing was competition aerobic. It looked, to Christa, like SoHo on speed.

Jasmine, heat, and thrills weren't the only things in the air. There was also the mouth-watering aroma of food. All around the edge of the terrace were small casitas offering an array of Miami delicacies. It was the new movement in cooking. Some called it New World Cuisine, others Floribbean, but whatever it was, it was both different and "now." Christa walked over to one stall. It was pure Little Havana, the kind of casita you found during the Calle Ocho street festival when a million Cubans ate, drank, and conga-ed for a week. Here were plantains, and beef tongue Creole; a pot roast simmering with sausage, fried veal and pork; paellas; baked chickens and piles of mixed black beans. Next door was the fancy stuff. It was a mango mélange, a passion fruit play, a citrus circus. The trestles were groaning with dishes in which the exotic fruits of the tropics had been drummed into service to bend palates and melt minds. Papaya, guava, kumquat, breadfruit, and yucca merged in happy, but unlikely combination with chicken and pheasant, with venison and sautéed grouper. Christa's stomach moaned in anticipation, but there were other things to think about at the party, and the first was a drink.

The waiters had clearly been recruited at one of the Suzanne Bartsch drag parties at Warsaw, the Beach's hottest club. The "girl" who now appeared at Christa's shoulder wore Op Art earrings over an extravagant Carmen Miranda gown. "Her" beehive hair was piled high and filled with bits and pieces of bric-a-brac that glinted in the strobe lights that were playing over the band.

"Can you get me a banana daiquiri?" asked Christa.

"I can get you a dyke with a banana if you want one, dear," said the apparition with the shake of a swan's neck.

Christa laughed, relaxing into the irreverence of the city that was now hers. The drink, when it came, was cool and frothy. A heavily scented white gardenia floated on its surface. She looked around her. There were several people she knew, but they could wait. She wanted to be by herself for a bit longer, alone in the crowd, the voyeur who could pick and choose. She wandered to the edge of the terrace and leaned out over the edge of the building. The rooftops of the Art Deco hotels stretched away before her, suffused from below by rich pastel shades of neon. The sun was now a burning memory, but over on the mainland the remains of its color singed the outline of the vast CenTrust tower and the Southeast Building, silhouetting them against the blackened blue of the sky. Cars, fireflies in the darkness, snaked across the causeway that joined the Beach to Miami; fairy lights twinkled on the cruise ships in their slips on Government Cut; the houses on Star Island, Christa's new home, gleamed against the dark waters of Biscayne Bay. She turned to her other side, toward the ocean, from which the warm breeze came. The moon was out, and its beams danced across the wide beach, painting the fronds of the palm trees in a phosphorus glow. Two luminous kites moved in clever synchronicity above the caramel sand, and Christa could just make out the two men who operated them. They stood together, their arms moving in intricate rhythms, muscle and bone seemingly controlled by a single mind. As Christa watched, a girl skated along the walkway of Lummis Park on purple roller blades. She moved slowly, lithe, liquid, her long legs stroking the sidewalk in what looked like a caress. Her mind was lost in Walkman sound as she glided along the edge of the beach, and Christa knew she would be dreaming Miami dreams, and that her beauty would make them all come true.

With an effort, Christa tore herself away from the visual banquet. Why didn't the world know the truth about Miami? Why did everyone think Cuban, and crime, drugs, death, and old age? All that had changed. This was no longer Joan Didion's Miami. It was no longer Allman's City of the Future. The future was now. Miami had awakened and, tremulous in the sunrise of its brave new world, it waited shyly for America to stop sleeping and to find it in the dawn. But there was a part of Christa that wanted it to remain a secret. While the unrecognized revolution unfolded, she, as one of the cognoscenti, could enjoy it. When the news broke, the developers and the businessmen would arrive by the planeload and the magic would crescendo, sicken, and so die, strangled by the wild exuberance of its own success. But that would be then, and this was now, and she was here. And somewhere out there in the crowd was the poet with the haunted eyes, in her town, on her turf, and to some delicious extent at a disadvantage to her. She walked to the edge of the dance floor, knowing he would not be there among the athletes of the night. Paradoxically, she didn't want to find him yet. She wanted to savor the thought of the moment, and to enjoy the anticipation of him as a special treat. She didn't want to rip the paper from an instant present. Instead, she wanted to turn it in her hand, to rattle it, to wonder for luscious minutes just exactly what she would find. She smiled. Peter Stein as a gift was an unusual idea. If he could know what she was thinking he would be horrified. Or would he? One knew so little about people . . . almost as little as one knew about oneself.

It was nearly time for something to eat, but, as she wandered toward the food, her eye was caught by a stall that offered, not food, not drink, but the future. STARLADY read the sign above, and below was a character who lived up to her billing. Christa recognized her at once. She had seen her snorkeling in the ocean, a great whale of a woman floating along as she searched for nonexistent fish on the sandbar off South Beach. She had seen her cycling, too, billowing along like a Dutch sailing barge, her wide-brimmed hat a capacious jib, the wide open spaces of her steppelike mammary land a more than adequate mainsail on her Ocean Drive voyage. And Christa had seen her in Sempers on *karaoke* night, her huge lungs puffed up like a prima donna's at Carnegie Hall as she belted out musical comedy that she would have preferred to have been taken seriously. Now here she was in a new role. Starlady.

"Hi," said Christa.

"Well, hello, dear. My goodness, you're living dangerously tonight."

"I am?" said Christa with a laugh. "You mean daring to say hello to the Starlady."

"Daring to say hello to someone rather more exciting, I sense."

Her arms were the size of Christa's thighs. Her hat was tasseled. What looked like ribbons cascaded down from an industrial-strength bra. But her smile was real. And her mind-reading act seemed mysteriously on target.

"Are you predicting a tall, dark stranger for me?" Christa laughed.

"We don't do those anymore in the age of AIDS, dear. They went out in the sixties when two very beautiful people were dreaming you up."

"Thank you. Can you do my fortune? Do you need to know my sign?"

"Heavens, no. I don't do sun-sign astrology, dear. It's bullshit. Anyway, any old idiot can see you're a Taurus."

"Not bad . . . a one-in-twelve chance," said Christa, suddenly unsettled. In the normal way she was about as metaphysical as a boot in the butt, but the Starlady had hit the target twice.

"Ah, a disbeliever. Much more fun," said the Starlady with a kindly laugh.

"So what *do* you do, I mean in terms of prediction?"

"I talk possibilities, likelihoods, influences. I believe we can change the future, but we have to try. I'm allowed to see the future through a glass darkly. It's my gift."

"Oh," said Christa. She felt nervous. It was rubbish, of course. But rubbish could play on your mind. To be standing here talking to somebody like this was itself an exercise in superstition. If you were told your future, would you be taken hostage by it?

"Have I seen you in Key West?" said the Starlady, her expression quizzical.

"What about Key West?" snapped Christa, too quickly.

"Not much, dear. I used to live there, that's all. No, wait a minute, that's not all. That's not all at all."

Christa stood stock still.

"Listen, dear, I don't want to sound dramatic, but I feel there's danger for you in Key West."

"Danger? What do you mean, danger?" It wasn't at all what Christa had expected, or rather wanted, to hear.

"Have you ever been there?"

"Once, twice. Spring break. A weekend at the Pier House."

"I used to do fortunes at the Pier House."

"What about the danger?"

"Oh, don't worry about it, dear. Probably a jellyfish sting, or a bad stone crab. Danger covers a broad spectrum in my psyche. Just be a bit careful in the lower Keys. I'm afraid my psyche's not too hot on defining city limits, either."

She gave a cheerful laugh, but Christa could swear she was covering something up.

Or was that, too, a part of the Ides of March act? Christa stood her ground, an anxious smile on her face. She wanted chapter and verse on the danger. But perhaps that was what she was *supposed* to want. By asking more questions, she would be revealing interest and that would put her in a subservient position. She decided to cut it off there and then . . . at the hauntingly unfinished business of unspecified danger in Key West . . . where she knew Peter Stein lived. She braced herself to turn away.

"Is that Christa Kenwood?" said the voice at her shoulder.

She turned toward the besuited man who hovered at her side.

"Lewis Heller! What a surprise! I didn't think you were coming to Miami. Why the hell didn't you come a day earlier? You missed my presentation."

"But not the excitement it generated, dear. There's a feeding frenzy out there. From what I hear, you're going to get silly money."

"There's nothing silly about money, Lewis." Christa laughed.

Heller laughed, too. He rubbed his hands together as if he were in the grease-manufacturing business. He was formidably smooth, everyone's brother Esau, from his patent-leather hair to the soles of his apparently varnished black lace-up shoes. In the publishing industry, in which he played the role of rapacious robber baron, Heller had once been described as an "oil well waiting to happen." Christa had met him several times in New York, and he had floated several indifferent publishing projects at her as a smokescreen for a baser motive that could best be summarized as "bed." She had never particularly liked him, but he was amusing, and powerful, and therefore potentially useful. People who were all those things were never all bad to Christa Kenwood.

"So you're not bidding, Lewis," said Christa.

"Got crushed in the rush, dear. It's Gadarene swine time. I heard Globe were getting ready to make *complete* fools of themselves. Seven figures, dear. Crazy, but I couldn't be happier for you."

Christa clapped her hands together in glee. She knew the interest in her book was phenomenal, but it was nice to hear it from Lewis Heller, the equivalent of the horse's mouth. And a million bucks was definitely above her wildest expectations.

"Well, I'll know tomorrow. The deadline is five o'clock."

"Get the champagne in, and expect the big offers at five to five," said Lewis. "Did you go to Stein's talk?" he added, changing the subject.

"Yes, did you?" It wasn't the moment to blush, but Christa managed it. Luckily, it was lost to the beady eyes of the publisher in the Day-Glo colors of the party.

"Oh yes. Oh yes. Mr. Peter Stein gives good verbals, doesn't he? I heard him once before. Not a stupid man . . . dear me, no . . . but rather *scary*, don't you think? I mean, *unsettling*. He's the kind of person who interferes with the digestive juices at lunch."

Lewis Heller made a moue of distaste. Anything that would disturb the oleaginous progression of his famous Four Seasons lunches would indeed represent a Maalox moment.

"I met him at the signing before his talk. I thought he was nice," said Christa, careful to mute her enthusiasm.

"Good God! 'Nice'? I'm sure Peter Stein's never been called that before. Nice! Goodness, Christa. Only you. Only you."

"What do you mean?" said Christa with one of her special smiles.

"Well, he's tricky, isn't he? A difficult man. Well known to be. Lives for his work and all that stuff. You know, suffers for his art. Cares deeply. Not much of a sense of humor. I mean, I sat next to him at a dinner once, and I was rattling away about one of his books . . . quite complimentary, nothing rude . . . and he turned to me and he said, 'Do you know what Marcel Duchamp said? He said "Those of you who cannot see, spare a thought for those of us who can." ' He said it just like that. Bloody rude, I thought. Still, I wouldn't mind having him on my list. Those blockheads who publish him wouldn't know a blockbuster if it sat on their faces. I could double his sales. Not that he'd let me . . . the pompous boor."

"I'm rather drawn to people who are obsessed," said Christa.

"Then you must like me. I'm obsessed with you." Heller laughed easily.

"Of course I like you, Lewis. Everybody likes you. I'm sure even Mr. Stein does." She couldn't keep away from him.

"Well, I'm famished. Shall we go and find something to eat?" Lewis Heller eyed a hovering drag queen waiter with suspicion. He'd have liked a drink, but the distaste of one extrovert for another was strong enough to steer him toward a nearby food booth.

It was a conch fest. There were vast steaming bowls of Bahamian conch chowder; sizzling conch steaks nestling on beds of Key limes; conch fritters with chili sauce; conch salads in half avocados, mounds of conch seviche on carpets of lettuce, cucumber, alfalfa sprouts, and Bermuda onions.

"Heavens, I'm going to conch out," said Lewis with a laugh. "I suppose all this is in honor of Mr. Stein's Key West abode."

Christa piled a plate high with marinated conch.

"Why do so many writers live in Key West?" she said, forcing herself not to ask "Why does Peter Stein live in Key West?" The word *danger* was scurrying around in her mind like a mouse.

"It's the end of the line where the dreams begin."

"That's rather poetic, Lewis."

"I pinched it from Thomas Sanchez."

"I wonder who he pinched it from."

"Precisely my own view of art, Christa. Something borrowed, something new. Never quite sure what all the fuss is about. At the end of the day, everything has been said before."

"What Sanchez *actually* said was 'Key West is the end of the American road, but also the beginning of the American dream,' " said the acid voice of Peter Stein. "I think Sanchez's version is rather better, don't you?"

They both spun around. The writer stood behind them. He was looking at Heller, his face full of scorn. Now he turned slowly to Christa and his face softened, as it had softened earlier when he had first caught sight of her at the signing of his books.

"Ah, Mr. Stein," said Lewis Heller. "Ah. Ah . . ." he petered out, uncharacteristically lost for words. A reference to their last meeting was not a conversational option. With regard to form, if not to content, this exchange of "pleasantries" promised to be an action replay of their first unfortunate encounter.

Stein ignored him.

"You've got to try the seviche. I make one just like it." He coughed suddenly, putting his hand to his mouth. It was extraordinary. When he had spoken to Heller seconds earlier, he had been totally in control, patronizing, socially merciless. Now, in the time it had taken to transfer his gaze, he was suddenly ill at ease, vulnerable, touchingly insecure. As if to cover his confusion, he reached for Christa's plate. He moved to the display, spooned a great scoop of seviche onto her plate and handed it back to her.

"There!" he said.

She smiled and dipped a fork into it, trying it.

"Mmmmmm. It's delicious. Lemon juice, red peppers, salt, pepper . . . sugar?"

"Key limes are the key, and Tabasco, jalapeños, a cup of coconut milk."

"So you're a cook, too?"

"Oh yes. Cooking comes second." He smiled a little-boy smile, pleased that she liked the seviche, pleased that he had had a chance to tell her about his culinary skills.

"Beware of Proust," said Heller with a vengeful smile. "Remember? 'All men end up doing the thing at which they are second best.' " He didn't wait for the Stein riposte. "Listen, you two, I'll see you later.

Got to go and say hello to Susan Magrino and find out who everyone is. See you later, Christa. Good-bye, Mr. Stein. Wonderful speech. Oh, yes, yes . . ." Lewis Heller wafted away from the potential conflict.

"Do you know that man?" said Peter.

"Not very well. A bit. Do you? He's a publisher, a successful one."

"He makes a lot of money."

"Why do I get the feeling that you're not much in favor of that?"

"Are you? You turned your back on Hollywood."

"Oh yes, I did, didn't I? I spurned the American dream that Sanchez found at the end of the American road."

"One mustn't confuse dreams with nightmares."

"Aren't nightmares just bad dreams?"

Peter Stein smiled as the semantics thickened. This girl was both clever and gorgeous.

It wasn't as rare a combination as people imagined, but it was always wonderful when you discovered it.

"Do you live down here, in Miami?" He cut across the conversation. He wanted to know more about Christa Kenwood.

"Yes. I've taken a house on Star Island. I've been here about three months."

"That makes you a native. You've come at the right time. Miami's on the move."

"That's what I think. It's been reborn. Lots of opportunities. It's fun, too, although I'm afraid I've reached the age where 'fun' is pretty hard work."

"How refreshing to hear someone like you saying something like that. I couldn't agree more. When I say things like that, everyone thinks, 'miserable fool.' Nobody could possibly think that about you."

"Thank you," said Christa. The blush was back. Her cheeks were burning. "Anyway, this evening is fun. This party is fun. I'm enjoying myself."

"I do believe I am, too." He laughed from the back of his throat and a wide-open smile lit up his suntanned face.

They were saying things to each other, but already they were meaning more.

Christa tried to sort out her thoughts. She had spent perhaps a total of five minutes in conversation with this man, but already she felt she could write a chapter about him. She had the overwhelming feeling that, at the deepest level of his being, Peter Stein was a soul mate. On the surface they were opposites, but somewhere down there, where his essence flowed, the river of her life merged with his. They were both deeply serious people, obsessed with goals, with winning, and being seen to win. That was what they shared. She could see it in his haunted eyes, and in the subterranean meanings that clung to his words. And of course it had been in the book of his she'd read, and it was in his reputation, and in the things that Lewis Heller had said about him. Those remarks had been intended to demean Peter Stein in Christa's eyes, but, instead, they had increased his attraction. But if, in their hearts, they played the same tune, they were playing at different speeds and with different instruments. That was the source of the delicious tension. Christa felt that at every second she was on the verge of having a fight with him. She had but to utter one wrong word, one misplaced sentence, one unworthy sentiment, and Mr. Peter Stein would not let it pass. He might try, but he'd blow a gasket in the process. Speaking his mind might not be a pleasure for him, but it would be an absolute necessity. And, strangely, she didn't fear him or his rapier tongue. In fact there was a part of her that longed to test herself against him. A perverse portion of her could hardly wait to see the fire flash and the sparks fly right here on the rooftop as the blazing sun sank in the marmalade haze, and the rock music raged through the warm night air.

"Ah, Peter, there you are," said a nervous-looking man in white shirtsleeves. A pudgy hand clasped the author's arm as if the newcomer instinctively knew that his prey would try to escape. "I've got some people from the Arts Council who are dying to meet you, and I've promised, so help me out, okay?"

Christa saw the look of horror flit across the Stein face. It was difficult to say what exactly had caused it—the touch of male flesh, always anathema to a man who deeply loved women; the thought of the collective Arts Council members dying in dozens from their absurd desire to meet him; the realization that he was about to be separated from her? The last thought felt best. She smiled at him. "I hope you find me again," said her expression. "I like to finish what I start."

He put out his hand to her, forcing his captor to let go of it. She put out hers to his. There was time to wonder what his flesh would feel like. Her mind had slowed down. She was aware of the excitement in her. This would be the first time they had touched, and if seeing was believing, touching was the truth.

So it was. His hand melted into hers, neither firm nor soft, just there, already a part of her. His eyes probed hers, speaking to her, and Christa throbbed with the illicit pleasure of the innocent goodbye. He squeezed her hand, as convention allowed, but there was poetry in the pressure, and he lingered longer than manners permitted. Christa prayed he would never let go. She fought to make her own hand as eloquent in the clasp as his, and she tried to promise him things that she hardly dared to dream about. Her heart was racing. Her breath came fast through lips parted in a smile of farewell that was also the smile of the future. And at the bottom of her, at her core, in her heart and in all the other places that knew such things, Christa Kenwood was full to the brim with the realization that one fine day they would be lovers.

4

Early Summer 1992 Palm Beach

"Steve, can you count to three and then shoot? I can't keep my eyes open for long."

Christa took a deep breath and her breasts broke the surface of the sea. She angled her face into the sunlight, eyes closed, and she felt its heat on her skin. Beneath her feet the sand was firm and the ocean in which she stood was warm as baby's milk. She tried to suppress her irritation by concentrating on the soothing sensations that wrapped her body like a womb. Photographers often made this mistake. They were so busy composing the picture that they forgot the model's problems. Direct sunlight made her squint, which meant a wasted shot, quite apart from the discomfort.

"Sorry, sweetheart, I keep forgetting you're human like the rest of us." Steve Pitts laughed. Christa was the only model in the world who could tell him what to do without getting her head bitten off. It wasn't just that she was numero uno. It was because she was bright, ballsy, and beautiful as hell; because she was more talented than anyone had the right to be; and because she wasn't afraid of him. Nearly everyone else in the business was, and Steve liked it that way.

"Now, what was it you wanted?" he continued. "One, two, three, and watch the birdie. Goodness, isn't this fun? Photography by numbers. Think where I'd be today if I'd thought of this in the beginning." His tone was sarcastic. Christa was his friend and he hadn't many of those, but friends had to be kept in line.

"You could always count in Mandarin, dear, if you wanted to be less banal." Christa laughed as she fought back at him.

"Don't speak the lingo, angel. Never had a Chinese boyfriend. Now Swahili, *that* would bring back the memories. Some say the African Queen was my finest hour."

The most famous photographer in the world stuck a hand on his hip and struck a pose. Everyone laughed; the *Vogue* fashion editor, not widely known for her sense of humor; the two assistants who held the reflector boards that focused the early morning light on the breathtaking Kenwood profile; the assorted hairdressers, makeup artists, and stylists who thronged the edge of the North End beach.

Christa smiled. She was enjoying this. She had forgotten the camaraderie, the back-breaking hard work, the pure physical satisfaction of a shoot. You gave your all for a specified period of time, and the joy of the job was that it had a beginning, a middle, and an end. She could actually see the fruits of her labor in the finished picture. It was so unlike the open-ended commitment to a business. Since she'd given up modeling to start her own model agency, she'd been walking a treadmill from which there seemed to be no escape. One of her girls had gotten sick, and it had been impossible to find a replacement in the time available. So, unwillingly, Christa had agreed to come out of retirement just this one time. Now she was glad she hadn't turned down Steve Pitts's anguished request.

"Am I too low in the water?" she asked. The diversion was over. Once again she was focusing on the job at hand, like the supreme professional she was. Models were silent screen actresses. Christa was asking for direction.

"No, you're beautiful as you are. Look proud. Look distant. Like a figurehead on a sailing ship. Head up a bit. Catch the light. That's it. Perfect. One. Two. Three."

Steve Pitts crouched low in the surf, as he angled himself for the shot. The magic-hour sunshine screamed in, its spears of light deflecting from the haughty angles of Christa's face. The brightness flowed over the shining wetness of her blond hair. It cascaded from her cheekbones, and bathed the strength of her jaw, and it lingered lovingly at her moist, high-gloss lips. Girls weren't Steve Pitts's bag, but he had been closer to the more beautiful ones than any other man on earth, and he had to admit that Christa Kenwood at sunrise took the cake. She was a dream on the shimmering surface of the sea. It wasn't just the powerful swimmer's shoulders; the surprising contrast of full, firm breasts, the rock-hard butt above the shapely, platform legs—it was her charisma. You knew the girl had it all, and the smoldering luminescence of her smile, the patina of her honey-baked skin, the dancing elegance of her constantly moving limbs, were just the packaging for the impossible-to-pass-by personality that sent the magazines flying from the racks in the bookstores and supermarkets of the world. The day she had retired had been a black one for all lovers of beauty, and Pitts was still hugging himself inside for his brilliance in persuading her to return to work to avert a deadline crisis for the *Vogue* swimsuit layout. It was like dying, and then being told by God you could return to life for a single day. Ten years of Christa Kenwood pictures would have to be concentrated into this last mind-bending photo session.

"Not too *Sports Illustrated,* Steve," said a thin, petulant voice from behind.

The titless wonder who spoke was the much feared fashion editor of the world's most prestigious magazine. Her tortured, dieted stick-like body made Olive Oyl look like a Rubens lady, as, through mean lips, she mouthed her request like a curse in church.

The frown that scudded across Christa's face was a cloud in a clear blue sky. She had nothing against *Sports Illustrated.* She'd done four covers for it, which was more than Elle Macpherson. It was the connotations of the remark. She was acutely aware that in fashion photography there were horses for courses. In their annual swimwear edition, *Sports Illustrated* went for overt sexuality as it aimed foursquare at the jocks who were the majority of its subscribers. *Vogue,* in contrast, prided itself on its avant-garde approach to what it liked to consider visual art. It cheerfully paid hundreds of thousands of dollars to photographic supermen like Steve because the finished result would be on the cutting edge of trend and a million miles from cheesecake. The insinuation was that Christa had forgotten who she was working for. Or, worse, that she had lost the knack during her year's retirement from modeling, and was now incapable of rising to the level of sophistication that *Vogue* demanded of its models.

Steve Pitts spun around in the sea like a whirlpool. His face registered instant outrage. He had been insulted. Christa had been insulted. Blood would now be spilled. That the Voguette was a power source in the industry didn't matter. He was too talented and too famous to have to think about things like that.

But Christa was there first.

"Are you worried about my breasts?" she asked with asplike innocence.

Olive Oyl *was* worried about the Kenwood breasts, but not because they would look out of place in *Vogue.* What worried her about them was that *she* did not possess them. Getting called "sir" by store clerks was wearing a bit thin. Models got under her skin, period, but almost invariably they were flawed. If perfectly beautiful, which was rare, then at least they would be stupid, or lacking in life, or poor, or socially beyond the pale. By concentrating on their deficiencies, jealousy could usually be kept caged. Christa, however, had unleashed the green-eyed monster and now it was on the rampage in the mind of the fashion editor. Christa was a physical 10, up to and including the trademark beauty spot below her belly button. She was rich. The Revlon contract had paid her three million dollars a year, and the advance on her book had come in at a cool million. It had been more than enough to finance the opening of her model agency, which would soon be competing with Ford, Wilhelmina's, and Elle. She was Social Register aristocratic. Her parents had been Old Guard Palm Beachers, and the now rented Kenwood North Ocean Boulevard home was just visible through the sawgrass of the dunes a mile up the beach. And it wasn't merely that she was loaded, grand, and beautiful. She was sparky, too, a live charm wire that lit up life around her. That was the hardest burden of all to bear for the plain fashion guru with the cold-broccoli personality.

But now a Siberian chill had descended on the beach. Instantly the fashion editor realized her mistake. The angst within her had bubbled out before her brain had been able to censor it. She attempted to retreat.

"No, of course I wasn't worried about your breasts, Christa. It's just that with swim stuff one has to be so careful, and you're so . . . well . . . fit . . . I mean, you work out . . ."

Christa laughed at the girl's confusion.

"Don't worry. No offense taken. I'll just strut my usual stuff and we'll leave it to good old Steve to rise above the level of pinup pix and *Sports Illustrated* staff photographers. Do you think you can water me down, sexually, Steve? You've been doing it to all the other girls for years."

Christa had taken pity on the fashion editor. Steve could go ballistic, and then he could only be handled by the strong and the brave. She was providing a diversion.

"Listen, dear, watering you down sexually would need more liquid than there is in this goddamn ocean. You're enough to make Dick Whittington turn. You, my love, are single-handedly responsible for the prevalence of the sin of Onan in the Western Hemisphere. It's a wonder the entire male college population isn't blind by now, or at least so weak they'd go up with the blind cord. Now, you horrid little vamp . . . head up and one, two, three . . ."

Christa giggled in delight. Steve was cooking with gas. He loved the backtalk. Unlike many other photographers, repartee relaxed him. His talent needed to be diluted. Now she could feel the energy that was always present in the best photo sessions. He was feeding from her. She was being charged by the current that flowed from him, as his clicking shutter orchestrated the sinuous movements of her body. She was losing herself in the moment, writhing in the sunbeams, twisting her limbs against the warm water, hardly aware of the beauty she was creating. Over the years she had practiced all the expressions and choreographed all the poses. Now she could fake sincerity and manufacture the natural without giving it a second thought. Few people understood the hard work that had gone into making this seem easy. It was the reason why it was uncrowded at the top of the modeling Mount Olympus where Christa lived.

As the sun rose, casting harsher shadows, the diffuse mystery light of the early morning began to disappear. Steve Pitts wasn't a Helmut Newton. He disliked the harsh reality of mere daylight, preferring to weave his visual spells at dawn and dusk when God was at work with his paint box and the earth and sky glimmered with an other-worldly glow. Christa knew, almost to the second, when he would call for the day's recess.

"I think we've lost it, boys and girls," he said at last.

His shoulders sagged. His thin arm fell to his side, the lens of the Nikon resting against the blue denim of his faded, rolled-up jeans. The cable was conducting the electricity of creation no longer, and he seemed suddenly drained as he smiled across ten feet of glassy sea at Christa.

She smiled back, knowing how he felt, feeling it herself, this little death at the end of art. She knew it had been good, very good, but was it on the film? That was all that mattered now, and the contacts wouldn't be seeable until tomorrow.

"You think we got it, Stevie?"

"It was you and me, darling. Can there be any doubt?"

"Not a lot." Christa laughed as she walked through the water toward him. The others were still there, but for all practical purposes they had gone. These two old friends had grown together on memories. This was another in the making. It was Christa's last modeling performance and she vowed there wouldn't be another. Hers would be no bullfighter's "final" farewell, no boxer's "last" exit, no superannuated pop-group's "ultimate" mass mind-grope. This truly was the end of the line . . . and Christa couldn't imagine a better finale. She was here, in Palm Beach, where she had survived her childhood. And she was with the brilliant photographer who had shown her the fun of a world that her WASP-ish family had never begun to understand.

He hugged her tight as she reached him. In the early days, she had been his protégée, and he had been her mentor. But in those days, he, too, had been climbing the lower rungs of the career ladder. They had grown together, learning from each other, and now it was difficult to know who had been responsible for whose success. Was Bailey a Shrimpton creation, or vice versa? Had Penn invented Lisa Fonssagrives, or were such relationships symbiotic, synergistic, each giving to the other, each essential, until the whole was infinitely greater than the sum of the individual parts.

"Just like the old times, no?" Steve gave voice to their thoughts.

"You'd think it would get easier," said Christa wryly. It was true. Over the years, she and Steve had stood knee deep in seven seas. There wasn't a pose she hadn't used, an expression she hadn't tried. And he had seen every possible permutation of light and shadow, experimented with each conceivable combination of lens, film, and camera. Still, it was difficult. Still, it was the hardest work. Still, there were the doubts that the shot was in the can and that the beauty had been captured on the celluloid. It seemed so unfair. Surely experience should mean that you didn't have to try so hard. But that was one of life's cruel jokes. The moment you slacked it showed in the work, and that meant that you had peaked and the vista stretching before you would no longer be the challenging upward slope of the mountain. Instead it would be the precipitous decline into the valley of career oblivion.

"What gets easier," said Steve, "is spending the loot, dear. I remember when the IRS, plastic surgeons, and podiatrists were just a gleam in my mind's eye."

"Steve, you *haven't!* I mean, plastic surgery . . ."

"I most certainly *have,* darling. If you don't use it, you lose it, heart-throb. And, having lost it, you have to get it back. I'm stitched up tighter than a mail bag at San Quentin. What do you think?"

He threw back his head and brushed graying hair from his temples. Two tiny scars said he wasn't joking. Christa peered at them closely.

"Jeez! Steve. You don't look any different."

"That's why I mortgaged my house to pay for the goddamn surgery, love. You're not supposed to look any different. I'm not trying to escape a murder one, and fool the viewers on 'Unsolved Mysteries.' I'm merely trying to fight the good fight against anno domini and keep nausea at bay among my younger friends. It's the very least an old poodle faker can do."

"What the hell's a poodle faker?"

"Oh, I don't know . . . it's a British expression for the kind of guys who send flowers, smell too good by half, and wear those silk eye masks to keep out the light at night."

Christa laughed.

"Did it hurt?"

"Not the operation. That was rendered painless by Steve Hoefflin and the first-growth claret in the Hermitage. The tab, however, was the purest agony."

Together they walked back to the beach, arm in arm, scattering scurrying crabs over the sand.

"Steve, are you busy right now? Do you fancy a late breakfast/early lunch at Green's? The Catholics ought to be out of there by now. There's something I've been wanting to talk to you about." Christa suppressed the pang of guilt. Agreeing to come out of retirement for the Pitts/*Vogue* shoot had not been totally without an ulterior motive. Okay, the girl they'd booked had canceled, but there were always other models. She'd wanted to soften her old friend up, because she wanted to pitch him a business proposition. The trouble was that it was an offer he could easily refuse. To get Steve to agree to the deal she had in mind, she would have to draw on the deep reservoir of their friendship.

"Don't tell me you want me to use all those broken-down old clotheshorses who pass for models in that agency you've started." Steve laughed, bending down to ring out the bottoms of his 501's.

"Steve, don't even *joke* about my girls." Christa laughed as she spoke, but there was a sharp edge to her words. With Steve more or less anything was on the humor menu. Her agency wasn't. It was her magnificent obsession. For years she had built her career as a supermodel, and she had even endured one wildly successful, but deeply dissatisfying, excursion into the jungles of Hollywood movie-making, but all her life what had really fascinated her was winning, and money was the method of keeping the score. Modeling had provided a ton of it, but modeling didn't last forever. There were new girls, younger girls, more "now" girls with trendier faces and up-to-date bodies that could do things that hers couldn't. She had learned one thing. To be successful you had to use the knowledge and the skills you already possessed. So she had decided to retire from Elle, and, to the fury of its owner, Johnny Rossetti, she had started up her own. But she didn't want to run an agency that was a carbon copy of all the others. Over the years she had dreamed up a totally original scheme. Steve Pitts was vital to its success.

A formation of pelicans swooped in fighter-plane formation against the royal-blue sky as Steve watched her warily. He knew this girl like the daughter and the sister he had never had. She was deeply wonderful in every way, but she was also as tough as old boots. Her parents had seen to that. Christa had often talked wryly about their "my way or the highway" approach to child rearing, and their "shape up or ship out" attitude had produced a girl stronger on wanting than on feeling. If Christa Kenwood's ambitions were thwarted, she would break off your legs like dead branches from a tree, and her eyes would be dry while she did it. The gorgeous package that wrapped her soul—soft, luscious, and voluptuous—told lies about her essence, because at heart Christa was a winner who would let nobody stand in her way.

"Okay," he said at last. "Let's do breakfast. My arteries could do with another coat of cholesterol. Is Green's still the 'Happy Days' diner?"

"Yeah." Christa laughed. "They redecorated it last year. It was closed for months and ended up looking exactly the same. Like your plastic surgery, I guess."

"Listen, dear, sticking yourself on hold while your enemies get older is the sweetest revenge. You know what they say . . . a stitch in time."

"Do you remember when we met, Steve?" Christa cut into the banter, suddenly eager for memories.

"Does one forget being run over by a steamroller?"

"A steamroller! Steve, I wasn't that heavy."

"Believe me, you were that heavy, darling. You were a sugar-sweet roly-poly pudding, all dimples and puppy fat and in the whole of my life I don't think I've ever seen anything more lethal."

"Steve!" She punched at his arm, laughing at what she'd been, able to do so because of what she had become.

"You bowled up to me, while I was actually shooting, dear, and you said, 'I can do that.' The poor Ford girl nearly had apoplexy. I'll never forget her face. It was *cerise.* I've never seen the color before or since."

"I didn't! I said something like 'I'd love to be able to do that.' "

Steve waved his hand in the air to dismiss the detail. "The point was, lovely, you were as far from being a model as I was from the state of grace."

"You said I was too fat, too short, and too stupid to be a model." Christa's tone was mock-accusing.

"I was being kind, dear."

"Well, you were wrong, weren't you, Mr. Svengali?"

"I wasn't *wrong* . . . it was just that until I met you, I'd always reckoned that faith moving mountains was merely a pious hope. If we'd patented whatever diet you used, we could be having fun buying Donald Trump at ten cents on the dollar rather than sweating blood on this boiling beach."

"I didn't go on a diet. I just stopped eating."

"That I can understand. What I never understood is how you *grew.*"

"It was an optical illusion."

"Done with determination rather than mirrors."

"Precisely." Christa pirouetted on the sand. She felt pretty. She was pretty. No, she wasn't, she was gorgeous. And nine-tenths of it had been willpower. "Don't you remember I used to make you crop me at the knees to give me extra height?"

"And we had to bandage your tits when big was out."

"But I drew the line at taking out my back teeth when all the others were doing it."

"It was about the only place you did draw the line."

"Like the time I said I could drive a car when I couldn't, and they shot the whole commercial in reverse gear, and then played the film back the other way."

"And the smoking shoot in France when you refused to smoke, and they had to center the whole theme around some babbling brook."

"They were the most successful ads Gitanes ever ran."

"Yeah, and Infiniti borrowed the idea of using nature and keeping the product out of sight. Shit, you had more front than Waikiki in those days."

"Nonsense. I just knew what I wanted."

"You, Genghis Khan, and Attila the Hun."

"I was sweet and impressionable."

"You were a Tomahawk missile with a halo and angel's wings."

"And you were God with a hangover."

"Somebody had to stop you from taking over the world."

"Was I that bad?"

"That good, I guess you could say. In all my life I've never known anyone want as much as you. It was the parent thing, wasn't it?"

Steve moved away from humor. In the old days they'd discussed things like this. Then success had seemed to make them irrelevant. But the pain of childhood never went away. It lingered on in the dark places and no "grownup" was ever totally free of it, certainly not Christa, certainly not him.

"My parents . . . Mary . . . losing them. Losing everything."

Suddenly Christa's eyes were full of tears. She fought to keep the feelings at bay. Feelings were things you weren't supposed to have. In her childhood, tears had been for losers. They were considered a weakness that did your family no credit and yourself no good.

"Parents are funny things," said Steve, wistfully. "You might not love them, but you're sort of sorry when they go."

"Oscar Wilde got it right. You start by loving them. Later, you judge them. You seldom forgive them. Yeah, I missed them. But Mary most of all."

"What was she like?"

"Oh, everybody's little sister. Cute, sparky, a pain in the butt when she hung around all the time. But, oh boy, did I love her. She was so young, but incredibly *alive.* I mean, my parents weren't ever really alive. They lived in some genteel state of suspended animation, but Mary was . . . oh, I don't know, I mean she had so much to look forward to. God, I wish I had her now. I'd just like to tell her things and show her stuff . . ."

"And after the car crash, the cash crunch," said Steve, unable to resist the sound of the sentence.

"Yup, sweet sixteen and less than zero money-wise. Mom and Dad kept up one hell of a show, but the bucks were long gone."

Steve smiled a bitter smile. He knew how she felt. On paper, their childhoods were worlds apart. His other-side-of-the-tracks beginnings had been characterized by desertion, alcoholism, beatings, beratings. Hers had been full of costly cotillions, sleep-overs, and summer camps. Christa's emotional deprivation, however, although subtle, had been no less wounding than his, and it had turned them into similar people. Now, their soft, hurting hearts were walled off in a brittle, self-confident package that allowed them to carve a ruthless path through lesser mortals on the way to their dreams. On paper they should be human wrecks, but each of them had chosen to treat the love deserts of their childhoods as a challenge rather than an obstacle. Maybe that was why they loved each other so much.

"Well, anyway, darling, you didn't take long to replenish the family coffers. But I can't imagine your parents would have approved of your blowing Brown to spend your life twitching about in front of a camera."

Christa laughed ruefully.

"They'd have been horrified. They were so insulated from reality. They didn't even have the home in New England that gave all their friends their 'world view.' Can you believe they were actually in kindergarten together? You and them would have been culture shock."

"You and *they*, dear. Goodness me, after all that money I spent on your education. Anyway, darling, they can't have been all bad, turning out someone as bright and beautiful as you."

"Oh, Steve." Christa laughed. "I bet you say that to *all* the boys."

"*Actually,*" said Steve, taking mock offense, "you were the one that could have saved me. If only you'd turned the light of your countenance upon me and given me a piece . . ."

"You'd have been horrified, Steve Pitts," said Christa, punching him on the arm playfully as she finished his sentence. "Your designs on my body were always strictly commercial."

"Sometimes I think the line between commerce and lust is a thin one," said Steve.

"Sometimes I agree with you." Christa laughed.

They walked on in an easy silence. Christa looked around her. Nothing had changed. Age had not withered Palm Beach, nor custom staled it. The multi-million-dollar beach houses, worn away by the sandpaper sea breezes, were as dilapidated as always, paint peeling, blinds torn and flapping in the wind, children's detritus littering the lawns. Every tenth house was the exception that proved the rule . . . a pristine palace put up by some tasteless parvenu who hadn't a clue what Palm Beach was about and whose leveraged business would probably go bust before he had time to find out. She smiled as she passed Mollie Wilmot's house. A few years ago poor Mollie had wakened to find a tramp steamer in her swimming pool, blown in by a high wind. Noblesse had obliged and the bemused South American greasers had been invited in for a posh breakfast beneath the Wilmot Picasso. Only in Palm Beach! Christa looked out to sea. Drift boats were fishing off shore. A couple of skindivers swam around a red flag in the shallows. A mile or two up ahead the skyscrapers of Singer Island, separated from Palm Beach by the narrow Lake Worth inlet, reminded the plutocrats from a safe distance what the real world looked like.

The concrete bulwark jutted out over the beach, and Christa felt the shock of sudden memories. It was Rose Kennedy's house, the clapped-out old Mizner they called the Kennedy compound. It had never been far from the news. The staunchly Republican WASP town had been appalled when Catholic Democrat JFK had gotten permission to build a helicopter pad in the compound when he had used the home as a Winter White House. They had been far less appalled a few months earlier when a Jupiter girl had claimed to have been raped there by Teddy Kennedy's nephew. The Palm Beach view had been that skinny dipping in the ocean at four in the morning with a loaded Kennedy represented consent to just about anything. The door to the beach, bleached white by the salt wind, was closed now against the world. But Christa could remember when it had been wide open. . . .

"Come on, Mary! Or you won't get a hot dog. You won't, I mean it."

"I'm coming, but I've got a splinter in my foot and it hurts, Christa."

"Are you two coming or not?" The four Kennedy cousins stood on the concrete breakwater, looking down at the two sisters on the beach.

"We're coming, for God's sake. Can't you just wait? Mary's hurt her foot."

"Teddy had his foot cut off," said Patrick with all the scorn an eight-year-old could muster.

"Can it, Patrick," said Teddy sharply. Only he was allowed to joke about his missing leg.

"We wait for you when you have asthma," wailed Mary from the beach in retaliation. She was sitting on the sand, her little foot twisted up to her face.

Christa walked over to her. "Let me see it."

"Look, there's the splinter."

"Yes, you're right. Here, hang on to me. They'll have a needle in the house."

They hobbled together through the wooden door to the beach, along the spooky corridor, up the steps to the lawn. At night, during beach parties, there would always be a Kennedy, a Shriver, or a Smith to spring out at you in the moonlight. Christa shivered at the far from unpleasant memories.

They had reached the top of the stairs.

Chris Kennedy stood there, a look of concern on his face. "Is it bad?"

"No, it's a splinter, but it's deep. I need a needle to fish it out."

"There'll be one in the house. Max, go and find a needle and some matches. We'd better sterilize it."

They laid Mary down on the lawn. The boys clustered around.

"Maybe I'd better go get Mom," said Teddy.

"No, don't. I can handle it," said Christa. "Now you're going to be brave aren't you, Mary?"

Mary bit her lip. "I think so," she said.

The needle arrived, big and gleaming. Great ceremony was made about sterilizing it. It was passed backward and forward in the flame until its end was jet black from the heat.

"It'll burn me." There were tears in Mary's eyes.

"No, it won't. I'll blow on it." Christa blew on it. The eyes of the four boys were on her. She had an audience, and a pretty neat audience, too. Maybe she'd be a surgeon when she grew up.

This would be her first operation.

"I shouldn't have blown on it. I could have put germs on it." Christa was lost in the role of doctor.

"Come on, Christa. Dad's doing hot dogs out by the pool. They were ready an age *ago." Patrick was hungry.*

"Okay, okay." Christa took a deep breath and eased the needle into her little sister's foot in the general direction of the black splinter.

"Ouch!" shouted Mary. It was all too much for a seven-year-old, the excitement, the pain, center stage, the thought of missing out on the hot dogs. She dissolved into tears.

"Stop it," said Christa sharply. "Stop it, Mary."

"Kennedys don't cry," said Patrick.

Christa twirled around on him. She *was allowed to criticize her family. Nobody else was.*

"My sister is not a Kennedy. She's a Kenwood, and Kenwoods are allowed *to cry," she snapped.*

Kenwoods *can* cry. Kenwoods *can* cry. Through the years Christa could remember the anger when she had said those words. Because of course, Kenwoods, like Kennedys, weren't supposed to cry. That was her parents' rule, and it summed up everything that had been wrong with her childhood. Her mother and father had never appreciated the basic truth she had been learning ever since, that to suppress emotions did not make them vanish. They lived on, bubbling beneath the surface, and they wrinkled the wallpaper of one's careful façade. They were painful, like the splinter in the little foot of her little sister, and they had made Christa cruel when she should have been kind and caring. Poor, poor Mary. If only now she could hold her in her arms. If only, somehow this minute she could be here again, asking questions, wanting attention, battling for a reaction from the big sister she adored. The sweetest little sister in the world had lived to see only four more summers.

Christa fought against the memory, but she lost.

The police car roared into the driveway, spinning around the central ficus tree and throwing out a spray of gravel. Christa had heard it coming from a mile away and had wondered idly which of the neighbors had been having a heart attack. She stood in the doorway, watching the flashing blue light, and preparing a remark about a wrong address. The cop jumped out, leaving the door open, and as he walked toward Christa she knew immediately that he had come to the right house. His face was white, and although he hadn't spoken, the frown on his face said he was worrying about the words he would use.

"What is it?"

"Miss Kenwood?" He was playing for time. He knew who she was. He was always having breakfast in Green's.

The clammy fingers were on Christa's flesh. There was no bottom to her stomach. She took a step toward him.

"There's been an accident, at the Kennedy curve. Your family . . ."

"Are they all right? They're okay?" shouted Christa. Her mom, her dad . . . Mary. They had gone to a lunch party. Christa had stayed home. The hosts had had no kids her age.

"It's bad," said the cop, his face saying that it was worse. "Your parents are both dead. Your sister was sitting in the back. She's still alive. She's asking for you. I'll take you there. We should hurry."

"Oh, God . . . Oh, God!" Christa ran to the car, her head in her hands. Somehow, shock had blanketed all feelings about her parents. But Mary, little Mary, alive and asking for her.

They roared along North Ocean Boulevard, the siren blaring.

"Is she all right?" Christa's voice came from miles away.

The cop, grim-faced, stared straight ahead at the road. "The paramedics are on their way," was all he said.

The sun beat down on the quiet sea to their left. In a minute they would be there.

"I'm afraid there's blood," said the policeman. They screeched to a stop beside the cop car that was already blocking off the road. The station wagon was on its side, its front and side crumpled by a silver Mercedes that was impaled in it like a spear. Two rag dolls sat in the front two seats, like dummies in a seat belt safety film clip. The difference was the blood. They were covered in it. Christa crammed her hand against her mouth. Another cop opened the passenger door.

"Come on," he said, holding her hand to steady her. She staggered from the car. Her mind was hardly working, but she knew she must be brave. Then she heard it.

"Ohhhhhhhhh! I'm hurting." It was the wail of a child. It was Mary, and it came from the depths of the car that was already a coffin. She ran then, pushing away the hand that held her. She ran to what was left of the window, and she hitched herself up. "Mary, oh, Mary, my baby, darling, it's me," she howled as the tears hurtled to her eyes and naked fear pricked at her guts.

"Christa? Christa! Oh, Christa, my legs."

Mary's stricken face peered from the gloom of the tiny space. Her eyes were wide with agony and terror. Her face was white as the face of Christ. One hand was free, the other was buried with the rest of her beneath the web of twisted metal.

"Darling, don't worry. I'm here. It's going to be all right.

"Trust me, Mary. Be brave, like always. It's me, darling. It's going to be all right."

"I'm stuck," said Mary. "I'm all stuck and crushed. I can't move."

"We'll get you out. They're coming." Christa felt the dread break through her. She turned and yelled at the top of her voice. "Get help, for God's sake, get help, someone. Do *something."*

She turned back to her sister.

"Oh, Christa, I love you," said Mary with the wisdom of a child at the end of life. "I love you so much."

"Darling, baby, oh, I love you, too, so much, so much."

A big tear filled Mary's eye. It overflowed, painting her bloodless cheek.

"I wanted to grow up like you," she whispered, and with the hand that could move she reached for Christa, touching her face.

Christa let her own tears come, melting the shock. She held her sister's hand in hers, sweaty and cold against her cheek, and she knew then it was nearly over. These memories would have to last for eternity.

"Remember that time," said Mary, "at the Kennedys', when you said we could cry."

"Oh, darling, don't talk. The doctors are coming. It's going to be all right."

"Kiss me, Christa."

Christa leaned in through the twisted window and lay her cheek against her little sister's. Then, with the tenderness of all her time on earth, she kissed her.

"Don't leave me, Christa. I'm so scared," whispered Mary, and Christa felt her shudder as the time came near. "Like when I was afraid of the dark and you let me sleep in your bed, but you wouldn't let me bring my teddies."

"Don't, Mary, don't! Oh, darling, I'm so sorry. I was so mean to you and I loved you so much. You were all I had. You're all I've got."

"If I get to look down on you, I'll look after you," said Mary, so small yet so very big at the edge of forever. It was all she had ever wanted . . . to be Christa's equal, to be included, to be loved by the big sister she worshiped.

"I'm cold," said Mary, "and I can't feel myself."

"Fight, Mary, for God's sake, fight." Christa held her tight, and tried to force her resolve into her sister's broken body. But her eyes were closing, as they had closed after the third story at bedtime, opening, again for a longer time before the endless sleep. Those had been such beautiful moments as tiredness and temper vanished and the morning of a brand-new day beckoned. But now there would be no tomorrows, and sleep was the dreaded enemy, the friend no longer.

"Oh, God, dear God, save her," said Christa. And she felt her sister's head move sideways against hers, her cheeks wet with Christa's tears, and the life fluttered free from her . . . as the arms of Jesus held her safe at last. Christa moved back and the wild sorrow rushed through her. And there on the hot road in the burning sun, she began to learn about loneliness.

Steve, oblivious to Christa's sad thoughts, was deep in his own memories.

"What a perfect place to live," he said, sniffing at the salt air and remembering the rotting, fume-filled odor of the Manhattan summer. "It must have been paradise for kids. Like having a vast sandbox in your own backyard."

Christa sighed. "Yeah, that part was great." Life went on. She was back. "We loved it, especially Mary. You know, endless cookouts, and snorkeling and sailing, and surfing and surfers . . . The grownups never went near the ocean. It was considered quite the wrong thing to have a suntan. We used to hang out with the wild and woolly kids from West Palm, who weren't supposed to be there. The town tried to keep them off the island, by making it impossible for them to park, but we'd tell them who was away in the summer, which was more or less everyone, so they could leave their cars in the driveway and hang out with us on the beach."

They were passing a house at which a small crowd had gathered. A candy-striped awning had been erected, and people were carrying white Igloo freezer boxes and trays of food to trestle tables that had been laid out under canvas. A beautiful girl in a skimpy bikini and Rio-type tan called out across the sand.

"Christa! Christa, is that you?"

Christa and Steve stopped.

Christa slapped her hand to her forehead.

"Hey, Steve, I'd totally forgotten. It's Memorial Day. Dina?" She called back across the sand.

Dina Hutton ran across the sand, laughing, and rushed up to Christa, hugging her.

"Christa! Christa! How wonderful! I didn't know you were in town. You beast! Why didn't you call? We're having a *party!* You've got to come to our *party!* You're just what we need. Don't say you've been working!" Her sunburned nose wrinkled in pseudodisgust.

Christa smiled apologetically. Her full makeup had given the game away. Palm Beach was about the only place on earth where work was regarded as a subversive activity.

"Dina, this is Steve Pitts, who is almost as old a friend of mine as you are. Steve, this is Dina, who spends some of the money that her ancestors made from a little company called E. F. Hutton giving the hottest Memorial Day beach parties in Christendom."

"How wonderful. A stranger in town. New blood. Any minute now you'll be telling me that he's famous and he *does* things, just like you, Christa. I feel quite *faint* with excitement. Well, anyway, we have the neatest reggae band that David shipped in last night from the islands on his boat. They none of them have passports or work permits or anything like that. They have to be history by tomorrow morning, or we all have to do time, according to all the old soaks who pretend to be attorneys." She giggled helplessly at the thought that on paper the laws applied to people like her. "Actually, getting locked up would be a relief after the season. Mr. Terlizzese got Mimi to design Palm Beach's only cell. It's apparently quite comfortable. And think of the *quiet. Such* a relief from the telephone."

"What do you think, Steve? Can we afford to take an hour or two off?" said Christa.

"Rum and reggae. Sure we can."

"Well, I'm sure there's some Mount Gay, somewhere. We often run out of food, but I don't think we've ever run out of drink."

Dina laughed at the ludicrous thought, and Christa recognized the upper-class shorthand. Palm Beach and Palm Beachers didn't change. Mount Gay, with the possible exception of Myers, was the "only" rum. It was drunk with tonic or club soda and a slice of lime from a paper cup, neither plastic nor glass being acceptable at the beach. It was never, *ever,* mixed with anything remotely resembling piña colada, fruit juice, Grenadine, or Angostura. *Those* were for sailing trips to the islands, and never for "home." But that was not all. There was also a mild rebuke in Dina's "some Mount Gay somewhere," because basically the drink of choice at Palm Beach beach parties was Miller Lite, Beck's imported beer, and cheap, but very cold, Italian white wine. The brand of beer was not negotiable. The wine could be anything but Californian as long as it was inexpensive and frozen to death. Confirmed alcoholics were allowed to bring battered silver hip flasks full of scotch that they were not expected to share. Outsiders had difficulty following these rules, which was the strongest reason for their existence. Parvenus could be forgiven for thinking that the very rich would drink very well, and that there would be an *embarras de richesses* of expensive and exotic booze at a beach party, dispensed no doubt by attentive servants. Wrong! The most impressive thing about the alcohol at an insider picnic was its quantity, not its quality. Moderation was the class enemy; the healthful, Californian "I don't drink too much because I'm always doing business" was the alien attitude; aggressive sobriety was strongly suspect unless it was well known that you were a card-carrying A.A. fellow traveler on a periodic "cure."

Dina Hutton's conversational smoke signals had flown way over Steve's head, but Christa, whose whole childhood had been an exercise in their recognition, read them effortlessly. She laughed out loud as she remembered the careless, callous snobbery of those far-off days. Social climbers had never been able to thread their way through the minefield of manners. They simply never understood that summer was a verb, that the right first name was your mother's last name, that Crimson, Old Nassau, and good old Eli were ivy-covered universities where you learned your most important lesson . . . how to drink.

A fat man strolled up. He wore a battered straw hat, with a brick-red and navy-blue band; a pair of beaten, buckled Gucci loafers, and a white T-shirt that read MILLIONAIRES ARE AN ENDANGERED SPECIES, TOO. His T-shirt carried the monogrammed initials JBW III in plain block maroon just below the left rib cage. Khaki shorts completed his ensemble.

"Atlantic have arrived with the ice," he said to Dina.

"Ah," said Steve, "the iceman cometh."

"What?" said the fat man. Dina looked blank.

"Eugene O'Neill," said Christa.

"What about him?" said Dina, her tone mildly irritated.

"He's going to be a little late for the party," said Steve wickedly. He was catching on fast. For literary allusions, Palm Beach was clearly stony ground.

"Danforth Wrightsman," said the fat plutocrat rudely in retaliation. He thrust his hand out at Steve as if he wished it had a sharp end. His belligerent chin said he was waiting for the hilarious joke that would be the recital of the stranger's name.

Christa hurried in to defuse the bomb.

"Hi, Danny," she said. "Remember me, Christa Kenwood? I was an angel in the Nativity play when you were a wise man."

"Someone knew a thing or two about casting," said Steve with a sarcastic laugh. It was clear he was referring to the fat man's lack of wisdom rather than to Christa's angelic deficiencies. The ambiguity of his remark, however, saved it from open hostility.

Danforth Wrightsman let out a snort of recognition.

"Of course you are," he said. "That's exactly who you are. You wore yellow panties." He appeared suddenly confused. Outsiders could be dealt with and demolished. Class brothers and sisters were of equal rank. Christa would have remembered the time he gave the second grade head lice; the volcanic facial eruptions that had destroyed his adolescence; the moment of uncharacteristic daring when he had set off the fire alarm at school.

Christa laughed at the aristocratic gaucheness. You didn't learn how to handle beautiful women at Porcellian, Scroll and Key, or Cottage.

"Couldn't I have worn something more romantic, like a yellow ribbon?" said Christa, her tone mock-plaintive.

"No, panties," insisted Wrightsman with the stubbornness of his species. "Aren't you a model now, or something . . . ?"

The word "model" was wrapped in tones of subtle reproach. Models were what your racier friends introduced you to on search-and-destroy evenings in New York. The ones that deigned to speak to you got taken to Au Bar when your wife was in hospital having the baby.

"Oh, Danforth, be an angel and get me a glass of wine, would you?" lisped Dina. She rolled her eyes skyward as he sloped off to do her bidding.

"Thanks." Christa laughed. "I'd forgotten what Palm Beach could be like."

"First time I've ever felt like slaughtering a member of an endangered species," said Steve.

"Oh, you mustn't believe Danforth's T-shirt," said Dina, closing ranks against the outsider. "Everyone's a millionaire here . . . at least!" She laughed to defuse any possible unpleasantness. "Including you, Christa. It must be so *exciting* to be a self-made woman, you know, like sort of *earning* your self-respect instead of being born with it."

"More like having it, rather than pretending to have it," said Steve Pitts sharply.

"Yes, well, anyway, lovely to see you, Christa, and you, Steve, but I'd better make sure that the ice person understands where to put it. Otherwise everyone will revolt, or be revolting or whatever."

She drifted away into the crowd.

"Steve!" said Christa, mock-scolding. "That's cruelty to dumb animals!"

"The hide on that animal is so thick she didn't feel a thing."

"Yeah, I think you're getting the hang of Palm Beach. Actually, they're not so bad. They just take a bit of getting use to . . . like about twenty years minimum."

"I'd rather do the time in the pen." Steve laughed as his shrewd eyes scanned the party. Social anthropology had always been his forte, and everywhere he was deciphering the subtle class clues. It was a beach party and yet everyone had made some sort of statement with their clothes. They were a million miles from either the 1920s classic Anglicism of Ralph Lauren or the wall-to-wall blue denim of the West Coast. Pants were torn and baggy, shirts loud or faded, shoes battered to kingdom come and stuck together in a couple of instances by white adhesive tape. Nearly everyone wore some version of an old-man-of-the-woods straw hat. The occasional person was dressed for something else, two for tennis, three for golf, at least half a dozen for vagrancy on the open road. Few had a tan and there was a totally preppy lack of interest in looking sexy. None of the men appeared to have heard of exercise, especially the ones who were dressed for it. Most of the girls, in contrast, seemed to be visiting the party for a brief interlude before returning to the gyms where they apparently lived. The food was anything but ostentatious and consisted mainly of chicken and potato salad. There were no hamburgers, no hot dogs, nothing at all that might require effort and detract from the main business at hand, which appeared to be drinking, and making fun of people you saw every day and had clearly lived with all your life. Not a soul looked like he or she had any intention of going into the sea. What did it add up to? That these people liked familiarity, contempt, booze, anything old, doing nothing, irreverence, failing to try, confidence. What they loathed were outsiders, displays of wealth, weakness, vanity, meritocrats, anxiety, enthusiasm. He failed their litmus test on several counts. They failed his on as many. But that was just the people. The beach, the sand, the booze, and the band were still there, and so was Christa.

"Come on, Christa, let's get a drink and some food and hit the sand and then I'll sit back and wait for you to proposition me."

"Okay, you got it." Christa laughed, but inside, the butterflies were loose. Steve hadn't forgotten the "something she wanted to talk to him about." Neither had she. Her future would depend on his answer.

A few chicken wings, a mountain of cole slaw, and two vast cups of Valpolicella later, they were side by side on the beach.

"Come on, darling. Shoot!" Steve could feel the uncharacteristic tension in Christa.

"Look, Steve, when I started up my agency I had a game plan, and it wasn't just to be a poor man's Eileen Ford. I mean, I think I can improve on the service the traditional agencies provide, and I know for sure I can give the girls a better deal than they get with sharks like Johnny . . ."

"Like presumably they won't have to go to bed with you for a start."

Christa smiled ruefully. Her fierce strength and her class remoteness had enabled her to circumnavigate the crass come-ons of Johnny Rossetti, the owner of the Elle agency, but she had seen corn girls from Iowa and suburban beauties from the Twin Cities get fed into the meat grinder more times than she liked to remember. Some had set their teeth and borne it in the name of ambition. Others had been won over by the music of the snake charmer and fallen in love with the man who didn't know what the word meant. They had paid for their mistake with bodies, minds, and souls. Christa shuddered as she thought about it.

"But what I really wanted to do was something entirely different."

She looked at him carefully. Was this the right moment for the pitch? She took a deep breath. It was as good as any.

"Listen, Steve. You know how in the movie business the big agencies like CAA put together packages—star, director, writer, script, and then sell the whole shebang to the studios. Well, I want to do that in the commercial photography business. If I had the top model on my books, and the best makeup people, the hottest stylist, and the number-one photographer . . ."

"You could go to Revlon, and Calvin Klein, and Levi Strauss direct, and bypass the ad agencies. You could charge a fee for the whole package, and you'd still earn your percentage commission on your client's earnings. The customer would only have to deal with one person, and all your clients would be at work. . . ."

Steve spoke out loud, finishing Christa's sentence for her. He spoke in thoughtful tones, sizing up the idea as he gave voice to it. Already he knew it was good. Very good. But it depended on several factors for its success. In order to swing the package, Christa would have to be able to deliver the top model, and the top model was Lisa Rodriguez. Even more important, she would have to deliver the top photographer . . . and the top photographer was him.

"Yes, absolutely, that's it, Steve. I mean, it would revolutionize the whole business. We could dream up the campaigns and then deliver the people and the finished product. It would streamline the whole process and we'd make a fortune. We'd only have to do it once or twice and then everyone would be using us."

" 'Us'? 'We'?" said Steve shrewdly.

"Yeah, us, Steve. I need you. I'd have to represent you. You're the key."

"So I have to fire poor old Peter, who's been my agent since the Stone Age, and I have to sail into the unknown with Christa Kenwood and her gaggle of girls on a wing and a prayer."

It wasn't a no. It wasn't a yes.

Christa talked fast. "Okay, I know I haven't any experience repping a photographer, especially one like you. But you're up there, Steve.

Peter doesn't have to get out of bed in the morning to get you work. All he has to do is pick up the phone, write down the bookings, and collect the cash. You're paying fifteen percent for someone who's effectively a bookkeeper. So, in the early days when you were relatively unknown, he earned his loot. He doesn't today. You're like an annuity for him. You don't owe him anymore. And I'd only want ten percent."

"Ah." Steve laughed. "The cash carrot. Your friends would be horrified." He waved a hand to encompass the ancient money whose affectation it was to pretend they'd never heard of the stuff.

"You're my friend. Have you got anything against cash?"

"Only my sticky fingers, darling."

"Think of all that extra 'poodle faking' you could do with another hundred thousand or so."

"And who, pray, do I take photographs of? Joking apart, you've signed some promising kids, but they're not exactly money in the bank. Okay, so I can invent a few, ram a few others down a few throats by calling in the IOUs, but it'll take time and I'd be spending goodwill capital. You're asking me to risk an awful lot."

Christa took a deep breath. The deal was still there, but she would have to pay for it.

"Okay, I'll handle you for five. You can be my loss leader."

"You make me feel like a can of beans," Steve protested.

"If the shoe fits . . ."

Christa could see it hang in the balance. Was this the time to play her trump? Once he started to say no, his speech might acquire a momentum of its own that would be difficult to turn around. On the other hand, if she revealed all her cards at once, she would have nothing in reserve.

"You wouldn't have to use my girls exclusively, Steve. You could continue to use your favorites from the other agencies. It would only be when we were selling a package that everyone would have to be 'in-house.' "

Steve was quiet for a bit. He sipped on the Valpolicella and winced. Its coldness was its most attractive quality.

"Look, darling, I love the idea. I love you. I admire you enormously. If anyone can make this idea fly, and I think it *is* a great idea, then you're that person. But somehow I wonder just who is going to pay big bucks for your package when there's no big-name model involved. Mike Ovitz has the stars as well as the directors, the writers, and the producers. It's chicken and egg. You won't get the stars until you can guarantee them the work, and you won't get the work until you can produce the stars."

Christa turned to face him.

"Lisa Rodriguez," she said simply.

"What about her?"

"I've got her. At least I've nearly got her. I know I can get her."

Steve Pitts's low, impressed whistle said it all. That was a whole different ball game. Rodriguez was off the centigrade scale in terms of hotness. He had used her several times, and he would cheerfully have block booked her through eternity if it wasn't for the fact that every photographer in the world was trying to do the same. She was the liquid dreams and pussy schemes of the Western Hemisphere's red-blooded males. Her sex appeal shone from the surface of her contact sheets. It was impossible to take a bad picture of her, and without appearing to try, she could make the clothes of the ultimate fashion victim look like the haughtiest, haute couture. Lisa Rodriguez looked good in everything and better in nothing, and any package in which she double-billed with Steve Pitts would sell for megabucks to anyone who had them to spend. But how the hell had Christa signed her? How on earth had she even gotten close to signing her? Rodriguez was with Christa's old agency, Elle. Lisa and Christa together had provided Johnny Rossetti with eighty-five percent of his profits. Christa had walked out on Johnny. Now she was starting a rival agency. Poaching Lisa Rodriguez would be an act far more substantial than the mere addition of insult to injury. Rossetti, the original wolf man, would have a cow. There would be blood on the walls, and the blood would be of Christa's type.

"You took Lisa away from Johnny?" he managed at last, his mind full of purple fantasies. Jesus! Christa had always been ballsy. It would be a wonder if she escaped a red badge for her courage.

"I'm *certain* I can get her. You know about Lisa, don't you? Johnny found her in one of those modeling competitions he was always holding. She'd run away from her family who live down in Miami, and he brought her up to New York when she was only fourteen and didn't know a street shark from a parrot fish. Johnny went the whole way with her—you know, group sex, Polaroids, scoring drugs for him when she was on trips to South America. She made it, despite all that, because she's tough as nails and makes Marines look like powder puffs, but she always hated Johnny for what he did to her. Now that she's a superstar in the stratosphere, she wants to use the height to dump on him good. Johnny's under the fan, Steve, and frankly I don't mind being there when he takes the hit. I've seen what he does to people. There was that girl who jumped under the train when he fired her. There were two others who were caught carrying his drugs and who are still locked up. They were too scared to finger him. He's roach droppings, Steve. He was always okay to me because I wouldn't take his trash and because I had his number and I didn't need him. He needed me. But I don't mind stealing Lisa from him, and I don't mind burying Elle business-wise. It's not just a pleasure. It's a moral duty."

Steve laughed. Christa Kenwood had not totally escaped her background. She was brutal like the upper classes, and like them, she considered herself untouchable. She felt the real world couldn't hurt her, because there was a sense in which, deep down, she knew she was superior to it. Gangsters, mobsters, crooks and thieves were colorful people, and about as menacing as the singers and dancers in *Guys and Dolls.* They might behave badly, and be deserving of punishment. Then it could and would be meted out to them as they overstepped the invisible mark. But dangerous they were not, because, ultimately, they inhabited that illusive ghost-land where social inferiors lived. Theirs was the insubstantiality of shadows and specters, and the very best they could do would be to clank a few chains in the guest wing at night. Steve knew better. Wild animals like Johnny Rossetti did damage, especially when stepped on. With their backs to the wall they would claw and scratch, and they were fueled by the high-octane gas of revenge. When Rossetti learned what Christa was up to, no solvent insurance company would be wise to take on her life.

"You're saying that Lisa will come with you to infuriate Johnny."

"Yes, and the fact that we get on. She trusts me. She believes in me. Oh, and I told her that you had agreed to sign with my agency. I think that was the most important factor of all." Christa giggled as she admitted her lie.

"Oh, I *see,*" said Steve, far from appalled at Christa's deviousness. The most important thing for winners was to win. He respected that. "And now, sweet Christa, are you pretending Lisa is in the boat just so that you can hook me?"

"No!" She placed her cards face down on the table. "She's promised to sign with me on the day she sees your signature on an agreement. You could have it in your contract that it was conditional on her signing. We could do it all together, like closing a real-estate transaction. Then everyone could see what the other was up to."

Again Steve was silent. It was an intriguing idea. It was original, had the flavor of excitement and adventure, and there was the distinct possibility of serious money at the end of the rainbow. When you got to his age, life had a tendency toward dullness. Getting there had been more fun than the arrival. Staying there was less fun still. Now, he was being asked to risk everything, and to jump from the warm womb of security into the bracing reality of the competitive jungle. Then there was Christa, the girl he loved more than anyone. They would be partners in a bold new scheme. The colors would be alive once more, the sounds sharp, the tastes tantalizing, as together they built memories for the future rather than relying on those from the past.

Christa was biting hard on her tongue. There was a time to stay silent, even when you desperately wanted to speak. Such a time was now. Anything she said would signal her eagerness, and eagerness in a deal cost cash. She was out of trumps. Her pitch was floating in the steam-heated air. It was up to Steve, and the past they'd shared. The reggae band chose the moment to strike up. "No woman, no cry," they sang, as the ghost of Bob Marley wafted across the palm-fringed beach. It was enough. In his mind Steve Pitts rolled over, legs in the air. Christa was too much. You argued with her like you argued with the Cat 5 hurricane that would one day level this island and inject a little much-needed adrenaline into the arteries of the sophisticates who surrounded him. Yup, Christa was irresistible. She had been irresistible way back at polo when she had interrupted his shoot and told him that he had to make her a star. She was irresistible now, as she lay against the sand like it was a lover and watched him with eyes that wanted.

"I'm in," he said simply. "It'll be a gas."

"Omigod, Steve, that's terrific."

She jumped up and her bikini top strained to hold on to its wondrous cargo. Sandy, like a leggy colt jumping up from the earth of a country corral, she leaped at him, burying him in her arms and kissing him. It was a peak moment. She wasn't a dreamer. She was a realist. What turned her on was getting things done. At a stroke, she had secured the foundation of her ambitious scheme, and it was built on rock, not shifting sand. Rodriguez and Pitts. Pitts and Rodriguez. She had cornered the visual beauty market. She had shut out the opposition from the commodities that no one could afford to be without. Now, it would merely be a question of inventing the price of the priceless. The cash mountain she had built from her modeling career and her book advance already looked like a no-see-um bite. Ahead were the serious bucks, the ones that would wipe out the memories of the genteel pseudopoverty of her childhood and fill the void in her life by allowing her to have what she needed more than breath . . . her very own way.

"Jesus, Christa, lay off, will you? Everyone'll think I'm straight." He laughed as she hugged him, falling back into the sand with Christa on top of him. She giggled, too, as she tickled and loved him. All those years ago he had changed her life. Now he had promised to do so again. What had they been saying about commerce and lust? Whatever. It was true.

"Goodness, sex at a Palm Beach party? What will people dream up next?"

The patrician voice, full of pseudosupercilious amusement, cut into Christa's vision of her wonderful future.

The Lilly Pulitzer reversible wraparound, a vomit-colored cocktail of lime green, pastel pink, and banana yellow, hovered above them. The preppy woman who wore it looked like she had a killer serve. Her legs were tree trunks, as wide at the ankle as at the knee, but wider by far at the thigh where it met an anvil butt. She was mahogany brown from the tennis court and she smoked angrily at a small cheroot.

"Now who is it that's managed to keep their hormones alive through the season? Christa? Is it Christa Kenwood? God, it is. Whatever you're taking, I want some of it."

Christa turned herself around with difficulty and stared up against the sun at the Amazon who threatened to blot it out.

"Shit, Muffy. How *are* you? I thought you lived in Wisconsin, or somewhere else in the middle."

"I did, with a marvelous man who beat me. Unfortunately, he fell off a horse, and then I got to beat him and that wasn't nearly so much fun so I jacked it in and came back here. Palm Beach is a masochist's delight, as I'm sure that gentleman you're torturing on the sand would agree. Can we be introduced?"

"Oh, Steve, this is Martha Kellogg. Martha, Steve Pitts."

In Palm Beach, second names were far more important than first ones.

"Pitts," said the Wagnerian figure in the skirt. "Pitts. There were some Pitts cousins in Maine, I think." She stared at him threateningly. It was not clear to Steve whether to admit a familiar relationship would contribute to good or bad karma.

"I changed it from Ball on my twenty-first birthday," he said defensively. He had the feeling that in Martha Kellogg even he might have met his Waterloo.

"How appropriate," she replied with a snort. "In this town all our balls are the pits. I should know. I give most of them."

"You do?" said Christa, surprised. Martha was a poor Kellogg.

"Yes, I'm working for lovely Bruce Sutka. Working *with* him, I should say. Like Nell Gwynne, I'm the flower girl. *Unlike* Nell Gwynne I do *not* get to make it with the Balkan royalty who are the nearest things to kings around here."

"God," said Christa, wrinkling her nose. "All those diseases."

"Times are changing, Christa. We did a culture the other day. Well not *hard* culture, like ballet and opera, but a Barbara Bush literacy promotion thing—you know, let's teach the kids how to read the *TV Times*. I had *terrible* trouble selling tables until I rounded up Fergie, who'll go to the opening of a Coke can as long as it's destined for a Cuba libre. She told blue jokes and threw bread until she hit Jack Van Buren in the eye. He wanted to sue, until I persuaded him that it would be unsportsmanlike because the British don't play the litigation game."

"Nothing changes in Palm Beach." Christa laughed. She was beginning to realize how much she loved this place, with its irreverence, its understatedness, the well-kept secret of its extraordinary beauty. The residents did a brilliant job of camouflaging it against the outside world so that they could enjoy it as their parents and grandparents had before them, and their children and grandchildren would long after they were gone.

"*Au contraire,* as the Frogs say. I found at least three things had changed when I got back from the prairie. Luckily I've forgotten what they are."

Christa laughed. "Listen Muffy, I'd love to get together with you sometime while I'm down here. I'm doing a shoot for *Vogue,* but we'll be finished this evening, and I'm going to hang around for a few days. What about dinner on Sunday?"

"Can't, dear. Mary Whitney's giving a huge party. I told her Sunday was a rotten day, but she said Sundays bored her and needed jazzing up. I don't suppose it matters, because Palm Beachers don't do

Monday mornings anyway. Listen, why don't you come? It's going to be totally over the top—gold-painted toy boys, alligators, salsa, lambada, and a band for the nightclub called the L.A. Guns who are apparently the very latest thing in androgyny. You know how Mary loves to be up to date. She'll horrify the locals, but she's got a house full of meritocrats down from sin city who'll think it's par for the Palm Beach course. Anyway, all the people we know'll be gone by eleven, so we can behave really badly and still be able to hold our heads up in Publix the next day."

Christa paused. Mary McGregor Whitney was giving a party. Mary Whitney, whose money was so old it had liver spots. Mary Whitney, Christa's old friend from Palm Beach days, who had turned her silver spoon into a platinum-plated fortune. Mary Whitney had started out designing clothes. Now she designed lives. She had *become* the American fashion industry. She was bigger than Estée Lauder, Calvin Klein, and Ralph Lauren rolled into one, and now Christa Kenwood had an invitation to her party. The two and two clicked up to four in her mind. What sort of person would buy a Pitts/Rodriguez package for a worldwide advertising campaign? Who would have the millions to hire the best? Who would be naturally drawn to doing business with an old childhood friend? The answer to each question was the same. It was Mary McGregor Whitney.

"Is that *the* Mary Whitney you're talking about?" said Steve quickly, vibrating on Christa's wavelength. The point of Palm Beach was becoming apparent to him.

"Yup, the real Mary Whitney, as the peasants are fond of saying," scoffed Muffy. "What an eager little beaver she's turned into. She's not content to merely spend the inherited loot. She has to make everyone feel guilty by being a success as well. Imagine wanting to design all those terrible clothes for the dreadful upwardly mobiles. Do you remember when she did it with the cop under the Jeep outside the 264 for a bet? She knocked herself out on the exhaust pipe because she insisted on being on top. Even as a teenager she was a bossy bitch."

"And she seduced Garretson duPont's younger brother at Dreher Park and he was only fourteen and had to go see a shrink to help him get over the experience."

"Can I ever forget?" The Kellogg laugh crackled like the cornflakes. "Old Trip duPont wanted her charged with rape, until Emerson Whitney bought up all the tables at his wife's prostate-cancer bash."

"Didn't the duPont kid become a Jesuit?"

"You bet he did. And his old man never spoke to him again, although Trip and Emerson kissed and made up. Now they play golf together every day at the Everglades."

"I guess there are some things you just can't forgive." Christa laughed. "Anyway, I'd love to come to the party. Will Mary mind?"

"Mary will be thrilled. She told me to invite all the okay Palm Beachers who weren't either dead or terminally ill. You appear to be neither, so I'll put your name on the list. Will you be bringing Mr. Bit, or was it Mr. Pall?"

"Actually Pitts, Stuffy," sniffed Steve.

"Steve, can you come?" Christa tried to signal with her eyes that it would be a great idea.

"Can't, love. I've got to get back. I'm doing an Evangelista cover for Cosmo at the weekend in Southampton. What a drag. I'd have loved to have seen Puffy's flowers."

Christa's mind was off and running. On second thoughts it might be better if the prickly Steve were safely in New York. If she was to land the biggest fish of all, there should be few distractions. Steve's mighty reputation might be a better sales point than his unpredictable personality. Mary Whitney and Steve Pitts might be a match made in heaven. It could just as easily turn out to have been manufactured in hell.

Martha Kellogg peered at Steve like she might a mess on the road. Her intentional mangling of his name had resulted in her becoming Stuffy/Puffy. It was not a good business. It wasn't a good business at all. That was the trouble with America. Nobody knew his place. The lower classes zoomed through life oblivious to their predicament. They simply didn't *know* that they were born inferior. Worse, they had zero desire to be you, and because of that they couldn't be manipulated, patronized, and stepped upon. How different life was for her English cousins, the Warburton-Stanleys. They had only to open their patrician mouths and recite the telephone directory and it would be game, set, and match as the middle classes cringed, bowed, and scraped. The battle was won by the accent alone. In Florida when you unleashed your Boston Brahmin, people reckoned that you talked "funny" and refused to accept your checks because you were clearly from out of town. It was no wonder that here the upper classes stuck close to their enclaves like medieval knights to their moated castles. It was the safe thing to do. She analyzed the situation. Pitts was probably the Kenwood screw. He was going back to New York. As retribution for the parvenu's rudeness, she would arrange for a rival to squire Christa to the party.

Her eyes narrowed.

"Don't you worry, Christa," she said wickedly. "We'll find someone to look after you at Mary's party. In fact I've got the ideal man for you. Oh, my goodness, yes, how perfect. What *fun* we're going to have."

5

Peter Stein stood on the swaying swim platform of his 43-foot Tiara and peered at the aquamarine ocean. It was top-to-bottom visibility, and he could see the reef clearly sixty feet below the boat. That was rare in the early summer, and it made him feel as good as anything could make him feel when he should be writing, but wasn't. Damn! There it went again. The siren of guilt. He tried to push it from his mind, concentrating instead on the outline of the submerged statue of Neptune that rose up from the coral. It reminded him of the bigger, more beautiful statue of Christ submerged in the Mediterranean waters off Porto Veneri. Still, it wasn't a bad attempt by his countrymen, who were usually far happier fine-tuning their psyches than their souls. He looked up to the sky, and then across to the shore where the Breakers Hotel, the symbol of Old Palm Beach, rose in monumental self-confidence from the shoreline. He had used it as a marker to find the approximate position of the reef—straight out for a mile from the fourth window to the right of the left-hand tower. The Impulse bottom finder had fine-tuned the ledge beneath him. Soon he would be in the garden, deep at the bottom of the ocean that he loved more than people, almost as much as his precious work, nearly as well as life. It was so peaceful down there with the slow fishes. He would be suspended in the eighty-degree water, buoyant, quiet, far from the difficult words that were both his cross and his salvation. There, in the silence, he could lose himself among colors more brilliant than reality, and shapes that gave substance to illusion. It was his escape. It was where his anger was softened, his vaulting ambitions tranquilized, his panic soothed.

"You want to do a loner?"

Ryan Van der Kamp twisted around at the wheel of the Tiara and eased the gears into neutral. He spoke quietly through chapped lips as he asked the question of his boss and friend. But already he knew the answer. There was one area in which Peter Stein was *not* blocked. His body language spoke volumes. His lean, wiry body was twisted as if it had done time on an Inquisitor's rack. Arms, business muscular, were firmly akimbo across a powerful chest, while his legs, long and strong, were cocked uncomfortably close to each other on the swaying platform. His shoulders were hunched, and his head burrowed down into the cavity they had created. His whole posture seemed a defense against the outside world, but Ryan knew it was not a defense based on fear. To the friend who knew him, Peter Stein's stance said clearly that his loneliness was a choice freely made. The outside world had been tested and found wanting and, as a result, when he needed inspiration he looked inward rather than out. His eyes carried the same message. Set deep at the bottom of a brooding brow they were brown, wide and intelligent, providing a window into the brilliant brain that would one day find a solution to the problems that so clearly plagued him. A shock of black hair, abundant and unruly, crowned the anxious face whose stark, troubling beauty seemed an insult to the mind of the genius inside.

"I guess," said Peter, wondering how he could waste fewer words.

Ryan smiled. He understood Peter as far as anyone could. They sensed each other, because each was no stranger to torture. Ryan's had been in Vietnam. His medals said he had learned well how to kill, but the scars on his soul told instead the story of his own emotional murder. Peter's wounds were self-inflicted, the endless suicide that was a life dedicated to his art, a ceaseless struggle for the perfection that the world acknowledged but which, to him, was always beyond his grasp. Now he would dive alone as he usually did. Of course it wasn't wise. Regular divers were horrified by his defiance of the accepted convention that you should always go down with a "buddy." But Peter didn't care. He didn't deal in "buddies." Apart from the daughter he adored but seldom saw, he was the ultimate loner, asleep in his Rip Van Winkle world of artistic isolation. If he was the sort of man who could have friends, he wouldn't need the escape to the ocean floor. And he didn't care about danger. That was a preoccupation of ordinary people with nine-to-five jobs, and mortgages, and silly holidays to look forward to. If something snuffed out his life now, then the struggle would be over. There would be no more battles with an empty page. Never again would he hear the accusing silence of the typewriter. The dammed-up words would be atomized and scattered amid the plankton, buried in the bellies of the fishes, consumed, eventually, by kids in the fish fingers of a thousand TV dinners. It would be a fitting end for the words he both loved and loathed, and he let out a short sharp laugh of longing for the normalcy that would never be his.

Ryan banged the boat into reverse, his eyes on the liquid crystal of the bottom finder. He wanted to be a few feet upcurrent of Neptune. That way Peter could dive the full length of the reef swimming with the flow, and he would pick him up at the other end. As a concession to safety, they were flying the red-and-white dive flag, but his boss never bothered with the inflated red ball that he was supposed to trail from his weight belt as a pointer to his position. Ryan didn't disapprove. It was tough enough trying to keep to your own rules in life without worrying about other people's. And it was only life and death. As a Navy Seal in the steamy jungle waterways of Nam, he had learned *they* were no big deal.

Peter Stein walked back through the transom door. He sat down and slipped on the Mares flippers. He emptied the antifog liquid from the silicon mask and placed it over his face, pulling back his thick hair to avoid breaking the air seal. He wore no wet suit. Next, he picked up the yellow aluminum bottle, the buoyancy-control jacket and regulator already attached, and he looped the fourteen-pound weight belt through the arm of the coat. He lugged the heavy breathing apparatus toward the boat's swim platform. Then he did a very strange thing. He didn't slip on the BCD. Instead he dropped the whole shebang off the stern of the boat into the ocean. For a second or two he watched it sink. Then he took four deep breaths, hyperventilating to depress the desire to breathe and, right hand on his mask to hold it in place, he dived head-first into the sea.

At the wheel of the boat, Ryan shook his head. What was Peter trying to prove? That he had the balls to free dive sixty feet and the cool to don the breathing apparatus on the bottom of the ocean. There was a bit of that in the gesture, but it was really a "my way" thing. Out of water it was always a struggle to manhandle the heavy equipment. Under it, the upward thrust from water displacement rendered it almost weightless. There were other advantages. It wasn't hot down there, and you didn't have to keep your balance on a swaying boat and a wet deck. But there were risks. If he was unable to find his air source on the bottom of the ocean he would have to complete a 120-foot return journey on a single breath.

Peter Stein kicked hard and arrowed down toward the bottom, blowing out against pinched nostrils to equalize the inner ear and sinus air pressure as he descended, exhaling through his nose to eliminate mask "squeeze." He could see the air bottle clearly on the ocean bed, as the sunlight flooded through the water illuminating the yellow tank against the coral. In seconds his starved lungs would be getting their meal of air. He looked to the right and left. The reef looked safe. It was early in the morning and there were no other divers about. Later the reef could get crowded. There were no big fishes either, except for a large lone barracuda about eighty feet away. There were indigo parrots, a shoal of small grouper, and a beady-eyed puffer fish directly below him. Nothing else. Six feet away from the air source he slowed. Where was the mouth piece or the spare breathing regulator they called the octopus? He was air hungry. He had just enough air left in his lungs for the return journey, but the decision whether or not to embark on it wouldn't wait for long. He circled the breathing device, swimming closer. The bottle was upside down, its first stage wedged between two rocks. A thin stream of bubbles rose up from the depths of the crevice. Damn! He would have to ease it out, and hope that no sharp-toothed Moray eel was lurking next to the bottle. It wasn't the lobster season, so he wasn't wearing gloves. In the usual way physical danger didn't bother Peter Stein, but he cared about his fingers. They did the typing. Losing them might assuage the guilt of block, but for sure it wouldn't help in the production of the masterpiece he had been struggling for two years to complete. He reached down carefully along the side of the bottle. He tried to ease it out. No way. It was stuck fast. Boom! A stick had hit the drum in his stomach. He was short of air. A struggle to free the bottle would use more. It would be sensible to head back up. To the amused eyes of Ryan Van der Kamp, ex-Navy Seal and holder of three Purple Hearts? Like hell! Perhaps he could ease out the regulator, or one of the other hoses. They all seemed to have been sucked into the thin black hole that God in his wisdom had placed on the ocean floor to irritate him. Once again he pushed his fingers down the side of the bottle to find its end. A smooth rubber tube slipped between his fingers. He pulled at it, but it was caught. He found another, but it, too, was going nowhere. Boom! Boom! Boom! The beat was regular now, and he could feel the adrenaline squirting into his bloodstream. His mind speeded as he realized he was doing something stupid, for reasons that were more stupid still. But still he couldn't give up. He could never give up. Was this the moment when a strength became a weakness . . . a fatal weakness here alone on the floor of the beautiful ocean that loved nothing more than to be a grave?

Shit! Peter Stein was angry now. It didn't take much. It never had. His fuse was short and it had burned fast. Forget fear. Screw panic. He was furious with himself for the pathetic macho gesture that had gone so seriously wrong. Okay, so he'd done this a hundred times before, but that merely increased the odds of something like this happening. He remembered the philosophical truth that in an eternity of time a monkey typing at random would unwittingly produce the entire works of Shakespeare. Sooner or later he was bound to arrive at the bottom and find the air unavailable to him. When he had confronted that hypothetical situation in his mind, he had always imagined he would simply turn around and return to the surface. It only went to show that the very last person on earth that you knew was yourself, and behind the mask Peter Stein smiled grimly as he realized that the most dangerous factor in this entire situation was his own personality. Whatever. A man had to do what a man had to do . . . whether or not there was an audience. His lungs bursting, he placed both flippered feet firmly on either side of the trapped air tank. He reached down and grabbed both slippery sides of the bottle, and he pulled with every ounce of strength he could muster. It didn't move, but he did. His right foot lost contact with the rock, and shooting forward, jammed itself into a crevice. His bare back brushed against the razor coral and he felt the shock of pain as the skin was peeled from it. But worse, far worse, the effort of pulling and the impact of contact with the coral forced the remaining air from his body.

"Oh, fuck," thought Peter Stein. "I'm going to die."

6

"So, Rob Sand, what's new in the land of the young and the restless?"

Christa stood upright at the wheel of the open Boston Whaler and her blond, salt-stained hair streamed out behind her.

Rob didn't know, or rather he could hardly say. Basically Christa was what was new. She had bounded into the Ameridive shop where he had just gotten a job as instructor, and while he was still trying to get his breath back, she had said she wanted somebody to give her a refresher scuba course. Private tuition. One on one. A pool session and a couple of open-water dives. She would provide the boat.

"I guess the tennis is kinda new," he managed, stealing a sidelong glance at her.

"Yeah, you said you teach diving in the mornings and tennis in the afternoons. That's a pretty heavy schedule."

"I imagine yours is pretty heavy, too."

He wanted to get back to her. She wanted to stay on him.

"Are you good at tennis? I guess you must be to teach it."

She looked at him openly, sizing him up. He was cute, but he was deep, too. The sun-bleached hair and the twenty-year-old muscles lied about the guy inside. That much Christa already knew from the two hours they had spent in the pool on Seacrest, from yesterday's open-water dive, and the long conversation they'd had after it.

"I'm better than those I teach." He laughed modestly.

"Come on, Rob, this is America. Sell it like it is."

"Okay, okay. I was in the semis of the all-Florida at Boca."

"That's better." Christa laughed and lunged playfully at the brown arm that was close to hers. She was drawn to this boy, and not just to his beauty. He was her opposite in temperament—quiet, thoughtful, introverted—but although he was modest, a trifle diffident even, he wasn't weak. There would be lines that Rob Sand wouldn't cross. It would be fun to find out where they were.

"So, who are you teaching right now? Anybody I might know?"

"I just started doing Mary Whitney. I suppose most people have heard of her."

"Wow!" Christa smiled as she let out the exclamation. That was like giving swimming lessons to a shark. Mary Whitney's tennis coaches did most of their hard work *off* the court. But surely not Rob Sand, with his on-the-sleeve religion and his strict moral standards. "How long have you been teaching Mary?"

"Just a couple of times so far. You know her?"

"I was at school with her. I've seen her a few times since. It's funny—I'm going to a party up at her house on Sunday."

"Great. So am I. Will you dance with me?"

"Sure I will, Rob, if you remember to ask me. But I expect the ladies of Palm Beach won't give you too many chances."

He blushed, and Christa felt guilty that she'd intended him to.

"What do you think of her?" she asked.

"Oh, she's okay. Sort of sarcastic, I guess. Doesn't seem to take things too seriously."

"Oh, she will. She will."

He cocked his head to one side, showing that he hadn't a clue what Christa meant.

"Are you planning to teach full time? Tennis and diving." It was time to change the subject. If Mary hadn't yet made her moves on Rob, it would be a calculated delay. There was no way to warn him. He was an adult. Just. Still, Christa felt the pang of something or other. It was best not to think what that something might be.

"No, I don't really know what I want to do long-term. Teaching's a summer thing till I finish school. I just want to do something worthwhile that the Lord would be proud of."

The way he said it was totally unselfconscious. God was in his heart and mind, and so God was in his words. Christa couldn't have uttered a sentence like that even if she'd had the sentiment to express.

"Have you ever thought of modeling?" She was acutely aware that this was probably not at the top of the list of activities of which God might be proud.

"I don't know anything about it."

"I do. You'd be a natural. You'd work all the time. Believe me. It's my business. I know."

"Thanks."

"No, Rob, it's not just an empty compliment. It's a business. You've got the look. If you did it for a few years, you could make some capital, buy a house. Then, later, you could go off and do something else. It's an idea, that's all."

Christa knew she wasn't carrying him with her. Rob's idea of male models would have been molded in South Florida. Modeling was certainly not the Lord's work. Hell, he probably thought it wasn't a *man's* work. Damn! She'd been thinking about starting a male section. He'd have been a great first signing. Steve Pitts would have gone nuts for the guy.

"How do you get into it?" He was being polite.

"I get somebody to take some pictures of you, but basically for you it's easy, 'cause I have an agency and I'm saying you'd be great." She laughed. "It's a bit like being found by Spielberg on the beach. But that's life, I guess. One guy's dreams are another's nightmares."

"Who found you, Christa?"

His voice was full of warmth. He liked her. She could feel it like the sun on her back.

"I got myself found."

He laughed. "I bet you did."

They were silent for a while as the boat banged across the waves, and the palm-lined beach floated past them.

"There, that's my house," shouted Christa suddenly. "The pink one, set back in the dunes."

"You own it?"

"I inherited it." Christa smiled as she spoke. What she'd inherited was a hundred-percent mortgage and a stack of repair bills. But that was then. Now, the rambling beach house, beautifully repaired and maintained, was five million and change.

"You live there by yourself?"

"Not often. I usually rent it. This summer it's rented. I used to live in New York. I've just moved to Miami."

"Mi*ami?*"

Rob had been born in Palm Beach County. Few natives of the Palm Beaches could see the point of the city to the south. There was a part of Christa that knew what he meant. It took some explaining.

"New York's a disaster area these days. Everyone's talking about getting out and quality of life and all that stuff, and they're right. When New York was the center of the universe like it was in the early Reagan years, you put up with the panhandlers, the muggers, the taxes, and the other shit because the whole place was 'now' and where it's at. The clothes scene was hot and that meant the photographers and the girls had to be there. Now everything's crumbling like it did in 'seventy-four. It was saved then by the deregulation of the securities industry and the boom on Wall Street. That for sure isn't going to happen again anytime soon, and all the guys like Trump who put up grandmothers they didn't have as collateral for overpriced real estate are hurting like hell. The city's in rough times. The action is moving west, south, overseas. Florida makes a helluva lot of sense. Low taxes, great weather, and Miami's opened up as a modeling center. You can't move on South Beach for kraut photographers and the New Yorkers have caught on. The magazines can fly their people down in a couple of hours or so, and all the art directors want to get out of Manhattan and pick up a suntan that doesn't come with built-in grime and a lungful of sulfur dioxide."

"I can see how you might want to get out of New York, and that the modeling is good down there with the weather and everything, but . . . I don't know . . . Miami is like sort of foreign, really. It's not just that it's sixty percent Hispanic but it kinda feels like it really belongs somewhere totally different."

"Get real, Rob. It's great because it *is* different. I was down at Bayside the other night, and I had dinner in a restaurant that was identical to one in Seville. The whole place is throbbing, and it's special. The night life is great, the lambada, the energy, the heat . . . I mean, in New York the kids are just churning in a vacuum, desperate to shock, and yet everyone's too jaded to *be* shocked. Miami is the future, I tell you, and it works."

Rob laughed. The girls he knew couldn't talk like that. They were small town. Christa was definitely big picture. Hell, she'd even starred in one.

"You make it sound pretty interesting."

"It *is* interesting. It's a fascinating city. And it just so happens that Lisa Rodriguez lives there. I told you she was joining my agency, didn't I?" Rob nodded and Christa smiled as she recognized her own tendency to bottom line it.

Lisa Rodriguez had been brought up in Miami and now, as conquering queens often did, she had returned to her birthplace. It was a fitting move, because the Rodriguez visual excitement was pure Spain. The heat of jasmine-scented nights wafted from her. You could hear the plaintive wail of flamenco as she arched her graceful back, sense the staccato rhythms of stamping feet as she sashayed across a room, hear the clapping beat of the *zapateados* as she bent forward to say hello. Yes, Christa's move to Miami made all sorts of sense for all kinds of reasons, but some of them were Lisa Rodriguez.

"What's she like?"

"A handful. You'd love her. All men do."

"It must be strange. Being a model, then giving it up and then repping models who are almost as beautiful as you."

Christa smiled as she heard the come-on. It wasn't true, but it was sweet. Lisa's beauty was cutting edge. Hers was five years old. She glanced at him. Once again there was color on his cheek. This time his own compliment had caused it. He was shy and gentlemanly, and not used to flirting. In fact, he was just the sort of guy that a tough girl like Christa was drawn to. It was the bimbos who fancied macho men.

"It's no problem," said Christa, playing his comment straight. "Models are a million miles from beauty queens. They get on pretty well together. I like women. Actually, I like them better than men . . ." She paused. "Most of the time," she added.

"How come you never got married? A lot of guys must have asked you." His voice was earnest. His tone said that it *really* was a puzzle to him.

"I was engaged once." She bit her lip. Oh no. Not this. But the mist was already thickening in her eyes. Damn it. Time was supposed to take care of these feelings. It hadn't. Ten years was yesterday. She could feel the touch of his lips on hers, the squeeze of his fingers in her hand. She could hear the roar of the track, smell the pungent aroma of fuel, hear the howls of the excited crowd. She could remember how alive she'd been, how frightened for him, how proud of him as she watched in delicious horror as she always watched when he was racing the cars he loved. Jamie Huntingdon was going to be her husband. The ring she still wore on her finger was the living evidence of his commitment. She was going to be his countess, and the whole of her life she would love him as she bore his heirs and ran his estates in the old country of which Palm Beach was a pale, tropical imitation. The screaming brakes, the rolling wheels, and the crash of thunder had ended her happiness and blotted out her future, and her stomach twisted now as it had twisted then as, before her eyes, the black acrid smoke and the bright yellow flames had burned the man she had worshiped. Yes, it was still bad, and it always would be. There would never be another to fill the aching void. Nobody was big enough to fill that chasm. Many had tried. None had been chosen. All had been found wanting.

"What happened?"

"He died. He got killed. He drove Formula One." She tried to make it matter-of-fact. But her voice caught on the last bit.

"He was a special guy?"

"He was easy to love." The tear squeezed out, and she shook her head and let the wind take it, turning away from him so that he wouldn't see the weakness.

Easy to love. It was the understatement of the millennium.

He had been fun, he had been joy, he had been the only person on God's earth who could relax her. Jamie had never worried about anything, had never criticized anybody, never experienced a pessimistic mood. Life with him had been laughter, an endless sand-box of pleasure, and each day had dawned more beautiful and exciting than the one before. Then, in a pall of smoke, the music had died. God, how she missed him. She longed for him, her whole body aching with the need that would never be filled, and sometimes she wanted her own life to end so that she could be with him, lazing in love in some meadow in Paradise.

Rob's hand was on her arm. His fingers squeezed their support. "He's safe with God," he said.

She smiled wanly through the mist as she turned to him.

"Yeah, God's your thing, isn't he? I guess he needed to have Jamie around . . . and my parents and my sister . . . sort of a greedy kind of guy . . ." Her voice trailed off in bitterness.

Rob said nothing. He had been here before. Mere minds could never understand God's mystery. Without faith nothing made sense. With it, everything did. There was no way of saying this to somebody who hadn't already grasped it. That was the problem. And he wanted to talk to Christa, to really talk to her. It was funny, she wasn't like the others. So many women saw him as the male equivalent of a bimbo. They thought his religion was as cute as his pectorals and his guileless smile. They patronized him, and listened with half an ear when he was speaking, because they were too busy looking, and lusting, and planning his fall from grace. Okay, that wasn't all bad. He used it. It got him jobs. It kept him jobs, and he could handle it, and them. But it pissed him off. And now when he found a woman he could really respect, like Christa, he wished he was better with words and he wished, too, that believing in God so deeply didn't sound so deeply dumb. Because he wasn't dumb. He was bright, and interested in things, and at Atlantic College he got good grades. Still, he was twenty and he had lived all his life in Florida, and Christa had eight or nine years on him, and eight or nine lifetimes in terms of experience.

"It's a question of faith . . ." he said at last, woefully aware of the inadequacy of his remark.

But Christa's faith was in herself. Misery wasn't for wallowing in. Nostalgia was a dirty word, and self-pity was an expletive she deleted. The thing to do was to get on with your life. If you were busy enough, there was no time for unhappiness. No time for unhappiness. That was her motto, and in a strange way, her motivation. She had thought about it so very often, and doubtless if she had not been born into the upper classes, who regarded shrinks as hilarious jokes, she would have had a chance to discuss it with a psychiatrist. Her basic problem had been how to get noticed by parents who weren't in the noticing business. Everything else had paled against the importance of that. The harder she tried to relate to her mother and father, the more distant they became. They were embarrassed by bodies, appalled by touch, nervous and skittish in the presence of public emotion. They laughed little but sneered a lot, and cynicism was their religion, and pessimism their forté. "Nothing will come to any good," was their world view and the best that could be hoped for in the life business was that the trust fund would see you through to a decently attended burial. Children were what you had to go to the schools you went to and to join the clubs that were yours. They married the children of your friends and, at the end of the day, they pushed up the daisies in the cemetery next to the church where you had done your living and your dying. In between, you existed, doing and saying the things your class fellow travelers did and said, and, as long as you kept your feelings under tight control, there wasn't an awful lot that could go wrong.

There had been only two ways to react to parents like that. You either beat them or you joined them. Christa could never quite work out why she had chosen the former. It had been a lifetime's work, and funnily enough the fact that they were no longer around as a bemused audience made zero difference to the way she carried on. The name of her game was to do things, to succeed at things, to set goals and to reach them. Her ambition was to dazzle the emotionally blind. In the careful world of her parents' quiet understatement, she was the rude noise. What didn't the children of the seriously grand do? They didn't become models. Right! No problem! She became the most successful model in the world. And what did the upper-echelon patricians regard as irredeemably common? The cut-and-thrust world of dog-eat-dog business. Wonderful. The model agency she had started would make Ford's look like a small-time operation. She substituted energy for the lassitude of her class; optimism for pessimism; extroversion for the corked-up constipation of her parents' social interaction. She didn't mind what she did, as long as her parents weren't indifferent to it. To irritate them, to anger them, to disappoint them, became her sole objective, but try as she might, the only reaction she got from them was apathy. All the time her parents petted their dogs, and gave their dinner parties, and regarded her with the affection and interest they reserved for the vast ficus tree that was such a prominent feature of the driveway to their house.

Shit! They were up there in heaven watching her. She would pull something out of the hat yet. It wasn't too late. It never would be. Once again she allowed herself to think of Jamie. Her life had almost changed with him. If he had lived to love her forever, the old ghosts and demons might have gone away and haunted her no more. But it hadn't happened like that. He had died and so had her sister and parents but they lived on to torture and torment her, and in some weird way to drive her on. So she laughed bitterly at the silliness of life and at its inescapability, as she forced herself back into the present. They were nearly at the reef. They were here to dive. It was time to get on with it.

"Here we are," said Christa, changing the subject and throttling back. "We'll anchor a hundred feet north of that Tiara."

Christa maneuvered the boat, peering over the side into the clear water. She killed the engine and heaved the anchor overboard.

The effort of climbing into the wetsuits in the ninety-degree heat was the distraction she needed. She was no longer looking back. She was looking forward. This was going to be fun, and it was great to have an experienced diver like Rob at her side.

He checked her equipment. "Okay, Christa," he said, taking control. "We'll do a sixty-foot dive for thirty minutes, or until we're down to five hundred pounds per square inch on the pressure gauge. Don't forget the three-minute safety stop at fifteen feet on the way up. What's the most important rule in diving?"

Christa smiled, grateful for once to be in the passenger seat. "Breathe normally at all times and never hold your breath under water," she intoned like a student in school.

"That's right," said Rob seriously. "And remember, we do a really slow ascent to avoid damage to the lungs."

"Yes, *sir,*" said Christa with mock deference.

"I'll swim down and check that the anchor's set. Stay close."

Rob sat on the side of the Whaler. Christa did the same.

"Dive. Dive. Dive," said Rob, and they both toppled over backward into the deep.

* * *

Christa kicked down in a head-first descent. She had been nervous. It was her first dive for ages, but now, wrapped by the warm ocean, she was already at home. To her left, Rob was swimming down toward the anchor to make sure that it was set firm on the bottom. He made her feel safe. He was so serious, so reliable—a real baby-boomer child, probably used to looking after parents who'd planned to remain sixties children forever. She smiled inside the mask. He was attractive, and she really liked him. But he was too straightforward for her, too one-dimensional, damn it, too young.

She looked around. She had half an hour of bottom time, and she wanted to make every minute count. As always, the beauty of the reef astounded her. Earlier she had mocked God's cruelty, but it was impossible to doubt his existence. All about her was the evidence of the Creator. This beauty could not be accidental. It had to have been designed, and by an architect who dealt only in perfection. The colors flooded into her mind, amplified by the silent slow motion of the deep. Christa breathed steadily, showering out a cloud of bright bubbles, and she sank gracefully to the bottom.

A conch shell caught her eye, nestling against a piece of coral and brushed by the frond of a sea fern. She reached for it. At once she felt an arm on hers. Rob was at her elbow, shaking his head, and pointing toward the shell with a clenched fist, the universal diver's signal for danger. Christa looked carefully at the shell and its surroundings. What had she missed? A Moray eel lurking nearby? A camouflaged scorpionfish that she hadn't noticed? A stingray covered by sand, that could react badly if frightened? She splayed open her hands. "Why danger?" she was asking. Rob reached for the slate around his neck. He scribbled on it and handed it to Christa.

"Poisonous conch," the message read.

Of course. Christa had forgotten that conchs could be poisonous. She smiled her gratitude and gave Rob the sign that said she had gotten the picture—thumb and forefinger together making a zero. Then she swam away from him toward the left. It was okay to have a guardian, and he had saved her from a painful rash, but she wanted to assert some independence, too. It was a reflex action. She liked to lead.

Almost immediately a violent motion caught her eye. Twenty feet beyond a ridge she had just passed an extraordinary scene was unfolding. A skindiver—way too deep at sixty feet—was wrestling with something that was stuck in the coral. As Christa watched, he lost his grip and fell back suddenly. She saw his shoulder sandpaper across a finger of razor-sharp coral. A cloud of blood came away with it, a thin film of crimson in the clear blue water. At the same time, bubbles exploded from the wounded diver's mouth. From their quantity it was obvious that he had just lost a lungful of precious air. The man was clearly in danger. He was hurt. He was out of air, and the surface was sixty feet away. Christa's legs threshed the ocean. She swam toward him, reaching for the spare regulator in the left pocket of her BCD. She was about to become the stranger's lifeline, embarking on the dangerous game of offering air to a drowning man. She prayed to

God he wouldn't panic. There was no time to alert Rob. He wouldn't be far behind, anyway. Rob would play it by the book, and the book said that diving buddies swam close together.

She was two feet from the lone diver. Still, he hadn't seen her. He was locked in his own desperate, private world. He had no idea help was at hand. She could see the raw wound on his shoulder, and now his foot appeared to be caught in a crevice. Christa could all but hear the alarm bells that would be ringing in his mind. At that moment he turned toward her, and she connected with the brown eyes behind the mask. She held up the mouthpiece, the one that was known as the octopus, and she reached for his left arm with her right one, drawing him in toward her. Unless he was a complete amateur, he should know how to do this. He did. His eyes widened. He jabbed down with his thumb on the "clear" button to expel water from the mouthpiece, and he jammed the octopus into his mouth. For long seconds he sucked greedily at the air.

As he did so, Christa tried to work out what had happened. A yellow air tank was stuck fast in a coral crevice at his feet. How the hell had it gotten there? Why on earth had the diver decided to take it off on the ocean floor? And how come he had managed to wedge it so deep, upside down, in the crack in the coral? Where was his buddy? Surely he couldn't have been so foolish as to dive alone. She remembered the Tiara on the surface. It had been the only boat there, and it had been flying a dive flag. She vaguely remembered there had been someone on board when she and Rob had begun their descent. She peered closely at the man she had saved, searching for answers in the shadowy face behind the mask. It was difficult to see what he looked like. His hair streamed out in the water, and the nosepiece of his mask hid most of his upper face, while the mouthpiece of his breathing tube distorted the lower part. His eyes, however, were clearly visible. They stared back at her. There was no fear in them. They flashed through the water in the way that angry eyes would, and it was with a shock of surprise that Christa realized they were signaling irritation. Gratitude, relief, humility, apology—all would have been appropriate emotions. Anger, however, was as unpredictable as it was unacceptable. Could she have gotten it wrong? She made the "Are you okay?" sign with her fingers. He didn't respond. Instead he helped himself to another deep breath from her tank, and he bent down to free his foot.

It was Christa's turn to be angry. Damn this idiot and his stupid arrogance. Helping an air-hungry stranger was a risky business. Sometimes they were so freaked they fought for your air and wouldn't give it up. And quite apart from anything else, he was using up her precious bottom time. For two pins she would snatch her breathing tube away and let him struggle toward the surface on his own. Trailing a vapor cloud of blood, he would be a tempting shark target. Maybe a hammerhead's teeth sunk deep into his tight little butt would teach the asshole a thing or two about safety, manners, and sociability. But even as she felt those things, Christa was aware of other emotions. The eyes that bored into hers were eyes that demanded attention. They were fierce and furious, they were tortured and tantalizing, they were tormenting . . . and they were tormented. The intensity of his expression shone through the diving mask, and the black Medusa hair, flying free in the ocean, emphasized the energy that flowed from him. For a single second, Christa Kenwood found herself breaking the cardinal rule of diving.

She held her breath under water.

Which was the moment that Rob arrived. Swimming thirty feet behind Christa, he had seen it all. As an experienced diver, he had already arrived at the bottom line. The guy in trouble was some macho novice who was diving alone. Almost certainly he had deep-sixed his breathing gear on purpose and then swum down to retrieve it. He'd seen other cowboys do the same stupid thing. Rob didn't often get angry, but the stranger's behavior had actually put Christa in some danger. That was unforgivable. The guy was breathing now. He was safe, but the scratch from the coral hardly seemed a sufficient punishment for his reckless behavior. As he swam up to them, Rob scribbled on his slate.

"Are you all right?" he wrote as a formal prelude to the fireworks that would follow.

The stranger peered at the slate and nodded once.

"Where's your buddy?" wrote Rob, thrusting the slate at the diver.

He deigned to reach for it.

He wrote slowly in a beautiful round hand that was a stark contrast to Rob's untidy scrawl.

"I don't deal in buddies," was his response.

Christa read it over Rob's shoulder. She couldn't believe the arrogance of the stranger. She grabbed the slate.

"Do you deal in thank-yous? They're usual when someone has just saved your life," she wrote angrily.

He snatched the slate from her.

"You didn't save my life."

He pushed it back at her, firing a fury broadside with his eyes.

"Are you a very stupid man?" countered Christa.

Something snapped inside Peter Stein. There had been dreadful moments in the last twenty years, but he couldn't remember one like this. All his life he had known one fact, and it had pulled him through the bad times and sabotaged all the good ones. What Peter Stein knew was that he was brilliant. He wasn't just clever. He wasn't merely "not stupid." He was a genius. The Pulitzer said so. The reviewers chorused it. The readers in their millions chanted the refrain. On the talk shows the hosts mouthed the truth at him. Now, at the bottom of the ocean, a woman with a better body by far than a Darryl Hannah mermaid was asking him if he was thick.

He stared in horror at the slate. He looked up at his wetsuited savior. She was watching him. She was waiting for him to communicate. What she wanted from him was words. But he couldn't find the words. Somewhere in the mess of his brilliant mind, they had gotten lost. It was a distillation of all the terrors over all the years, but somehow it was worse because of all people this girl had a right to his writing. The panic was strong inside him, stronger than when he had thought he might die. On the bottom of the ocean, the hero of American literature had writer's block.

Then, at last, there was merciful movement in his fingers. It wasn't Nobel Prize–winning literature. It was hardly Pulitzer material. Only the most devout fan of minimalism would have considered it "great writing." Peter Stein, however, was as relieved as hell when he managed to scratch out—

"Thanks."

Now there was only one word in his mind. *Escape.* He bent at both knees and he pushed off from the bottom as if jumping for the moon. In diver's language it was known as an emergency ascent, and Peter Stein remembered to do the strange thing that the diving manuals demanded. As you rose toward the surface, the pressure of the water decreased and the air in your lungs expanded. If you didn't get rid of the air on the way up, you risked a ruptured lung. The solution was to breathe out as you ascended, and beginners were encouraged to shout loudly underwater so that their instructors could actually hear them performing the safety maneuver. It jelled perfectly with his mood.

As he shot upward, Christa heard quite clearly the extraordinary noise he made.

Peter Stein had found at last the perfect description for his humiliating experience.

"Aaaaaaaaaaaaaagh," he screamed.

Christa watched him go, bewildered by the intensity of their brief encounter.

Rob scratched furiously on the slate.

"What an *asshole!*"

"Mmmmmmmmm," murmured Christa, nodding her head. But oddly, in her heart, she couldn't agree. In fact, her heart was behaving strangely. It was pumping hard. It was leaping around in her chest. As she looked down at the slate, she was not reading Rob's irritable diagnosis of the stranger's character. She was concentrating instead on the single word "Thanks"—the one he had found so very difficult to write. Already she had forgotten his irresponsible behavior. She could remember only the burning brightness of his eyes, his wounded shoulder, the desperation of his precipitous departure. Who was he? Who would he be? From what private hell had he summoned up his departing scream of the damned? She wanted to know. But she would never know. He had been a man in trouble at the bottom of the ocean. She had rescued him. She would never see him again.

7

"Muffy, I don't mean to be rude . . . and usually there's nothing I enjoy more . . . but where the hell's Bruce? I'm paying him fifty big ones. I shouldn't get palmed off with the sidekick for those kind of bucks."

Muffy Kellogg didn't like being a sidekick, but she smiled a sickly smile to pretend she didn't care.

"Oh, he'll show later, Mary. Don't panic. You know Bruce. It's always all right on the night. He likes to stoke up the anxiety levels. It makes for a better party."

Mary McGregor Whitney's lip curled. She peered around the flower-bedecked terrace as if expecting to find a coffin on it.

"Muffy, let's get one thing straight. I don't panic. I never, ever panic, dear. And I don't give a shit about the party. All my parties are disasters. I give them to get back at my 'friends.' What I *care* about, sweetheart, is value for money. I've paid for Bruce Sutka's butt and now I want to see the tight little thing mooning at me, okay?" She laughed to emphasize that she meant what she said.

"I'll get him over right away," said Muffy. She cursed inside. God, she hated being the poor relation. Working for a living was *so* demeaning.

She picked up the cellular phone as if it were something the cat had brought in. It made life simpler, but it was totally non–Palm Beach—along with faxes, Ferraris, and fornication.

Mary Whitney's arm shot out to forestall her.

"Later, Muffy. First, I want a tour of the disaster area. And I want to see the seating plan. That's always fun. Did you remember to put the Partridges next to those Phipps cousins whose son ditched their daughter for a salsa dancer in Miami? *They* should find plenty to talk about during the lambada cabaret."

She laughed a throaty laugh, throwing back her long neck and letting the severe geometry of her sixties-style cut fly about in the beach breeze. She felt good. Business was booming, and business set the rhythm of her heartbeat. The first quarter's results had arrived that morning from the accountants in New York. Whitney Enterprises was running thirty percent ahead of last year, despite the recession. At this rate the full year would top a billion bucks in sales. If you valued the whole shebang at the average industry multiple of ten, it meant her company was worth ten billion dollars. Not that she would ever sell it. Whitneys didn't sell the things they owned. It was considered the worst possible taste.

"So what's the story on the roses?"

"A hundred and twenty long-stemmed roses per table of eight. Fifty tables. That's around seven thousand with spares. They fly into West Palm from New York tomorrow afternoon in an iced compartment. The buds will open in time for the party."

"And next day they'll be garbage," said Mary Whitney. Muffy could swear there was relish in her voice at the conspicuousness of the consumption. Not for the first time, she wondered what weird mutation in the Whitney genes allowed her to enjoy blowing ten thousand bucks on blood-red roses. It was so nouveau riche. She suppressed the shudder of revulsion. When the lilies, orchids, and gardenias were thrown in, the money spent on the flowers for this single evening could have put her brother through college—not that the wastrel had either the energy or the inclination to go.

Mary Whitney walked across the terrace to the colonnaded balcony. She leaned over it, skinny elbows perched on the faded stone, and looked out to sea. The ocean was flat, its color the aquamarine of the Caribbean. Below her, on the grass, men were draping fabric over black metal frames as the "nightclub" took shape down by the beach. She peered from side to side, surveying the immaculate ten acres of her oceanfront estate, the old Mizner house lolling grandly on the multi-million-dollar lot. She sighed. Money might not buy happiness, but it for sure allowed you to spread some misery around. She turned to Muffy. "Is anybody coming who's even vaguely amusing?" she asked petulantly.

"I suppose you mean 'famous,' said Muffy with a sarcastic laugh. As a Whitney social equal, albeit a cash inferior, she was allowed the odd potshot at the plutocrat.

"Don't knock fame, dear. It's just another method of keeping the score. It has to be earned with a little thing called talent. Of course I realize that here in trust-fund land, that's a dirty word."

Muffy laughed, pleased that she had scratched the surface of the Whitney skin.

"Well, apart from the New York glitterati who are staying with you, I'm afraid the list is a little short of 'household names,' unless you include the dependents of the heroes who gave us Listerine, Kleenex, and Corn Flakes. Now who's amusing? God, is *anyone?* Oh, I almost forgot. Do you remember Christa Kenwood? She's down here with some creep photographer, doing a shoot. I found her on the beach, and invited her. I hope that was okay. She's fun *and* famous and you did give me carte blanche on the Palm Beachers. She used to be one of those."

"*I* know Christa Kenwood," sneered Mary Whitney. "She lives in the real world, Muffy. She might have gone to the Day School with us, but she got out, dear. She escaped, like me. She's done a ton of stuff for the company. She's a star and a sweetheart." Mary paused. "Do you remember her yellow panties?" she said at last.

"Danforth Wrightsman was going on about them on the beach. Funny the things that stick in one's memory."

"I heard she gave up modeling and opened an agency," said Mary thoughtfully.

"What a bizarre thing to want to do. I suppose those yellow panties were trying to tell us something," scoffed Muffy.

"An agency in Miami, I heard. It's getting hot down there on South Beach. Pretty cool idea. Good. I'm glad she's coming. Brighten up the evening for the heteros . . . if there are any left. Put her at my table."

"I already have."

"Who's sitting next to her? It should be somebody who'll fall hopelessly in love with her and ruin his life as a result . . . you know, divorce, a messy court case, suicides." Mary Whitney laughed delightedly at the thought.

"Actually," said Muffy slowly, "I thought it might be amusing to sit her next to Peter Stein."

8

"I'll drive."

Lisa Rodriguez stepped forward and took the wheel of the boat. The boy she replaced flattened himself against the seat to make way for her.

"Okay, fine, Lisa," he mumbled, pretending that he was giving her permission to steer. He swallowed hard. Among the silky hairs of his chest, the gold crucifix leaped on its chain.

"Where's the speed thing?" snapped Lisa. She turned and stared hard at him.

For a moment he was speechless. The Rodriguez gaze had scooped out his guts. It was too much. She was too much. Her butt alone could make slaves of people. It platformed out from slender nut-brown thighs, the crowning glory at the end of her long, luscious legs, and her naked buttocks were separated from each other by a pencil line of the luckiest black material in the world.

"Where?" barked Lisa. She waved an imperious hand over the instrument panel.

"The levers with the gold tops," spluttered José del Portal de Aragon. His stomach was a vacuum. It wasn't just the Rodriguez beauty. It was also the fear of what she would do to his precious boat.

She showed him.

Her right hand shot forward and jammed itself against the four accelerators.

The roar of the coupled 450 Mercruisers coincided with the great leap forward. Lisa was slammed back against the white leather of the driver's seat, her rump cannoning happily into the soft upholstery. José, however, was not so lucky. In the cramped cockpit of the powerboat, he was positioned in the no-man's-land between the driver's and the passenger's seat. Now he had lift-off. He flew backward like a Parthian shot, lost his balance, and crashed in a heap of winded flesh onto the sun platform in the stern.

"Shit," he howled.

"Hang on," screamed Lisa into the howling wind. She knew she was way too late with her warning, but she didn't care. At the peak of her beauty and fame, caring was for others.

She could feel the throb of the engines beneath the soles of her feet. The shock waves climbed her legs and curled contentedly around the smooth contours of her butt. The vibrations wrapped themselves around her, running up the inside of her thighs, plucking at the suddenly awakening core of her. Legs wide apart for balance, she braced herself on the heaving deck.

At the back of his half-million-dollar custom Cigarette, José picked himself up. He was more sophisticated than most twenty-one-year-olds, but he knew he was out of his depth. Lisa Rodriguez was two years younger than he, but in the ways that mattered she was ancient evenings. He stared helplessly around him as the sea rushed by. She was doing sixty miles an hour. Thank the Lord the ocean off Miami Beach was smooth. If a novice driver hit a wave at this speed, it would be a short good-bye.

"Be careful," he shouted into the breeze.

"Be careful . . . shit," Lisa screamed back. To emphasize her point she pushed the "speed things" as far forward as they would go. "Pedal to the metal," she murmured to herself.

The Cigarette obeyed. The engines roared to maximum revs. The Speedo kept the score. Seventy and rising.

José crawled toward the cockpit. A good day on a supertuned boat like this was getting home with three out of four engines still running. Even if they didn't capsize or hit anything, the mechanic's bill alone for this outing could run twenty thousand bucks. But, despite the danger, and the threatened financial hit, he didn't feel bad. Instead he felt light, wonderful, elated . . . because, of course, he was in love.

He made the safety of the passenger seat and crawled into it, grabbing the guardrails gratefully. Half a mile to the right, the shore was a blur. They had sped past Bal Harbor, and now the skyscrapers of Miami Beach were falling like nine-pins. At this rate, lunch at Los Ranchos in Bayside looked like a non-go. It was next stop Key Largo. He debated whether he could make that point, and he stole a look at the Amazon who was so totally in charge of his life. It was pointless. The wind said so. So did the mind-numbing sound of the engines. And so did the Rodriguez breasts, thrust forward in the breeze, dominant, daring, defiant of anyone or anything that stood in her way.

But, perversely, just as José surrendered, Lisa hauled back the throttles. It was as if the Cigarette had hit a brick wall. It stopped dead in the water. Its mountainous wake surged forward. A wall of salt water descended on the stern, soaking the engines with their delicate fuel-injection systems and splashing over the expensive leather of the sunbathing pad.

In the silence that followed, Lisa Rodriguez said, "Wow! This baby can move."

José wondered if it would ever move again. The calculator in his brain tried to add up just how many thousands it would take to get it to move. If salt water had gotten into the fuel lines, then his gargantuan allowance wasn't going to hack it. Jeez! It would be the carpet in his father's study and deals done with the devil in exchange for the cash infusion that would be needed. A promise to go back to school; a summer job in the Madrid offices of one of his father's companies; some best-behavior dates with the dog who doubled as the Florida senator's daughter.

"It's better not to stop so suddenly," he managed.

"Stop fast, go fast, live fast," said Lisa, laughing.

"Love fast?"

"Love even faster, José." Her tongue painted sensuous lips. "With those who know how to keep up."

In case there should be any doubt about her meaning, she looked down his body, past the flat boy's stomach, to the already stirring pale pink boxer trunks.

"I'm glad you came back home," he said softly.

"I didn't come back home. Miami isn't my home. The world's my home."

She tossed her hair in the hot breeze as she tried to deny the childhood that nobody could ever escape.

"Here," she said suddenly. "You steer."

José hurried to obey, one ear tuned to the rhythm of the engines, the other to the unpredictable strains of Lisa's emotions.

He flipped the wheel to the right. They hadn't overshot Government Cut . . . either by accident or design. Maybe the Rodriguez daredevil spontaneity was more apparent than real. Lunch at Los Ranchos looked safe.

"Didn't you like Miami?"

"Which Miami? The living dead people? SoBe and the trendies? Cubans still crying in their *cortidijos* over the Bay of Pigs?" She laughed a scornful laugh. How could he be so naïve? Miami was not black and white. It was everything in between. It was the rainbow colors of "Miami Vice" and all the drab and dingy earth hues of a decaying Third World city at the bottom of America. It was old Spain, bourgeois "now," the city of the future. It was fun and dull. It was sad and gay. It was cosmopolitan and parochial. Above all, it was the city where she had fought the war of her childhood, and the exciting town she would now stoop to conquer.

José looked puzzled. The Aragons had sensed which way the wind was blowing and gotten out of Batista's Cuba with their loot when Castro was still a guerrilla in the hills. Now, the Aragon sugar plantations were Florida's biggest business after tourists and citrus. So he hadn't a clue what Lisa was talking about. To him, Miami was the twenty-thousand-square-foot palace on the Bay, boats and seaplanes and checkbook parents and more cousins than grains of sand on the private beach. It was private tutors, the base for trips to the Andalusian bull ranch near Seville, the Avenue Foch Paris apartment, the brownstone in the Big Apple on Sutton Place. The camera shops, the seedy barrios, the nervous opulence of Downtown were all part of the looking-glass world beyond the tinted windows of Aragon stretch limousines.

"I guess it is a funny place," he said at last to paper over his inability to analyze any world that wasn't his. He stole a sidelong glance at her. Where was Lisa's mood heading? His heart thumped against his chest. Oh, shit, she was beautiful. And famous. Her starlight would shine all over him at Bayside where he parked the Cigarette on weekend evenings. He would walk her around, and all the idiots who were his friends would see that José del Portal de Aragon was more than just his shiny boat, his platinum plastic, and his megarich old man. But it wasn't just that. His whole body was on fire with lust. Did she do it with kids like him? Where could he find the words that would smooth his path to sexual glory? What to do? What not to do with a goddess like Lisa Rodriguez? Every millisecond would be a manhood test, and the fear and excitement flowed within him because nothing had ever mattered as much as this.

"We met once," said Lisa suddenly.

"What?" José hadn't expected that one. Obviously it was a mistake. When he had first set eyes on her, at a party given by a friend of his father's, he had fallen in love. Flying high on good champagne, he had found the words to invite her to lunch, and for reasons he still couldn't understand, she had accepted.

"A long time ago. There was a party in the Grove, given by some people called Almodovar. I asked you to dance."

"I'd have remembered, Lisa. Nobody could forget you. Not me, not anyone."

He swallowed. It was true, but he felt strange. There was an edge to Lisa's voice. What was coming might not be good.

"I wasn't beautiful then. I was fat and I was ugly and I was poor. My dress was made from old drapes and I made it myself."

He said nothing. He hadn't been a very nice teenager. His gut told him that the past was about to take away the toy he wanted with the desperation of the spoiled rich kid.

"I said, 'Will you dance with me?' and it took me an hour to find the courage. Do you remember what you said?"

"I think you got it wrong, Lisa. I never . . ."

"You said . . . you said . . ." Lisa Rodriguez looked straight ahead. "You said, 'Aragons don't dance with peasants.' "

He gulped hard, but she hadn't finished.

"And then, while I stood there with tears in my eyes, you turned to your friends and you said, 'Unless they are very pretty,' and you laughed and laughed and they laughed, and then I ran away."

The throb of the engines papered over the agonizing silence. José didn't know what to say.

He couldn't remember the incident. But it sounded like him at fourteen. His backbone had been constructed from cash and carelessness in those days. And in these, for that matter. There were two alternatives. He could deny it, or he could apologize for it. True to character, he tried to do both.

"Listen, Lisa, I think you've got it wrong. I'd never have said something like that . . . especially not to you, but if I did . . . if I did, then I'm very sorry, really, I mean . . ."

He watched to see how he had done. Not well, he suspected.

"Oh, I don't mind. It's a little thing. It hurt me then, but lots of things hurt me then. I shouldn't have asked you to dance. I shouldn't have been poor. I shouldn't have eaten all those sticky cakes. Everything bad that happens to you is your fault. And everything good that happens to you is your triumph. I don't believe in accidents. You'd dance with me now, wouldn't you, José."

She cocked a brown leg onto the passenger seat, and adjusted the strap of her thong over her hip bone. The minimal bra was plastered to the underside of the breasts that didn't need it, and suddenly the air around her was thick with the scent of lust. She turned toward him, the famous lips parted around the perfect teeth, and she smiled the Lisa Rodriguez million-dollar smile at the silly little boy who had once wounded her.

He smiled back in relief. He was still a contender. For some reason he would never understand, she hadn't blown him away.

"We could go dancing tonight," he said, his voice falling over itself in enthusiasm. He was so caught up in his own needs, he hadn't picked up Lisa's deeper message.

"Let's see how you do at lunch," said Lisa, unleashing a gurgling laugh that was equal parts flirtation and scorn. The butterfly of beauty had flown free from the ugly chrysalis that this boy had once wounded. But she was the same Lisa Rodriguez, and she had never forgotten how to hate.

He stood tall at the wheel of the Cigarette as he turned the boat into the Bayside marina. Good-looking chicks on powerboats were known around Miami as "deck furniture" and he had a museum masterpiece beside him. The pride of pseudopossession puffed up his muscled chest as he flicked the gears and manipulated the throttles beneath the admiring glances of the lunchtime crowd. He backed into an empty slip with maximum people exposure, gunning the powerful engines and flipping on the stereo to top volume until the whole marina was rocked with the violent bass of "Wild One." Look at me, he was saying. Look what I've got. Look *who* I've got. See, therefore, who I am.

He threw a rope to the dockhand, with a haughty "Please don't touch the boat," and he hurried to position the fenders and tie up before reluctantly killing the souped-up Mercruisers that were such a potent part of his masculinity.

Lisa watched him, smiling. She drummed on her thigh in time to the music. He was quite cute with his tan, tight muscles, and taut butt. In another world she might even have liked him, as a sweet joke of no consequence on a slow afternoon in the sun. But it wasn't another world. It was this one. And José de Aragon was a symbol. The world might agree that Lisa's circumstances had changed, but how could she prove it to *herself*? The answer was here, beside her in the eyes that had once been filled with mockery and scorn when she had dared to ask the pretty aristocrat for a dance. The eyes sang a different song now. They were full of lust and longing, of fear and humility, chockablock full of admiration for the person and the body and the beauty that Lisa Rodriguez had created from the psychological wreckage of her childhood. Here, at her side, was the living proof that she was no longer the person she had once been.

"We should have a drink before lunch on the boat," said José in a tone of voice he had copied from his father. "I make a neat martini."

"Like all good preppy American boys," said Lisa.

"Would you like one?" He ignored the "American" remark. Cubans would always be Cubans, both to themselves, and, less fortunately, to the American WASP establishment who would never totally accept them. As far as the New World was concerned, aristocrats came exclusively from the Old World. Third World "aristocrats" existed only in their own imaginations.

He hurried below into the slinky cabin of the powerboat and grabbed a silver shaker, some ice, and the "right" gin. In an elaborate gesture of macho, he passed the bottle of Vermouth over the shaker to show that he knew how to make martinis strong. He shook it over his head as if it was a talisman to ward off evil spirits. He poured a large shot into a glass and handed it to Lisa. In José's world, the first thing you did with a woman was fill her with booze. The second thing you did was to tank up yourself. It was an insurance policy. It often made for a disastrous conclusion, but it for sure dulled the memory of it. That way, at least, you weren't inhibited from trying again.

Lisa took the drink and tossed it back as if it were lemonade. She'd learned booze and harder things in a school far tougher than any José had ever dreamed about. She caught the look of admiration on his face.

"Are you working down here?" he said at last.

"I'm going to be. There's a new agency that's just opened up. Owned by Christa Kenwood. I'm probably going to go with it."

"Christa Kenwood, the model?"

"Ex-model," said Lisa firmly.

"She made that movie . . . *Summer People.* It was a blast. She's really a turn-on."

Lisa Rodriguez stifled a mock yawn. There were few enough women in the world she considered genuine competition. Christa was one of them.

"Isn't it taking a chance to go with a new agency . . . I mean, when you're so successful. Who were you with in New York?"

Lisa looked at José, as if seeing him for the first time. That was a shrewd remark from a megabuck, narcissistic airhead. Clearly he'd been listening to the grownups.

"Elle. Rossetti's purple harem. Listen, baby, when you're as big as I am, you don't take chances. Other people do. I could be with an agency *you* started, and still work every hour God sent. Make me another drink."

He scurried to obey.

"I met Rossetti once at Aussi in Sag Harbor. He's a pretty cool dude. Jeez, what a job." José whistled his admiration. If his father would allow it, he'd be a fashion photographer. Great way to pull chicks.

Lisa's laugh was a snarl. She had never known the meaning of ambivalence until she'd met Johnny Rossetti. She could still remember the mall in Boca where they'd had the model competition. Rossetti had been sitting in the row of judges, predatory as a hovering falcon, as he had sized up the meat at the market. He hadn't needed to look twice at Lisa Rodriguez. He'd whispered to the know-nothing local judges who fronted the traveling Elle pulling machine, and she had won. It had been the turning point in her life. Before that moment there had been no victories, after it there had been no defeats. Rossetti had pressed the fast forward on the video of her life. Champagne and caviar at an expensive bar had been followed by a sleeker "I'll-make-you-a-star" pitch than the prepubescent Lisa had ever heard at the movies. The first-class one-way ticket to the Big Apple had been delivered by courier the next day, and the apartment above the Elle offices on Madison was the heaven that Lisa had always dreamed of finding. It had taken her a month to discover what in her heart she already knew . . . that the lunch would not be free. And then she had met the "other" Johnny Rossetti. The one she was about to bury deep in the shit.

"What did you think was so cool about Rossetti?"

José didn't answer right away. What was cool about Rossetti was that he had access to wall-to-wall beautiful women and knew how to use and abuse them. That wouldn't play well with the fiery Rodriguez.

"Oh, I don't know, he seemed kinda . . . intelligent," said José with a dismissive wave of his hand. "He didn't really talk to me."

"He's as thick as his dick," barked Lisa. "He's the sort of guy who thinks a magazine is a book and Shirley MacLaine and Jane Fonda are intellectuals. You think he's cool because he screws a lot."

There was no answer to that.

José felt like his second martini.

"Maybe he's got a Don Juan thing . . . like he's gay and trying to prove he's not." José paused. It was a reach. "They talked about that in psychology," he added by way of explanation.

"Could be, Sigmund Freud, because the first time he screwed me he had a Filipino baseball player clamped on behind."

José was finishing his drink. Now he gagged on it.

"He didn't," he spluttered.

"He for sure did. I was thirteen and he wasn't superstitious."

José fought to find the priorities. Rossetti was a *faggot?* Psychology was *real?* Lisa Rodriguez did . . . orgies?

Then, like a slow moon rising, the more adult ramifications dawned.

"He *made* you do that . . . like it was *rape?*"

Lisa paused. "No, it wasn't rape. He didn't force me to do it. I didn't *want* to do it, but I needed the things he could get for me, and that was what it took. You wouldn't understand about needing things."

José suppressed a smile. Lisa could get some things wrong. He *needed* a Testarossa. His friends were beginning to laugh about the Porsche. Hell, right now he needed Lisa Rodriguez. The emotion was almost painful.

Lisa stood up, uncurling herself like a flag. She stuck out a leg, threw back her shoulders, and angled herself against the vertical sunlight. She was totally aware of what the harsh rays would do to her. They made her diamond hard, painting her long body into a short shadow, and emphasizing her absolute power, over the world, over men, over boys like José.

"Come on. Let's go eat," she said. "I'm bored of sitting on your silly boat."

She slipped into the cabin, threw on a T-shirt and a white micro skirt, and in minutes they were parting the lunchtime crowds at Bayside, Lisa streaming ahead, José trying to appear cool as he swam in the wake of her glory. On every side the Hispanics slipped into recognition mode. Lisa was *their* star, like Gloria and Julio. They talked to him, not to her, plucking at his sleeve and asking, "Is that Lisa Rodriguez?" A few muttered "*hombre*" to show respect for any man who owned this woman for even five minutes. José brushed them all away, and he smiled the inscrutable smile of the guy in charge.

It was better, or worse, at the restaurant. The usually ice-cool lady of the lectern was confused as she recognized the supermodel. A posse of smirking waiters showed the couple to the best table in the window, and two of them almost collided as they vied to pull out the chair for the dream girl.

Lisa sat down heavily. She peered around the room at the rubber-necking fellow lunchers.

"They've put us in the psycho section," she said out loud. "I remember this place. It's good," she added. It was old Spain, from the faded tile floor to the oak-beamed ceiling. The chairs were studded brown leather, the walls covered in old tapestries, the tablecloths sparkling white, hanging down in tented folds to the floor. A guitarist picked out a Sevillana.

"Some champagne?" said José hopefully.

"What else?"

"What kind do you like?"

"The wet, cold fizzy kind." Lisa Rodriguez didn't play brand names. Popular novelists had done that game to death.

"Bring me a bottle of the most expensive champagne you have," said Aragon arrogantly. "People argue about the best," he added to excuse his pomposity. "About the most expensive there can be no argument." He'd heard his father say that. And his father had mistresses for mattresses.

Lisa smiled. Whatever else he could or couldn't do, this boy would give good restaurant.

"Your father's cute," said Lisa, cutting through to the subconscious.

"He thinks so."

"I can see where you get it from."

Oh, boy. The stick and the carrot. The lash, then the cash.

"Thank you." He looked down. She was smiling at him. The business guys at the next table wanted to be him. They were a still life, food poised at open mouths, eyes fixed lasciviously on his lunch date. He could see her braless breasts through the plain white T-shirt. They were probing at the cotton as if looking for an escape route. They were sharp and pointed and going up, goddamn it, like the breasts of Masai girls at a circumcision ceremony in Social Anthropology 101. He reached for the champagne with a hand that shook.

"Tell me about *your* parents," he said.

To José it was a diversion. To Lisa it wasn't. She went white. Her hands clenched the tablecloth. Her voluptuous lips thinned. Her eyes flashed fire.

"What about them?" she snarled.

"Oh, nothing really . . ." said José, stepping back from the abyss that had so unexpectedly opened at his feet. But Lisa wasn't going to let it go. A genie had been summoned by the lamp. It would be given air time.

"I hate them." Her voice was a hiss.

"I think everyone sometimes, I mean . . ."

"Shut up!"

The silence ticked like a bomb. Then, with the compulsiveness of a child picking at a sore, Lisa began to speak.

"Okay, you asked me about my parents. I'll tell you all about them. My father died when I was six, and he was a peasant, a carpenter. The kind of guy whose daughter your family didn't dance with, right? And he was perfect and I loved him all the money in the world. In all his life he only did one incredibly stupid thing. He married my mother."

"You didn't like your mother . . ."

"My mother is a *WHORE!*"

The whole restaurant heard it, heard, too, the bang as the Rodriguez fist landed its hammer blow on the table, knocking over her glass of the most expensive champagne. But the Rodriguez confessional was not over. Her voice was pickled in venom as she continued.

"My father had been working on some cabinets for a dealer in the Gables, and he had a heart attack . . . and . . . and he died . . ." Tears tried for her eyes, but her eyes were too angry for sorrow. "And the guy came over in his disgusting gold-plated Cadillac to drop off my father's tools and he saw my mother, and my mother saw him, and they liked each other, immediately, right there. They liked each other, and my father hadn't been dead for more than a few hours. I mean, he was dead in the hospital. My mother had just gotten back from the hospital, and she was smiling at this guy and he was leering at her, and I was there *watching* it. It was so horrible. I was six, but I knew. I can see them now. He was leaning in the doorway, and she was looking past his great belly at his car, and he was flashing his fat hands and they were all golden rings and shit, and he was like made of grease, his hair stinking of cologne and there was my mother with cash-register eyes pushing out her tits at him and coming on like gangbusters . . . and you know what he said, you know what he said . . . ?"

José didn't know.

"He said, 'Do you want to take a ride in my car?' "

"She didn't . . ."

"Oh, but she did. She did it. And she's been riding ever since. I ran. I remember running down the street and screaming at the top of my voice, because of course they wanted me to go with them. But they went anyway. She went for that fucking ride in that fucking car . . . and in *two weeks* we moved in with him." She paused to fill herself up with the fuel of revenge. "And you know what? They got some other guy to finish the cabinets."

José swallowed. Conversations like this were no part of his sheltered world.

"And do you think that's it? You think that wasn't enough? Oh, there was much better. There was a whole lot better than that. He waited until I was eleven. Maybe that was the one decent thing he did in his filthy life. I gotta give him that. But at eleven he reckoned I came of age. He raped me in the Jacuzzi, and he near as goddamn killed me, because the last thing I remember before passing out was the bubbles turning red with my blood."

Lisa Rodriguez was shaking. José could feel the table vibrating beneath her hands, rattling against her trembling thighs. She'd reached him now, not in the lust zone where she ruled him anyway. But somewhere else. His heart was filling up with tenderness and sympathy. There was something so fine, so proud about this wounded beauty. She'd been to dark places he would never know. She could love and hate with an awesome intensity he could never match. He prayed that one day he would be able to feel as she felt. Could she show him how?

When she continued, Lisa's voice had softened. It was matter of fact, morning-after-the-hurricane now. The damage had been done. The task was to clear up the wreckage from the storm.

"They found a bent doctor to put me right, and the moment I could walk I was gone. But you know, she never left him. My mother knew everything, and she's with him still. They have a neat little house on the bay and he keeps a sixty-foot powerboat outside it on davits. And I guess he still runs a few drugs, deals some k's, rapes some kids. Just the sort of guy any mother would want to call her old man."

"Isn't there anything you can do, we can do? I mean, this is America." José tried to put into words his belief in the system. When Aragons spoke, everyone listened—cops, judges, politicians, journalists. It was impossible to grasp that in the forest of the poor the cries of torment went unheard.

"It's old, it's finished, but it lives on in here, and here."

Lisa tapped her head and her heart. "There, it will live forever."

"It's why you came back to Miami?"

"Yes, it's why. I'm somebody now, somebody they would like to know and be known by. They'll see me on the news, and in the magazines and in the gossip columns, and they'll hear how much loot I take home—more than they'll ever have. That's what my mother cares about. Money is her language. You can't talk to her in any other. I want to be even richer and more famous, until I'm all she can think about and until her sleep is full of the nightmare of me. And all the millions she let slip through her fingers. That's what I want. That's what makes me feel good."

But even as she spoke, Lisa knew it wasn't enough. Somehow spelling it out loud underlined the inadequacy of her retribution. Living well was a wimp's revenge. It was the path of action for those with too much sense and too few balls. The idea hit her quite suddenly. A thrill of excitement bubbled within her, and she gripped the table, in awe of herself and her invention.

"Can we have some more champagne?" she said.

It was the totally unexpected voice of the sensuous woman, emerging phoenixlike from flames of bitter anger.

They ordered food that neither now wanted, and Lisa was Lisa Rodriguez once more. She talked of modeling assignments in places that José dreamed of visiting, and she dropped the names of girls who visited his dreams. She was New York and Paris and London and Milan, floating above the world he admired on a cloud of sexual sophistication, bewitching him with the tantalizing reality of her illusion.

She had one purpose, and she set about achieving it with single-minded determination. During lunch she had to hook José like he had never been hooked before. Slowly, but surely, she wound him up. Her hand snaked across the table to touch his arm. Later, her fingers played with his until the flush of hot excitement was all over the bits of him she could see. She laughed when he joked, and she mocked him gently. When he stepped uncertainly, she reined him in. The whiplash of her resolve cracked in the air near to him. Her control bit was reassuring in his untutored mouth. She led him on and drew him out, until he talked with a brilliance he didn't know he possessed. All the time the love light grew in his eyes as it was meant to, and Lisa Rodriguez crept nearer to her goal. She leaned across the table toward him until he could smell the scent of her breath on his face.

Then she whispered sweet secrets in his ears as she showed him her body up close, and he squirmed and lost track of his sentences in the hot lust soup in which he was swimming.

The champagne trickled into his mind, loosening the clutches of reality, and it vapored into hers, hardening her resolve.

He looked confused, but he had something to say. She nodded her encouragement.

"Lisa . . . I don't know you very well, but . . . but . . ."

Her leg found his beneath the table. She pushed against it. He pushed gratefully back.

"But I love you."

She laughed softly, and the promise was in her sultry eyes. Her leg pushed harder against him. He had gotten away with it. He had told Lisa Rodriguez that he loved her, and her leg was still hot against his. He was lost in the vastness of the moment. The restaurant had gone away. It was the two of them, locked in the present, but dreaming of the future, and José's life took flight on the wings of angels.

Through the mists of holiness, the waiter shouted in church.

"Can I get anything else for you? Some dessert?"

She looked up at the interloper, smiling sweetly.

"We don't want anything else. Please leave us alone for a bit," she said.

The precious moment hovered on the brink of extinction, but Lisa was not about to let it go. She leaned across the table until her face was inches from his, and she made it more beautiful than she had ever made it before.

"You're still hungry," she whispered.

"I am?" he managed.

"Eat me," she said.

"What?"

"Do it now. Here. Do it right here."

The shock and the excitement collided on his face. He smiled to hide his confusion. His cheeks were on fire. He didn't know what to do. He had to be shown. He had to be told.

Lisa's voice was commanding.

"Pretend you've dropped something. The tablecloth will hide you. Do it quickly."

He paused. He looked around. He looked down. His chest was heaving. Lisa saw the beads of sweat on his upper lip.

"*Do* it."

Her order cut through to the part of him where desire drowned reason. He disappeared. Now, beneath the table, José was already preparing to obey her.

Lisa let out a shuddering sigh of satisfaction. She looked around her. A column partially hid the table from the restaurant. The other diners were deep in conversation. Nobody had noticed.

She reached down beneath the table and found his head. She guided him toward her, her hand firm against the back of his neck, and she eased herself forward to meet him. Her micro skirt slid up her legs, and she pushed herself down deep in the chair, knees crushed tight together.

"Take off my panties," she whispered.

She felt his fingers tremble against her thighs. With her left hand she pushed against the seat of the chair, lifting her butt an inch or two from the seat. He reached for the bikini briefs, his movements fearful yet eager as his fingers fumbled with the elastic. She squirmed beneath his touch and the excitement spiked through her. Her lips were dry. Her heart hammered against her chest. All around lurked the danger of humiliation, the dread embarrassment of discovery. But the lunchers lunched on, oblivious to the passion that was building in their midst.

He was drawing them down, over her thighs, her knees, down her calves. She slipped off her shoes. Her panties were gone. He ran his hands along the inside of her thighs, parting them, and she splayed her legs open for him, leaning back in her chair and thrusting out her pelvis.

"Oooooooh!" She moaned softly at the touch of his hands on her skin, and she smiled in anticipation of the pleasure to come. She closed her eyes. Beneath the white of the tablecloth, she could feel her steam heat build. She was damp with desire, wet and wanton, as she basked in the beauty of the moment.

His lips were against hers, hovering at the brink of her. She could feel his breath, warm and nervous next to her heat. He was nuzzling near to her, burying his cheek against the inside of her thighs. She pushed them together, clamping his head between them. She squeezed them tight, feeling the rasp of his masculine skin against the creamy softness of hers. And now, in the velvet trap of her, he touched her with his tongue, and Lisa shuddered with delight. He was gentle at first, finding his way in her wetness as his tongue explored her. He lapped at her lovingly, reverently, as he savored the extraordinary intimacy, its edges sharpened by danger. But his passion was too strong for clever love, and Lisa's impatience was too great. On either side of his head, her thighs imprisoned him. Now, with both hands she reached beneath the table and clasped them behind his head. He was her captive. There was no retreat. She had him. He existed for her pleasure.

"Make love to me with your mouth," she murmured.

She felt his tongue disappear into the depths of her. Like a dagger it pierced her, long and hard, reaching into her heartland and setting her mind ablaze. His head was crushed against her, by his force, by the force of her, and she ground her hips against his face to increase the friction. The restaurant was still there, but the faces of the crowd were blurred now by the intensity of her desire. She threw back her head, and her mouth was open as her breath shuddered in her throat. His lips were closed over hers, drinking shamelessly from her desire. His tongue probed her, licking in long strokes from the slippery depths to the tiny tip of her pleasure source. He lingered there, at the knot of love, pushing out, pressing down in the triangle of joy, and she moaned her delight as her hands tightened at the back of his neck. He was drowning in her. She was a fountain at his face, slick and wet at his lips, and he fought for breath in the lake of her lust. He tried to pull back to breathe, and her hands relaxed for the minimum moment, before tightening once again to force him forward into her core. Her legs were wide open now, her butt pushed forward to the edge of the chair as her whole body welcomed him.

And then she felt the first wonderful quickenings in the pit of her stomach. Beneath the table he sensed the message on her quivering lips of love. The rhythm of his tongue beat faster, lashing her toward the goal both wanted. She was galloping on now, legs threshing around his shoulders as he buried himself desperately between them. He was fighting for leverage on the slick slopes of her, and she fought to ride him, the saddle of her bound tight to him in the ride to liquid glory.

"Oh *God!*" she said out loud. She could hold him no longer. Her whole body was melting. Her muscles had no power, her limbs were losing their coordination. In front of her eyes, the room was a purple haze and she steadied herself, clenched fists supporting her straining butt and lower back as she struggled to keep the contact that would be the passport to bliss.

"I'm going to come," she whispered, her voice breaking in her throat. It was a wish and a command. A prediction and a promise. Beneath the table his head threshed from side to side, up and down. She felt his whole face making love to her, tongue, teeth, his eyes, his hair. He reached up with both hands and he pushed her straining thighs apart, splitting her open as he fought to lose himself in her damp body.

Lisa took a deep breath. Her head rolled over to one side, and then back again. She battled to hold on, even as she prayed for the moment of release. How could she stay quiet through this? How could she fail to scream her pleasure at the crowded room? Her knuckles were white as they grasped the seat of the chair, suspending her whole body in space as she sought to thrust it at the face of her hidden lover.

"Oh, nooooooo," she moaned, as the awesome feeling took her. It lifted her up, feather light on the wind of the storm, and it cast her down, heavy as lead, as she crashed into the crescendo of her orgasm.

9

Lisa Rodriguez was at the wheel of the Cigarette once more, muscular legs apart, her head pushed forward into the breeze. José stood by her side, a puppy dog, his adoring eyes fixed on the mistress who was now his master.

"Where are we going?" he yelled above the roar of the engines. His tone insinuated that he was prepared for a journey to hell and back. He had zero idea that the voyage to Hades was not going to be round trip.

She didn't reply, but she laughed into the wind and reached out to ruffle his hair. It started as a gesture of affection. But halfway through she changed her mind, and she thrust his head away from her as he nuzzled in her shoulder.

The pain flashed across his face, but he still had the memory to hold on to.

"I've never done that before." He laughed, wanting to talk about the restaurant, to have the incredible intimacy acknowledged.

"And you never will again."

He looked at her quizzically. What did she mean? What did she ever mean? But her face was set hard as the course of his boat. It flew across the water like an arrow, joined to the surface only by the churning propellers as it planed across Miami Bay. There was something terrible happening in her eyes. They were on fire with hatred. His stomach turned. Surely he wasn't her target. He could still taste her on his lips. He had been her lover. It was too soon to become her enemy. He fought back the desire to ask her what was the matter. Where *were* they going? Lisa looked more focused than he had ever seen her. They weren't just driving aimlessly. Her whole posture spoke of single-minded purpose. She was leaning over the wheel, her furious eyes scanning the shore ahead, her breasts pointing like weapons at her unknown destination.

She turned to look at him, and their eyes met. Her smile was cruel, a snarl of encouragement and threat.

"José!" she said.

"Yes, Lisa."

"Come here and sit by me."

She patted the seat on the far side of her, easing her all but naked body back to let him pass. He sat down on the seat next to the side of the boat, and her brown shoulder rubbed against his.

Once again José dared to hope, but he couldn't get rid of the feeling of foreboding. Lisa Rodriguez was good news and bad news. The nice was always followed by the nasty, the nasty by the nice.

But now, apparently, she had changed gears on her mood once more. She curled up on the seat, one languid brown arm on the wheel, and she dangled out her foot. It tangled playfully in the chain of the crucifix he wore, her painted toes nestling among the sparse chest hairs of which he was so proud.

"I loved it . . . back in the restaurant," she said, her voice husky.

"You did? So did I. Lisa, I mean . . ."

What did he mean? That he loved her? That he wanted to marry her? That he wanted to walk tall forever next to the most beautiful girl in the world. But José never got to find out what it was he wanted. Whatever it was, it was not wanted equally by Lisa Rodriguez.

She straightened her leg at the knee like a piston. It shot out, foursquare into the concavity between José's nipples. He went backward, his face silly, unable even to register surprise. His legs pointed at the sky, and his head went down and he shot like a bullet over the side of the speeding Cigarette. His splash was swallowed by the wake, and Lisa didn't bother to turn around to watch him surface a hundred yards behind the boat.

"Get a life, José," she murmured as she dismissed him from her world.

She'd got one of her own. She'd stuck it together from the cracked pieces of her childhood, and it hadn't been easy. Perhaps it was never supposed to be. But the breakages had been painful and the hideous memories lingered. Now she would wipe them out.

She pulled back on the throttle, and picked up the binoculars. For a minute or two she swept the shoreline, until she found what she was looking for. The house was waterfront, but it wasn't particularly grand—a far cry from the plutocratic palaces of Star Island and Biscayne Bay. It had been built right on the water to take advantage of the view, and a sleek black speedboat bobbed beyond it on the dock. Lisa sighed her satisfaction. His boat was there. The package that was his pride, his joy, and his masculinity was docked in front of his home. Even from this distance she could tell that it was brand new. It looked like an Aronow catamaran, sixty feet long, four monstrous black engines attached to its back. There would be no change from two hundred thousand for a powerboat like that, and Lisa felt the thrill and the fury as she realized that she was looking through the glasses at her mother and her stepfather's entire net worth. The boat and the house together had to be a million bucks. Her dead father could never have imagined that kind of money, but it was the dreams of it that had sent her mother to live with a fiend before her father's body had cooled in his grave.

Then she saw the movement. Surely she couldn't be that lucky. But yes, someone was standing in the companionway to the boat's cabin. She adjusted the focus and strained her eyes. It was him. He was fatter now. His hair was longer at the back but balding on top and it was as greasy as it had ever been. Around his neck was the same medallion that had banged against her breasts in the Jacuzzi, and the red bubbles that had bubbled then were now bubbling in Lisa's heart. Her hand reached forward to the throttles of José's boat, and she thrust them forward. The boat accelerated, and now, over its razor-sharp bow, she could see the man she hated as if through the sight of a gun.

What would he be doing there on the back of his thunder boat? Drinking a beer, calling a dealer on his cellular phone, or just lying in the sun and enjoying the good life on a summer's afternoon? She smiled grimly. Her mother would be inside the house, polishing and cleaning the possessions she had sold her soul to own. She would be singing in her high-tech kitchen, or dusting the multichannel TV that would be too big for the small drawing room, and all the time she would be unaware of the menace that lurked in the middle of the waterfront view she'd bought. She wouldn't be thinking of her daughter. Lisa had been trouble in Paradise, part of the baggage of her old life to be discarded as she embraced the new one with such indecent haste. And now Lisa laughed as the engines throbbed beneath her feet, because she was back. She was back.

"I'm back, Mother," she screamed into the breeze. "Your little baby has come home."

She was near enough now to see him clearly with her naked eye. And he had seen the Cigarette. Professional interest would be registering in his evil eyes. He would be comparing José's boat with his own, calculating its cost, wondering why it was speeding toward the shore.

Lisa spun the wheel. She would draw the last drops of revenge from this moment. He could see her in profile now, as the Cigarette made its wide turn. Lisa could swear she could see him smile, and her mind tuned in to what would be his thoughts. Hey, beautiful rich bitch in your big boat and small bikini, give me the time of day, drop in for a drink, hang out for awhile. Lay your hand on my upholstery, touch my chrome, feel the power of my engines. He waved. He actually waved at her, and, as hellfire burned in her hurting heart, Lisa waved back. There was only one thing the piece of shit didn't know, and it would cost him everything. He didn't know who she was. Nor did the little woman who had appeared in the plate-glass window of the drawing room to watch the charade. Her mother had a duster in her hand, and on her face would be the long-suffering frown of the subservient woman as she watched her husband attempting yet another flirtation in front of her.

The boat, and Lisa's life, had turned full circle. Now, once again it pointed at the target. She was a hundred and fifty yards from the house that had never been her home, the same distance from the two people she hated. She looked at the fuel gauge. The boat held maybe three hundred gallons and it was three-quarters full. How many gallons were in the tank of the Aronow? Maybe the same again.

She had slowed to make the turn, and now she all but stopped to savor the moment when her old life would end and her new one begin. She had no doubts. There was only a longing for the deed she would do. Inside her there was nothing but the frozen lump of loathing.

She took aim with the bow, and she pushed the levers that fired the missile that would be the boat. It happened so fast. The target screamed toward her, magnifying in size, until she could see every detail. She stood up on the driver's seat to show them who she was as she speeded closer, and she saw in both their faces the recognition and the terror as they realized what her presence meant. His face crumpled in horror as his brain computed the collision course. He stared into her eyes, rooted to the spot by terror as he peered into his own infinity. The Cigarette was a bomb, and the boat on which he stood was a powder keg. He would be killed by the impact, but the bits of him would be deep fried before they hit the water. His life flashed before him as it was supposed to do, and through it all played the theme music that was Lisa Rodriguez. He had time to see up close how beautiful she had become, better than the magazines, more alluring than the commercials, bigger by far than that time in the Jacuzzi all those years ago when he had sealed his fate. He opened his mouth to scream the scream of the damned, and even as he started, he knew he would have no time to finish.

Lisa saw his mouth open, and in her soul she heard his cry. It was balm to the pain, absolution for all the years when she allowed his crime to go unavenged. But it was time to go. To savor death, you had to live. She braced herself and leaped sideways. When the fuel tank of the Cigarette met the gas tank of the Aronow and the orange ball of flame exploded into the sky, Lisa Rodriguez was swimming safely ten feet beneath the surface of the bay.

10

"It's incredibly boring," said Mary McGregor Whitney. The faces at her boardroom table blanched. Discouraging words had been heard. All around them was the paraphernalia of a top-end advertising pitch, the audio-visual aids, assistants scurrying about, models trying to look languid amid the atmosphere of hype and fear. White, Whelding and Blankheart had put their best foot forward in their presentation for the Whitney Enterprises "India" fragrance campaign, and now Mary Whitney had stamped on it.

The agency head chose his words carefully.

"Of course, it's just an idea, Mary. I mean, we don't have to go this way." He waved his hand in the air to dismiss the presentation that he and a dozen of his top aides had spent the last six months and a million bucks dreaming up. "Can you give us some idea of where you think it goes wrong?" he added, his voice dripping with humility.

Mary Whitney drummed her fingers on the table. "So you want me to provide the 'creativity' I pay you for," she said.

"No, of course not, we can go away and think again. We want to do better. It's just that you are so brilliant and we value . . ."

She signaled him into silence.

"The idea for India," she spoke slowly as if to a dense foreigner, "was to capture the romance and sophistication of a distant country with an ancient civilization and a deep appreciation of beauty. The India of the Raj was opulent, mysterious, untouchable, yet real. The trick is to draw out that essence, bottle it, package it, and market it to the masses who buy my stuff. Your India, Mr. Blankheart, has the soul and excitement of a tacky ethnic restaurant in the Bronx. *Your* India, kind sir, is not even Madras, let alone Vindaloo. It has the piquancy and flavor of a curry powder from some colon-conscious yuppie health-food store on Madison. If your India was a rubber, dear, your mistress would be in deep doo-doo."

Blankheart paled. He had asked for it. He had gotten it. And he had to like it. He laughed nervously. Was the mistress crack a shot in the dark? He hoped so.

"Maybe you thought the Indian models were a little obvious?" he tried.

"I have nothing against the obvious," sniffed Mary. "But what's obvious to me clearly is not obvious to you. What this campaign needed was not a load of callow, down-trodden anorectic female doormats whose only virtue is the racial cards they were dealt at birth. What this campaign needed was a star."

"Like . . ." Blankheart had gone blank. He looked up and down the table in desperation for help with a few names.

"Like Lisa Rodriguez," barked Mary Whitney into the frantic silence. "God, you *have* heard of her?" she added, her voice thick with scorn.

"But she's sort of . . . Hispanic," stuttered Blankheart, the words stumbling out before he'd had a chance to think them through.

"So from now on only blacks get a chance to play Othello, do they? Well, well, well, silly me. Shows how little I know." Mary Whitney sat back in her chair. It was fun to throw her weight around, and it was astonishing how subservient grown men could be once you had them on the run, but deep down she was wondering if the colorless India presentation wasn't trying to tell her something. The very fact that Blankheart and his advertising cohorts had failed to find any excitement in the campaign just might be the idea's fault rather than the agency's. Did America, where her perfume would be sold, know or care about India? Only ten percent of her fellow countrymen had bothered to apply for passports, and sometimes she didn't blame them. From the redwood forests to the New York islands and the Gulf Stream waters, there was something for everyone. Why traipse around the Third World when a Winnebago could take you around the first one and you never had to miss "Wheel of Fortune"?

And then there was the question of the smell of India. When she'd stayed for a few days at the Taj in Bombay the essence of India had not been so much mysterious, opulent, and untouchable as frankly biological. The trick had been to avoid stepping on it in the street as you fought off the flies and the beggars.

She let out a short, high-pitched laugh at the thought. What on earth had she been thinking about? A scent called India? It was quite ridiculous. She must be going senile. She'd have done better to call it Iraq, and cash in on the Desert Storm enthusiasm like all those L.A. musicians and stars with their dial-a-patriotic-song. Why hadn't all these fools around the table told her? Why had they blown a million of her dollars on a scent whose name could as well have been Beirut? But of course she knew, and once again it was her fault. She was a one-woman band. It was the way she had always been, and would always be. She liked courtiers around her, not advisers, and mostly it worked because she made so few mistakes. Here was one of them. But even as she realized she had screwed up, Mary Whitney looked on the bright side. A million bucks was deductible chicken feed compared to the cost of a major campaign that turned into a major bomb. In the fickle world of fashion, disasters had a way of setting off chain reactions. If India was a dud, now was the time to recognize it and to pull the plug on it.

"Do you know what I think?" said Mary Whitney.

They didn't, but they all leaned forward to find out.

"I think India is a disastrous name for a scent."

"Oh," said Blankheart. Confusion reigned. Was she joking? Almost certainly not. You could tell when Mary Whitney was joking in the same way that you could tell you were being whipped.

Blankheart recovered first. "I must say, I did have reservations . . ." He proceeded warily. He wanted to stay in tune with his most valuable client, but he was aware that he was laying himself open to being blamed for not voicing his objections earlier.

"Bullshit," snapped Mary. "Anyway, the damage is done. India is dead. I shall have to go away and dream up something else."

"Something Hispanic . . . if we want to use a star like Lisa Rodriguez?" said Blankheart, cunningly.

Mary Whitney looked at him carefully. He tensed, waiting for the lash of her tongue. But none came. She continued to watch him, and she tapped on the Honduran mahogany of the table with a Cartier pen. She looked up at the ceiling, over at the four-million-dollar Rauschenberg, out of the window over Central Park. The silence was impregnated. A thought was growing in the mind of the megacouturier. Had Blankheart sired it?

"It may be not such a bad idea to come at this whole idea from a different angle," she said at last, speaking slowly. "Perhaps we should start not with the scent, or its name, but with a star. If we have Lisa Rodriguez, the rest will be detail. She could sell lingerie to Martians whose bits and pieces didn't match hers. It's called the sex factor. Okay, here's what we do. We get Rodriguez. We sign her for an exclusive, say a year, maybe two, and during that time she only works for us. Tie her up. We get to own a lease on her. And everything else comes later, with Lisa as the linchpin of the campaign."

She stood up. "There, that's settled. At least that's simple. All you boys have to do now is to sign Rodriguez and then you can all piss off and play golf . . . or whatever it is you do in your spare time. And now, if you'll excuse me, having flown all the way up here for your . . . 'show.' I now have to fly all the way back again. I wish I could say it had been a pleasure."

She stalked to the door, flanked on either side by assistants. One opened the door for her. The other closed it behind her. Mary Whitney was gone.

"Shit!" said Blankheart into the gaping vacuum she had left behind. "How the hell do we get a supermodel like Rodriguez to agree to an exclusive?"

"She's with Rossetti's agency," said someone. "He's a dick, but he's for sale. We should be able to work something out."

"I think there might be a problem with Rodriguez," said one of the account executives. "I caught a flash on CNN a minute or two before the meeting. She's in jail in Miami. Drove a speedboat into her parents' waterfront house. Blew the pair of them to kingdom come."

11

Johnny Rossetti was too cool to run, and too anxious not to. So he sort of loped, like a wolf on amphetamine, and Miami airport flashed past him, a video on fast forward. The woman two paces behind him didn't have his long legs, and so to avoid losing him in the wall-to-wall Hispanics, she trotted bravely in his wake.

"I can't believe they screwed up on the limo. I can't *believe* it," he muttered to himself, adjusting his sunglasses and his tie at the same time, as if neatness would be some protection against angst.

"I guess your secretary didn't speak Spanish," agreed the woman, looking around her disdainfully. To many New Yorkers, Miami was South America.

He didn't reply. The limo was a minor inconvenience. Lisa Rodriguez wasn't. Together the duo exploded out into the superheated air and grabbed a taxi.

"What's the address?" barked Rossetti.

"Shit, it's somewhere in the bottom of my bag. Does he know the police station? He looks as if he might."

"Ah, pleez station. Pleez station, no problem," said the black-toothed Mexican driver. It was apparently a well-known destination.

They piled in. Thank God the cab was air-conditioned.

"Well, there are your palm trees," said Rossetti. It seemed to mean they were in the right town. He sighed. In the modeling business, days were allowed to be difficult. But he couldn't remember a roller-coaster one like this. It had started out like wild dreams, the best day of his life so far, and then, just as suddenly, it had turned into tragedy. That morning, as Johnny had sat in his all but deserted office, Blankheart had called. That in itself was strange for a Saturday.

"Is Lisa Rodriguez available?" he had asked on the telephone at 9 A.M., minutes after Johnny and the secretary had arrived. He had come through on the private line as befitted two head honchos discussing a star.

"What have you got, Don?" Rossetti had replied. Blankheart calling personally meant it was a biggie. A couple of weeks on location for a major campaign. A booking for one of the big collections.

Blankheart had gone straight for it.

"Listen, Johnny, I had a meeting with Mary Whitney yesterday. She's launching a whole new line of fragrances, scents, bath essences, soaps, the whole bit. It's going to be major, and I mean megamajor, the biggest thing she's done so far . . ."

"And you want Lisa to do some print ads and some commercials." Johnny had zipped in to take the punch out of the Blankheart pitch. He had sounded bored to disguise his excitement. Excitement cost cash in the deal.

But Blankheart had had better things to offer. Much better.

"Not so dull, Johnny," he had crowed. "Nothing so dull. Mary wants Lisa to be 'The Whitney Girl,' the spirit of the campaign. She wants her signed on maybe a two-year exclusive, no other work, morals clauses in the contract . . . the works. You did say Rodriguez is around and kicking, didn't you?"

"Of course she's around. Whaddya mean, 'is she around?' Jesus, Don, I don't know. An exclusive for Rodriguez would be incredibly expensive. Have you any idea what she earns? I mean, we're talking the income of banana republics here. Then there's the effect-on-the-career angle. Modeling isn't an annuity. Next year there's new girls. I've got fourteen-year-olds in here that can burn your balls off. I know Whitney's big but, boy, are you going to need a budget?"

"Listen, Johnny, it's me, Don Blankheart. I'm in the same line as you, remember? I know what's involved here. If you can't pitch the bigs, Johnny, let me know right away. I got things to do I should have done in my last lifetime."

"No, no, Don, I just wanted to spell it out. I mean, I'd have to talk to Lisa. Maybe I could talk her around. You know how close we are. Lisa was my invention. She's like a daughter to me."

"Ha. Ha." Blankheart had laughed into the B.S., insinuating that he knew the score. Fathers who behaved to their daughters as Rossetti was rumored to have behaved toward Lisa tended to have the keys thrown away on them.

Rossetti had ignored the gibe. Inside his mind the math had been coming together in orgasmic harmony. For two years they could be talking five million. Maybe more. As always, the trick had been to find out just how eager Blankheart was. His mind had switched into calculator mode. Probably five was low field, and he had a fifteen percent deal with Lisa. He would take out three-quarters of a million, minimum, maybe the straight million if he could wind them up a bit. It was the best sort of money for an agent. Once the contract was signed, there would be nothing to do but count the money. There would be none of the hassle of booking and managing the complicated Rodriguez career over two back-breaking years.

"No, Don, what I mean is that Lisa takes my advice. If you can persuade me that the money is right, the photographer is kosher, and that the whole campaign is going to be handled in the right way . . . and I know how you work, so that's no problem . . . I'm sure we can sort something out."

"Where's Lisa now?"

"She's in Miami. She's got family down there. I discovered her down there, you know."

"Yeah, someone was saying she was down in Miami. But she's cool, right?"

That had been the time when the insects had come out to play on Johnny's back.

"What are you asking, Don? Do you mean, 'Is she freaking? Is she doing blow? Is she pulling a number with some loser?' No, she's cool. She's just taking a day or two off. She's entitled, and she's the biggest pro on my books. She can handle Whitney's smell thing in her sleep. She's the number-one girl right now . . . we all know that."

"Since Christa flew the nest."

That had put the stranglehold on Johnny's fast-developing euphoria. When you ran an agency, it was always bad karma to lose a girl you didn't want to lose. It was poison gas to lose an earner like Christa Kenwood. He still hadn't gotten over it.

"You know what? No, you must have heard. I guess she told you all about it."

"Told me what?"

"Nah, forget it, Johnny. She's a big loss. I just loved to use her. Had the old Grace Kelly class-and-sex act."

"Told me *what,* Don? You mean her selling that book for a big one?"

There had been a pause.

"Told you that she opened a model agency."

"She didn't. I mean . . . she can't."

"Yeah, for sure she did. We had a head sheet came around yesterday. Based in Miami. Not too many girls, not too great looking, but, yeah, Christa Kenwood Agency, located down there in the Art Deco bit, what's it called, South Beach . . . a few miles down from the Fontainebleau where you used to have all those modeling contests. Remember?"

Johnny had fought not to lose it. On the one hand was the Rodriguez five million. On the other was Christa Kenwood's *agency?* His stomach had spun. His guts had knotted. His psyche had roller-coasted. He had looked down. On his blue silk shirt a small knot of moisture had emerged. God, it had been *sweat.*

He had taken a deep breath. He had fought to stay calm, but his mind was filled with visions of Christa Kenwood bleeding. An agency. A competitor. She hadn't just left him. She'd dumped on him. How long would it be before she was trying to poach his girls, or worse, his bookers. Christa, who'd always been loved by everyone. Christa, who'd written the definitive beauty book and sold it for a million-buck advance. Christa, who was closer to Steve Pitts than God to grace. Pitts would use the broken-down old nags she'd scraped together for her head sheet, even if arthritis had rendered them immobile. She'd be able to exist for a bit on her contacts alone. For long enough to drive him mad, anyway. He had clenched his knuckles and rapped out a rhythm on the table. From that moment on, Christa had been an enemy, top of a long list. From that millisecond she could expect the same treatment as the other names on it. And, unlike the Nixon hate list, which many regarded as a superior honor to the Congressional Medal, the Rossetti scroll was an uncomfortable place to be. He personally guaranteed it.

"Now that you mention it, I think she did say something about trying to get it together in the agency business. I told her to go ahead, but not to use her own money." He had laughed a nasty laugh as he had told the lie. "I guess you won't be doing any business with her, out of courtesy to me, I mean, what with this Lisa thing coming up," he had added.

"Nah, no sweat, Johnny, unless she wants to rep herself. But then I guess there's no action in her taking a percentage of herself. Anyway, Johnny, get back to me on the Rodriguez thing. As you can imagine, I need to know yesterday. Whitney doesn't screw around except on the tennis court. I want to give her good news. She doesn't like the other sort."

"I'll be back to you before the end of the morning, Don. I hope we can make a deal. It's always good to do business with you."

He had jumped up and bounded out of his office, to the open plan area where the single secretary who worked on Saturdays sat. His smile had been fifteen percent of five million dollars, but when he saw the face of his employee it had gone into fast fade. Her features had been twisted into an Oscar-winning depiction of terminal gloom.

The secretary had come right out with it.

"I didn't want to interrupt your call with Mr. Blankheart, because I listened in and heard the offer, but . . ."

"But *what?*"

"Lisa Rodriguez has been arrested in Miami. She drove a powerboat through her parents' house on the waterfront, and the whole thing exploded and they're both dead. The answer machines are solid with messages from journalists."

* * *

Johnny Rossetti shifted his butt on the scuffed seat of the taxicab as it sped through the streets of Miami. It had taken him half an hour to get hold of the criminal attorney and another half an hour to get to Kennedy to pick up the private plane south. In between, he had filled himself in on the cellular phone.

"Let me try this once again," he said to his attorney. "Lisa's story is that she was driving this rich Cuban kid's boat, and she goes 'Let's drop in on my parents and surprise them,' then he falls overboard, and she gets the controls all muddled up and then she jumps overboard, and boom, good-bye, Mommy and Daddy."

"Mommy and Stepdaddy. Stepdaddy was apparently a dealer, and the reason the boom was so big was that the Rodriguez boat cut through the dealer's boat on the way to hitting the house. Both gas tanks exploded. It was lucky the whole block didn't get torched."

"It's a shitty story." Rossetti pulled his damp collar away from his neck. On any other day this would be a major disaster. On this particular day, with the Whitney contract offer still ringing in his ears, it was an epic tragedy.

"Actually, it's not such a bad story, because the Cuban backs it up. And he's big-bucks believable, according to his attorney. The family is sugar and they've got all sorts of hitting power in the Big Orange. The cops are walking in ballet shoes. The dealer's no big loss. He had vice files a foot thick. They want to believe the Cuban. The tourist people want to believe Rodriguez. She's an institution down here. All the radio shows are saying she's innocent, and elections are coming up."

"The Cuban kid just fell off his boat? Was he loaded?"

"Yeah, he'd *lunched.* I guess if you're some spoiled rich kid of twenty-one you don't drink iced tea when you take out Lisa Rodriguez."

"How far apart were they when they were picked out of the water?"

"Mmm, that's the problem. Two miles. But Lisa says that when he fell out, she panicked. She didn't know how to handle the boat and she was frightened she'd mash him in the propellers if she tried to pick him up. So she drove on to her parents' house for help. Then she thought the clutch was the throttle, or the other way around, and the thing took off like a rocket and she jumped off and that was it."

"I see. And if she did want to kill them, she'd presumably have to have a motive, and nobody knows of one, do they?"

Rossetti was remembering. He was remembering the rock-hard under-age Rodriguez body and how it had frozen like ice when he'd made her for the first time. Later, loosened up on dope, he'd heard the story of the Jacuzzi and the dealer who'd moved in with her mother. There was a motive all right. But for now, thank God, it was secret.

"That's it," said the attorney. "No motive. She didn't see her folks much, but there's nothing to suggest a major falling out. The homicide guy was pretty impressed by that point. And the other thing is, if it was premeditated murder, you have to suppose that the Cuban kid was in on it, or, if not, that she somehow got him off the boat and then wasted her parents with it. It's highly unlikely that he was an accomplice. Apparently, he hardly knew her. And if she pushed him off the boat, he'd be the first one to say so. I mean, that was *his* boat, and she blew it up for him."

"Yeah, no kid would lie to save Lisa's skin. That's for sure," said Johnny, and he laughed because he knew what Lisa Rodriguez could do to a man, any man. Jesus, if he himself hadn't come with armor plating, Lisa would have done it to him. After ten minutes of the Rodriguez treatment, a megabuck Cuban brat would crawl five miles over broken glass to lick her painted toe. Mere perjury would be blowing in the wind. And this Aragon had apparently been with her for the best part of twenty-four hours. The only mystery was why he hadn't admitted to driving the boat.

"I think we're out of this one. I really think so. So does the Aragon lawyer. He's quite cocky about it. Keeps saying, 'This ees my town, señora, this eesn't the Beeg Apple. When you get down here, you just put in the bills and let me do the talking. The policemen here, the Coast Guard, they are all beeg friends of mine.' "

"And if they don't charge her, then this is a media fest," said Johnny Rossetti. He was feeling better. He liked "up" lawyers. He liked female lawyers. Hell, he liked women. The legal eagle from

Downtown was looking better by the minute. If she didn't watch out, she'd get lucky. For a minute or two he was silent. Maybe this minus could be turned into a plus. One thing had been worrying him because he couldn't figure it out. Blankheart had clearly heard about Lisa's Miami problems when he'd called that morning. But if he knew that Lisa was a homicide suspect, why the hell had he offered her the Whitney exclusive? It was the kiss of death to an endorsement deal for the model to have bad publicity. He had even referred to the morals clauses that were always inserted into those kinds of contracts. Now, however, he could begin to see Blankheart's position. He would have had his Miami people look into this. If they had concluded that Lisa was about to be freed, her name cleared of any suspicion of wrong-doing, then at a stroke she would be at the center of a storm of publicity. She would be the tragic figure who had, through no fault of her own, killed the parents she loved. The poor girl goes away to make her fame and fortune and returns to show her folks her material spoils, only for disaster to strike. The publicity would merge with the launch of the Whitney campaign in a blissful synergy as it was announced that Lisa would be its star. Everyone would be too busy counting the money to laugh on the way to the bank.

"I think we're here," said the attorney.

They, and the entire Miami press pool, were "there." They pushed up the steps through the dense crowd, and made themselves known to the policeman who was fighting the losing battle to keep the journalists out of the building.

"Go up to the fifth floor. You'll see the door marked HOMICIDE. The detectives and the others are expecting you."

They were quiet in the ancient elevator. The optimism of the taxicab already seemed far away. Johnny stared at his polished shoes. His attorney looked at him. The elevator stopped. The door marked HOMICIDE banged behind them, and a police sergeant showed them into a large office. It needed to be large. Everyone was there.

In the middle of the crowd sat Lisa Rodriguez. She was weeping quietly, but Johnny reckoned he knew her inside out. In his book, she was capable of any and every crime up to and including matricide and patricide. The tears were her concession to the role of orphan that she had killed to play. Standing next to her was the captain of Homicide, slap bang in the middle of a spotlight that he clearly enjoyed. He frowned a lot to show that this was a serious business, but a half smile kept breaking through to give away his game. To his right were the Aragon team. The boy was smart in an Italian suit, smirking a lot, except when his father looked at him. Then he would study the floor and assume the sort of pious expression you saw a lot of in church. The father, stern and patrician, was the only one who looked pissed off by the proceedings, but even he seemed to be getting some pleasure out of it . . . the exercise of power, probably. A lifetime spent making hundreds of millions paid off at times like these. It was what the money was for, a potent demonstration that all the hard work had not been wasted. A barbershop quartet of Aragon lawyers hovered about their boss, and the smallest and most ebullient of them welcomed the duo from New York.

"Ah, Mr. Rossetti, how good of you to come, and so fast, and welcome too, Señora Feinstein, from the esteemed New York firm of Vogel, Silverberg and a hundred others from the masthead on your fax . . ." He laughed to show how at home he was in this situation, all sleek grease and expensive suit, his neat little mustache gray in patches, his teeth stained slightly from the Havanas he chain-smoked all day.

"Well, it's a very sad day for us all, and of course, mostly for Señorita Rodriguez and her terrible tragedy . . ." the lawyer intoned.

On cue, Lisa failed to suppress a sob. She buried her head in her hands and looked miserable. Inside, she *was* in turmoil. She, herself, could hardly work out whether or not her tears were an act. She had done the deed. She had lanced the pus-filled wound of her hatred, and now she found that the relief was all mixed up with an alien form of pain. It was her mother she minded about. Somehow her terrible betrayal of Lisa's father, her callous disregard of her daughter's fate had been wiped out in the holocaust that Lisa had unleashed. And what was left was the blood that was thicker than tears. She had grown in her mother's belly. She was part of her, even though she had loathed her, and there had been happinesses in those far-off times . . . the beach, Christmas, and all the Disney days of a South Florida childhood. And there were other things to remember now that she had gone. Half of Lisa's remarkable beauty had come from her mother. Her beloved father had loved his wife, and wanted her to be happy, and well cared for . . . and safe. How would he be feeling, on some hillside in Paradise, as he looked down and saw what his daughter had done?

The tears came faster in the confusion, as the thoughts tumbled around in Lisa's mind. It wasn't guilt, exactly. It wasn't even regret.

But it was something, the weird sensation that right and wrong were somehow applicable to her damaged but triumphant life, the alien feeling that perhaps there were principles that were more important than winning, and fighting, and getting her own way.

She blinked away the tears and looked around her, cunning still, and terminally shrewd in her moment of doubt. These fine feelings must not be allowed to destroy her. She was still in mortal danger. Things seemed to be going her way, but any delay before dropping charges . . . a referral to a grand jury, the decision of the police to investigate further . . . would be a body blow to her career. Anything less than total exoneration could be disastrous for her. So she used the tears, and the sorrow that wasn't completely surrogate, to her best advantage. It seemed the smartest thing to do.

* * *

The policeman was talking. "I think I ought to say for the record that my department has concluded its investigation into this case, and we have examined the possibility that this was not an accident." He paused.

Lisa's sobs intensified. José looked at her as if he was seeing the face of the Virgin Mary. Even father Aragon, who, after all, shared his son's genes, looked touched by her sorrow. "However, there is no motive. And we have the evidence of the only eyewitness, Mr. José de Aragon, a man whose family is a pillar of respectability in our community. And then we have the character of Ms. Rodriguez herself, a person Miami has always been proud to claim as its own . . ." Again he stopped, peering around the room to watch the effect of his words. Everyone was nodding. The sugar baron was adding up the IOUs. The Aragon lawyer was beaming. Lisa looked consumed by the enormity of her personal tragedy.

"So, let me just say that it has been agreed with the offices of both the Medical Examiner and the State Attorney that this was a tragic accident in which no one was at fault, and I can only say how deeply sorry I am that this terrible event has occurred."

Johnny Rossetti wondered if this was the moment the champagne would appear. It was an absolutely joyous occasion. The air was thick with the atmosphere of mutual congratulations. Only Lisa seemed locked away from the celebration, and Johnny had to admire what he was certain was her act. He had never seen her look more beautiful.

A vision of the Whitney contract flashed in front of his mind. A voice in his head said quite clearly, "five million dollars."

Lisa stood up. She took a deep breath and shuddered. A smile broke through her tears, like the warm sun after a cold rain. She turned toward the captain of Homicide. She knew what was expected. It was time for her to deliver her part of the unspoken, unwritten deal that had just been done.

"May I just say thank you, from the bottom of my heart, to our wonderful Miami police department, and especially to Captain Hernandez, who has worked so hard and so thoroughly on this investigation and yet who has always been chivalrous, and kind, and considerate in this terrible time. I have returned to Miami because I have always loved it, and I love it because of the wonderful people like you, Captain, who live here . . ."

Captain Hernandez was shining like one of the president's mysterious points of light. Later, he was due to appear on a couple of the local news programs. The *Herald* wanted a profile. "Hard Copy," "Inside Edition," and "A Current Affair" were circling like sharks, and there had even been an exploratory call from "NBC Nightly News." Captain Hernandez had indeed been chivalrous, kind, and considerate to Lisa Rodriguez, because he had seen this case from the very beginning as a one-way ticket to promotion. Major Juan Hernandez, the man who could handle the limelight, the *hombre* who knew how to look after the lady that Hispanic America worshiped. The voters wouldn't forget that, and neither would the mayor who always remembered what the voters wouldn't forget. Okay, in a perfectly righteous world investigations would not have been concluded so quickly. But a dealer was a dealer was a dealer, and a dealer's wife was always an accomplice. In the Hernandez book, the "accident" . . . and it probably *was* an accident . . . was the kind he would have liked to have seen more of.

"And I would also like to say sorry to a very sweet boy who has been caught up in all this through no fault of his own, and, and . . . José, thank you."

She smiled at him. He sent back a look of slavish adoration. Lisa was feeling better. The remorse, if that was what it had been, was fading. The hell with them all. This was her party. All the bit players were feeding off her as usual, but that was okay. It was a way to know that you were a winner, and winning made all the struggle, the hard work, and the pain worthwhile. The fat cop would ride to promotion on her fame. The spoiled rich kid would get a chance to boast to his grandchildren about the time he had had his way with the supermodel, and all for the price of a lousy boat. And even the father, slipping surreptitious glances at her out of the side of his face, would be scoring points somewhere. Lisa would have bet a month's income that the slimy billionaire would be on the telephone within the week, talking yachts and planes, and long weekends at Cartier. But Lisa was not yet finished. There was still more revenge to savor.

Because across the room was dear old Johnny. Johnny had never raped her in a Jacuzzi, but he had turned her on to cocaine when she was fourteen years old, and when she was high on that, he had floated the heroin at her. He had held her arm and showed her how to inject it, and when she was all strung out for a fix, he had taken photographs of her doing things so disgustingly bizarre that they had failed to be included in a textbook of sexual perversion that she had once read. She had clawed herself back from the brink, despite his Svengali influence, and brick by brick she had built her mighty career until she was untouchable, beholden to no one, safe in the fortress of her money and her fame.

All the time she had learned the lessons of her life. People dumped on you, even the ones you loved. If you let it, the world would do unspeakable things to you. The only remedy was to be strong. Then they would not merely leave you alone, they would bow and scrape at your feet, and you could walk like a god among them, and you could drink deep on the cup of revenge. Her stepfather had paid the price for raping her. Her mother had been sent to hell for marrying him. José had been turned into a murderess's accomplice and fined a boat for calling her a peasant. Now it was Johnny's turn. Oh yes, it was. It was his turn now.

She walked across to him.

"Thank you for coming," she said.

It was hardly enough, thought Johnny. Once again the Rossetti insects were back walking. He peered at her suspiciously.

"I'm so glad it turned out okay. Jeez, kid, you had us worried. What a terrible thing, a terrible business . . ." he added.

"Yeah," she said. "That was a real piece of bad luck, wasn't it?"

She knew he knew. She knew he knew she knew he knew.

And she knew he couldn't prove a thing.

"Listen, Lisa, I've got to talk to you in private. You're not going to believe what's happened."

"Good news?"

"Only the best."

"No," she said. "The best is over."

Her smile opened up her perfect teeth. They looked to Rossetti like the tombstones of her parents.

The captain was walking over to them. So was the Aragon lawyer. Rossetti couldn't hold it in any longer.

"Don Blankheart called and offered you a two-year endorsement contract at Whitney Enterprises. I don't know, but it could be worth five or even more."

He stood back to watch the effect of his bombshell.

She rocked gently as she took it in. Her head was cocked to one side, and she smiled as it registered.

"Five million dollars," she said at last. Then she turned and pirouetted on her heel, snapping her fingers as she did so. "Hah! Five million dollars," she said again.

"Isn't it wonderful?"

"It is wonderful, wonderful . . . for me."

"For us," Rossetti corrected her. Seventy-five percent was better than fifteen percent, but fifteen percent was better than peanuts, and she'd be the one doing the work.

"No, no, Johnny, it's wonderful for me, but it's not wonderful for you at all."

"What are you talking about?"

"I was waiting for the right moment to tell you, Johnny, and you know, I think this is it."

"Tell me what? What is this horseshit?"

"Tell you that you are no longer my agent. I quit. I'm history. I'm no longer with Elle."

Johnny's mouth was open all right, but the words wouldn't come out.

Eventually they formed, like tea leaves at the bottom of a cup.

"You've gone with another agent?" he spluttered.

"Yeah," said Lisa Rodriguez. "I've gone with Christa Kenwood."

12

Key West

"Are you working, Daddy?"

She stood in the open doorway, a naughty smile on her face, and she pushed the door backward and forward, swinging against it. She wore a straw hat with a black band, a pink T-shirt saying BORN TO BE BEAUTIFUL, black cut-off work-out shorts and ice-cream-for-the-feet candy-striped sneakers. At five years old, she was dressed to kill her daddy.

Peter Stein leaned back in his chair and smiled.

"Oh, Camille!" he said. "No, I'm not really working." Was sitting in front of the typewriter working? Was he writing while merely thinking about writing? Would all this blocked angst finally be undone by the psychic plumber? Who knew? At the end of the day, who cared? Nobody asked a writer to write, and carpenters probably had problems too, though right now Peter Stein couldn't imagine what they might be.

"Good," she said. "I'm in." She ran to him and he swiveled around in the chair and flung his arms around her as she cuddled into him, laying her head on his knee. For seconds they were still, loving each other, but he knew that wouldn't last. Camille was never still, always asking, always wanting . . . a bit like him, really, but it was so adorable in a child.

"You're writing a book," she said. To Peter it sounded suspiciously like an accusation.

"Yes, I am, and it's very hard."

"I'm not stopping your book, am I?"

"No, darling, you're not. I'm stopping myself."

She giggled. "You can't stop yourself. That's not fair."

"It isn't fair. You're right. I'm not being fair to myself."

"You're a silly daddy," she said, but she nuzzled in to show him that she didn't think he was at all silly, that he was in fact the most perfect daddy in all the world.

"Did Louise let you come up here?" said Peter cunningly. The big fat nanny was always trying to get extra time for the daytime soaps.

If Camille could be filtered up into his writing room, strictly forbidden territory, her charm could be guaranteed to keep her there through "Santa Barbara" and most of "Days of Our Lives."

"No, she was watching TV and it was *boring*, so I came up here. Daddy, can I play with your typewriter?"

Can I scratch your Stradivarius? Can I stomp on your Steinway? Can I play darts with your scalpels, Daddy?

"Yes, darling, but be careful with it. Daddy loves his typewriter very much."

"As much as me?" Accusation.

"No, darling. Daddy loves you more than anything in the whole wide world." It was true, but only just. Because there was the book inside that wouldn't come out, the book that had been gestating for two miserable years. He loved that, too, and hated it for the pain it caused and would cause until some future book washed away its memory.

She sat up on his knee and hammered at the keys.

tthjtnbfnfhhfffkhjkkkereeiu34riuyerjhidejivejoweojwloe

"Look. This is for you, Daddy."

She ripped the paper from the machine and handed it to him with a smile of pride.

He looked at it carefully.

"What does it say, Daddy? Read it."

"That's very good, darling. I can see two words, nearly three. That's two and a bit more words than I've written all day and I think they're good words. *Hide* and *jive.* That's what writing is all about these days. Hiding and jiving."

"What?" She held her head to one side, and her hat wobbled and nearly fell off. He had to kiss her. God, she was so divine.

She wiped off the kiss with the back of her hand, but was pleased by it.

"Do you hide and jive, Daddy?"

"Yes, I sit in here all day for years on end, and then sometimes I go off to places like Miami and everyone makes a big fuss of me and I ride in long cars and drink champagne and everyone tells me how clever I am."

She cut through to the bottom line.

"It's not your AMI. It's Louise's AMI."

"Well, it's my Ami *and* Louise's Ami, I guess." He laughed, remembering the "undertoad" of Garp's world.

"Can you read me your book at bedtime? Has it got animals in it?"

She took hold of the lapels of his open shirt and stared deep into his eyes, melting his heart as she intended.

"Oh, darling, I wish I could, but I think you'd find it very boring."

"Like Louise's TV?"

"No, *not* like Louise's TV. Boring in a different way. Boring to little girls, but not to grownups." God, conversations with children were so frightening. They clarified things. Maybe his book would be boring to grownups and fascinating to children. It depended on the adult. It depended on the child. Hell, was there any difference at all between the two, except experience, the name men gave to their mistakes.

"What's it called?"

"It's called *The Dream I Dreamed.*"

"Why?"

"Because I saw a line in a novel by someone called Victor Hugo. It said, 'Life has killed the dream I dreamed.' That's what my book is about. It's difficult to explain, but dreams are the things that get us going and we have to pretend they are real, otherwise life would have no meaning. But in the end, dreams aren't real, and reality kills them, and when they die we are very sad."

"Do we cry?"

"Yes, if we can, we cry."

"Because our dreams are dead?"

"Yes, and because reality crushes our spirit."

"Ooooooh. I don't want to be crushed. Not before supper."

He laughed. She'd snapped him out of it. The melancholy, that hovered around him like a shroud.

"What are you having for supper?"

"Fish fingers in the micro-rave."

Peter Stein grimaced. "Microwave," he corrected her absentmindedly. In his mind he was weighing the scales. He had been sitting at his desk for three hours. He hadn't dredged up a word, let alone a sentence. He should break for the day. The excuse was forming in his mind. But you never knew when the words would suddenly form like rain. If he was sitting at the typewriter he would be ready for the word storm, should it come. If he was somewhere else, the precious moment would be wasted.

The decision made itself as it always did.

"Come on, Camille. Daddy's going to cook you dinner. Okay? We're going to have one of our famous candlelit dinners for two."

She whooped her excitement.

"I'll put on a dress."

"We'll cook first. Okay, let's go see what we've got."

Together they clattered down the mahogany staircase of the old Conch house.

"You're a better cook than Mommy," she said, taking his hand.

"I try harder at cooking than Mommy. She tries harder than me at other things, and she's better at those things than I am."

"Like what?"

Peter Stein fought back the temptation to unload the list—

Dressing up.

Spending money.

Being unfaithful.

Being lots of fun.

Being alive.

Being happy.

"Oh, Mommy's warmer and kinder than me, and she's a better mommy to you than I am a daddy." Was that fishing?

"I think you are both nice to me," said Camille with the scrupulous fairness of the very young. "I wish you lived together. Mommy says you don't live together any more 'cause you're cold." She squeezed his hand. "But you feel warm. I think Mommy's wrong."

"I don't think Mommy's talking about my temperature. She's talking about my personality."

"Your poisonality. You're not poison."

He laughed. "Some people wouldn't agree with you."

The kitchen was lean and spare and stripped for action, like the piles of neat blank paper stacked next to the Stein typewriter. Cooking, like writing, was serious business. You had to get it right. Peter opened the fridge door. He pulled out some shrimp he'd bought in the market at seven that morning. From the freezer he took a silver packet marked "swordfish," bearing yesterday's date. He'd caught it late evening on the way back from the Dry Tortugas. He put the dish of shrimp and the swordfish side by side. Next, he washed his hands, dried them with the care of a priest at mass, and then he began to lay out the things he would need on a scrubbed, scrupulously clean maple chopping board. Camille stared at him, fascinated by the ritual. She knew from experience that helping Daddy cook meant watching him.

"Can I set the table?" He was never very interested in that, but

Mommy just *loved* to do it. She grabbed some knives and forks. "It's easy when I stay with you, 'cause you don't have any friends," she said as she pranced through to the dining room.

Peter smiled. Yes, he was alone. It wasn't really a choice. It had just happened. And it was true there weren't many friends, because friends were work, and tricky and mostly stupid, which he found difficult to forgive. They took up time and they wanted things from you, and he could never think of anything of value that they gave him in return. Above all, they were part of the reality that was the enemy of fantasy, and as such they were dangers to his precious writing. Friends enjoyed strangling the dreams you dreamed.

He worked fast, like a surgeon with a life to save. Olive oil, vinegar, Dijon mustard, pepper, rock salt, some finely chopped chives for the vinaigrette. Some endive leaves, finely sliced radishes, paper thin cut tomatoes to make the plates of shrimp beautiful. The swordfish steaks, lightly buttered and salted, laid out side by side on the grill. The salad was uncompromisingly green. The French bread, fresh from the morning market, warmed in the oven. New potatoes, firm not soggy, brushed with butter and garden mint. There was a jar of his own mayonnaise in the refrigerator, and a bottle of Montrachet in the icebox. Last, but far from least, he made the Shirley Temple that Camille loved.

Louise wandered in from the study, her eyes thick with soaped infidelity and bleached passion.

"Oh, are you cooking Camille's supper?"

"No, I am preparing the pope's breakfast."

"I didn't know you was doing that."

He *presumed* she meant the dinner. With Louise's I.Q. you could never be certain.

"Daddy, you *are* cooking dinner." Camille giggled.

"I was attempting a joke with Louise, but I don't think she's back from Santa Barbara yet," said Peter with withering scorn. He couldn't stand the flesh mountain that looked after Camille, but you weren't allowed to be too rude to nannies in case they decided to take a walk.

"Listen, Louise, as I'm already doing the heavy lifting, perhaps you could go and get everything together for tomorrow, and I'll put Camille to bed after we've eaten."

"Oh, Daddy, I don't want to go back tomorrow. Can't I stay in Key West with you?" She ran to him and wrapped herself around his leg like a limpet.

He felt the tug at his heart where he was meant to feel it. She was the only one who had ever touched him there, the only one who ever would. He had never loved before. It was as simple as that. He had married with the enthusiasm of a social scientist for a field project, and when the time had come for divorce it had been as friendly a separation as between college roommates heading off in the world's different directions. He didn't hold it against his wife that she had had affairs. Given that all his passion was focused on work, and the one-time-around nature of life, it seemed the bright thing to do. It did hurt that she'd left him for a psychiatrist. That seemed gratuitously insulting, especially as the man practiced psychoanalysis, the pursuit of the unhappy in the futile search for a more meaningful unhappiness. Luckily, Camille was too young to have been indoctrinated into the mysteries of penis envy and the Electra complex. But boy, if the dread buzzwords ever passed her lips, he was going to have serious words with the mouth merchant from Pasadena who had taken on his wife.

"Come on, darling, remember our dinner. You're such a big girl now. Let's light the candles."

She sat as still as she could through dinner, but that wasn't very still. She didn't eat much, but she tasted everything, and she tried to be serious like he was. Every now and again she crawled onto his knee and got him to feed her, and she whispered in his ear that she loved him, and she wondered why that made his eyes get misty.

"Are you all right, Daddy?" she asked suddenly.

He laughed through tear-filled eyes. How could one so young ask a question like that?

"Yes, of course. I'm fine. I'm just happy, that's all."

"What will you do when I'm gone?"

"I'm going up to Palm Beach to see a friend of mine. I do have a *few* friends."

"Who?" Camille looked suspicious. She liked to have her daddy to herself.

"A very old friend called Mary Whitney. She's giving a party and I'm going up there on my boat."

"Do you love her?" Oh, faithless father.

"No, of course not. She's just a friend like the ones you have in school. She's very funny and makes me laugh."

"Maybe there'll be pretty ladies at the party in pretty dresses."

"Maybe it's time for me to tell you a bedtime story about a beautiful little girl who found a magic wand that could bring cuddly toys to life."

That did it. Daddy was strong meat. He wore his daughter out. Bed and a long lovely story sounded terrific. He led her upstairs and tucked her in, and he rubbed her back as he made up the story. No block now. This was easy, because it was not judged, by him or by the world. Perhaps all writing should be like that, for fun, not for pride and money, but to send people happily to sleep to dream good dreams.

She was gone. She hadn't waited for his dramatic ending with its carefully crafted twist. She had left his lovable characters and fearless heroine suspended in thin air and passed on them all in favor of the joy of sleep. Now her little chest rose and fell and sweet breath blew through her parted lips.

Peter Stein pulled the blanket over her. He bent down and he kissed her forehead.

"I love you, Camille," he murmured. "If it weren't for you, I wouldn't know how."

13

Christa hurried across the lobby of the Intercontinental, and she tried to remind herself that this was Miami and not some city in the tropics. All around her, South America lazed and loitered. Patent-leather-haired men bent solicitously over the painted hands of Nina Ricci-ed flamenco dancer look-alikes, while effervescent, well-behaved children skipped around their ankles. Spanish syllables hissed and lisped, and even the Muzak was pasodoble as the bemused American waitresses served the sherry they were used to pouring into soup. But Christa was not concentrating on the culture clash. She was thinking only of the make-or-break meeting that was about to take place. She was thinking only of Lisa Rodriguez.

By sheer bad luck she had missed the drama that had captured the hyperactive attention span of America for a record-breaking thirty-six hours. She had decided to stay until the day after the Whitney party, but her old friend Noreen Rouse had asked her to come on a dive trip to the Memory Rock reef in the Abacos. She hadn't been able to resist it, and so, while Lisa's drama had filled the airwaves, Christa had been incommunicado in the Bahamas.

The bottom line was that Christa, the would-be agent, fingers supposedly on the pulse, had been the very last to find out that Lisa Rodriguez had orphaned herself with a speedboat. The moment she'd arrived back and heard the news, she had spent a nerve-racking couple of hours trying to find Lisa. When she'd eventually tracked her down, the supermodel had been guarded.

On the telephone, Lisa had not sounded like someone who had accidentally burned her family and spent a night in jail as a murder suspect. In fact, she had sounded like her usual self-confident self. She had seemed chiefly concerned by the possible effect of it all on her career, so much so that Christa had the surreal impression that the whole thing was some bizarre publicity stunt. They had both agreed that no long-term damage had been done, apart from the psychological wounds that Lisa must have suffered, and then Christa had probed carefully to see if Rodriguez had made any final decision on the agency move.

"I want to talk to you about that. Can you come down to Miami this afternoon?" Lisa had replied.

"Of course. I can be with you in a couple of hours."

"Great. Oh, have you heard from Johnny?"

"No. Should I have heard from him?"

"I just wondered if he'd called you."

The "about what" hung in the air.

Christa's stomach had done the elevator thing. Had Lisa changed her mind? Perhaps she had decided to stay with Rossetti after all, had told him of the Kenwood poaching effort, and now he was furious. Or, there was the optimistic possibility. Lisa intended to leave the Elle agency and had already sent Rossetti the "Dear John." In either scenario Rossetti would now be a Cruise missile targeted at Christa's head.

"Have you talked to Johnny recently?" she had managed in the quest for clarification.

"Yeah, he and his lawyer creamed into the cop shop when it was all over, all cock and congratulations, and tried to take the credit for springing me."

"I'm sorry I wasn't there for you, Lisa. I was in the Bahamas and the news never filtered through." Christa was acutely aware that she had lost brownie points. Hot agents weren't supposed to be out of touch with the world for a nanosecond, let alone when their prospective top clients were aiming powerboats at parents.

"Listen, I was there for myself, Christa. I always have been. I didn't need anyone, least of all Johnny Rossetti. Anyway, you're not my agent yet."

Silence.

With a superhuman effort, Christa had kept her mouth buttoned.

"Okay, Lisa, I'm on my way. I'll be there in a couple of hours."

It had taken Christa ninety minutes to get to the Intercontinental. Now, there was a long wait between Christa's knock and opening of the door to the penthouse suite. Lisa looked preoccupied, distant rather than sad. She wore a shirt that read I DON'T DO MORNINGS and nothing else at all.

Christa hugged her tight, and then stepped back to look at her.

"I'm so sorry . . ." she started. She had rehearsed a speech on the I-95, but somehow she knew all along that it would be superfluous. It was.

"It's over," said Lisa, putting an end to solicitous sorrow with a flick of her hand. Her toasted parents were still in the morgue, not yet having achieved coffin status, but it seemed that to Lisa they were already ancient history. Christa, herself no stranger to family brutality, found it a tour de force of emotional toughness.

"I'm having a brandy," added Lisa. "Do you want something?"

"Is there any wine?"

"Yeah, I think there's some in the mini-bar. Help yourself."

Christa walked over to the fridge. The room looked wrecked. Lisa, however, looked perfect.

"You're very brave," said Christa.

"Fortune favors the brave," said Lisa with an enigmatic smile.

There was no answer to that. Christa undid the top of a small bottle of wine.

Lisa raised a shot glass of cognac and took out the amber liquid like Wayne in a Western. She smacked edible lips, breathed, "Aaaaah, that's better," and sank down into an armchair.

Her next remark was totally unexpected.

"Do you know Mary Whitney?" she asked suddenly.

"Sure I do. She lives in Palm Beach. I'm going to a party at her house tonight."

"You are?" Lisa sounded impressed, which was unusual.

"Why?"

"I'm going to be working for her."

"Really?"

Things were moving fast. They weren't far from the nitty gritty now.

"Mary Whitney is going to launch a whole new perfume line. It's going to be a vast campaign, and they want me as an exclusive contract model. Two years. Big, big bucks."

"That's wonderful, Lisa." But only wonderful if you're with my agency. Christa was suspended over the abyss.

It was better to get it over with. "I guess the offer came through Johnny."

"Well, yeah, it did, but I told him to get lost. He went ballistic. Then I told him I was going with you, and he went the next thing, whatever that is."

"You told him you're coming with me. You *are* coming with me? For real? For sure?" Christa felt the bubbles in her chest. Lisa equaled Steve Pitts. Two plus two stars made a star agency and a star owner. At a stroke she had gotten her own way, had won whatever she was trying to win, had proved the goddamn point.

"I said I was, didn't I? Once I've signed, you can do the deal with Whitney Enterprises and Don Blankheart. Johnny's going to try and cause all sorts of trouble. You know that, don't you?"

"If I'm handling you, I'll deal with Johnny. Forget him. He's history."

"Oh, I'll *never* forget him," said Lisa, her full lips suddenly narrow. "Seeing his face when he lost his share of me was the second best moment of my life so far."

Christa didn't want to know about the best one.

"What sort of money are we going to go for, Christa?"

"We'll have to find out how badly they want you. That's the key. On a 'loss of earnings plus a premium basis' I imagine they'd have to go five plus. But if they're set on you, the sky's the limit. Maybe I could find out from Mary."

"At her party tonight?"

"Maybe."

The idea suddenly occurred to Christa.

"Hey, why don't *you* come to the party? I mean, looking like to die and winding them up. Oh, no . . . of course you couldn't . . . I mean with all this . . ."

"Shit, I look *great* in black," said Lisa. "I've got this Alaïa thing that's like really obscene."

"Are you sure?"

"Can you get me invited?"

"Oh, no problem. No problem." Christa paused. There was no

time like the present. "Listen, Lisa, drive back with me to Palm Beach, and stay the night. I've got a contract in my hotel. You could sign it, so it's all sort of legal, and then we can go to the party and I can start dealing like a dervish on this Whitney thing."

"Okay, fine. That sounds great. I really feel like a party. You'll have to stay close and tell me who to screw."

Christa laughed.

"At Palm Beach balls everything is on the menu *except* sex. If you see somebody who looks like Mr. Right, you know the party is fancy dress."

Her heart sank momentarily amid the wild excitement of the moment. Who the hell would be the bore who'd be sitting next to her at dinner?

14

"Can you show me the Western grip again, Rob? I seem to have lost the plot."

Mary Whitney smiled slyly in the bright sunlight, as he walked toward her. This wasn't the first tennis coach who'd speeded her pulse, and it wouldn't be the last. But there was something about Rob Sand that added up to much more than his serve, his backhand, and his deep blue eyes. He was fatally attractive, the sort of boy who could become one of her rare magnificent obsessions.

He wrapped his arms around her from behind, and on purpose she pushed back at him, feeling his hard body crushed against her as she allowed him to adjust her grip on the racket. He was damp with sweat and she liked that. It was one of the reasons she insisted on playing at a time when only mad dogs and Englishmen were about.

"There," he said. "I don't really know if it's the right grip for you, Mrs. Whitney."

"I like it, Rob," she purred. He let go of her, like he might a hot potato. There was a flush on his face that wasn't the heat. At twenty, the Sand hormones were clearly in working order, even if she was old enough to be his mother, perhaps because of it. Forty was a dangerous age. But then so was twenty. It was thirty that was safe and dull.

"You want to hit some more balls before we start?"

"Oh, yes, I do indeed," said Mary. She stared at him with sex-ray vision. He was incredibly good looking. The best so far by a mile. The ad on the board at Palm Beach Atlantic College hadn't produced before. Now it had dealt a diamond. She walked toward the baseline, exaggerating her movements to show off her wiry body, as if modeling the tennis outfit that she had designed for herself. Okay, she didn't win prizes, but her tits were big and bold still, and kids of a barely screwable age tended to like that.

He was back on the other side of the court now, protected from her lust by the net. For now.

Thwack! She took the rising ball and curled her racket over the top of it like the big boys did. It went over low and kicked up with the topspin. *Thwack.* Back it came with knobs on. Mmmm. He was good. Junior Wimbledon standard at least, and brown as a berry, all golden juicy delicious. Could he learn to love her as much as God? That was the bad news, or was it the good news? In the battle for Rob Sand's postadolescent attention, she had a rival her own size. The Almighty.

"When you hit one, do you do it for Jesus?" she called over the net. She kept her smile inside. *Thwack!*

"I believe everything is for Jesus."

Thwack! He was deadly serious. He'd got God bad. It was an occupational hazard in Palm Beach these days, especially among the young and the attractive. Cool dudes hung out at the First Baptist's Chapel on the Lake. Dweebs took drugs like their sixties parents. In the generation game, it was the kids' revenge.

She zapped the ball way out of court, and bent over to pretend she was exhausted. Her scheming brain hummed on. This boy wouldn't be cashable. Not for a bit, anyway. She'd have to wade through a morass of tantalizing moral inhibitions before he dropped his defenses and surrendered like the others.

Thwack!

"Hang on, Rob. Spare me. Save me. I'm feeling faint."

He vaulted the net, all long brown legs and coordinated muscle. He was fat-free, a gorgeous low-cholesterol meal, all clean and healthful, the sort that could only do you good. Mary licked dry lips as he loped, worried, toward her.

"I told you it was too hot to play. We should have waited till later in the afternoon. You should drink some water."

She allowed him to lead her to the water fountain, leaning heavily on his arm. Heavens, he had the street cunning of an Iowa farmboy. His wholesome mind hadn't dreamed that he was a sexual target. Or had it? One of the nicest things about Rob Sand was his ability to surprise her.

Mary Whitney flopped into a director's chair and patted the seat of the one next to her. He sat, too.

"Thank the Lord for water."

"Amen," he actually said.

She looked at him, trying to keep her mouth shut. Drooling at her age was a no-no.

"Are you a Christian, Mrs. Whitney?" he said at last. He looked at her through wide blue eyes, then quickly looked away.

Mary Whitney knew the format. This was not a "Christian-as-opposed-to-an-Arab/Jew/Buddhist" question. This meant "Are you on the Christian case dusk to dawn and dawn to dusk?" Given what the world knew about Mary Whitney, it was not a very perspicacious question. There was only one way to answer it, given the game plan.

"I'd like to be," she lied.

He seemed relieved by her answer.

"It's changed my life," he said simply. "I know it sounds crazy to say this . . . to someone like you, I mean . . . but it could change yours."

She took his hand. He let her have it. Outside the Christian context, she wouldn't have had a prayer. She squeezed it sincerely. She rubbed it religiously. She put it on her bare thigh and breathed her longing at him.

"Maybe you could show me how," she said.

In the V of his vest she could see a tuft of soft blond hair. Below the cotton of his shorts there would be another. Woof! Mary *did* feel faint.

"I'm not a teacher . . . I mean, I don't teach Sunday school . . ."

"I know that, Rob. I know you're not exactly . . . qualified, but you can teach me by example, by your enthusiasm, by your excitement. That's how people like me learn."

"I'd like that." He seemed less than sure that he would. "Have you got a Bible?" That was firm ground.

"There must be one or two in the library." Mary Whitney didn't quite succeed in extracting all the sarcasm from her reply. This was hard work, in the heat and the steam. It was so much easier signing checks. And she really ought to have a nap before the beastly party.

"Do you want to hit some more balls?"

"No, I think we've had enough balls for today." To her Mortimer's friends, that would have been quite a good third-Martini joke.

He stood up.

"Okay, then, Mrs. Whitney, I hope you enjoyed the lesson, and I'll see you tonight at the party. You're sure it's all right if I wear a suit."

"Anything in the world will be all right, as long as you promise to ask me to dance," breathed Mary McGregor Whitney.

15

Mary Whitney lay still on the four-poster bed, unable to sleep. Through the open window came the myriad noises of party preparation. The telephone rang.

"Mrs. Whitney, I have Christa Kenwood for you."

The steamy visions of Rob Sand, stretched out on her private altar of lust, faded. Christa Kenwood, her old yellow-pantied friend, was on the line. What did she want? Mary needed to know, not least because it was rumored that Lisa Rodriguez, the supernova model that Mary intended to hire, might move to the fledgling Kenwood agency. If Rodriguez had been hot before, she was hotter now, blazing in the glare of heightened public awareness since her bizarre boat trip.

She scooped up the telephone.

"Christa, darling, Mary. How *are* you? How wonderful to hear from you. I'm thrilled you're coming to my party."

"Hi, Mary, yes, isn't it exciting? I come into Palm Beach and fall in with Muffy and everyone. It's just like a Day School reunion."

"Muffy said you were *modeling* down here."

"And other things. Like, I've just signed Lisa Rodriguez for my new agency. Isn't that *exciting?* I think she's just the best, don't you?"

It was classic understatement, and meant to be.

"Is she here in Palm Beach?" said Mary carefully. "Is she all right after that terrible thing in Miami?"

"Oh, she's *wonderful.* So brave. So tough. She's a survivor. I can hardly believe her strength. Listen, Mary . . . that was what I was calling about. Would it be a big problem to bring Lisa along this evening? She's staying with me here at the Brazilian Court and I didn't want to leave her at the hotel while I came to the party. I think it would do her good. Can I bring her?"

"Of course, bring her. Have you told her how dreadful it will be? Outsiders have such inflated expectations of Palm Beach parties."

Christa laughed. "Don't worry. She just doesn't want to be alone right now. She'll probably wear black, if that's all right."

"Totally appropriate, dear. All my balls are wakes. She'll be the only one properly dressed for it."

"Great, Mary. Thanks a bunch. Longing to see you. Bye!"

"Oh, darling," said Mary, catching her before she went. "Listen, sweetheart, can you come half an hour early? I'd just love to have a little chat with you before all the awful people turn up. You know what it's like when the dreadful music starts."

"Okay, darling. I'll do that. Catch up on all your news that I don't get from Liz Smith and Billy Norwich."

"Yes, yes. Ha! Ha! All the dirt. Oh, and darling. Do you ever read books? I've put you next to a dear sweet old thing at dinner who keeps winning prizes for his scribbling. Have you ever heard of Peter Stein?" said Mary Whitney.

A silence boomed down the telephone.

"Christa?" said Mary. "Are you still there, dear?"

"Oh yes, sorry, I'm here."

Christa was there . . . just . . . but the world seemed to be spinning on without her. For a breathless moment she had been left behind. Had she heard of Peter Stein? There was no answer to that question when she was busy contemplating the fact that she would be sitting next to him at dinner. It had been six months since she'd met him in Miami. At countless moments she had prayed that he would call her, and at countless others she had dreamed up excuses to call him. But he hadn't made the first move, and she hadn't been able to bring herself to do so. Pride had been too strong. And so, with time, the memory had faded, and she had picked up his book, *Death of a Friendship,* less frequently and had read his inscription to her less often. He had never gone away. The chemistry they had generated that night lingered on like the subtle aroma of flowers, permeating her life, and promising a present in some distant future. Now, apparently, the moment was about to arrive.

"You haven't fought with Peter Stein, have you darling?" said Mary Whitney hopefully. "Most people have. I can't promise you a pleasant evening, dear, but I think I can guarantee a lively one." She cackled in delight at the thought. "At least you'll be awake, which is more than you'll be able to say for the rest of the poor lunks at my party."

"Oh yes," said Christa slowly. "I think I'll be able to keep my eyes open for Mr. Peter Stein."

16

"Come in, darling. This is my library. Isn't it a joke? Imagine, a library in Palm Beach, where nobody's read a book for years. My grandfather bought the books by the yard from some dealer in London. I looked at some once. *Incredibly* dull, and almost certainly worth *millions.* Anyway, what about you? My goodness, you look younger than you did at the Day School, and what a beautiful dress. I can almost see through it, dear. Still with the yellow panties?" Mary Whitney cackled in delight as she ushered the shimmering Christa into the dark, paneled room.

Christa smiled. Mary Whitney made life look small. She was a bully, redeemed by a mighty talent and a voracious appetite for life. If you gave as good as you got, you could survive her. If your energy flagged for a second, you were gone. Right now, Christa knew she was going to be softened up for a deal. So she steeled herself.

"How's your backhand these days, Mary? I always remember you were a small-ball-game freak."

"Ha! Ha! How clever of you to remember. Well, I keep working at the lessons. You know, grinding away. I've got a wonderful teacher. Fully paid-up member of the God squad, but buttocks like a dream. You ought to check him out, dear. Put a bit of beef into your serve."

Christa sat down in a deep sofa. This wasn't the moment to tell Mary she knew Rob. At school Mary had always had a problem with sharing.

"Let's get some champagne or something we're not allowed to drink in this town, like absinthe or crème de menthe . . . something to bring up the wind, anyway. Have you ever tried Cointreau and Pepto-Bismol? It's actually not bad, if you stick it in a blender."

"Yeah, let's have a bellini or a buck's fizz or something like that."

Mary picked up the telephone. "Bring some bellinis to the library."

She sat down opposite Christa.

"Rifat?"

"Mizrahi."

"Breast job?"

"Nope, all my own."

"God, how depressing. I'm a complete scalpel junkie. I've reached the stage that if I'm not stitched up I don't reckon I'm alive. Then there's the gland treatments. I've wiped out the monkeys in entire regions of the Amazon jungle and I still feel like shit. It isn't easy being a billionaire these days, I tell you."

"Come on, Mary. You look wonderful. You know you do. You're the only person I know who's as good at pleasure as business."

"Well, fun *is* important, isn't it? It's a far better revenge than success. And talking of fun, what about you and the lovely Lisa Rodriguez teaming up? That was a pretty shrewd signing for a brand-new agency, wasn't it? And I bet Johnny Rossetti is not a happy camper. Goodness, he must be deeply pissed." She clapped her hands together in delight. "What a little shit he is."

"I haven't talked to him about it, but he's probably no longer in my fan club. He was unhappy about me going. Me plus Lisa has probably halved him."

"And the rest. Good. He deserved it. Do you remember that young girl he got on heroin, the one who was crazy about him and topped herself? Haden Beast exposed it in *New York* magazine. Not a nice story. Ah, here come the bellinis. Come on, Christa, let's get wasted."

"*Before* the party?"

"No chance *during* it, dear. The guests are far too sobering."

They sized each other up over the rims of the flute glasses.

"Mmmmm, delicious," said Christa, playing for time. The first one to move would reveal weakness. That would cost money somewhere in the deal.

"I have a little man somewhere in the bowels of the house who does nothing all day except squeeze fruit."

And you prance around all day cracking nuts, you brassy old ball buster, thought Christa.

"The company seems to be doing well," said Christa, treading gingerly on the outskirts of the subject.

"Yes, it is," said Mary, stifling a yawn as she played the ancient game. "I've got a rather good plan for selling a whole new line of Mary Whitney scents. It would be a biggish campaign, probably over a two-year period. I've got an interesting idea for a theme."

"Is it India?"

Mary started, but recovered quickly. "As the inexperienced honey-mooner said to his wife . . . no, yes, well, it was India, but it isn't anymore. How did you hear about it?"

"Oh, the grapevine," said Christa with a dismissive wave of her hand.

"Ah, so you may have heard on a similar plant that I was vaguely interested in signing Lisa on an exclusive basis to peddle the stuff."

" 'Vaguely interested'?"

"Well, it was an idea of Blankheart's. I don't get too closely involved in the small print of these things," she lied.

"Sounds like a big campaign."

"Not small." Mary watched Christa with gimlet eyes.

"You'd need a pretty big girl to carry a campaign like that. Wouldn't do to go off half cocked with the also-rans. Still, it's lucky you're not real gung-ho on Lisa, 'cause she's not really ready for an exclusive. Wants to play the field a bit more. Doesn't want to get too tied down. She's a real free spirit. And tricky to handle if pushed into something she doesn't want to do. She can be a bit of a fireball."

"I'm sure," said Mary, her voice icy, "that if her parents could still talk, they would agree."

"Mary!"

But Christa wasn't really shocked. This was all strictly business.

"Well," said Mary with the semblance of finality, "if the great Lisa Rodriguez doesn't want Whitney Enterprises, then Whitney doesn't want her. Pity. There would have been some big bucks. For her *and* for you."

"Of course, you could always come up with a number. If it's big enough, who knows, it might change her mind. After all, we're not talking immortal souls here, we're talking beautiful faces and bodies. Lisa's talent *is* for sale . . . but only at the right price."

"Listen, dear, Lisa Rodriguez's soul, if she has one, is about as valuable as a virus. Her bits and pieces are what my company want . . . wanted . . . vaguely wanted."

She bit her tongue. Shit. Christa was good. Very good. It wasn't fair that she looked like that and could deal like this. But then nobody ever promised that life would be fair.

"Incidentally, where is she now? Did she come with you? I hope you didn't leave her around downstairs. She might start a fire."

"Don't worry, Mary. She's in safe hands. I left her with Rob Sand. He showed up early, too. Got the time wrong. He's showing her around."

"He's my tennis coach," said Mary Whitney through clenched teeth. "Do you know him?"

"He's my diving instructor. He does me in the mornings, you in the afternoons. And I agree about his butt."

"Hmmmm. I didn't know he was rent-a-dick to the world and his wife. Still, I suppose one musn't be too greedy, and there *are* a few thousand Rob Sand clones in the county."

* * *

Mary Whitney tried to stay calm, but inside she was seething. Damn it! Why was Rob so important to her? Why did young men have this power over her? But of course, she knew. It had all started with the anorexia, so very many years ago. Sloshing around in the money molasses of the Whitney childhood, there had been absolutely no reason to be good at anything. All were automatic winners. Everyone had prizes. Until fourteen she had toed the party line of the super-rich, and then she had discovered dieting. She could even remember the moment she had started her determined pursuit of thinness. Her father had told her at breakfast that she was putting on weight . . . in front of everyone. She had gone on a diet and immediately she had found that she was frighteningly good at it. The pounds fell off her, her periods stopped, and her bones began to push through her skin as she exercised, dieted, stole laxatives and diuretics from the medicine cabinet, and refused to put anything into her mouth that would stay in her body. The thinner she got, the thinner she wanted to be, and, as she became progressively more emaciated, she would recoil in horror from the vast fat person her distorted self-image showed her in the mirror. Her whole life began to revolve around fear of fatness, as she pursued her warped goal with a fierce energy. They had force-fed her in the hospital when the doctors had finally been called in by her worried parents, and she had fought the weight gain with a determination that had astounded even the hardened psychiatrists. She had made herself vomit; had loaded herself up with water before the daily weighing ritual to make it appear that she was putting on weight; and, on one occasion, she had resorted to swallowing lead fishing sinkers to give the illusion that she was complying with the doctors. Later, when they passed through her, and the weight came off, the shrinks were at a loss to explain it. Eventually she had been turned over to a psychotherapist and the reasons for her obsession had been revealed. It was explained to her that her real fear was not of gaining weight, but of growing up. In her heart, she wanted to remain a child, free of responsibility, safe from the demands of adulthood, of sex, of meaningful grown-up relationships. It had made sense. Mary Whitney had always thought of herself as a child, a willful, determined child who would force the grown-up world to obey her. Now, the years had passed but the psychological chains of her early life still bound her. She looked always for youth. She wanted to be surrounded by young boys, by kids young enough to be her children. They were unthreatening to her, and they wouldn't ever learn her secret . . . that despite her age, she, too, wanted to be a child and that she would pursue her goal with a focused determination that bordered on madness.

But Christa knew nothing of the Whitney psychological profile. All she knew was that she was getting the upper hand in the deal. Now she piled it on.

"Oh, I don't think there are many guys like Rob. I think Rob's kinda special. Anyway, he said he was going to show Lisa Rodriguez the tennis court. They sure made a cute pair."

"Well, if he gets raped, I shall hold you personally responsible," said Mary, trying as hard as she could to sound light and bright.

They stared at each other, the Whitney irritation lasering out at Christa. Everything could and would be used in the deal now. Mary's temper was turned on. That was points to Christa, but it meant the gloves were about to come off.

"By the way, Christa, have you actually *signed* Lisa yet? I mean, Blankheart's offer went through Johnny. If Johnny had a current representation agreement with Lisa at the time of the offer, then he might want his cut if it should ever come to a deal. That might leave you in a sticky position. After all, you could hardly expect Johnny to behave like a gentleman when you haven't exactly played the gentle lady."

Christa leaned back to play the hardball.

"Actually, Lisa had a yearly agreement with Johnny. It had expired at the time of Don Blankheart's offer. It wasn't renewed, and yes, she has signed with me. So Johnny is history. But it's all academic anyway, because as of right now, Lisa is out of your scent deal." She just managed to stop saying, " . . . and into your tennis coach."

"Mmmmmm, all very convenient," muttered Mary. Usually she could browbeat people into submission, but Christa could not be blasted off the map by the awesome Whitney armory of cash, class, and Teflon-coated balls. It was deeply frustrating, because, of course, Mary Whitney just had to have her own way, and having her own way meant having the best model in the world for her perfume campaign. Compared to that, mere money was an irrelevance. The trouble was that Christa knew her secret. Christa knew that to Mary Whitney, zeros were the round things with holes in them that you stuck on the end of checks.

"So, who will you get to do it?" said Christa, smiling gently at the edge of victory.

"Oh, I don't know . . . I mean, there's that girl from Zaire who's hot . . ."

"I heard she wasn't a girl."

Mary Whitney was on the run. The best was the best was the best. The rest were bullshit. She wasn't convincing Christa. She wasn't convincing herself. She tried one last tack.

"What I *really* think is that the girl isn't the vital ingredient here. The important thing is the photographer. I'm going to use Steve Pitts. He can make anybody look like a dream. You know that better than anyone. *He's* going to be the linchpin of my campaign. As far as I'm concerned Lisa Rodriguez can go find some more family to blow up."

"But you haven't hired Steve, Mary."

Mary waved the mere detail away with her hand.

"Steve's no problem. Anyway, how do you know I haven't hired him?"

It was time for the *coup de grace.*

"Because I'm his agent."

"You're *what?*"

"I rep him. He's signed with my agency."

Mary Whitney stood up. She walked to a cupboard and pulled out a bottle of brandy. She walked back and stuck some in the remains of her bellini. Okay, so now it was a champagne cocktail.

"Steve Pitts and Lisa Rodriguez," she said as she sat down.

"Yes," said Christa.

Mary Whitney put up her hands in surrender.

"All right, all right, you little shrewdini," she said sweetly. "You win. It's only money. How much of my loot do you want? They say you can't take it with you, but between you and me and the gatepost, I was intending to try!"

17

"Do you want to see the tennis courts?"

Rob looked away from her as he spoke. He kept trying to remind himself that she was only his age. In God's eyes he was her equal. He needn't be impressed by her. But, that body, and her face, and the fame. It was nearly too much. He tried to hide the fact that he needed to swallow, and he took a deep breath instead.

"Is that where you strut your stuff?" Lisa laughed as her words played with him, mocking him slightly, not too much, not too little.

"I guess."

"Then, okay. I want to see them."

He felt her provocation in the pit of his stomach. He saw it, as her tongue licked lips that needed no wetting.

"This way." He walked ahead of her where it was safer, but he could feel her eyes on his butt.

"What's it like teaching Mary Whitney tennis?"

"It's cool. She's a neat person."

"I heard she liked to ball young guys."

She had caught up with him. She cocked her head to one side and smiled seductively as she eased the conversation into sexual gear.

He smiled, despite himself. Hell, he was only human. It wasn't bad to lust, just difficult to think of God when you were doing it.

"She doesn't give me any hassle," he said.

"How long have you been on the job?"

"Three days."

"Ah," said Lisa Rodriguez, doing something barely legal with her mouth.

He turned toward her, suddenly exasperated. The big-name girl with the good-time body had been dunked too long in the sin juice of the city. She couldn't understand his longings. She wouldn't know about his church, and his friends, and the life he was building for the glory of God.

"Listen, I teach tennis. Period. Nobody uses me. I serve only the Lord."

"Wow!" said Lisa. "I'd forgotten I was in the deep South."

She laughed, but her laugh was thoughtful. The boy with the muscles had revealed a new dimension. She just loved those.

"So you're into Jesus."

"You make it sound like some trendy cult."

"Isn't it?"

"You find sneering easy, don't you? People who sneer a lot have usually been through a lot of bad times. Have you?"

Lisa said nothing. She had lost the driver's seat. The cute hick had thrust her out of it. She could feel the red on her cheeks.

"And you read shrink books, too? I thought God and psychiatry were enemies."

It was the best she could do, but she'd wanted to do better. Usually boys were safe toys. This one had pricked her.

"If you love God, you don't have to know things. You can feel them. That's a pretty dress," he said. A blob of tenderness had welled up inside him. The supermodel was human after all. He had just seen the color of her psychic blood.

"Thank you," she said crossly, marching by his side. "I'm in mourning." She looked at him slyly. There, that would pay him back. If he was a Jesus freak, then death and mourning would be buzzwords that would conjure up care and concern. Especially parents. That would be heavy duty.

He stopped. They had been walking through a ficus-lined pathway. She stopped. She felt the pang of guilt, and something else. The hell with it. She fancied this Rob Sand more and more each minute. She'd never been around people like him. All was fair in lust and war.

"I'm sorry," he said. Clearly newspapers weren't his thing. "Should you be here at a party?" he added, letting his puzzlement out of his mouth before he realized that he was being judgmental. "Not that it's my business . . ."

Lisa laughed, making it sound brittle and brave. All models were actresses. Hardly any actresses were pretty enough to model.

"My parents were killed in a big accident. It was my fault. I'm still in shock, I guess. It hasn't sunk in yet. I just couldn't handle being alone."

Rob's eyes widened. The information was hitting him at all sorts of levels. Dead parents. Two at once. In an accident. This was the girl who'd tied his tongue a few minutes ago. Then he'd been unkind to her, and felt a little sorry for her, and now the whammy. As a Christian it was a test. His action was reflex.

"Will you pray with me?" he said. His voice was urgent. It was the only possible thing to do.

Lisa looked as if she'd been sandbagged from behind, absolutely astonished. Rob realized his request was virgin territory for a girl who would hardly be able to remember virginity. That made it better. He reached out for her hands, and she surrendered them, a weird expression on her face. He sank down to the grass of the pathway, and she sank down too, her black micro dress charging up brown legs.

"I don't really . . ."

He closed his eyes, and she petered out. He held her hands tight and strong, pouring the power of his belief into her, to shore her up, to help her pass through the moment, to gain strength for the sorrow beyond.

"Oh, God, whose infinite wisdom can never be known by mere minds, have mercy on Lisa. Help her to see that her tragedy is part of your Divine Purpose, and give her the will to learn to love you. Make her strong, dear Lord, in the trial that is her life right now, and help her to realize that those she loves are safe forever in the arms of Jesus."

Lisa felt the lump grow in her throat. Oh, jeez! That was incredible. Boy, he had reached her. Talk about a line. Unfaked sincerity. The *best!*

She wouldn't let go of his hands when he'd finished.

"That was *very* beautiful," she said, staring deep into his now open eyes. "I mean, where do you get words like that?"

He was embarrassed now.

"They just came," he said. It was true. They had come automatically. From God. From nowhere else. He felt his heart surge in his chest. God had spoken to him, and he had spoken for God. He was grateful to the Almighty and to her, for the opportunity she had given him to be close to his Maker. He started to get up, but she held him there on his knees. The hands that had captured hers had themselves become prisoners. The religious moment was fading, another was building. Somehow the emotions did for both as the electric beauty of holiness merged into the tingling excitement of human togetherness.

There were tears in her eyes. There was love in his heart. He adored God, and here before him, more beautiful than nature, was God's hurting creature. She was God's creation. In loving God, he must love her.

"Come closer," she whispered.

In a dream he leaned toward her, drawn by her hands, by the magnet of her parted lips, by her gentle command.

Their faces were close in the fading light of evening. Behind her head, the Palm Beach sunset burned the blood-red sky, the palm trees placed like notes in a symphony of beauty. His eyes roamed across her face, drinking in her loveliness. He could smell her sweet scent, feel the warm breath of her fan his cheek, and he held back to preserve the moment that was already so very close to a sacrament.

She lifted his hands up to their faces, as if to pray, and she leaned over the top of them and placed her lips on his. She breathed out, bathing him in a baptism of breath, as her mouth trembled on the brink of his.

"Kiss me," she murmured.

Rob's breath shuddered from his lungs as he surrendered. In his heart there was conflict. In his body there was none. Her lips were the sacrament. It would be an offense against nature to refuse them. He leaned across to her. Her face was so close, her beauty taunting him, here at the brink. He could smell her now. The scent of her filled his mind—sweet, alluring, unshackling his feelings and setting them free in a dangerous, wonderful world where nothing was controlled, nothing certain. He tried to make sense of it, in the seconds before it was too late. It wasn't right. It was crazy. It wasn't decent. He didn't know this girl. She was a stranger. They were in public, at a party. Any minute someone could walk by and find them here . . . but his head moved forward as his heart stood still.

She was smiling at him, and for a second Rob saw himself and his endless dilemma reflected in her eyes. They had met minutes ago, but already she was peering into his soul. She was laughing at the pools of guilt she could see there. She knew all about his repressed feelings, his fear of his own lusts, the all-embracing love of God that confused him even as it gave him peace. To this beauty who knew the underside of his life, Rob Sand was an open book and it was with a thrill of excitement and horror that he realized it. And now her lips would dissolve his doubt on the path to a greater ecstasy. He closed his eyes as if darkness could hide sin. It amplified the aroma of her, but still she didn't touch him.

She hovered there by his lips and he felt the evening breeze at his shoulder, the gentle current of her breath at his mouth. He would let her do this. He was passive. She was in control. If she took the initiative, he would be blameless. But his heart hammered against his chest as he told it the lie it didn't believe. Now in the blackness there was the beginning of panic. He wanted the kiss. Could she be teasing him, here on the edge of intimacy? He opened his eyes into her smile, and he moved the millimeters she had always intended him to move.

Her lips were dry, and his were, too. They brushed against each other shyly, nervously, pretending that there could be a chaste end to this. Their mouths met in quiet exploration, but already the tingling excitement was winging its way through their bodies. She put out her tongue to touch him. Wet and wonderful, it parted his trembling lips, coating them with moisture. Her tongue lapped against his teeth, firm, probing, and he moaned out loud as he tasted it with his own. She brought up her hands to hold his cheeks and he reached out to steady himself against her, their fingers tender in this anxious prelude to the storm that would come. They squeezed together, thirsty for each other's liquid, wanting to drown in the wetness of passion. Rob felt the joy as thought went away. His mind was fading. His body was taking over. Here was a simple world of complex pleasure. At last he was free to feel, and his mouth fed from this girl who had liberated him, as the blood sped through him, pulsing and pounding in his veins. She moaned into his lips as her tongue invaded him and he fought back in the kiss, using the power of his arms to draw her into him, forcing his tongue into her mouth in an unrelenting counterattack of lust. She bent away from his onslaught, and he leaned over her, pushing her head back with the eagerness of his desire as he ground against her. Teeth clashed, tongues merged, and the tides of their saliva flowed together, as they battled to climb into each other's bodies, to live and luxuriate there in the steamy moisture of intimacy. There was no shame and no thought of discovery. The world had gone away. There was only the kiss.

She tore herself away from him, pushing on his chest with her hands and arching her neck. Sweat glistened at her forehead in the fading light. Her wet lips, slick with longing, were parted. Her breasts, painted, too, with a sheen of dampness, heaved in excitement against the cotton of her jet-black dress.

"Not here," she whispered.

For a brief moment reality was back, sticking itself like a dagger into the velvety magic of lust.

They were still on their knees, still holding each other, still burning with terrible desire, but now there was a decision to be made.

Behind them the great house was ablaze with light in the gathering dusk. Away to the left the floodlit sea lapped gently against the beach. But up ahead there was darkness. The tennis pavilion was not a part of Mary Whitney's party. Rob stood up. He drew her up with him, and she smiled at him in the conspiracy of lovers. He walked quickly, leading her in the twilight, and he prayed to some pagan, alien God that the moment would not pass. The building loomed up ahead, its stone columns thick as trees. He led her up the steps to the veranda, threading past the chaise longues and tables where "spectators" sipped iced tea. The double doors weren't locked. He turned to look back at her. She was there in the moonbeams, her face lit to perfection by the flickering light. She moved in nature's strobe, throwing back her head and posing in the way that only Lisa Rodriguez knew how. She took his breath away as she wanted to, and her hand squeezed his as she promised herself to him.

His hands fumbled on the latch of the door. There was no air inside him. His throat was dry. His stomach was knotted tighter than a hangman's noose. He had never felt like this. The slow bliss of God's love was quiet, gentle. But this was the raging exhilaration of a fire fight, a battle for the ultimate joy here, now, not in the life hereafter. He tried to swallow. He tried to stay afloat on the roaring adrenaline river that gushed inside him. He tried not to think of the vast, throbbing part of him that struggled against the tightness of his shorts.

She was close behind him, backlit by moonlight. Her scent was in his nostrils. Her hand moved softly on his butt. He found the latch. The door was open and inside was the womb luxury of the Mary McGregor Whitney tennis pavilion. A vast chintz sofa, double deep, dominated the room. To the left were the showers and the sauna. To the right, the marble mosaic Jacuzzi, and the Mr. Steam cabinets. At the back of the room, beneath the high windows, and flanked by twin areca palms, was a marble massage table on a marble plinth that looked as if it had been shipped through the ages from the Senate in ancient Rome.

He turned to face her. It wasn't his game. It was hers. She stood and looked at him, up and down, and she smiled slowly. His chest was heaving. His nostrils were flared. He still held her hand and his was hot, his grip uneven, too firm, too soft, in the desperation of the unpracticed lover. But in his pants she could see his wild desire. He was straining for her, hot and big and more capable than his young mind would ever know. She breathed out, savoring the moment. He stood before her, unexpected, undeserved, but so very wanted. The suit was all wrong, of course. Too tight; too new; way, way too cheap, but that made it even better. It said that Rob Sand knew few of the things she knew, needed almost nothing that she needed, except the most important thing of all. She moved toward him, standing up close, her breasts flattened against his chest. She put both arms around his narrow waist, and she whispered up into his face.

"I'm going to show you heaven here on earth," she promised.

He shook with desire in her arms. She could actually feel his body tremble in the aftershock of her words. And she could feel, too, the mammoth evidence of his emotion. It was hard as steel against the pit of her stomach, and although she stood still and he did not move, the restless heart of him, caged and angry, was alive against the cotton of his pants, the cotton of her dress.

She sank down to her knees. All the time she held him close, falling down his body like water in a shower. Her lips brushed against his shirtfront, the buckle of his belt, coming to rest millimeters from the part of him she would have. For long seconds she stayed there, her hands on the taut muscles of his bottom, pulling him toward her, his pelvis captured in the bonds of her arms. Her cheek lay against his pants. The material was hot, radiating the fire below. She moved her face against him and her breath caught in her throat as he moved against her. Even now she knew Rob's secret. She could tell he was vast, bigger by far than she had ever known. Suddenly, fear flew into the delicious mélange of her emotions. Could she handle this? Could it be done? Ohhhhhhh. The moan rumbled from the back of her parched throat, and then her hands were fumbling to find the pull of the zipper. She drew it down, terrified of what she would find, thrilled by the awesome prospect of it. The boxer shorts exploded into the gap in the dark blue material, stretched to the limit as they battled to contain him. It seemed that at any second they would tear apart and unleash their captive to ravage her face. And, right now, she wanted that, more than life, more than breath.

Rob could bear it no longer. He reached down and freed himself. Lisa leaned back as it sprung at her, and the bottom fell from her stomach as she saw it. It was long, oh so long, longer than the distance from the tip of her forehead to the place where her swan neck met her broad shoulders. But it was thick, oh so thick, thicker than her wrist, broad as her wide-open mouth as she watched it in panicked wonder. In amazement, she touched him. The burning heat seared her fingers. She could feel the blood coursing within him, the shining skin stretched tight as a drum around his passion. She reached down to the base of him, to the sweat-soaked hairs, and then down, and back farther to the fetid jungle between his legs. She breathed in the musk of his maleness, savoring the wild aroma of untamed youth, and her heart took flight above the steamy moment.

"Oh, Rob," she murmured, hardly knowing what she meant, but wanting to hear the sound of her voice to tell her this was real and not some fevered dream. Her fingers traced the outline of his hugeness, lingering on the taut veins, marveling at the steel of him, at the slippery tenseness of his tip. She laid her lips on him, and his hands moved helplessly to the back of her head, pleading silently for her to do the thing that she wanted so very much to do. She knelt up straight. She took a deep breath and she placed the end of him at her lips. First she touched him with her tongue. She rested it there, in homage, at the opening, not moving, just letting the wetness of her merge with the moisture of him, the heat of their bodies fan the furnace of each other's flames. Then, her tongue began to move. It traced a small circle at the tip, but soon, thirsty for him, she flattened it against him, lapping at him, licking him, first like a lady and then greedily, like the hungry child she was. She sucked the top of him, and then she ran her tongue down the sides of him, nibbling at the base, running up again to the peak with its tiny fountain of molten desire. The groan rumbled from the back of his throat and she felt his hands tighten at the back of her head, willing her to the next stage, but too gentle to force her. She looked up at him as her tongue pleased him. His head was thrown way back in abandonment. He was still dressed for the party, neat in his awful suit, but now the center of his soul was bared to her. Soon it would be inside her body, crammed into places it could hardly go, and she would split herself apart for him and the pain would be the gilt on the gingerbread of her ecstasy.

"No!" His strangled murmur stopped her on the brink. He looked down at her, his face twisted in anguish. "I can't," he said.

The flood tide of Lisa's passion collided with the breakwater of his unexpected words. She smiled, her expression quizzical. He didn't mean it. Against her face his body was screaming yes.

He backed away from her, and she felt the pain of the parting.

"What's the matter?" she whispered soothingly, trying to hide the panic in her voice. She had to have him. Now. Nothing had ever been as important.

"It's wrong," he said. He tore his face away from hers. How could she understand him? They spoke the same language, but to exchange meaning you had to have had experiences in common. "I mean . . . it's a sin. There has to be love. There has to be commitment." He actually stammered as he spoke the word.

"There just has to be this." Lisa was as certain as he was. She reached out and curled her fingers around the part of his body that was making his tongue a liar. She squeezed it, making him moan, and he didn't try to stop her. He was suspended there, on the horns of a dilemma so deep and dreadful it could never be resolved. The only hope was delay. But there seemed no way to stop what had been started.

"Please . . ." His eyes, too, were asking for mercy. She could help him do the right thing. She was his only chance. Lisa knew that.

"It's all right," she murmured soothingly. She let go of him and smiled up at him, her lips parted, her breath rushing through them. She angled her face to catch the moonlight that streamed through the high windows at the back of the pavilion, and she reached up for her breasts. She massaged them with both hands, kneading the already tense flesh, and she took her nipples between thumb and forefinger and she squeezed them tight beneath the black cotton of the Alaïa frock. All the time she watched him. Yes, she would help him. In his hour of need she would be there for this boy. Lisa Rodriguez was a girl you could count on. Mercy dripped from her lips. Goodness filled her heart to overflowing. She reached inside the dress. She wore no bra. She pulled out her breast and she showed it to him.

"Oh, God . . ." It was a prayer. It was a blasphemy. He watched her breast as if it were an executioner. In the moonbeams, in her hand, it lay there, indescribably lovely as it was meant to be. Her nipple throbbed against the taut brown skin, full to overflowing with her lust, and the perfect proportion of her breast arrowed through to the part of him that she had captured. Slowly, she stood up, her height emphasized by the deliberation of her movements. She uncoiled herself like a serpent, impossibly beautiful. Her left hand still held her breast, but her right hand reached for the hem of her skirt. She hooked her fingers beneath it, and she lifted it the millimeters that made the difference. Mesmerized, his eyes followed her. They feasted hopelessly on the triangle of white panties, framed against the sculpture of Lisa's thighs. He swallowed the dryness in his mouth as his heart beat against his ribs. In all his life he had never seen anything as wonderful.

She knew that. It was all she knew, all she had ever known. No other body could resist hers. It had never happened. It never would. This boy would fall as the others had fallen, but it was sweet that he had tried to fight against her. It was better than sweet. It was adorable. And she laughed at the silly thought, because it was the first time in her life that she had ever been grateful to God.

Rob's stricken eyes moved to her breast. Again he swallowed. They moved back to the panties, brilliant white against the brown of her thigh. A thin, damp line bisected them. Her lust was visible, too. Dear Lord, give me strength . . .

She walked toward him. He took a step back. With the sinewy grace of a cat she slipped down her panties, stepping out of them as she moved forward. They lay there, on the bleached wood floor of the pavilion, and to Rob they were the white flag of his surrender. He gulped. Still she held up her skirt, so that he could see the heart of her love, glistening in the uncertain light. Still she held her breast on the platter of her hand. The combination of delicate beauty and lascivious lust was too strong for his defenses. Behind his back was the hard edge of the marble massage table. Before him was the body of the most beautiful girl in the world.

She pushed her leg between his, crowding against him, her face smiling close to his, her breath fanning his face, as she dared him to refuse her. He put both hands behind him on the cold slab. Already it felt like the tombstone on the grave of his good intentions, the altar on which he would be sacrificed to the devil. She crushed herself against him. Her thighs were tight against his. His heat was drowning deliciously in the wet fires of hers. She reached down and held him, moving him against the already slippery skin of her thigh. With both hands she guided him, up to her firm stomach, down to the silken hairs, rubbing him gently against the velvety lips of her love. Always she stared deep into his eyes, so that he would never forget how beautiful she was, how strong, and how impossible to resist.

"You're going to make love to me," she whispered. "You're going to do it now." As she spoke, she stood up on tiptoe, and with both hands she guided him to the place he longed for, the place he dreaded. For long seconds he stayed there, throbbing against her steam heat, nestling against the soft lips that guarded the entrance to her. He knew it was too late. He knew it would happen, but even at this time he could see beyond to the guilt and the recrimination. But that would be then. This was now. He closed his eyes. He held on to her bottom, and he thrust forward into the heaven that would also be his hell.

He threw back his head, as the awesome feeling took him, and he growled both his passion and frustration at the woman who had tricked him. The roar exploded from his throat. His powerful hips thrust forward. He sank like a spear into the depths of her, lifting her up into the air, her legs dangling helplessly on either side of his straining thighs. He opened his eyes to watch the triumph and the wonder in hers. They were big and round, astonished by the hugeness of his passion. Her mouth was open in amazement, and the wind whistled from her lungs at the force of his invasion. All over her face was the realization that she was the leader no longer. There was excitement in her eyes, and there was fear on her trembling lips, and now she winced in delicious pain as she prepared her body for the trial to come.

He spun around, and laid her down on the cold marble of the massage table, still deep inside her. She looked up at him, her expression pleading with him to be gentle, as her mind willed him to be rough. She splayed her legs wide apart, fighting to make space for him, and she moaned her pleasure at the fullness, at the tightness, wondering if she would be able to contain him. Her dress was around her waist, her naked breast crushed against the material of his jacket. The heels of her shoes slid against the marble as she tried to steady herself for the onslaught. Above her face, his eyes were hooded with desire. He had become an animal. He was no longer human. All his finer feelings, his doubts, all the noise of thought had vanished from his mind. Now, as she had intended, she would reap the whirlwind of his lust. Wet like a river, her hot bottom slipping and sliding on the cold stone, she bucked beneath him as he reared inside her.

"Rob! Rob!" She didn't know what she meant. She knew only that she wanted to make contact with him. Her body was ablaze with a deeper pleasure than she had ever known, yet she wanted more. She needed to know that he was there, and that the gorgeous monster she had created would not hurt her, might even learn to love her after the passion of their bodies had been spent.

He couldn't answer her. He was lost in a world he had denied for too long. His young body had been jammed like a coiled spring into a box. Now for this blissful moment, he was free of the ties that for so long had bound him. Beneath him was Lisa Rodriguez. She was painted around him. He was alive inside her, gripped tight by silken walls, held captive by the body that for this short time he also owned. That was all he knew. It was all he cared about. Later there would be a reckoning. But the future would have to take care of itself.

He moved roughly within her. He had no rhythm. It was about being there, an invader in a strange land, marveling at the feel and the touch of it, exploring, plundering, having his own way. He pushed to the roof of her, ramming her between the rock of his desire and the hard place at her back. He withdrew to the entrance, hovering at the brink, threatening, blackmailing her, forcing her to choose between the terror of his reentry and the horror of his departure. And all the time he grew inside her, pouring the blood of his desire into her until she could do nothing but flow against him. He was punishing her for what she had done to him, but she was all the women, all the temptresses through all the years who had thrilled him with their siren voices and turned him spinning in his bed at night. She was at war with God, but God's creation, too, the hand of the Designer so evident in the glory of her beauty. So he beat her with the weapon of the Lord's vengeance and she moaned her pleasure as she shook beneath the divine retribution.

He could feel her hands on his butt, clutching him to her when he withdrew, pushing him away as he thrust into her. In a dream he held her, too. His fingers marked her bottom, as he held her in a vicelike grip. His stomach was slick with her passion, slapping down wetly against hers as he rampaged inside her, twisting from side to side, reveling in the glory of total possession. Then, at last, they found a rhythm. They moved together, no longer enemies but allies in the search for pleasure. She arched her back and pushed against him as he thrust at her. The sweat stood out on her brow, on her arms, at her lips, as she allowed him to separate her body into parts that felt they might never touch again. She battled to relax, to open up, to make room for him, but at the same time there was only tightness and wonderful wet friction as she made over the gift of her body to the young lover who knew nothing about love. In the maelstrom, she tried to think. Already, in the middle of this mind-bending moment, she was thinking about the next time. He couldn't be let go. He must be kept close, chained to her by bond of lust or love, until she had taught him everything, used him up, and wrecked his life. Only then could he be thrown away, useless and spent, the pieces to be picked up by the God she had replaced.

"Ooooooooooh." Her own cry drowned her thoughts. She felt the well-known feeling. It started at a single point in time, a flicking, sweet second of mystery when everything changed and the end of the beginning became the beginning of the end. Her senses sharpened.

She knew to pay close attention now. The moments had to be milked of each last drop of ecstasy. She clenched her fists tight and listened to the music her body made. The bass thumped in her ears. The treble was tight and taut in her nipples, at the nape of her neck, in the tingling fullness of the part of her that wrapped him. It was beginning to make the sense it always made. The sounds were coming together, conducted by the remorseless baton of her lover. She felt the sweat pour shamelessly between her breasts. The cleavage of her butt was drenched with it, and the heady scent of her wetness was filling the room and steaming up her mind. She dared to reach down and feel the point at which he pistoned into her. Her wondering fingers traced the amazing contours of him, until her hands were slick with her own passion.

"Rob!" Again just his name, but now it was full of meaning. It was her signal to him, his name and her faraway eyes and her desperate fingers. He seemed to hear her, out there on the astral plane of his joy. They must come together, the roaring, flaming fighter plane merging with the bucking deck of the carrier at sea. In the controlled crash landing of orgasm they would both win, and so he held back as she sped forward, and he accelerated as she slowed, and all the time they moved closer to their destination.

Lisa tried to hang on. Her fingers clawed at the smooth stone. Her legs clamped tight around his heaving body. Her head thrashed from side to side. She opened her mouth and moaned in the agony of her ecstasy, and her cry grew as she came nearer. It was enough. Her abandon released him. He rose up one last time, and then, as he descended, he flowed into her like a raging, undammed river. His whole body was rigid against hers, perfectly still at first, apart from the rain of passion that played inside her. And then he began to tremble. It began as a fine tremor, the rumble of the distant quake, and then, slowly, he started to lose his coordination. He shook against her, his legs hammering against hers, his feet shuddering on the hard stone. It was as if he were disintegrating, a device held together by a single purpose that had now been achieved. There was only one constant—the fountain inside her, damping the fires from her own explosion, and setting him free from the terrible pleasure of his.

At last he was still, and she smiled up at him, wiping a tear of sweat from her eye.

"That was better than church on Sunday, wasn't it?" she said.

18

Mary Whitney descended the staircase. Below, in the grand hall of the house that was not quite a home, her guests looked up, as they were supposed to. It was called making an entrance, and she was carrying it off quite well. Parties were about shepherding. You herded the sheep this way and that, corralling them together, stampeding them, stuffing them full of food, shearing them, and, occasionally, cutting their throats so that you could see the color of their gushing blood. Right now they were guzzling champagne and martinis in the hall so that they could watch her come down from on high to visit with them. There would be flesh pressing and verbal jousting, information gathering, and Machiavellian manipulation, and only then would the sheepdogs in the guise of waiters steer them through to the balcony where they would get their first whiff of the food.

The roar of conversation quieted as they bleary-eyeballed their hostess. This was Palm Beach, and already the WASPs were flying high on magic wings of tip-top booze.

Muffy and Bruce Sutka, who would get the blame for the party, hovered at the base of the stairs.

"It all looks wonderful, dears," she intoned as she reached them. "Pity we had to spoil it all by inviting the beastly people."

"They're getting high fast," said Muffy. "I think it was a mistake not to have the canapés."

"Balls," said Mary. "Then they wouldn't want the larks' tongues and sauté of camel's eyelashes or whatever lah-di-dah rubbish you're giving them for dinner. Look, Bruce, I know I'm a little dense, but can you remind me of the theme for this funeral? It's not immediately apparent."

Bruce giggled in delight, quite unfazed by the acid Whitney tongue.

"Lambada, dear. Catch the sounds. Grab a load of the luscious Hispanic extras vamping the crowd. Wait in eager anticipation for the steamy couplings of the cabaret."

Mary peered around the room. A dozen sinewy Hispanics twirled among the bemused Palm Beachers, striking poses and gyrating in time to the Latin beat of the piped music.

"Goodness," said Mary. "Is that what they are? I hope the paramedics are standing by. The hearts around here haven't speeded up in years. There are bound to be fatalities." She tossed her head and smiled. The thought of death was so comforting. Could there be *anything* nastier than eternal life?

"Do you want to mingle a bit before we point them at the food?" asked Muffy.

"Let the dog see the rabbit," said Bruce.

"It's my party. *I* do the funnies," said Mary Whitney. "You did the décor. Talking of jokes," she added maliciously. Suddenly she darted into the crowd and plucked at a sleeve. She had actually seen someone she wanted to talk to.

"Peter, darling, this is wonderful. How perverse of you to come to my party. Still, I know how it is with you writers. You'd rather go to a traffic accident than sit in front of an empty page."

Peter Stein smiled back at her. Mary Whitney was the only person in the world who could raise a smile from him on the subject of writer's block. She was right, of course. Parties to him were root-canal work, especially Palm Beach ones where intellectuals were an endangered species. But anything was better than the lonely struggle to find the words.

"Nonsense, Mary, this is research. You're a lifetime of source material in a single evening. You are my sole entrée to the secret world of women."

He bent over to kiss her, and she came back, European-style, for the other cheek. Her eyes sparkled.

"Rubbish, sweetheart. I wouldn't know a woman if one sat on my face. It's men I know about, darling. And I'll tell you something for nothing. It's high time we got you laid."

Again he laughed, throwing back his ruggedly handsome face and allowing the laughter to wash over him, like bracing water from a cold shower. God, it felt good to laugh. Cousins was right. It was the best medicine.

"Anybody in mind?"

She looked him up and down. He was incredibly good looking, but it was far more than that. He looked so *interesting.* Across a crowded room, you knew that small talk would simply not hack it with Peter Stein. The suntan, the hard body inside the ancient dinner jacket, the subtle flecks of gray in the tousled hair, were the introduction. But soon you would be mesmerized by the delicate lines around the mouth, the brilliance of the flashing brown eyes, the way his hands seemed to conduct his words, emphasizing them, rubbing them out, building them to a crescendo in your ears.

"I think it had better be me," said Mary Whitney. It was only just a joke.

"But I'm too old for you . . . and I don't play tennis."

"Villain, you know my secret." But Peter had raised a good point. Where was the Jesus freak? He'd been showing the Rodriguez tart the house. They'd better not be out there in the bushes. She craned her aristocratic neck around the room. Nope, the bimboy was absent. A frisson of irritation exploded on the glacial side of the Whitney heart. Damn! Maybe she should take a quick tour of the grounds before dinner, and nip anything nasty in the bud.

She turned back to Peter. "How's *Dream* coming along?" That was quid pro quo for the tennis crack.

He winced. "There have been quicker books."

"Listen, dear. Art is like sex. The longer it takes, the better it is. Talking of which, I've got you a dreamboat for dinner. Christa Kenwood. There, how about that? If that's not charity, I don't know what is."

Peter Stein couldn't control the blush that roared across his face. The Christa Kenwood name had painted it all over his cheeks.

He spoke quickly to hide his confusion. "Christa Kenwood, yes, I met her once. The model. The actress," he managed.

"Given it all up to run a model agency. Actually, a rather successful one. Now," said Mary. The vision of the check she had just agreed to write Christa for the Steve Pitts/Lisa Rodriguez campaign package flashed across her brain and threatened to make it ache.

Peter wasn't used to being surprised, and he was doubly unused to surprises being so pleasant. The book fair seemed like only yesterday in his mind, and he had never forgotten the girl who'd impressed him so deeply. He had intended to see her again, but he'd been endlessly sidetracked at the party, and when he'd searched for her later, she'd gone. In Key West, stretched out on the unforgiving rack of his novel, he had thought about her often and of how he might see her again. But he had forgotten how to play the dating game and all the potential telephone conversations he'd had with her in his mind had sounded deeply horrible as he had rehearsed them. Now Fate was giving him a second chance. He would have her captive for maybe two hours. If he couldn't construct something for the future on the basis of that, then it was time for the monastery.

"A model agency?" he said at last. "I'd never have thought of her doing that." It was true. She'd seemed so bright. A model agency, even a successful one, was a little disappointing.

"Don't underestimate Christa Kenwood, sweetheart," said Mary Whitney. She had picked up on his seeming disapproval of Christa's career choice but had totally missed out on the excitement that now bubbled beneath his cool exterior. "In fact, it is now a Whitney rule that one should never underestimate *anyone* who wears yellow panties. Listen, darling, got to run, but I'll catch you at dinner. You're at my table. I thought I'd concentrate all the neurones in one place, rather than spreading them out thin."

Peter Stein watched her go. Yellow panties! God, Mary got odder by the minute.

But there was a strange feeling in his heart as he reached out and grabbed a passing glass of champagne. Could it actually be that weird thing called "happiness"?

19

Christa kicked off her shoes and hoped the Whitney telephones weren't tapped. Come on, Steve. *Be* there. The answer machine clicked on.

"Hi, this is Steve. I might be here. I might not. Say something after the beep. If I like you, I'll pick up. If I don't, I won't. And if you have fragile self-esteem, console yourself with the thought that I might not be here after all, but I would have picked up if I'd known it was *you*. Beep!" He actually made the noise himself.

"It's Christa, asshole," said Christa. "Are you back from Southampton?"

"Christa, darling, what's up?" Steve answered instantly.

"Steve, I've got the most *incredible* news. I've just sold a package to Mary Whitney. A two-year campaign for scent and bath stuff, you name it. We're getting *mega*bucks! Funny money! It's three solid months of location shooting with Lisa. Can you *believe* it?"

"Serious poodle-faking money?"

"You're in for a million dollars."

"Shit. That's a cottage on Shelter Island."

"And it's only the beginning, Steve. It's our first deal, and it's paydirt. We can milk this for years."

"Until my looks go." Steve laughed.

"With this sort of loot they need never go. You can block book Steve Hoefflin each year and give yourself a new face every Christmas."

"Jeez, Christa, how did you do it?"

"I did it when I stuck you and Lisa together. The best has to have the best. The price is irrelevant. Remember, I told you that on the beach. Hey, listen, Steve, one thing. You've got to be nice to Mary, okay? Kiss butt, whatever it takes."

"I'm puckering up, buttercup. For a mill, I'm anybody's. I'll even let Lisa blow me up. How is she, by the way? Not poor, I imagine, if I get to score a big one."

"God, that's reminded me. She's taken Rob Sand, Mary's tennis coach, for a tour of the grounds. I hope to God she doesn't make a pass at him."

"Is he male?"

"Precisely. But I think it'll be all right. He's very religious."

"Yeah, and Lisa's so plain."

"Don't, Steve. This is a good-news telephone call. Actually, you'd really like Rob. He's incredible looking. Make a great model. I tried to sign him, but I think he thought I was a white slaver or something. I keep forgetting that Florida isn't New York."

"Mmmmm. Sounds neat. I had a backhand once. Perhaps I could rediscover it. Where are you? Is that music in the background?"

"Yeah. Mary's giving her ball. I came early and did the deal. I'm flying at around sixty thousand feet. I still can't believe it."

"Well, those Palm Beachers'll soon shoot you down."

"I'm sitting next to that writer, Peter Stein. Have you ever met him?" Christa's heart was pounding. Were days *allowed* to be as good as this one?

"Heavens, what on earth's he doing in Palm Beach? I thought he was a sackcloth-and-ashes sort of a guy. His books are *incredibly* depressing, but after you've read them you sort of feel that you know all the answers. I heard he's working on one called *The Dream I Dreamed.* There, that should give you an opening while you're trying to pry his nose out of your cleavage."

Christa laughed. "I don't have a cleavage."

"Listen, darling, with tits like yours, you always have a cleavage. It's not so much a physical fact. It's a state of mind."

"Did you ever read that book he wrote about what it was like to be a child?" Christa wanted to stay on the subject of Peter Stein.

"Yeah, it was quite clever. On one page was what the child did and said. And on the other was what it was thinking—like simple thoughts, but in complex adult language. It was a sort of an intellectual's version of those Travolta movies about talking babies. He got a Pulitzer for it. *Child's Play,* it was called. I flicked through it at Doubleday once. Not bad, if you find children even remotely interesting."

"The jacket blurb said he was married, with one child," said Christa.

"Uh-oh! Actually, divorced with one, if you can believe *People* magazine."

"Steve, surely you don't read *People,*" was Christa's diversion.

"I get to it sometimes at the checkout after I've done the tabloids. You've got to remember, I'm not as young as I was."

"Nonsense, you're far younger than you were. Any minute now with you it'll be 'hello womb.' Then you can write a sequel to Mr. Stein's book."

Back to Peter Stein.

"Christa, I know Stein is a fascinating subject, and I would dearly love to be a fly on the wall when he falls in love with you, but do you think we could spend just a little bit more time on my million . . . like how am I going to earn it, and spend it, and what do I have to do to show my gratitude . . . ?"

"Oh, for sure, but look, darling, I can't talk now. I'm sitting in Mary Whitney's library and it's time for dinner. I'll call you first thing in the morning, okay? Don't celebrate too hard. And think location, God knows where. Remember that time we did the shoot on the houseboat in Kashmir? I got conjunctivitis and you did all the pix using the rest of my body. That was genius."

"That, dear, was desperation."

"Love you, Steve. We're rich." She put the telephone down. There were three things on her mind. Mary Whitney, the whereabouts of Lisa and Rob . . . and a Mr. Peter Stein.

20

Mary Whitney hurried along the path. Her brow was furrowed, her arms swung like clubs at her side, and her head was lowered like the battering ram at the gate of a medieval castle. She wasn't angry, but she was all stoked up, ready for a fight. Of course, she could be wrong, but one was seldom wrong when emotions were involved. In affairs of the heart, the bad news was invariably true.

She even had a probable venue for the "infidelity." The tennis pavilion was as likely a love nest as it was inappropriate. Yes, if they were doing it, they would be doing it there, adding insult to injury in the way that the unfaithful so enjoyed. Quite suddenly she stopped. What on earth was she going on about? Rob was the tennis coach. At this point in time he was nothing more nor less than that, despite her track record and her long-term intentions. Okay, so she fancied him rotten. That was hardly a sexual contract. In theory he was free to make out with anyone he chose. But theory sucked. It always had. It always would. What mattered to Mary was what she felt, however illogical, however perverse. Her empire had been built on intuition, and the ability to guess what people would be doing in the future before they had a clue about it themselves. She and Rob were lined up to be lovers. It hadn't happened yet, but it would happen. Who cared that the time frame was out of whack? The nitty gritty was that her sexual target was two-timing her with the best-looking girl in the world.

She started up again, a new spring in her step. The pavilion, cloaked in darkness, loomed up ahead. What would she find? Would they be in flagrante, postcoital tristesse, or in one of those dreadful tête-à-têtes that constituted modern foreplay? Why were the words for it all in Latin or French? Because the English hadn't a clue how to screw. That was why. Shit! She marched up to the door.

She peered into the blackness. Blackness stared back. She put her hand on the doorknob. Once again, she paused. She had just agreed to sign the Spanish hooker for megamoney. Was this the best way to meet the star of her vast campaign? Or was this a discretion-is-the-better-part-of-valor moment? She smiled in the darkness. A woman had to do what a woman had to do. But, as she eased open the door, business was stirring uncomfortably beneath the green layers of jealousy that blanketed her mind.

She walked into the pavilion. There was nobody there. Her eyes adjusted to the darkness. Oh, yes, there was. Still as corpses, two people were lying on the massage table. She marched over to the light. She switched it on. Yes! Oh yes! God, what a dreadful moment, but how wonderful it was to be *right!*

The lovers were blinking. That was just about all they were doing, but it was *not* all that they had done. Lisa Rodriguez was below in black. "Mourning," Mary had time to think. She was in a rather good Alaïa from the new collection. The big buttons on the belt were a nice touch. Mary would steal them for her spring show, make them a little bigger, a little shinier, and three not two. Dyads were last year. Triads were next. Her skirt was up around her waist. Her panties were at Mary's feet. One of the knock-out Rodriguez tits was caught in the beam of a 200-watt downlighter. The boy had already put it away, and Mary couldn't work out whether that was the good or the bad news.

His suit was wrecked, and the better for it. It looked now like a cosily crumpled Armani rather than the ghastly Lord and Taylor forty percent polyester it was in real life. His face was red, from exertion not embarrassment, and his hair looked like he had used it to wash dishes. He lay on top of the supermodel as if posing for Rodin in a sculpture studio in which, for some strange reason, nudity was banned. Mary Whitney had never seen him look more wonderful.

She stood there, one leg thrust aggressively in front of the other. It was all she could do to keep from throwing her left arm into the air, because one thing was more certain than death and taxes—Mary Whitney had first service.

Her lip curled around the delivery.

"I was so *very* sorry, Lisa," she said, "to hear about your poor parents."

Lisa Rodriguez smiled a slow smile. Things like this didn't faze her. They pleased her. It was what her life was all about. Making chaos, stirring things up, getting her own back on the vicious whining world that had wrecked her childhood. She knew the score and the stakes. She had seduced the tennis pro, and tennis guys were the Whitney thing. The business bitch with the billions was furious because Lisa's looks had undermined the God-squad propaganda before the Whitney dollars had a chance to do it. It was as simple as that. Nobody had the moral high ground here. It was about power, and irritation, and who could get away with what. What did Whitney care about the most? Her business or her horizontal dancing? The Kenwood package was the stake in the poker game.

"Mary Whitney, I presume," said Lisa.

Mary ignored her.

She turned toward Rob. She wanted to hurt him, but he looked like he had been hurt already . . . confused, terminally embarrassed, deeply adorable.

In mid-invective, she softened her sentence. "God's always going on about people loving one another. I guess you believe in taking him literally," she said.

Lisa Rodriguez scooped her breast back into her frock. She disentangled herself from Rob's legs, smiling all the time, and she eased herself off the massage table. She smoothed the skirt down to the top of her thighs, and she walked toward Mary. She bent down and picked her panties off the floor. Then she stood up, and a foot or two from Mary, she put out her hand.

"I'm very pleased to meet you," she said. "And I'm really looking forward to working with you on the perfume campaign."

Mary Whitney, a superb bully, had to admire it, had to admire her. She had never seen Rodriguez up this close before, and she was a work of art. The steamy lovemaking had added to her beauty. She was positively luminescent, shining with charisma and a hypnotic sexuality. Of course, she would have to go. Lack of respect on this scale could not be tolerated . . . or could it? For a second, Mary saw the vision. She saw the scintillating sensuality of the Rodriguez features staring from the billboards and the pages of the sweet-smelling magazines. She saw the Whitney scent flying from the displays in the up-market department stores and classy pharmacies, and she heard the blissful music of the pan-American cash registers. There was only one guarantee that the campaign would be wild dreams, and that guarantee was standing in front of her.

Mary swallowed. Could this unhappy business be forgiven if not forgotten? Could she wrap her teeth around a piece of humble pie? It hung in the balance of the moment. Not for long. Mary Whitney knew that there was only one way to be successful. You had to focus all the energy. All the ambition had to point in the same, simple direction. You could have other interests. But they had to be meaningless. She took a deep breath.

"It's a pleasure to meet you," she said at last. "Now, if you don't mind, we're all about to sit down to eat so we ought to hurry back. I bet you two have worked up a superb appetite." She smiled a glacial smile, as she sank to her bottom line. Perhaps there might still be an opportunity for blood sports later. After all, they were both sitting at her table for dinner.

21

"Hi, we meet again."

He had arrived at the table early, hoping that she would, too. He didn't want their second meeting diluted by strangers.

"Peter Stein! Well, hello! What a wonderful coincidence. Of all the people in the world, I never expected to see you in Palm Beach."

They stood facing each other across the table.

He watched her, drinking her in. There wouldn't be time for this once the conversation started. He knew somehow that it would take all his concentration. She was even more beautiful than he remembered. He tried to work out why. It wasn't merely the superb arrangement of her features. It was her energy. She seemed surrounded by a bubble of scrubbed effervescence. He wanted to think "radiant," but she wasn't that remote. She was touchable. She was the girl next door, if you were *really* lucky. You simply couldn't ignore her. Some people were like that. Was it some invisible aura? Pheromones? Or was it just a cunning mixture of body signals, clothes, and gestures that conveyed subliminally the confidence, the sense of purpose, the antineurosis that drew him to her. She stood there, hands on the back of a gilt chair, smiling at him. She was pleased to see him. It was obvious. And she was wide open to anything that might happen. Everything about her said so—the smile, the cleavage of her understated black cocktail dress, the throw-away camellia stuck to its bodice.

"Palm Beach is one of my favorite places." His shy half smile said he was being half sarcastic.

She took him in. God, he was attractive. It was more than the craggy good looks. It was his posture. He held himself at an awkward angle, one that seemed to have been chosen specifically for its lack of comfort. It threw you off balance, but at the same time it kept you on your toes. His darting, deep-set eyes emphasized his unsettling aspect, while curly hair, tousled and barely combed, added to the impression of dangerous anarchy. How much of her feelings were subconsciously culled from his reputation, from her memories of his stage presence at the Miami Book Fair, from the Pulitzer that sat on his shoulder like an invisible parrot? It was difficult to say, but she wanted to know. Soon she would find out. God, his eyes were amazing. Wait a minute! They reminded her of someone. Who?

He bent down and picked up a place card, holding it between thumb and forefinger, as if it might be mildly contaminated.

"You've drawn me," he said, "and somebody called Stanford Vanderbilt." His voice was flat, but there was a hint of mockery as he said the Vanderbilt name. He managed to insinuate that he was laughing at the world, at the party people who were partying, and at anyone at all who would have a name like Stanford Vanderbilt.

"I was at school with Stanford," said Christa. "He's very grand." She laughed to show she wasn't impressed by Vanderbilt grandeur, was more interested in the literary kind that Peter represented. "Don't worry, I'll be talking to you" was the shorthand.

"Yes, he sounds grand, doesn't he?" said Peter. Was that a whiff of insecurity? thought Christa. Vanderbilts didn't get on with Steins. Nor, on the whole, did people who'd been to school with Vanderbilts, even though they might be prepared to laugh about Vanderbilt "grandeur." There were few groups on earth who were totally unimpressed by mighty intellectual reputations. The WASP establishment was one of them.

Christa walked around the table. She, too, picked up a card.

"Lord, you're sitting next to Lisa Rodriguez."

"*The* Lisa Rodriguez."

"Oh yes, the genuine version." She laughed, teasing him. He wouldn't be comfortable around media fame. Very subtly, her remark highlighted that.

He picked up on it right away. His eyes flashed once, then darted back to a marginally less easy neutrality. Goodness, he was sensitive. She hadn't meant to have a dig at him.

It was just her way of saying things, the light backtalk of the upper class at parties. But it emphasized what she had known all along. Conversation with Peter Stein would be a tricky business. Right now, to Christa, that felt like dangerous fun.

"Surrounded by models," he said. Was there the tiniest hint of disapproval wrapped around his last word?

"A big change from academics!"

"Actually, most of my friends are fishermen," he said. He looked at her, still smiling, but only just. "Fishermen" seemed to have been designed to trump Vanderbilts and models.

"Fishermen sound like *lots* of fun," said Christa, moving it along.

Both were aware that their conversation had taken on a life of its own. Neither was steering it. Both seemed content to let that happen, and yet there was a mutual anxiety. They wanted very much to like each other, to add depth to the mutual attraction. Would it be possible?

Christa wandered around the table checking the names of their fellow diners.

"Anna Wintour, editor of *Vogue.* One for me. Her husband, Professor Shaeffer. He's a child psychiatrist at Columbia. One for you. Mary Whitney. I guess she's mine. And Rob Sand. Yours. He's a diver and a tennis pro, which, I guess, is not a million miles from a fisherman."

"So we are on opposite sides, are we?" Peter Stein smiled at her performance. She wasn't afraid of him. That was nice. And she was very, very pretty, pert, forceful, and just a little bit slinky sly.

"Only if you want to be." She gave him the head-on smile. He held it hard. He didn't look away. Most people couldn't cope with it. Where on *earth* have I seen those eyes before? thought Christa.

"Wonderful," said Mary Whitney, knifing up to the table, a smooth Stanford Vanderbilt in tow. "You've met. Two of my *favorite* best friends. Now, you have to show Peter how to enjoy himself, Christa. And Peter, you have to show Christa how to be a little more sensitive. She's just taken me to the cleaners in a deal."

She sat down, grabbed the linen napkin and shook it with a flourish.

"Where is everyone?" she said to no one in particular.

"I think Lisa and Rob were on a tour of the house," said Christa.

"Oh, I found them. They're getting cleaned up."

"What did you think of your new Whitney girl?" said Christa, wondering what the hell Mary meant by "getting cleaned up." Her stomach did a couple of revolutions.

"I think she has a terrific future on the tennis court."

Oh, God! Surely not. Was the contract still intact?

Mary read her mind.

"Don't worry, darling. The deal's done. But you won't mind if I insist on a thirty-page morals clause, will you? Ah, here are the Shaeffers."

Anna Wintour, cool, pixie-faced *Vogue* editor and fashion panjandrum, sidled up to the table, her husband at her side. Peter Shaeffer had read *Child's Play.* He made a beeline for Peter Stein.

"And here at last are the children," said Mary Whitney.

Lisa and Rob had arrived. They looked not so much all cleaned up as all washed up. Christa rushed over to them.

"Lisa, you met Mary. How wonderful. And Rob, did you look after my star client?" She spoke fast, well aware of the currents that swirled around the table. Across it, she could see Peter Stein watching her.

"Let's all sit down and eat," said Mary Whitney.

She said it firmly. Everyone did as they were told.

Waiters pounced with the champagne.

"*What* fun," said Mary Whitney, and she let out the nastiest laugh that anyone at the table had ever heard.

"I detect bad vibrations," said Peter to Christa. He didn't bother to lower his voice.

"No way," said Christa, aware that the color on her cheeks was exposing her lie. "Lisa is a new client of a model agency I own, and we're going to be working for Mary Whitney. It's really exciting."

That was the truth.

He looked at her. His eyebrow arched. "Sounds terrifying," he said with the hint of a smile.

"Yeah, okay, it is." Christa smiled, too. He was sharp as a knife. Not much would get past him. Was that a writer's talent, or just his?

"What's terrifying?" barked Mary Whitney.

"I imagine that working for you would be," said Peter, totally unfazed by the aggression in his hostess's voice. Christa looked at him again. He was not a frightened man. He was used to doing the frightening. Mmmmmm. She had always preferred her men with soft centers. But there was no law against changing your mind.

"What on earth would you know about it, Peter? You've never worked for anyone in your entire life." The calmness of his response had already softened her tone.

"Neither have you, Mary."

"No, thank God," agreed Mary. "Work is the curse of the thinking classes. It's far too valuable to be wasted on someone else." She laughed to show that they hadn't had a row.

"I wouldn't dream of working for someone else," said Lisa Rodriguez.

"Surely, when you do a *Vogue* cover, you're working for Anna," said the suave voice of Stanford Vanderbilt.

Anna Wintour, who had cultivated detachment to a fine art form, stared into space.

"It's an attitude of mind," said Lisa. "I do everything for myself."

"You're wrong," said Rob suddenly. "You should do everything for God."

An uneasy silence descended. God could produce those.

"Well, it was certainly a pleasure to witness your work on his behalf this evening," said the acid tones of Mary Whitney.

"God created nature," said Lisa, smiling broadly. She crunched her legs together beneath the table. The echo of him lived on, deep inside her.

"And the devil to tempt people," said Rob Sand. His face was stricken. The caviar lay untasted on his plate. His whole body radiated despair.

Christa wanted to get up and hug him and tell him it was okay. He was way out of his depth here. He was the voice of simple decency among the jaded sophisticates, and however much he prayed, he hadn't a prayer in this company. He made her feel like a mother, warm, protective, deeply concerned. Whatever had happened earlier, he was being punished for it. Christa was prepared to bet anything that he wasn't to blame.

"Ah," said Peter. "The Manichaean heresy. How seldom one hears it nowadays when the devil is so out of date and mental illness has taken his place."

"But surely," said Christa, "the Manichaeans believed that God and the devil were unrelated, independent powers. They wouldn't subscribe to Rob's view that God created the devil to tempt people."

"What?" said Peter Stein. His mouth hadn't dropped open, but a neon sign on his forehead said that it wanted to.

"You're absolutely right, Christa," said Professor Shaeffer. "The Manichaeans developed the ideas of Zoroaster/Zarathustra. Their devil was a coequal of God's, not God's creation."

"How very clever of you to know," said Peter Stein to Christa. He meant it as a compliment. It *was* clever. He was astounded that anyone as beautiful as Christa would possess information like that. Unfortunately the patronization of his thoughts was not hidden in the tone of his words.

"I learned to read as a child," she said. "Now I can even do it without moving my lips."

Christa couldn't help it. It had slipped out. He had found her weak spot. He hadn't done it on purpose, but that scarcely mattered. Her psychic blood had been shed. She was acutely aware that she was his intellectual inferior. Now, inadvertently, he had let her know that he thought so, too. How on earth does a dumb blonde get to know about religious philosophy, was the thought running around in his mind. His words had given her a window on it. Well, shit, she *hadn't* gone to college, but that didn't mean she wasn't allowed to know things. The sarcasm of her counteroffensive lingered in the air like an aftershock.

Peter's face registered the rebuke, and his response was instant. He'd gotten Christa Kenwood wrong. She was somebody else entirely. The girl was merely a tricky, touchy looker who slid through life on her sexual attraction, and the millisecond people stopped drooling over her she turned nasty. Okay, he had made a remark that *could* have been considered marginally patronizing, but it hadn't been intended that way. It had been meant as a compliment. Knowledge of the nuts and bolts of the Manichaean heresy *was* clever. People who ran model agencies, ex-models, former actresses, on the whole, in his limited experience, weren't conversant with it. Hence his remark. But if he had been patronizing unintentionally, she was now being gratuitously rude. How did he know that the pushy cow who rented out beautiful girls to the glossy magazines had fluked an A in Divinity 101? That hardly made her Einstein. Actually, she'd probably picked up the information from *Reader's Digest* on the john. It would be the only time in her day she wouldn't be busy being superficial.

"Knowing how to read must be an advantage when you're playing Trivial Pursuit," he said.

Christa's head shot back. She'd intended to rap his knuckles. He was supposed to fall into a confused silence, and surface a bit later to find himself forgiven. Instead, he had mounted a counterattack that demanded a stinging response.

"Oh, I find Trivial Pursuit mere child's play. Didn't you write a children's book once?"

Peter Stein's eyebrows met in the middle. His forehead was a concertina as the frown devoured it.

"That 'children's book' won a Pulitzer Prize," he growled through clenched teeth. "Have you read it?"

"No, but I think John Travolta and Kirstie Alley must have. They keep making all those funny movies about it."

Peter Stein smiled an evil smile. It was war, and he would win. He always won, especially against women, especially when the weapon of choice was words. His anger merged into a cruel anticipation of victory. Tears would be the signal of her defeat. He would make her cry in front of everybody, and the terrible insults to his precious work would be avenged.

"I suppose," he said with a sneer, "movies and magazines are the borders of your world."

"And Manichaeans," she shot back. It was a neutralizer. Minutes before he'd complimented her intelligence. Now he was saying she was thick. She was pointing out the discrepancy.

He stared at her carefully. The girl had claws. She was quick, street smart from a lifetime of hustling, probably. But God, she was great-looking, and she was more real now. Her personality was filling out before his eyes. Mmmmm. Was he actually enjoying this?

"If you had read *Child's Play,* you would understand that it is about nothing so crass as a talking baby. It is a perceptive, and I like to think very original, examination of what it is really like to be a child. Children, lacking words, find it difficult to explain. Adults, lacking memory, are poor at it, too. It is difficult both to think thoughts and to remember them if you don't have a decent vocabulary. Wittgenstein was responsible for that particular insight."

He had changed tack. Now he employed the slow, patient delivery of the teacher to a dense class. He leaned back in his chair, and his angry eyes softened. He was de-escalating the crisis. Instead of going for the knockout blow, he had decided to take his time. Mockery and sarcasm would be his weapons. In the long haul, Christa would be worn down by the power of his intellect. It would be more fun that way, playing cat to her mouse. Anyway, the girl had shown a surprising aptitude for the cut and thrust of one-liner conversation.

"It's difficult to imagine you as a child," she said. "Was it miserable, your childhood?" The injection of the personal into the conversation was an escalation of the fight. Concentration was now total. They were getting to know each other fast.

"I've rather given up on 'happy' and 'unhappy' labels," he said, somewhere in between condescension and surprise at the turn in the dialogue. He paused. Yes, his childhood had been miserable. She'd gotten that right, and it was a topic he'd always avoided in publicity appearances. So her shot in the dark had hit home. Or was she genuinely perceptive? Miserable children tended to make miserable grownups, and aggression was a favorite disguise for misery. Could she know things like that? "I suppose, for what it's worth, there have been more cheerful childhoods than mine," he said.

Peter Stein smiled grimly. He didn't usually do understatements.

He'd done one now. On paper, his childhood had been picture perfect, but only writers realized that paper knew nothing. The agony had had one source. His father. Even now, the very thought of him could conjure up the bile. Julius Stein had always done the clever thing, and the clever thing had been to escape with his entire family from the Warsaw Ghetto before its glorious, and disastrous, rebellion. Peter, not yet one year old, had no memories of the horror, but his father had born the scars of the Holocaust, and, it seemed to Peter, had spent the rest of his life attempting to transfer them to him. His father had been one of the most respected psychiatrists in Europe, a psychoanalyst and a friend of Freud's, but he had never learned to speak English and, when he had arrived in America, it had been long, bitter years before he had been able to practice the art he lived for. A cold, calculating intellectual, a steely surgeon of the mind, who believed that all adult behavior was programmed in childhood, Julius Stein had never learned how to love. He had treated his son as if he were an irritating, unpredictable experiment that failed continually to confirm the data he was expecting. Peter had learned at an early age how to confound the father who believed he was too clever to be confounded. As a result he had found himself diagnosed as an intractable neurotic with an all but untreatable narcissistic personality. To be regarded as a patient by your own father was not the firmest foundation for great father/son bonding, and as he had gotten older, it had gotten worse. Later, for some strange reason, his father, an intellectual snob with a classic European education, had settled on the fiction that his son was stupid.

The cleverer Peter revealed himself to be, the firmer became his father's illusion that he was an intellectual minnow. No success at school, no amount of praise from his teachers, none of the accumulated evidence of the younger Stein's vast brain power could dissuade Julius Stein from the view that he had sired an idiot. It became the stick with which he beat his son. And disproving his father's false thesis became the weapon with which Peter tortured his father. The mutual hatred had grown and grown, until there was hardly anything else in the lives of either. Peter's mother had been a pawn in the deadly male game. Julius Stein patronized and looked down on his bird-brained but beautiful wife. Peter Stein placed her on a pedestal, and generalized his love for her to embrace her entire sex. Conversely, men of all shapes, sizes, and forms became the enemy. And through it all, an endless and inescapable refrain, was the desperate desire for brilliance, and acceptance of his brilliance, that was doomed never to be satisfied. Now his father was dead, but his father's legacy lived on. "I suppose there have been more cheerful childhoods!" Hah! Oh yes, there had. He had never been hungry; never less than wonderfully educated; never cold; never dirty; never short of culture; never without money in his pocket. But he could never remember being loved. And of course that was the only memory worth having.

He came out of the dream. Christa's beauty was back in focus. She was talking to him. What was she saying?

"I imagine writing must be a bit like exorcism. The ghosts frighten you. So you light the candle, write the book, and ring the bell on the talk shows, and abracadabra, they're gone."

He laughed, despite himself. She had surprised him again. She didn't just know things. She thought things. And if she was capable of thought about writing—the ultimate mystery, and Peter's obsession—then they had more in common than he had dreamed. Still, her insults were not forgiven—although it would be rather nice to find a plausible reason to forgive her.

"What people usually say is that writing is a form of self-analysis, of psychotherapy. You get rid of your conflicts by laying them out, putting them in order, and in effect defusing them by pouring the cold water of reason all over them. But shrinks are merely priests of a secular religion, so I guess your analogy is in line with the popular wisdom."

He laughed what sounded to Christa like a superior laugh. She didn't stop to wonder whether she was being hypersensitive. Her inner monologue was off and running. Oh, thanks a lot, Mr. Stein. I just mouth the crass guff the others spout. Is that the case? Is that what you really believe about me? What a nasty little chauvinist there is inside that brilliant, liberal, cunningly handsome exterior. You like to beat up on girls, don't you, Mr. Stein. Why? Was that Mommy's legacy? Did she play Virgin Mary to your God in your "uncheerful" childhood? Do you ever give anything back to that female place from which your cute baby curls once poked out at the world? Shit, dickhead; duck, baby! I'm going to splatter you all over the caviar from the Caspian sea.

"A friend of mine once said that your books were incredibly depressing, but that the reader walked away from them with the sense that they had all the answers. That's how I feel about meeting you. Depressed, but knowing the answer."

He couldn't resist it. "What answer?"

"That you are the most arrogant, self-centered, insensitive person that I have ever had the misfortune to meet."

Her eyes flashed fire as she spoke. She had Stein's number. He was Machiavellian man. He pursued his horridness beneath a smoke-screen of sentences. Behind the camouflage of his intellect he took potshots at the world, and the disguise enabled him to get away with it. Well, Christa knew him now. She didn't deal in words. She dealt in emotions. If she felt put down, insulted, patronized, then that was what had been intended, however much this word merchant might deny it. He could shout "foul," "overreaction," "paranoia," but he would be blowing in the wind. She was onto him.

" 'Arrogant,' because I insinuate that your thoughts are not totally original? 'Self-centered, insensitive,' because I don't fall on my back, legs in the air, when the famous model/actress shines the light of her overexposed countenance upon me? Please! There are people in this world who take thinking seriously. They don't just turn on the mind tap at parties and spray their silly thoughts at the assembled company. I care about art and literature and the human predicament. You care about butts and tits and the cash you sell them for. That's the difference between you and me. Please have the simple good sense to recognize it."

There! That would get her. The bimbo believed she had a brain behind the beauty. Now he had skewered her presumption. She was back in the boudoir where she belonged, a ballsy bourgeois harridan who had finally bumped into a brick wall.

He leaned toward her like a tree on a stormy heath, and his eyes blasted into hers. His words shuddered in Christa's ears. His eyes burned holes in her brain. Then, quite suddenly, she recognized him. He was the diver at the bottom of the sea. He was the guy who'd screamed as he'd fled. He was the man whose life she'd saved. The eyes behind the mask were the eyes before her now. There was the same fury, the identical angst. There wasn't a shadow of doubt about it.

Her smile started at her jaw and broke upward into a glorious dawn all over her face. Winning the lottery would have nothing on this. Mr. Peter Stein, the vicious biter, would now be bitten as he had never, ever been bitten before.

"Done any diving lately, Mr. Stein?" she said.

"What!" He blinked. She twinkled. "What do you mean?" he added, but already his eyes had lost their certainty. His hand raced to his head and fumbled with the black unruly hair.

Christa clapped her hands in simulated bimbo-esque excitement.

"Oh, everybody," she trilled. "This is sooooo funny. Listen to this. You must listen to this." She spun it out until she had the table.

They were her audience. Mary Whitney, quizzical, prepared to be amused; Vanderbilt, languidly smiling; Shaeffer, honestly interested. Rob Sand was rapt, leaning forward to capture any Christa word; Lisa Rodriguez petulantly yielding the stage to another woman; even Anna Wintour was momentarily back from the private Mars she had been visiting. Peter Stein alone wasn't ready for this speech. He was red with embarrassment and rage. The mainframe computer that was his mind had run the program. Christa Kenwood, who at this moment in time was the person he hated more than anyone on this earth, was also the beautiful mermaid who had saved his life.

"I've just remembered where I saw Mr. Stein before. Rob and I met him out diving, and I saved his life."

Peter swallowed hard. There was no answer to that. His red was turning white. For the second time in a few short days, this fiend from hell was going to humiliate him. He clenched his fists beneath the table. He looked around him. Could he escape? No. Not this time.

"You saved his *life?*" Mary Whitney gave a delighted laugh.

"How on earth did you do that?" said Lisa Rodriguez. Both women had their antennae tuned in to the trouble ahead. They could hardly wait to reach it.

"You tell them, Mr. Stein," said Christa.

Peter cleared his throat. He tucked a finger into his suddenly tight collar. On his chest he could feel sweat, the stuff you were supposed never to let them see.

"Well, I don't know about 'saved my life,' but I was, stupidly, diving alone . . ."

He petered out, turned to Christa, and said, "I had no idea it was you."

"Come *on,* Peter, tell us more. What a splendid story," said Mary Whitney, crunching on a piece of melba toast like a lizard on a roach. "You were out diving, and . . ." she prompted.

"I was out diving, stupidly, alone . . ." tried Peter. He heard his words like echoes in a madman's mind. How often could they be repeated? Could the needle remain in the groove until this dreadful moment had passed? No. He ground on. "And I got my foot caught in a crevice. In fact, I got stuck."

"And your air ran out?" prompted Stanford Vanderbilt.

"Well, actually, I wasn't wearing scuba gear."

"He was skindiving at sixty feet," said Rob Sand. He had been astonished to learn the identity of the mystery idiot who had broken all the rules of diving. Now he leaned across the table, his face a mask of righteous indignation, as he ladled the sarcasm into his words.

"Isn't that a bit deep for skindiving?" said Lisa Rodriguez, spelling out the accusation in Rob's statement. She could read body language. The scribbler was on the rack. Christa was in Nirvana. Lisa had seen them fall out earlier. Peter Stein was going to emerge from this story as a pale shadow of his former self. Lisa was a student of human discomfort and she saw it as her role to amplify it wherever she found it.

"I sometimes . . . occasionally, for fun, I drop the gear over the side and dive down to retrieve it. It's probably a silly thing to do . . ." He peered around the table. They were all nodding at stupid, silly Peter Stein. They smiled smiles of patronization and superiority, because they already had the gist of this conversation. The braino had screwed up, and the beauty had saved him, and now the art hero was in court, and they were judge, jury, and executioner. It was a fun situation in which to find themselves.

"Anyway, to cut a long story short . . ."

"Oh, don't do that," said Mary. "We all want a *long* story from the storyteller, don't we? Lots of motivation, and character building, and psychological profiles. Come on, Peter, indulge us." She leaned back in her chair. It was her party. She could be sly if she wanted to.

"Christa arrived . . . luckily . . . and gave me some air, and I was able to get back to the surface with no damage done." There. That was as long as it would get.

"But what I can't understand," said Vanderbilt, "is how you didn't recognize Christa. I can see how you might not recognize her under water with her mask and breathing stuff on, but when you both got to the surface, and you thanked her and everything, then surely she'd be totally unforgettable."

Peter looked at Christa. Would she be merciful? She would not be.

"By the time I got to the surface, Mr. Stein had roared off in his boat."

"But you gave him *air,*" persisted Stanford Vanderbilt. The upper classes cared about nothing except the manners they maintained maketh man. They would cheerfully slit your throat if you crossed them, but they would be scrupulously polite as they did so.

"Surely not," said Mary Whitney.

"He never thanked her properly," said Rob bitterly. Having your life saved was one thing. Having it saved by someone as wonderful as Christa was quite another. Stein's lack of gratitude boggled Rob's mind.

"You didn't thank her for saving your life?" said Lisa Rodriguez, her head cocked to one side. She had never thanked a woman for anything, nor would she, but hypocrisy was her second favorite vice.

"I'm sure Mr. Stein had his reasons," said the professor, showing the solidarity of intellectuals.

"I'm longing to hear them," said his wife.

"It was an awkward moment," said Peter at last, "but it wasn't a life-threatening one. That's a little dramatic. Anyway, I did thank Christa." He squirmed in his chair. He never answered to anyone. His whole life had been built around the need to avoid that. Yet here he was experiencing the third degree and about to be proven guilty. It was intolerable. It would have to end. But he knew his last words hadn't ended it. He had said two things that implicitly contradicted each other. If she didn't save his life, why the hell had he needed to thank her? Okay, a lawyer could have reconciled the apparent paradox, but there were no lawyers at this table. It was a table peopled by winners who dealt only in the big picture.

"After a little prompting, he wrote 'thanks' on my slate. Then he bugged out," said Christa with a cheerful laugh. "I must say I would have expected something a little more fulsome if I'd known it was Mr. Stein. His books are pretty long-winded."

"I think you ought to say thank you now," said Rob Sand. It sounded suspiciously like an ultimatum.

Silence. Nobody said a word. They were all looking at him.

Peter Stein stood up. He laid his napkin down on the table. It was a personal Epiphany. He had been pushed too far.

His voice quivered with fury as he spoke.

"You can all, singly and collectively, go fuck yourselves," he said. And he pushed back his chair, turned around, and he walked away.

He threaded through the tables at high speed, weaving like a slalom racer as he headed for the exit. Somebody reached up for his sleeve, hoping to introduce himself. He brushed away the supplicant hand. Nobody else tried to block his escape.

"Wow, Christa!" gasped Lisa. "You sure as hell lit his fuse." She sounded jealous that someone had hijacked her role as chief fuse lighter.

"I've never been so insulted in my entire life," huffed Stanford Vanderbilt. With the arrogance of his species he had already forgotten that the Stein advice had been directed at others besides himself.

"He needs our forgiveness," said Rob gently.

"Well, all I can say is that if hate turns to love, it's wedding bells," laughed Mary Whitney, not remotely put out by the precipitous departure of her star guest.

Christa said nothing. She was in a state of shock, but it was not Peter Stein's words or actions that had caused it. What was freaking her was one astounding emotional truth. She wanted to see the bastard again.

22

"It would be a help, Mary, if we could know a little bit about the scent, mainly the name, I guess. I mean if it was India, which I gather it isn't anymore, we'd have to be thinking Kashmir or somewhere like that for the location," said Christa.

"Christ, not Kashmir," moaned Steve Pitts. "Eye infections, tummy upsets, flies . . . and that's just on the airplane."

Mary Whitney eyed the photographer carefully. At a million bucks he wasn't cheap, but he was the best. He'd have to hold the funnies, though. Especially on the morning after the night before.

"No, we've rubbed India off the map of our lives," said Mary Whitney, reaching for her coffee cup. "And in its place we have a gaping void. But that's mere detail. All scents are the same. What you're selling is excitement, romance, and sex . . . disappointment, in other words."

"Oh, come on, Mary, you're the biggest romantic I know. When did you last find sex disappointing?"

"Last night, in the tennis pavilion, dear."

"Sorry I asked," said Christa.

"As I was saying," said Mary with an arch look, "scent is about lovers, unfortunately. And lovers love beaches, and bare bodies, and tarts who look like Lisa Rodriguez making eyes at some poor unfortunate man. So let's do that, okay? Luckily, Florida is on our doorstep, so there is no immediate shortage of sand. Actually," she allowed a little alien enthusiasm into her voice, "I've had rather a good idea for this scent."

They were listening. Mary McGregor Whitney didn't fool anyone with her terminal pessimism, her understatement, her perennial pretense that life was a bore sent personally to plague her. Her track record gave the lie to all that. It was a façade, nothing more nor less. The truth was that Mary was business brilliant and art smart. The megabucks said so. Steve, who had just arrived from New York on an early plane, leaned forward to hear the "good" idea that would be better than good.

"Scent bottles are so useless, and so ugly, and in these days nobody wants to spend money on rubbish except the psychos who pay the going rate for modern art. I dreamed up a bottle that would be shaped like a seashell, really beautiful, opaque, and with a fabulous texture. You'd wear it around your neck like a piece of jewelry, on a simple, brightly colored string necklace. Everywhere you go, you take your scent with you. You can wear it on the beach, in the sea, in bed . . . Anywhere you want to turn on the boy you're with."

"I *love* it," said Christa. "The new thing is swimsuits and Lycra exercise gear that you can wear to the beach and the gym, and then wear in the evening, too. Round-the-neck scent goes beautifully with that. Hell, you can even be thoroughly British about the whole business and skip the shower in between."

"The British never exercise, dear. Bodies are for hiding over there. It's why they're not allowed to wash. But, yes, you've got the thrust of it, Christa. This is for the young and the faithless, who hate handbags and never know from one moment to the next when they are going to need to smell delicious."

"Marvelous, so we can shoot here, in pseudocivilization. That takes one helluva load off my plate. Lots of lovey-dovey stuff on the sand, young hard bodies, smoldering eyes. It'll be just great. Any ideas for specific locations?" said Steve.

"Mmmm," said Mary absentmindedly. "Christa knows South Florida as well as anyone. I suppose I do, too, come to think of it. Sanibel's quite atmospheric if you dose up on the Avon stuff for the no-see-ums, and I guess the Abacos are great if you interpret 'Florida' loosely. Lots of good spots down in the wilder and woollier keys. The Dry Tortugas off Key West are beautiful, and Christa will be able to pick up where she left off with our good friend Peter Stein. If *The Dream I Dreamed* ever gets delivered, we'll all have to thank you for it, Christa, you in your role as savior of his life." She laughed brightly, catching the blush that spread across Christa's face.

"How did you get on with him?" said Steve.

"It was not a success."

"Christa drove him crazy. We all got told to perform an act that I feel sure is anatomically impossible, especially for women, and then he walked out on my party. One has to give him taste points for *that.* It was a disaster."

"Oh, Mary, it wasn't. It was a wonderful party."

"It might have been okay for you, dear. You were spared the tennis pavilion hors d'oeuvres. The moment this thing is history I'm going to turn that Rodriguez bitch into steak tartare."

Christa laughed at the expression of transcendental sadness that Mary Whitney, half joking, had assumed. Whatever she had witnessed in the tennis pavilion, it hadn't changed her decision to use Lisa in the shoot. Nothing else mattered.

"Which brings us to the other thing," said Christa. "We need a boy."

"Yes, I know, but do boys need us?"

"For the shoot," said Steve. Mary's sense of humor was a little too close to his for comfort. He had caught an early flight to Palm Beach because he was raring to go. He'd already thrashed out a game plan with Christa on the telephone. The first thing had been to get the broad details of the perfume, to decide on the visual thrust of the campaign, and to choose a location. The second part was the boy.

"Well, why should I care who you use? We've got the best girl, and, I'm told, the best photographer. The boy is incidental."

"We want to use Rob," said Christa.

"Rob! 'We'?" Mary Whitney was seldom surprised. She was now.

Christa took a deep breath.

"Listen, Mary, putting personal feelings aside, he would be wonderful for the campaign. We've got Lisa, whose profile is stratospheric. A complete unknown to play off her would be perfect. I'm telling you that, camera-wise, he's got what it takes. This morning I had him come over and I introduced him to Steve. Steve agrees. He's even more enthusiastic than I am, and Lisa's over the moon. She can be tricky. It would be great if we can work up good chemistry between her and the boy. All in all, it makes sense."

"And now I suppose you're going to tell me you've just signed Rob with your beastly agency and you want a billion dollars for my tennis coach. Just remember, darling, that we were coasting along quite happily on fifty bucks an hour until your road show hit town."

"He doesn't even know if he wants to do it. He doesn't know if he *can* do it. I floated the idea. That's all. We had to run it by you first."

Mary Whitney said nothing. She was sizing it up. Suddenly, everyone wanted Rob. Lisa. Christa. Steve Pitts. Damn it, *she* did. Christa's interest was supposedly platonic. She guessed the photographer's wasn't.

"And what exactly did *you* think of our Rob, Mr. Pitts? I think we should know."

"He's a natural. Christa's right. He's got tomorrow's face, today's body. There's an innocence that will offset Lisa's over-the-top sex appeal. I think it would be a magic combination."

Steve Pitts wondered if he'd gone too far. It was true. The boy had turned his motor, professionally . . . and otherwise. That made it so much easier. It meant he could give just that little bit more to the shoot as the personal juices merged with the creative ones in the steamy artistic stew.

Mary Whitney's beady eyes peered into his soul.

"Weeeeeell," she drawled. "It seems that my little discovery has captured hearts all over the place. Let's just hope that he can move the merchandise like he can shift the hormones."

"Is that a yes?" said Christa.

"Listen, darlings. You're the pipers. Play your tune. But just one thing, boys and girls. Don't come bleating to me if this ends in tears."

Mary Whitney drummed her fingers and scowled and looked out to sea across the lawns that looked like they had been manicured by Georgette Klinger. And she wondered why the hell it was that she suddenly felt so angry.

23

Le Bilboquet is the trendiest restaurant in New York. Few people know that, and the regulars like it that way. There are several reasons for its low profile. There is no sign outside to say what it is called. You can't make a reservation. It is smaller, but far brighter, than the black hole of Calcutta. Then there is the persona of Jacques, who runs it. He is adorable, but French, eccentric, and difficult unless he knows and likes you. For a long time the Bilboquet did cold food only. They hardly had a kitchen. Now they do, and the hot dishes no longer have to be ferried from across the street. The crowd is Euro, but not trash.

Balkan ex-royals, Sotheby's girls, haute preppies, and top models rub shoulders, literally, with the New York/Hollywood aristos like Hoffman and De Vito. The tables are so close together, every lunchtime is a party. If you turn up at twelve forty-five and look the part, you will get seated. If not, you will be kept hanging around on the sidewalk until all pride is gone. This is barely bearable in the summer. It is possible only for stoics and extreme masochists in the winter.

Johnny Rossetti, however, the exception that proves the rule, had a permanently reserved table for four at Le Bilboquet. Only if he had not arrived by one thirty was it given away to someone else.

Today he was there, and today he was more than usually irritated. This morning he had read the press release about Christa, her agency, Lisa Rodriguez, Steve Pitts, and Mary Whitney's perfume campaign. He sucked crossly at a mind-numbing Bilboquet bloody, and dreamed of revenge.

The girl opposite him, her back to the crowd, would have put anybody else in the restaurant into a supremely good mood. She was about six-foot-two, a black beauty with moonlike eyes, full, pert breasts, and lips that looked like they could only do you good. Mona was an Elle girl in every sense of the word, but she was also Johnny's girl, his special one . . . happy and contented in the Islamic role of "favorite wife." The girl across the table on Johnny's left was a contender. She was white, or rather honey brown, the legacy of a Seychelles shoot. Her blond hair was page-boy perfect over an altar boy's complexion. Blue eyes, a determined chin, and a pouting mouth were what you could see of her spectacular good looks. But her best part was hidden. Nestling cozily on the Bilboquet banquette was the choir boy's butt that Johnny Rossetti couldn't get enough of. This was Sissy, and Sissy and Mona were both friends and rivals. Right now, both were trying to pry Rossetti out of his evil mood.

"I never thought Lisa would leave," said Mona. "I mean, you *invented* that girl."

Johnny crunched on a celery stick, ignoring the attempt at solidarity. He waved across the room at Howard Stein, the nightclub wizard. Au Bar was where Johnny got cognaced out at night.

"And Christa really pulled a fast one. She never told *anyone* she was thinking of opening an agency," agreed Sissy, throwing back her head to catch the eye of a Yugoslav prince on the other side of the restaurant.

"Yeah," said Rossetti, letting his disinterest hang out. Models weren't big on information. They tended to specialize in background commentary, a sort of conversational Muzak for which he had acquired a taste over the years. Not today. Today was different.

He eyed his girls. They were money to him, but more than that. They were games, they were tricks, they were toys for the boys. They were beautiful pawns on the chessboard of his life, expendable, useful, and once in a purple moon they metamorphosed into queens. Christa had become a queen. So had Lisa. And now both of them had dumped on him. He took out the rest of his drink and signaled for another. The Hine hangover was lifting as the Absolut reinforced his alcohol stream. But it didn't make his mood better. It just meant he was angry with a clearer head.

"What's South Beach like these days?" he said at last. Surely these girls could tell him *something*. South Beach was the new hot Miami modeling destination. He'd passed on it three years ago, when the Art Deco renovators had looked like they were fighting a losing battle against the crackheads, the homeless, and the geriatrics who'd seemed to people the streets. This year, apparently, it was happening. Ford's had opened a branch office, so had Click and a whole host of others. What had started as a German invasion had turned into an American jamboree, in which all the magazines from *Vogue* downward were taking part. Word was that South Florida had eased L.A. into third place as a model-agency location. It was bad news that Elle wasn't there. It was worse news that the fledgling Christa Kenwood agency was.

"It's great," said Mona. "We always stay at the Park Central, which is really neat. And there's this great restaurant, Oggi's, and Mezzotinto, where we all go eat."

"Mezzanotte," said Sissy, pissed that Mona had gotten to go first. "And then we go down to Semper's, which is this cool piano bar, and later, when we're all zoned, we go dance at Warsaw."

"An' the music is so loud it makes your heart sort of vibrate in your chest. I mean, it's really wild, and all the assistants who think they invented the scene in New York are all sort of put down because they always thought Florida was like nowhere, and now it's wilder than anywhere . . ."

Mona had taken up the running. She paused to see if she was uttering encouraging words. Rossetti stared back at her, his face blank.

"Do you two want some blow?" he said. Bright eyes brightened. Oh yes, they did.

He reached into his pocket and passed Sissy a packet. Both girls stood up. Conversation in Le Bilboquet ground to a halt. Top models standing up was superb spectator sport. How high could they go? How tall was the sky? Black and white, four luscious legs, four tight gluteals, hardly hidden at all by identical black Lycra skirts. Way-to-go, Johnny! If only sex was as good as it looked.

The chat started again as his girls beelined for the john, spilling drinks, nudging shoulders, squirting hormones among the cheerful lunchers. Johnny sat back in his chair. Christa had creamed him. She'd stolen his income, filched the most lucrative campaign in the history of high-fashion advertising, taken the top photographer out of the equation. She'd opened a rival agency in the hot new spot, and already its total for the year would surpass his. This wasn't competition. This was war. Nations fought for their oil, their living space, their openings to the sea. It was a question of survival. But it was more than that. It was personal.

He stared around the restaurant. Its mood was light, frothy, like a good soufflé, as the rich and careless cracked their jokes and flirted harmlessly. But in his corner, revenge was the dish being cooked, a great leaden suet pudding of hatred and malice, and already Rossetti could see it landing like a bomb on the head of Christa Kenwood.

His girls were back, flying high.

"Hey, Johnny, that girl of yours wouldn't lay that stuff on me till I *kissed* her. You catch that? What you hirin' these days, gay girls? Jeez, baby, where did you learn to *kiss* like that?" She talked and laughed loudly so that the people around could hear, and Sissy laughed, too, in the conspiracy to lighten Johnny up. He liked that, two girls getting it on. It made him feel good, and then he was generous with his drugs, and had a word with the bookers so that they got to work more and make more bread, and score a little bit more of the fame they craved.

"Don't listen to her, Johnny. Mona's been shining out to me ever since Peru. She plain wore me down, that's all. Shit, Mona, did you see that tourist *freak?*"

He smiled indulgently. He knew what they were doing, and he liked it. They were trying to please him. And after lunch, after a few more drinks, he would give them their chance to do it properly. Mmmmmmm! That would be nice. Sometimes he felt that love was too good for men to make.

He looked at Mona. He looked at Sissy. Which would be the instrument of his revenge? Which was the more malleable, the more trustworthy, the more expendable? Mona had been the main event for six whole months. Her time was up, and she knew it. So she was afraid, and desperate to hold on. She would want to believe the lies that were his promises. And that would leave Sissy to him, and a vacant spare-girl slot which maybe the British cockney could fill, or the Brazilian with the Ipanema legs and tits like torpedoes.

"Mona," he said.

She turned toward him, her lips and eyes luminous, her heart banging on the coke. She smiled at him. She was still his number-one girl. He was still her career doctor, dealer, her lord and master. Nothing had changed. Nothing would change. Nothing *must* change.

"Mona, I want you to do something for me."

"For you, Johnny, anything." She breathed the sincerity into her words.

"I want you to go work for the Christa Kenwood agency," he said.

24

Christa slunk into the bookshop. It was cool and dark, a refuge from the bright vulgarity of Duval Street. It reminded her of London, or the Village—a place where readers took reading seriously. There were no garish dump bins of best sellers, no banners, no great stacks of books browbeating you into buying them by sheer weight of numbers. There was space to walk about, a couple of chairs for browsers, and a rich Dickensian aroma that reminded you that books were food for the mind, and not just a fast snack for the imagination between subway stations.

She knew what she was looking for, and again the feeling of unreasoning guilt washed over her.

"Do you have any of Peter Stein's books?" she asked the girl behind the counter.

"Just that wall," was the unsmiling answer. Christa followed the pointed finger. It was a slight exaggeration. The shelves bore the books of the homegrown talent, and Stein was not alone and in excellent company. Hemingway, McGuane, Tennessee Williams had all feasted on the dripping tropical loneliness of the town at the end of America, and so had the impossible man whose life she'd saved. There were ten copies of *Child's Play*. She picked one out. She turned it over. His face accused her. Scavullo had captured all the aggression and the angst, and the charm, too. She smiled down on him. He stared crossly back at her. Christa put the book on a table. She had decided to buy it. Now she looked at the other titles. *No Man's Landing,* according to the blurb, was a passionate antiwar hymn about the courage of a conscientious objector. Set in Vietnam, it examined the bravery of a man who refused to kill and contrasted it with the lesser heroism of those who unthinkingly obeyed orders, who asked no questions and dreamed no dreams. She placed a copy on top of *Child's Play.* Then there was *The Man Who Loved Men.* "A heterosexual's fascinating flight of imagination into a gay man's world," said the inside of the cover. "Peter Stein's essay in compassion and empathy is the very stuff of creative genius. He does his research in his own soul." Three books. Three totally different subjects. But already Christa could identify the common theme. Peter Stein's heroes were outsiders. They dared to defy convention. They passed up ease for a life of stimulating difficulty, and when at last they died they were at least hauntingly alive. Conscientious objectors, homosexuals, children, were all on the outside looking into the cozy, adult, normal world. As such, they were uniquely placed to provide the insights that turned good books into great ones. Christa's pile was now three deep. It was threatening to go higher.

"I get three bucks a book," said the voice at her shoulder.

She spun around. Oh, God, no! Oh, God, yes! His head was cocked to one side, questioning her. His face was darker than she remembered it, his teeth whiter, his extraordinary eyes more compelling. He wore baggy khaki shorts, beaten topsiders, a simple white T-shirt, and his hair, relentlessly tousled, was a poem about anarchy.

"Oh, heavens, you frightened me. You've caught me buying your books."

"I have, haven't I," he said, allowing his eyes to twinkle. "I hope you survive the depression they will bring."

She blushed at the reference to the party. The words they had exchanged were printed on the pages of her mind.

"Actually, they sound fascinating. You made me angry the other day. I guess I wanted to hurt you."

She smiled straight back at him, as she recovered from the initial shock. Christa didn't do apologies for saying the things she'd felt. Neither, apparently, did he.

"What brings you to Key West?" His question was intense, not small talk.

"I'm scouting locations for a big shoot, actually for Mary's company."

"In a bookshop?"

"I came in to get out of the heat." Christa blushed as she lied.

"I come here sometimes to get out of the world."

"I'd have thought a writer would want to get away from books."

"Writers want to get away from themselves. Books are an escape hatch, as long as they've been written by someone else." He laughed a short, mirthless laugh that seemed only to emphasize the deadly seriousness of what he was saying. He looked absolutely tragic, as he stood there, his shoulders bent by the burden of his art.

"You make it sound like blood, toil, sweat, and tears."

"It has to be done," he said simply.

"I guess advertising shoots don't have to be done."

His silence said that he agreed, but it was different now. He didn't want to belittle her. Perhaps because he knew the perils attached.

"Which should I read first?"

"Oh, I think the children's book." His smile was warm now as he reminded her of what she'd said about *Child's Play,* but he left it there. He didn't labor the point.

"That's the one you like best?"

"Dislike the least. It's difficult to be satisfied. There's always a better way of saying something."

He waved away the problem, somehow emphasizing its magnitude. Critical acclaim of the quantity and quality heaped on his work was clearly as significant to him as the sound in the forest unheard. The judge sat inside, not out, and the judge was a hanging judge.

Christa felt the strange excitement. She'd been here before, at the book fair in Miami, and the memory danced from the shadows, and cavorted in the front of her mind making beautiful shapes and swaying to the wonderful music.

"What are you doing now?" she said suddenly, almost fiercely, and she waved her watch as if it meant something. "I mean, do you want to have lunch with me?"

He seemed genuinely surprised. He peered at her closely, sizing her up as a person to lunch with. He looked around, and then he stared back at her and his hand worried at his hair as if it might be too tidy for a restaurant. He wanted out. He wanted in. He was De Niro doing ambivalence.

"Yes," he said, shooting it out to stop himself from changing his mind.

"Good. Great! Where?" Christa couldn't help it. She'd always been pushy. Relief surged through her. She was going to see this man for longer. She hadn't gotten much further than that.

"Oh, dear," he said. "I don't have any money or cards or anything."

"I have. It'll be my treat. After all, you allowed me to save your life." She just couldn't help it. The desire to get underneath his seriousness was too strong to resist. She ducked mentally. But he laughed. And again he looked at her, as men looked at her, like all the men through all the years, but this time she knew it mattered. He was watching her body, and her breasts, her lips and her hair. She could sense that he was warmed by the warmth of her, and charmed by her charm, and Christa was grateful for all the gifts that God had given her . . . and lunch was to come.

She bought his books and they walked out into the street. The summer heat wrapped them up in its wet slinkiness.

"Do you know somewhere?"

"A few places." He walked fast, dodging the tourists, and Christa sensed some unwritten rule that forbade talking and traveling. The moped that he signaled her onto reinforced the feeling. Soon they were zipping through the crawling cars, down along the docks, past fishing boats and sailing yachts, to the old part of Key West. There was no nonsense about helmets, and the sultry breeze played with Christa's hair, reminding her of the unreality of it all. At first she avoided holding him. Instead, she rode the bike like she might a bucking bronco, trying to anticipate its swerves and swoops, and clinging onto the saddle with both hands and thighs. Then she relaxed. She leaned forward and laid her hands lightly on his hips. Something was happening. Her fingers were strangely sensitized to the faded cotton. She could feel his taut waist. The smell of him merged with the smell of the sea. Christa had never felt so much energy. It beamed from his back, enveloping her in an aura of supercharged angst. He was hunched over the bars of the bike, engrossed in steering it. But it was only a step in his life, a mere moment passing. Soon it would be gone, and she would be gone, and that gave birth to a pang of regret that was as painful as any Christa had felt.

Suddenly he veered to the left. The bike slid in a slalom turn and screeched to a halt, leaving rubber marks on the forecourt of a tiki hut bar at the water's edge. He turned around. On his face was the smile of an unruly schoolboy. "There! I frightened you. Wasn't that fun?" it said. It wasn't irritating. It was deeply charming, especially coming from him. Christa didn't feel like a judgmental parent. She felt like a co-child. It was no longer a mystery that he could write a book like *Child's Play.*

"We should eat here."

It wasn't the "restaurant" she'd expected. There were tables in the open air, sun-bleached and much hacked up by knives. There were stools that looked like they had hit people. There were people sitting on them who appeared to have been hit. A beaten-down barmaid tended the beaten-down bar. A blackboard said grouper was the catch of the day. Weathered ropes cordoned off the eating area. There were bits of buoys, fishing nets, and a couple of old anchors scattered about in a passable imitation of a nautical Broadway set. But this was the genuine article. If the booze hadn't robbed the bar's patrons of their memories, they would have sworn to that.

"Hi, Donna. Late last night?"

"Hi, Pete. More like early. Sun was up, anyways."

Pete? The diminutive was a shock. She had never met a Peter so far removed from a Pete.

"How's the grouper?"

"It was feelin' better in the Gulf Stream 'round six this morning."

"Squeeze some Key lime on it, and tell Seth not to hold back on the garlic. Two of those and a couple of bowls of conch chowder to start. Ice-cold bottle of chardonnay, and we're in business." He turned to Christa, almost as an afterthought.

"You don't mind my ordering for you."

"It's fine. It's your town." It was, somehow. Why did writers love Key West? Why was Peter Stein the eighth and last Pulitzer Prize winner to live there? People had speculated about it. It was a frontier, a place surrounded by water, the Freudian symbol of the unconscious mind. Did ideas grow easily here, in the fetid heat, nourished by anarchy, and fertilized by the loneliness of a place whose nearest large city was Havana? Certainly it wasn't a follow-the-leader thing. Stein wasn't here because Hemingway had been here and Audubon, and Frost and Merrill. All around them were people who looked like they couldn't read. And in the middle was the writer, pulling out her stool for her, as if it were a gilt chair at the Plaza. Gulls and pelicans wheeled overhead, a charter boat maneuvered itself into a narrow berth a few feet from where they sat, and Christa Kenwood couldn't remember when she had been more excited.

"It takes a bit of understanding," he said, reading her mind. "It looks laid back, cool, quiet, but it's a strong place. You have to be brave to live here. It's rich meat. If you can stay calm in Key West, it's a magic garden."

"Calm in Key West. Sounds like a good book. Do you stay calm here, Peter Stein?"

She smiled at him as the wine came, and he smiled back, well aware that this chance meeting was already a success, perhaps even threateningly successful. He had thought about her often since the terrible evening in Palm Beach and the dread embarrassment on the ocean floor. He remembered her smile most of all. Its wide openness. Its lack of guile. The way it warmed you like sunlight on a cold back. He remembered her sparky intelligence, and her refusal to be browbeaten or placed into all the slots he had wanted to hide her in. He remembered her as an equal. That more than anything, apart from her body, and her breasts, and the extraordinary poise of her, a posture so perfect that her body language was more seductive than any he could write, or dream of writing. Now, she sat beside him, in his place, this girl who had bought his books, and insulted him and, oh yes, who had more or less saved his life.

He bypassed her question. He was too dangerous a subject.

"Hemingway stayed calm here, you know. Despite all the Sloppy Joe myths, he didn't drink that much here. He got up with the sun. Turned out the books. Never worked as well before he came, or after he left."

"You all live here, but you don't write about here."

"McGuane does. Hemingway did in *To Have and Have Not.* But you're right. I don't know. 'Why' questions are so difficult, aren't they? Because we're American, and terminally optimistic, there's always supposed to be an answer to them. I prefer 'when,' 'what,' and 'where' questions. You can get a stranglehold on them."

"Perhaps it's because wherever you are there's too much reality. Reality breeds contempt. Fantasy is fueled by distance. Memories are the best research."

He couldn't resist it. "Yeah, misery loves company. Happiness is just an illusion. Absence makes the heart grow fonder."

He smiled to take the sting out of the put-down. Her eyes flashed fire.

"Mine *weren't* clichés," she said.

"No, actually they weren't. I'm sorry, Christa. I'm a cynic. I'm not good at conversation. I guess it's like a kid pulling the wings off flies." He had surprised himself. It was nearly an apology.

Her face softened immediately. "No, it's okay. It's my fault. I shouldn't talk to you about writing. I don't really know anything about it, and you want to relax and get away from it. I understand that. It's just nice to talk to someone like you, I mean someone who does thinking for a living. You're quite impressive, you know. Maybe even a little frightening. But then I don't have to tell you that. It's your trademark, isn't it? Peter Stein, scourge of dimwits and sufferer of fools ungladly."

He sipped carefully at the wine and watched her over the rim of the glass. She passed all the tests.

She was the one who was impressive. She hit the right notes time after time. He more than liked her. He fancied her. Yes, he did. He wanted to touch her body. He wanted to touch the hand that lay on the table, calm in Key West. He looked at it. The long, delicate fingers were waiting for him.

He cleared his throat.

"I'm glad I found you in the bookshop," he said suddenly. It sounded like a marriage invitation.

"*Are* you?" said Christa. "I'm glad you said so. I was beginning to wonder." She cocked her head to one side. Bang, bang went her heart. God, this was like Pavlov with his beastly dogs. The guy blew hot and cold and she salivated to the sound of his bell.

"Luckily, I express myself reasonably well on a typewriter. Perhaps writers ought not to be allowed out. They see normality as the enemy. They're always trying to escape it . . . drink, drugs, Key West. I don't mean that you're normal . . . I mean you are . . . but actually I find you very interesting . . . I mean . . ." There was no way to say it. None at all.

She laughed at his dilemma. He lived by the word, but words were difficult for him. They meant too much, maybe. They had to be flawless.

"Don't panic! I know what you're saying. It's almost what I was saying earlier when you accused me of spouting clichés. Artists have to escape the intolerable clutches of reality. Like neurotics, they have to build ivory towers. The trick is to avoid the psychotic's fate and end up living in them!"

"That's very well put."

"Thank you, Peter Stein. Actually, it's been said before. I modified it."

"I know, but you modified it rather well. Everything's been said before. Writers are merely spin doctors."

The waitress dropped the conch chowder as if it were a cluster bomb. It slurped and slopped and slid about, but most of it was still there to eat. Tender pieces of conch swam in the steamy tomato base. Peter Stein emptied some chardonnay into it.

"Better than the sherry they have down here."

"Where do you stand in the great booze/art debate?" she said.

It was a gentle probe. Where were his weaknesses? Were they ordinary ones, or more exotic?

"They cancel each other out. Drink gives the imagination a kick in the butt, and then screws up the ability to describe the ideas it sets free. Writing is odd and it's about oddity. Even when a writer describes the mundane he has to do so in an odd or unusual way. Otherwise it's dull. Mood swings are a help, up or down, and both depression and mania have an affinity for alcohol. I think most writers drink because they are genetically programmed to experience emotional extremes. That's why they write. That's why they drink."

They were silent for a moment, thinking the same thoughts. Not about drink and writing. About other things.

"Conversation isn't the same thing as dialogue in a book, is it?" she said.

He laughed, knowing what she meant, but uncertain whether he was prepared to admit it.

"It's three-dimensional dialogue, I guess."

"Intonation, body language, facial expressions make a difference, but the real difference is that conversation is never about what it seems to be about."

"What's our conversation about?"

He wanted to see how far and how fast she would go. She was a bull of a girl, a gorgeous, beautiful Taurean missile that would rampage into a heart and tear it to pieces. Even, maybe, a cold, strong heart.

"It's about getting to know each other."

"You want to hurry that up, don't you?"

"Yes." She paused. "I do." She looked at him, disarming his aloofness with her honesty.

"Sometimes things can't be hurried. Sometimes they shouldn't be."

"Sometimes they can be. Sometimes they should."

"I guess that's true, too." He smiled and scooped up a lump of conch. She'd whacked his mini-rebuke back to his baseline. She was right. Words were feelings' smokescreens. What they did best was tell white lies. He was sensitized to her. His mind was racing, faster, clearer than the magic moments when the typewriter took over and dictated his own book to him. It was a firefight of chat, and the stakes were bodies and minds. The conch slipped from his spoon. Splosh! Back it went to the tomato bisque. A huge globule of soup took flight and landed on his shirt.

She moved more quickly than he did. The pile of paper napkins were in the calm hand, mopping, rubbing, dabbing at his shirt and the chest it clothed.

"Oh, damn," he said, making ineffectual wing motions with his hands, like some superfluous conductor of a seasoned orchestra. He didn't mind about the shirt. He minded about his clumsiness, or rather his clumsiness being revealed to this nonclumsy girl. The incident was thick with meaning, but the meaning would be lost in the telling—her mother to his child, a move to take control, shortcuts on the road to intimacy.

"Thank you very much."

"You're welcome." It was better than she had gotten for saving his life.

"We never talk about what you do," he said, distancing himself from the situation, yet aware of the significance for him of her touch. Peter Stein had always been inaccessible. It was an art form of his. He reveled in his status as an untouchable. Now her hand had been on him, and she was inside the mind that nobody was allowed to visit. She was touring the stark disaster area up there, planning drapes, moving furniture, letting light into the austere barracks of his brain.

"Think of me as a business," she said, smiling. "My books are open. Probe away."

"In fact, I know quite a lot about you. I saw your movie. I saw you do a morning show about it. You were very good in it. Why didn't you do any more?"

"Have you ever done the Hollywood bit?" It was an answer.

"Sometimes they ask me to do scripts when they're disappointed Dostoyevsky isn't available."

"Precisely."

"The money's not bad, I suppose," he added with zero conviction.

"It's not the kind of money *I* have in mind." Christa laughed. "And I'd rather not learn in the supermarket that I'd had secret twins by a green alien from outer space. I was in Publix yesterday. The *Weekly World News* headline said Princess Grace's body had been stolen. The *Sun* exclusive was that she was alive."

"Obviously, she stole her own body."

"Yeah, that's next week's. 'Princess Grace arrested for grave robbery. Show-biz lawyer hints at insanity defense.' "

Peter was laughing, *really* laughing. God, it felt odd. God, it felt good. "That's funny," he said, surprised again by her, surprised by himself and his reaction to her.

Their laughter quieted. It was going so well. The sun beat down on them. The soup was being taken away, the grouper was arriving.

"James Merrill got Key West right," said Peter. "Heavenly colors, swell fish."

"Fascinating people," added Christa, twisting on the rheostat. She watched him, chin balancing on the tips of her fingers, elbows on the table.

He smiled at her, a coconspirator now. Their past had gone away, or been redefined. The bad times were really the good times. It was funny that they had once fought. It had been a wonderful misunderstanding. Insults and bloody mindedness were now honesty, self-respect, strength.

"How long are you here for?"

"Oh, I don't know. It depends on the photographer, Steve Pitts. He's really doing the work, scouting the locations. He wheels me in if he can't make up his mind, which is once in a blue moon."

"So you're footloose." The "fancy-free" hovered in the gentle breeze.

"Yeah, it's pretty unusual for me, but it's a nice place to be it."

He looked down at his plate. He was going to ask her something. It wasn't easy for him, apparently.

"Look, there's a sort of literary conference going on at the moment. And they've asked me to give a speech, and I said yes and it's tomorrow evening. Afterward there's a free-for-all discussion. Would you by any chance like to come . . . as my guest? It'll probably be incredibly boring . . ."

"I'd love to."

"You know . . . there's never been a right time to say what I should have said . . . about what happened when we were out diving. Thank you, Christa. Things looked pretty bad."

She held his eyes, honest eyes now, maybe even gentle eyes.

"Better you get to eat the grouper than it gets to eat you," she said, defusing the moment.

"I mean it. Thank you," he said again, his voice earnest. As if to emphasize it, he reached out and laid his hand on top of hers.

"That's okay, Peter."

But was it? His touch was electric, confusing her mind with its shuddering intensity. But he wasn't gripping her hand. His fingers lay across hers, soft as a silk sheet on a hot night. She had amplified the feel of him. The surge tide of adrenaline that flowed within was her production, not his. But it was so wonderful it mustn't stop. She turned her hand around beneath his, and their fingers closed together in an embrace as tender as any in her life. For long moments their hands negotiated there, and they stayed still, savoring the moment of togetherness as their souls came close, circling each other around the campfire of emotion that was building, building inside each of them.

"After lunch," he said, his voice small in the storm of feeling, "would you like to come back and see where I live?"

"I think I would," said Christa.

25

It was a writer's house. Its Conch exterior, gingerbread New England, gave way to a bare Bahamanian entrance corridor. There were no pictures, no furniture, nothing to suggest that anybody lived here.

Peter stood back to let her pass. He breathed in as she did so, filling his lungs with her smell. He felt young again, a guilty adolescent doing something a little dirty. He was experiencing her. She didn't know she was being experienced. He was a voyeur in the bushes, feeding from molecules that came from her body. Then, as the thoughts hurried across his mind, he caught himself doing what he always did when faced with a new and exciting situation. He was wondering how he would describe them in a book. Damn! The scribbler wouldn't get lost. However hard he tried, he couldn't get used to the idea that life was for living, not for reading or writing about. It wasn't a research project. It *was* the art. The recording of it was merely incidental, no matter how well it was done.

"Mmmmm. It smells good, like a home," said Christa, her subconscious vibrating in tune with the olfactory currents that swirled in the corridor. It smelled of old wood and new polish, and, now, of Calvin Klein's Obsession because she was there. She turned to face him in the dim light. Where to? It was his house. It was his move.

She tried to keep her excitement bottled. This was crazy. They'd had lunch, a wonderful, magnificent lunch, and he had invited her home, and she had accepted. It wasn't like her. It couldn't be like him. But they had held hands, or rather held fingers, and touch didn't lie. Not that touch. Not those feelings. The future hovered in front of her. How would it happen? Would it happen? She tried to work out what she wanted, but her thoughts wouldn't think to order. There was only the heightened awareness, the strung-out emotion, the jagged edge of threatened sensation.

"Would you like to see where I write?"

He had arrowed to the heart of the matter, and surprised himself in the process. Camille was the only other girl in the world who was allowed into his writing room. It was a secret place, his private part, where he suffered in silent solitude, and where he flew to the peaks of experience. He dreamed dreams in that room from which the world would recoil in helpless horror if they were to be made public. He unleashed ideas in that room that would have been happy in the mind of God. And in between were the mundanities, the ceaseless search for escape, the lists, the doodles, the unwanted coffee, and all the detritus that served as steadfast allies to the empty page.

Christa had an overwhelming desire to say, "I'd like to see where you sleep." It was mammoth in its lack of propriety. It trembled on her lips like an oath in church. She bit them to close them.

"Mmmmmm," she murmured for the second time in a minute. Could she handle this? She didn't seem suited to the job. This was cat and mouse in the jungle. One false step and all could end in a firefight of embarrassment and humiliation. It had to be a cunning guerrilla war. But assault was her usual method of attack, and total offense was her plan for defense, too. The trouble was that Peter Stein's tactics were the same as hers. Somebody was going to have to step out of character, if disaster was to be averted.

He led her up the narrow stairs, their feet clattering on the polished mahogany floor. A long landing was flanked by French doors that overlooked a balcony. A walkway joined the balcony to a separate building that was buried in a mass of dense foliage. The fronds of a banana tree wrapped it, birds of paradise licked like flames at its sides, coconut palms leaned over it, fingering its roof with their leaves as if tickling the back of a lover. This was their destination. Peter opened one of the doors and together they walked out into the midafternoon heat.

Christa kept thinking of children. It was a children's tree house, a Tarzan world, far from civilization, where a child wrestled to turn adult complexity into simple sense. The weathered boards beneath her feet groaned as she stepped on them. The foliage rustled around her like the skirts of starched nannies. A rocking horse, its paint peeled by the rain and the sun, heightened the impression of child's play. Was this the secret of writers and writing? Was it a child's rejection of the grown-up world? Was writing the refuge of the nonconformist who was determined to earn his living far from the petty dictates and preoccupations of lesser mortals and their bizarre institutions? Whatever. She was being invited into his special room, far more intimate than his bedroom. It was a room full of ghosts. She could feel their eerie presence from the terrace where she stood.

The room was locked. The key that Peter pulled from a deep pocket was large, like the key to a medieval keep. He opened the door and stepped inside, looking around furtively, as if unsure that the room was ready for a stranger's eyes. Had he left his socks out? Had he tidied his closets? Would the grown-up visitor complain that toys had been left on the floor as a hazard to feet?

"Here it is."

He stepped back as if baring his soul. He looked around his room. He looked closely at her. Could she see the invisible things that he could see? Could she see all the messes and the dead ends, all the triumphs and the tragedies that lay piled up in the corners? Was it accessible to her? Was *he* accessible to her?

She zeroed in on the neat pile of paper that lay next to the typewriter. She walked toward it. The book lay face down.

"What's this? Your new book?"

"Yes. It is."

"Does it have a name?" Christa wondered if this was the famous unfinished *Dream*.

"Yes. It does." It was better than "What's it called?" Less good than "What's it about?" He swallowed. He had to do better than these monosyllables. "It's called *The Dream I Dreamed.* Hugo," he added. Then, "Victor Hugo."

"The one who wrote the Broadway musical," said Christa with a smile. Perhaps they could laugh about this now. He smiled. They could.

"It's a bit depressing. About how reality unravels the illusion of dreams."

"But you end up knowing things." She laughed.

"Hopefully." He laughed. "Knowing what I know, anyway."

She walked toward him like a model on a catwalk, slow but sassy, calm and confident. She sent her butt swaying in the still air, and she let out the smile that should have had a license. She stopped a foot in front of him.

"Just what *do* you know, Peter Stein?"

He swallowed. She could see his Adam's apple bob. There wasn't meant to be any answer to her question. It wasn't a question. It was an invitation. She stood her ground, daring him to move. He stood still, not daring to. She was inside his space. Her invasion couldn't be ignored. She was the aggressor. It was retreat, or . . . Her beauty mocked his indecision. It was all there, in front of his face, a beauty more real than it had a right to be, close, available, sure not to be available for long. He tried to get his mind right, as the feelings sloshed around inside him. Was he ready for this . . . commitment . . . to this girl from the other side of the universe to his? There was his lover, over her shoulder, staring at him in shock/horror at his potential treachery. Who would dream dreams for the book if reality scored such an early knockout over illusion? The paper screamed its protest. The blank pages howled their agony in his mind. In front of him, the perfect face of the girl was the flesh-and-blood rival to the pulp he had written and the pulp on which he would write. It was now or, perhaps, never. The moment was passing.

"Come and look at my view," he said, his voice mangled. He tore himself from her force field and walked around her to the table. He straightened the perfect rectangle of *Dream,* as if in a gesture of conciliation for his so-near betrayal. He pointed to the window.

Christa followed him. Her heart was beating fast. It had been so close. Deep in his eyes she had seen him want her. A war had been fought there. He had resisted, but he had been weakened by the battle. Now he would be riddled with regret. She looked out of the window at the view he'd wanted her to see. A small pool, sparkling clean, nestled in the exuberant jungle. A hammock dangled between two royal palms. Across the treetops, scattered like paving stones on an ill-kept lawn, were the white roofs of half a dozen houses. It was a metaphor for Key West. Civilization on the edge of the primitive, an uneasy equilibrium between order and chaos, the sort of lonely front-line where the right balance could be kept between looseness and tension, between freedom of imagination and the discipline needed to describe it.

"Can I sit at your table?" she said.

She sat, not waiting for his okay. "This is where it all happens." She was quiet, trying to summon up the feelings he would feel on his lonely mornings above the beckoning pool. He was standing beside her, out of sight, but there, like the shrink hovering at the head of the couch, like the priest in the confessional. She reached out to touch the keys of the typewriter, and she tried to visualize the words forming themselves from nothing on the paper. The only thing her book had in common with his was the word used to describe them. Hers had sold for maybe more than what *Dream* would fetch and yet she would be ashamed to see them standing together on the same bookshelf. Her beauty book had been a self-advertising career move designed to glorify the cult of Christa Kenwood and help sell all the things she wanted sold. His books were the voice of his soul. The difference between their personalities was vast. She was action. He was thought. He had to catch fish down there in the vast depths of the grandest canyon. She recoiled from the enormity of the process. There had to be a simpler way of struggling through life. Hers was simple. She made goals and she hammered balls through them. Lots of sweat, but no problem. He struggled with motivation, and what targets and why targets, and he knew when he found a question and an answer that there were a trillion other worthy questions, and a quadrillion other better answers, and an infinite number of ways to capture them in words.

"It isn't easy, is it?" she said to him.

"Not for ease our prayer should be."

"But for courage."

"If it doesn't sound too pretentious."

"How much do you get for them? Up front, I mean. Loot. Big ones. How does this shit pay?"

She changed the subject, brutally. She didn't really know why. Was her crudeness a form of self-defense, the attack she favored when threatened? For a second there, she had questioned herself. She had wondered deep down if maybe Peter Stein was a superior being to herself, and that line of thinking was a Christa Kenwood no-no. Now, she twisted the art thought to cash talk, and she didn't care if the conversation squeaked in pain. It was okay. Artists might suffer, but the successful ones got paid and paid well. Chipping coal out of rock a mile down wasn't exactly harp strumming on cloud nine. What was the big deal about butt-sitting in a house with a pool, letting your mind hang out for money? A chance would be a fine thing for most of struggling humanity. Yes, maybe Stein's prayer for courage *was* pretentious. Maybe *he* was pretentious. She swiveled around in the chair to face him and find out.

He was smiling at her. He was ahead of her. He had her drift.

And it seemed he was relieved. The goddess was flawed after all. Insecurity had poked its head above the glacial surface of her sea.

"I don't take an advance. I get royalties afterward. I like it better that way. It takes some of the pressure off."

"You're joking."

"I'm not. It's unusual, but some people do it. Updike does."

Christa's attack as defense petered out. There was a new emotion. Disbelief. Bewilderment. Stein was an important writer, but she was an ace businesswoman. Not to take an advance would make zero business sense. It offended against her natural order of things in the way that an unwieldy sentence might offend against his.

"But Peter, your books are best sellers. You have to be worth a premium to the publishers over and above what you earn as a percentage on book sales. And you're a serious author. I mean, your stuff isn't trash. It's a prestige deal for any publisher to have you. Other writers will want to go with the house that publishes you. Agents will think of your publisher first when they have a hot project. I mean, you must know all that."

He waved it away with his hand, in a gesture that seemed to be waving away her life and her values.

"I can't get interested in all that," he said with a laugh.

"What does your agent say?" If the incompetent is capable of speech, thought Christa.

"I don't have one."

She shook her head. Okay, here was the Achilles' heel. The guy who could shift the art couldn't cut the deal. There wasn't anything new about that. Having your head in the clouds didn't give the best vantage point to see what was going on in the gutter. What the hell did she mean . . . "gutter"? Business wasn't the sewer. It was the sidewalk where the real people lived. People like her. The people who bought the books of the fake people, the pretentious people, the pompous people. She took a deep breath. She was winding herself up again. But why? To escape from the thought traps she kept allowing herself to fall into. Peter had hardly said a thing. This whole conversation was being driven by her.

"Is that wise?"

Somehow she managed to wash the scorn out of her question. At the end of the day, *she* was an agent. It hurt not to be needed, but it was never cool to let that show.

"Probably not, but it's the way I work." He nearly stopped there, shutting her out. But he didn't want to shut her out. "I have a wonderful editor, who understands me and my work, if that's possible. And World has been a superb, supportive publisher. I don't need a middleman. And I don't need any more money. It sits about as it is in dreadful dull things that bankers and accountants know about. It just gets in the way."

"The servant who did the safe thing on the talents didn't exactly shine with his master," said Christa.

"I don't have a master . . . or a mistress."

She'd walked into that one. The coldness had left his voice. He was amused again. He was playing with her and he was winning. Christa could feel the red high up on her cheeks.

"The way I see it is this. In any financial deal there's a winner and there's a loser. Somebody does better out of it than somebody else. If you don't make them pay top dollar for your books, they are richer and you are poorer. You owe it to yourself to get the best deal you can. Who cares about the money? You can give it away if you like. Hell, you can even give it back to *them.* I just can't bear the idea of someone laughing at me, and thinking he's smarter than I am."

"Ah, so that's what you can't bear, is it, Christa Kenwood? I was wondering when I was going to find that out."

"Don't you feel like that?"

"Maybe it's a mistake to imagine that other people are exactly like you."

"They are."

She was deadly serious, so serious that he had to laugh. Her face was turned up toward him. Her jaw stuck out. He always imagined he'd cornered the market in egotism. Apparently not. Christa's world began and ended with herself. Others existed only insofar as they mirrored her thoughts and opinions. Was that self-respect or the sin of pride? The answer was unequivocal. It was self-respect, and the thing that made it so was charm. She was awash with the stuff. It sprayed from her eyes. It dripped from her lips. It floated in the air around her, a magic mist of attraction that made her words irrelevant and her body beautiful overkill. He reached forward to her shoulder and he touched her.

"They are, aren't they?" she persisted, but the smile was already turning up the corners of her mouth.

"If you say so," he said. His voice was low now. He wouldn't fight her anymore. He would love her.

She reached up for his hand, closing hers over it, and allowing her smile to spread. They were together again. The little wars brought them close, pushed them apart. She knew it would be like this, with them. They were the same people in different worlds doing different things. They were both strong and fierce. Both were bullies, short-tempered, but deeply honest and unashamed, proud of their honesty and independence. They would rush to disagree. They would not shirk pain. They would hammer at each other until each could fight no more. But at the end of the day they were equals, and the firm foundation of their fatal attraction would be unshakable admiration.

She stood up to face him, as she would always face him, and the song in her heart was a slow, sweet melody because of what they would do now, because of what they would become.

He held her waist as she moved in toward him. His breath shuddered from his body as she closed against him. She pushed her breasts to his chest, and he pushed back, loving the feel of them. Her lips, like a mirage, were in front of his. Thirsty, he bent down to them. He took them greedily, unable to be gentle, because he had temporarily forgotten how to love. She stood before him, glowing in the privacy of his inner sanctum. He felt the power of ownership course through him. He would take her now, this girl who had fascinated him, and infuriated him, who had intrigued him and saved him. They had ridden the roller-coaster ride to intimacy. Now it was time for rewards, punishments, and all the ambiguous ecstasy of the war of bodies. He moved one hand to capture her head, fearful she would try to escape him. The other was behind her neck, buried in the richness of her hair. He crushed her lips with his, and he opened his mouth, forcing his tongue on her, bending her head back to feed from her. She didn't fight him. She fought to be devoured by him. Her own mouth opened wide, and she tangled her tongue with his, and they splashed together in the wet bath of love.

Her hands moved to his waist, to the front, to his hard stomach. She reached down, and at the same time she stood up on her toes to drown in the liquid kiss. He was hard everywhere . . . his bottom, his thighs, the muscular arms that wrapped her tight in the womb of longing. She could feel him against her legs. Rampant, unashamed, he pushed and thrust against her through the irrelevance of clothes. He drank from her mouth and radiated the heat of his desire through her trembling body. They battled in the kiss, trying to become each other, to climb inside each other's body in the blissful union that would be the end of self. They were wanton, making damp noises of passion, past embarrassment, lost in lust, as they ground together in this their first embrace. The urgency was total. This contract must be signed in the warm blood of love. They must merge, and commit, and learn the ultimate secrets, so that never again could they be strangers. After love, there could be hate, there could be anything, but it could never be subtracted from experience. This moment would live on in both their lives, unforgotten, perhaps even unforgiven, but undeniable, like day and night and the beauty of holiness.

Through the mists of longing, Christa tried to understand what was happening. Who had done this? Peter? Had she? The answer was that *they* had done it. They had moved together, drawn by the gravity of stars, unstoppable, each irresistible, as they had hurried destiny. Their attraction was monumental. She was ablaze with passion, wanting only to drown in the sweat of this man's need. He must own every inch of her and use her for the pleasure that would double as her own. A delicious humility flowed in her veins. He could break her in two with his arms. His mouth could tear her apart. He had become a body, no longer a mind, and she was soft for his hardness and dry for his wetness, and strong in her longing for the communion that would come. She rubbed herself against him. Lewd and lascivious, she moaned her joy, muffled in the prison of his throat. Her hands reached for him, desperate for the rawness of touch. Her skirt hitched up her legs, pushed by the friction, crushed and crumpled already by the making of their love. She thrust against him. Her panties were slippery around the furnace that screamed for him, and he crushed blissfully against her, reaching down now to her straining butt, holding her buttocks, forcing her pelvis against the part of him that needed her. He pulled up her skirt to her waist, his mouth still plundering hers. His hands roamed over her silken panties, marveling at the firmness of her muscles, at the smooth hot skin of her lower back, of her upper thigh. His fingers dipped down into the silk and traced the contours of her butt. They wandered to the edge of the cleavage, sticky already with the sweat of Christa's passion. He held the tight flesh, his fingers on her buttocks. He drew her closer. His hardness thrust at her panties, sliding on the dampness, threatening and promising the so-soon future.

She could bear it no longer. She fumbled for the opening, her fingers foraging for the buttons. She forced her forefinger into the slit of the material and tore upwards freeing the fly. She reached in, and she found him, hot and hard and huge in her hand. She wrapped her fingers around him, encasing the violent strength, the leaping, throbbing tautness of the part of him she wanted. He moaned in the kiss, not resisting her, his eyes closed to focus on the beauty of her touch. She freed him from his shorts, and now he was against her thigh, skin on skin, blood rushing against blood. She reached for him with her other hand, one on the back of him, one on the front, as if trying to cage him forever, for her alone. Then she guided him to her wetness. She rubbed him gently against the front of her panties, soothing his heat with her liquid, damping his fires with the wetness of her lust. She breathed in, savoring the scent of her own longing, and she pushed away from him with her upper body, withdrawing her lips from his. She wanted to watch him at this moment. He stared hungrily into her eyes. His mouth was parted and wet from hers. His breath panted through bared teeth. His chest was heaving.

His arms were around her waist, holding her there, and she swayed back and away from him, pushing in with her butt below, so that the distance that separated them at the top was balanced by the closeness that joined them below. Now, she moved him as she pleased. She was the conductor of the orchestra of his want. She rubbed him against the scented skin of her thigh, slick with lust. She imprisoned him between her legs, squeezing him tight. Then, loosening her grip, she allowed him to slide free only to take him once more into captivity. She held the shaft of him, and rubbed the point against her core. She buried it in silk until it sank millimeters into the glistening heartland, separated only by the sheath of panties from the home it wanted so desperately. He reared against her, trying to tear the material and sink deep into the warm welcome of her liquid body. But she stopped him, driving him onward, upward, until his rushing blood screamed its protest in the ever expanding prison that contained it.

His legs buckled with the strain as he thrust out at her. The smile of longing on her face comforted him. Soon this ecstasy would end, and a greater glory would begin. He had never wanted like this. He wanted to see her body. He wanted to know every inch of it, every detail, to find the wonderful imperfections that would give new reality to her beauty. He wanted to see her breasts, naked, revealed, defenseless before his probing vision. He wanted to touch the nipples of this girl, to hold them, hot and tight in his mouth so that his tongue could love them, and he could feel them grow in wonder. He wanted to lay his cheek against the flat of her stomach and to dip his tongue into the sweet mystery of her navel. He wanted to be in all her forbidden places, at home, in his home, until her body belonged to him as completely as it did to her. There would be time for all that later. In sleepy slow time they would discover each other, and every longing would be satisfied as desire turned to love. But now there was necessity. He had to have her. He had to have her now, screaming her surrender as he flowed into her and anointed her with the passion that would signal a brand-new day. So he moved forward, forcing her back across the room. Still tied in his arms, her back was against the edge of the table. She felt it. Her eyes widened. She willed him to do what he must do.

"Yes," she murmured. It was a groaning, moaning acquiescence in passive passion. This man would own her for these minutes. When they were done, she would be his and he would be hers. There was no time, no inclination, for gentler love. She wanted him now. Before it was too late. While it was so early. She didn't want a bed. She didn't want soft music, softer talk, and plans for the future. She wanted to be taken, standing up, fully clothed, with her back on the table where he wrote his art. She wanted to be had there and then, howling her relief, and she wanted the memory of the moment he entered her to linger in this room. Later he would not be able to be in it without thinking of her, nor to leave it without regretting that she wasn't there. She would leave the imprint of her joy on the molecules of his room, and from now on his lonely slavery would be further tortured by thoughts of her. She reached down and hooked her hands into the elastic of her panties. She pushed them down her trembling legs, to the knees, freeing herself for him. Then she put both hands behind her on the table for support and she waited. Sweat beaded on her brow and on her upper lip. It ran like a river beneath her arms and on her stomach. It merged in harmony with the juice of her lust on her inner thighs.

He reached down and held himself, positioning himself at her eager opening. He looked down in wonder at her bared lips of love, glistening petal pink in the mound of blond hair. He guided the tip of him to her. He rested there in dread anticipation of a pleasure more complete than he had ever known. It was too good. There was no right to this. To take it would be to lose the moment. So he waited long seconds, drinking in the magic. He was more focused than he had ever been, yet more humble as he contemplated the joy that was about to be unleashed.

"Please," she whispered.

"Yes," he said, once, sharply. He plunged into her, past the shy portals of velvet longing, pinning her to the wood at her back, pushing deep, deepest into the place that was already his own. He rammed against the soft roof of her, lifting her body from the floor with the fierce force of his entry. The air exploded from her lungs, as the momentum took her. Her hands gripped the table. Her knuckles were white with the strain as she rode him.

Her eyes widened in wonder at the feeling. Her body had been invaded and it was no longer hers. It existed to surround the conqueror. She felt the incredible tightness, the sensation of being whole at last. She touched the ground only by tiptoe, a voyager rocketing to stars that were already exploding in her brain.

Her orgasm was instant. It pealed from the clouds of bliss in a flash of lightning and a bang of thunder that rocked her soul as she battled to stay standing. Her legs shook with the force of it. Her mouth opened and she shouted his name to tell him what was happening, to say sorry it was so soon. "Oooooooooooh!" It went on and on, rumbling in her bowels, darting to her toes and the tips of her fingers. Her blood boiled in her arteries. The tears of passion rolled down her cheeks. The fountain of ultimate pleasure played around the center of her joy.

The instant it was over, it started to build once more. He had hardly moved. One terrible thrust, one single-minded invasion, and she had fallen into the jingle-jangle moment of total abandon. But now, she could feel him shift inside her, surfing on the foaming sea of love she had unleashed. He moved back, forward, still far from a rhythm, but an explorer now in the silky depths of her, sliding on the waves of her lust in the search for yet more sensation. She tried to move around him, retreating as he advanced, pushing back as he withdrew, but her balance made a slave of her. She was caught deliciously between the rock of his power and the hard place that was the table at her back.

She signaled to him with her desperate eyes. She wanted to sink down to the floor, to be taken by him there. She wanted to fight back in the love war. She wanted to give as well as to receive.

He lowered her down. His strong arms were beneath her soaked body, taking the weight of her, and he was still inside her. Her right arm swept across the smooth surface of the writing table as she surrendered her balance to him. She couldn't control it, and it caught against the edge of the neat pile of paper. *The Dream I Dreamed* crashed down, a ticker-tape confetti, floating, cascading, flying to the floor.

For a second, panic gripped her.

No other thing could stop the love, but this.

But he didn't hesitate. He knew what he was doing, and he did it. Slowly, with tenderness, he lowered his lover onto a floor covered like a sheet with the pages of his precious novel. She felt the pages beneath her butt. She felt one buckle up, soaked already by her wetness, crumpling in the crevice of her bottom. Oh no! Oh yes! There was a defiant gleam in his eye, a crazed awareness of what would be done. He lay her down on the shroud of his art, and his hands slid on the papered floor on either side of her torso. She lifted up her legs and wrapped them around him, opening herself wider. She tried to work out what was happening, and immediately she knew. Here, now, she was more important to him than his work. Yesterday, tomorrow, that had not been, and might not be. But now it was the truth. The meaning of his symbolic action was crystal clear. The love they were making was on the pages that once he had loved more than anything.

"Oh, Peter," she moaned. In answer, he pushed gently into her.

"It's all right, Christa," he whispered. "It's all right."

26

"I don't know."

On a moonlit night, at a sidewalk table at the News Café, the nucleus of South Beach's social life, Rob Sand looked like he didn't know. But it didn't matter. His knowledge was not his point. At least, that was what Lisa Rodriguez thought. She had never seen him look more beautiful. She leaned across the table so that he could see the sunburned nipples beneath her dress, and she smiled a devilish smile.

"Rob, believe me. Believe Steve Pitts. Hell, believe Christa. She *really* wants the best for you. You know she does. Okay, Steve fancies you. I fancy you. We're not bullshitting you, but I guess you could question our motives. But Christa, I mean, you trust Christa's judgment, don't you?"

It was difficult for Lisa to get another woman's name past her lips, especially sandwiched between a couple of compliments. Somehow she managed it. Needs must when the devil drove, whatever that meant. Anyway, Christa wasn't a rival. Christa was cooled out way up there on some ambition cloud of her own, with no time for the distractions that Lisa lived for. Christa was maybe the second-best-looking girl in the cosmos, but emotionally she belonged to some dead limey. That suited Lisa just fine.

"Yeah, I do believe Christa. I mean, you, too, and Mr. Pitts, but Christa's kind of . . . oh, I mean, like pure."

"And I'm not pure," purred Lisa.

Rob looked surprised, not realizing at first what he'd said.

"Oh, yes, I'm sure you are, Lisa, but Christa really understands. When she talked to me about the modeling, she really sympathized with my problems. And we talked for hours, about everything. My past, my ambitions, about God."

"You did?" Already Lisa was regretting the good press she'd given Christa. "Never speak well of a woman" had always been her motto. Now she'd broken her first commandment and it had rebounded on her.

"What else did you talk about?" she asked quickly.

"What do you mean?" He sipped at his Coke.

"What do you think I mean?" The Rodriguez lips, which had once been an invitation to a fun party, were now as amusing as a writ in a restaurant.

"I don't know what you mean." He laughed. "I don't know what you mean a lot of the time. You talk in riddles."

"I mean, do you want to get in Christa's pants?" She tried to keep the snarl from her voice. She barely succeeded. Hiding her feelings wasn't Lisa's strong suit.

"That's a terrible thing to say," said Rob. He was shocked, and he looked it.

"I didn't *say* anything. It was a question, Rob. Do you want to ball her? Do you dream of screwing her? Do you pray for a chance to take her panties off?"

"I don't have to sit here and listen to this," he said. He stood up. He looked stricken. The people at the next table, almost sitting in their lap anyway, were transfixed. They knew who Lisa was. Now the young male model was going to walk on her, and she was jealous. Jeez! This was Page Six in the making. Musto and Saban would love it. How much did Norwich pay? Could the Christa they were talking about *possibly* be Christa Kenwood?

She reached out and held his hand.

"I'm sorry, Rob. I'm really sorry. Don't go. Forgive me." She wondered about a God botherer's buzz phrase like "Have mercy," but she held it back as a reserve.

He allowed himself to be drawn back to the table, but he was confused. Lisa was Lisa. She was a bombe surprise on a short fuse. She said terrible things all the time and then forgot she'd said them, or didn't mean them, or both. She wasn't deep-down bad, she was naughty, like a bored but energetic child. The Lord would forgive Lisa because she didn't mean to hurt. Anyway, she was fun, and an education, and she cooked things with his hormones that he didn't know could exist. But she had reached him on the Christa thing. Why? Because a part of it was true. Christa was special. She was like an angel, an embodiment of the kinder and gentler America that everyone was looking for in vain. She was clever, and brilliant and maybe a little bit ruthless, but somehow that wasn't what you saw. More important, it wasn't what she made you feel. And forget "you." He was thinking about him. Yes, he liked Christa more than he knew. Lisa had opened the private box with the key of her crudity. Rob loved the way Christa listened to him, her quietness, her peace. He liked the way she could discuss God without being embarrassed, and without sneering. Morals for her were real, not something you learned in an ethics course at college. She was on his wavelength, and when she had begged him to give modeling a try, he had been persuaded. And yes, he was aware of how she looked. He knew all about the serene beauty of her face, the smile that God had given her and her alone, the body that swam like a mermaid and moved with the slinky grace of a serpent in the garden. He didn't want to ball her, screw her, and pull down her panties. But maybe he did want to lie with her beside some bubbling river and talk to her, warmed by sunlight, their fingers touching, their bodies close, the scent of her breath on his face, the sound of her words caressing his ears. And he wanted very much to take her to his church. He wanted to stand beside her in the chapel of the First Baptist down by the lake and watch the sun set over the Everglades, as the lights twinkled in Palm Beach and the yachts moved slowly in the twilight on the Intracoastal waterway. He wanted to pray with her and for her, and to be with her.

Rob sat down as the bombs that were his thoughts exploded in his brain. His life was changing, all at once. The simple had become complex. The future was dangerous, but infinitely more exciting than it had ever been.

It had to do with the people. It was impossible to know what motivated Lisa, and Mary Whitney and Christa. They lived their lives as if they were chased by demons, chasing moonbeams, at a frantic pace and with a barely controlled desperation. His life had never been like that. Back in Okeechobee it had defined peace, and certainty, the decent poverty of a family that lived for God. He worshiped his father, a carpenter who had never said a cruel word or thought an unpleasant thought, and he adored his mother, a kind, gentle woman who had never asked for anything or regretted a moment of her dear, sweet life. All Rob had ever wanted was to be like them, and to be close to the God they loved. There had never been the remotest question of rebellion. Against what, and for what possible reason? He felt no need to assert his individuality. He had no need for money, success, for material things. The Lord had always provided and would continue to do so. It was a matter of trust.

But here, near to this wild strange woman, the will of the Lord, his own will, seemed weaker. In the ordinary way that would have been cause for alarm, and perhaps it was, but it was wonderful, too.

Lisa watched him closely. Jealousy had sent her over the top. Had she retrieved the situation? She hoped so, because she intended this night to be a fiesta and a movable feast rolled into one. Hemingway couldn't write this evening. *She* was going to. *A Moveable Fiesta.* Rob was about to be introduced to South Beach, the most exciting café crawl in America and the hot spot of the future, and he was going to be shown it on the arm of the girl that Miami worshiped. She just prayed she hadn't pooped her own party.

"It's okay, Lisa. It's the way you say things. I guess I'll get used to it. My folks would have been devastated if I'd said things like that."

"You were lucky. My folks wouldn't have been listening."

She bit her lip. Her dad would have listened. But she'd been so young then. The memories of him were blurred and, however much she tried to sharpen them, they faded. The horror was far stronger than the warmth. He had died, and the guilty had lived. It was the only argument against God she knew. But in the absence of Divine retribution she had filled the vacuum, and now the slate was clean, apart from the pain inside, the pain in a little girl's heart that wouldn't go away.

"God is always listening," said Rob gently.

"In this life you have to be your own God," said Lisa dismissively. She wanted out of the God chat. That was asking for trouble. What she wanted was what all girls wanted. She just wanted to have fun. Now. And fuck the future and fuck the past. And later, when the night turned to day and SoBe tired, she wanted to fuck this boy on the sand by the sea. The early risers on the balconies of the Art Deco hotels could watch. Shit, that wasn't so much for a virgin to ask.

"So what are we going to do tonight?" said Rob. He, too, didn't want God drawn into the evening. One day he would show Lisa how to love God. The time was not now.

She brightened.

"Well, it has to be carefully managed like all the very best spontaneous evenings. We have some more drinks here and watch the paseo. Then, around nine, we go eat at Mezzanotte, and we drink some wine. Then we go play billiards if we're not too zoned, and we walk some more, and then we sit around at Sempers and listen to Lola sing, and we find some friends maybe and hang out, and then we all go dancing at Warsaw. After that, it's kind of optional. Decisions sort of make themselves by that stage."

"I've never seen anything like this place. I was down here seven years ago and it was like a no-go zone. What happened?" said Rob.

"Isn't it great? The Philly mob turned it around. They bought some hotels on Ocean Drive, put in some loot, restored the Art Deco stuff, and the crack dealers and street trash wafted away. I *wonder* why. It's funny, 'cause the Philadelphia guys always had the reputation as the mob that couldn't shoot straight. Anyway, the whole thing hung in the balance until maybe early 'eighty-nine and then bingo, critical mass and now this."

She waved at the crowds that bobbed along the sidewalk past their table. They were pretty people, and when they weren't that pretty they were state of the trend. It looked like Prince Street on a good day. It was the sixties Kings Road updated, Ibiza at its zenith, Marbella before the Arabs. You could pick out the models. They walked tall and proud in a way that transcended their beauty, surrounded by the powerful aura of their physical self-respect. Everyone knew to wear black, even the Germans and the Scandinavians who made up a large percentage of the photographic contingent. The guys wore round glasses with metal frames, hair was pony-tailed, ears were ringed. All walked slowly, going everywhere, going nowhere, and the leisurely pace of the crowd came all the way from Spain via South America. The homegrown Americans had picked it up, but it was foreign still, an attitude that clung to Miami like the smell of Cuban cigars to an empty room.

"I've never seen so many models in one place."

"I heard there are ten separate crews down here . . . everyone from Patrick Desmarchelier and Grace Coddington doing a *Vogue* shoot to Swedish magazines you've never heard of. New York is still bigger, but the models get lost there. Here, it's like ten blocks. You walk out of your hotel room and you're part of the party. Hey look, there's Mona."

There was Mona. She was swinging along like a panther on uppers, trailing a swarthy Arab who looked like a lesser pet.

Mona saw Lisa the second Lisa saw her.

"Lisa, baby, great to see you, honey. You look like sweet dreams." She towered over the table, her legs like stilts, her tits a tent over their heads. The scent of her rained down from heaven.

Lisa's eyebrows shot up. This was the Rossetti main squeeze. At least she had been last week. But Lisa was now a Rossetti enemy, so why was Mona coming on like gangbusters? To impress the Arab, probably. Yes, that would be it. One thing was for sure. The "great to see you/sweet dreams" jive was gush slush. In the normal way, Mona wouldn't put Lisa out with piss if she spontaneously combusted, and vice versa. Still, tonight was party night and parties needed people, even if you didn't like them.

"This is Rob," said Lisa briskly. "And this is Mona. Mona works at the agency I used to be at. I guess you're the top girl there, Mona, aren't you . . . *now?*"

Mona laughed to say she'd caught the gibe and was letting it go. She held out a hand for Rob's. Flames flicked from her eyes. He stood up. "It's nice to meet you," he said, as if he meant it.

"You can sit down, Rob," said Lisa.

"Oh, and this is Abdul. I can't do his second name. It sounds like you're clearing your throat. He keeps a yacht at Lauderdale. One with bedrooms."

Lisa looked Abdul up and down. Later he'd ask her to adorn the boat with bedrooms. Arabs always did. Who knew? For a fifty-grand ring, she might throw one his way. He smiled slyly at her, not at all put out by his introduction.

"Hi, Abdul," was all Lisa gave him up front.

"It is an honor," he lisped. Lisa smiled. He'd gotten one thing right.

She turned to Mona.

"How's Johnny?" she said. She was always happiest at the heart of the matter.

"Not happy right now, honey. You know that enemy list he always raps on about. You and Christa are equal number one. 'Nuff to make you squirm in your shoes, ain't it?" She laughed cheerfully to show that her enemy list didn't dovetail with Rossetti's.

"You want to sit down, Mona, and join us?"

"Sure, baby. Let's party."

Abdul was clearly a meal ticket without a vote. But he seemed grateful to be in the Rodriguez orbit. He drew back a chair for Mona and eyed Lisa while he did so. Rob looked at Mona. Mona looked at him. Lisa looked at both of them.

"Mona's a Buddhist," she said suddenly, to everyone's obvious surprise.

"And myself, I am a follower of the prophet Muhammad, and young Rob a Christian unless I am much mistaken, and possibly Lisa a Catholic. So we are an ecumenical council here in Miami," said Abdul, pouring oil on waters that looked as if they'd acquired trouble from somewhere.

There was a nervous silence. Mona wasn't looking at Rob anymore. Rob wasn't looking at Mona. In her own inimitable way, Lisa had just ordered both of them not to.

"Let's have some drinks," said Lisa, signing the peace treaty.

Abdul clicked his fingers. A stunning micro-skirted waitress was there immediately.

"What about some champagne?" said Abdul. All religions managed to agree on that.

"So, what's Johnny doing about it?" said Lisa.

"Oh, you know Johnny, same old Johnny. Drinkin' and thinkin'. Schemin' and dreamin'. I don't go for his jive no more. All that 'baaaaad white boy' shit don't play with us black dudes from the deepest part of the pit."

"Come on, Mona, wasn't your dad a doctor?"

"Whatever. Johnny's pissed, and he ain't nice to be near. That's the truth. I'm outta there."

"You walked on Johnny?" There was respect in Lisa's tone.

"Better believe I walked."

"Out of the agency, too?"

"Yeah, out of the agency," said Mona. She sounded defiant. The champagne arrived.

"You going to Ford's? Elite?"

"I'm going to get high, honey. An' I'm goin' to let Abdul take me to the Abacos. An' I'm going to listen to *his* crap for a week or two before I get sick of it."

Abdul joined in the general laughter, clearly enjoying the irreverence. You didn't hear stuff like that wafting out from behind a veil in Arabia.

Rob leaned across the table, eager to be of assistance in a stranger's hour of need.

"You ought to join Christa's agency," he said. "It's just starting, and I know Christa wants lots more models."

"She does?" said Mona. She looked at Lisa. Was the toy boy allowed to say things like that? Were they worthy of airtime?

"Yeah, maybe. I think Christa's looking. You could give her a try. She's down in Key West with Steve scouting locations for a Mary Whitney campaign. She'll be back tomorrow," said Lisa without enthusiasm.

It was cold water, but not ice water. Lisa was number one, but she was realistic enough to realize she couldn't be the only one. Anyway, as a black girl, Mona wouldn't be direct competition. And it would be another one in the eye for Johnny. His own screw, going to Christa and underwritten by some camel jockey with billions and a boat with bedrooms. It wasn't the very best joke in the world, but it tickled her sense of humor.

"Where does she hang out?" said Mona, trying not to appear too interested.

"The agency has an office in the Central. Christa has a house on Star Island. If you do mornings, you could drop in. She's back late tonight."

"Isn't this fun?" said Abdul, raising his glass. "To all of us. To Mona's career, and to your agency, and down with Mr. Rossetti, who is not really a gentleman."

He waved his glass in the air as if it were a wand that would make

Rossetti go away and cement the brilliant future of the sitters at the table.

"Yeah," said Lisa. "I'll drink to that." As she did so, she realized that yes, she was having fun, and that there would be more fun to come. Lots of it.

Rob, who didn't drink much except the occasional Bud, joined in the toast, and the bubbles fizzed on the way down and the moonlight caught Lisa's profile, and the soup inside him started to simmer. He breathed in the heady atmosphere of South Beach and wondered why Abdul was smiling at him and he looked across at Mona who was moving like a snake to the Muzak, clicking her fingers and boogeying in a way that he found charming and very un-Florida, and he, too, realized that he was having a good time, and that it was going to get better.

"Blame it on the bossa nova," said Mona, swaying to the rhythm and thinking how brilliantly she had achieved her objective and how thrilled Johnny would be. Tomorrow she would infiltrate the Christa Kenwood agency. In her role as the viper in its bosom, she would have nothing to do but to wait for the command to sting.

"Blame it on the bossa nova," she sang, "the dance of love."

27

Lisa Rodriguez led the way into Mezzanotte. It was the only way to fly. This was fame's top trick, the provision of restaurant tables when there weren't any. It made the supermarket tabloids bearable. The guy at the lectern had his standard speech ready about booking and waiting at the bar. It died in his bull neck as the supermodel flounced in. Her butt grinding like a pepper mill, she stalked up to the maître d'. All around, the Miami cognoscenti slipped into recognition mode. The decibels of the restaurant's conversational hum were decimated.

"Miss Rodriguez," he said, washing his hands as if they were dirty. "Wonderful to see you."

She deigned to know him, and extended a silken cheek. The maître d' hit heaven. He leaned forward to accept the peck as if it were the sacrament. She said nothing as she made flesh contact with the minion, and she looked at the ceiling as if she were suffering for England. He stood back, his face flushed by the brush with fame, and then the trouble started. Lisa Rodriguez came with a party of four. They had to have a brilliant table, but there weren't any. The bar was four deep with drunken desperadoes, their stomachs rumbling and their pride melting. Everyone who'd scored a table at the hottest restaurant in America apart from Mortons was hanging on to it for dear life. The lingerers were drinking so much coffee they risked caffeine psychosis. None of them would sleep for a week after this. But still they ordered drinks, and more stimulants, and they laughed and shouted, and rubber-necked and hung out, chockablock full of the joy of being in the right place at the right time. A look of steely determination crept over the maître d's face. A table of losers would have to be found and removed. It was as simple as that. Would they go quietly? Who knew? Shit, who cared?

He stared around the crowded restaurant. The pretty people couldn't be removed, nor the less pretty locals, nor the drug guys who spent cash like water and ran on short tempers. What he needed were some tourists who'd fallen on the place by chance in the early hours before it was full, and who'd overstayed their welcome. His eyes lighted on a middle-aged couple with no suntans. That was a no-no on South Beach unless you were a night person from the Big Apple, where you were allowed to look like a ghost.

"Ms. Rodriguez, if you would have a drink with us while I organize your table, I would be most honored," he said.

"Okay, champagne," she said without smiling. "French," she added.

He scurried away to do her bidding. She looked at Rob, standing like a god at her side. Half the restaurant were doing the same thing . . . the female half. But Lisa didn't mind. He was hers. He just didn't know it yet.

"You booked?" said Rob. He'd missed it all.

"I'm permanently booked." She laughed. "Stick with me, darling. You'll never go hungry."

"Or thirsty," said Abdul, thoroughly encouraged by the whole business. In the capital cities he frequented, he stuck to the restaurants where they knew him and his money. Otherwise, he was just a greasy nobody. Now he was basking in fame's reflected glory. Lisa's price had just gone up. A week on the boat for an afternoon at Cartier. Less wouldn't hack it. No way.

"Well, la-di-da, Ms. Rodriguez," said Mona. "Ain't you the homecoming queen 'round these parts?" She couldn't resist the implication that this was a Miami thing and that Lisa couldn't deliver the bacon outside the boondocks.

"Lucky we're not in Palm Beach county," said Lisa. "We'd have run into problems. You wouldn't have gone with the color scheme up there."

"Ha! Ha!" laughed Abdul.

"They don't really do Arabs either," said Lisa. She was smiling now, the reassuring smile of the psychopath with a sharp ax. Only Rob was safe. She slipped her hand into his as the champagne arrived.

Abdul was bulletproof. He laughed. "Actually, my king has a house on Palm Beach," he said. Nobody bothered to ask him who his king was.

Conversation in the restaurant had regained its momentum, but shifted its subject. Now everyone was talking about Lisa. The men and the great-looking girls thought she looked better in "real life." When you were a beauty, you didn't have to be a beast. The nearly pretty girls thought she was a disappointment, while the plain ones thought any conversation about models was dull, and could it please be moved onto something more interesting. Nobody was neutral, but everyone was watching her, and muttering about burned parents, megabuck deals, and who the hell was the guy by her side with the balls to be scoring her?

The tourists were being bundled away. The table was being made up in record time.

"Anybody got any blow?" said Mona.

"Can that stuff around me," said Lisa sharply, for Rob as much as for anyone.

They sashayed through the diners like the wedding group through a respectful congregation. The waiters buzzed around the table. The group sat down. Lisa and Rob, facing the room, took the pole positions.

"What do you think, Rob?" She put her hand on his knee beneath the table.

"I think it's a pretty excitable place."

The table next door was wired. Three macho medallion men, deep brown from island trips on their Cigarettes, sat with four blondes who would have liked to have been models if they had not been too short, too muscular, too old, or too stupid. One girl was perched on the lap of a guy who was trying to eat his lasagne. From the loudness of her conversation, it was clear that she was zoned. Now she fell off and hit the floor hard. She lay there, quite still. Nobody at her table lifted a finger to help her.

Rob jumped up. Lisa's arm shot out to hold him back. "Sit," she whispered. She knew the score. Sure enough, after a minute or two, the girl got up. Her attention-seeking gesture had bombed. She climbed back onto the lap of her hulk and smiled as if she'd just done Everest. His only concession toward recognizing her return was to shift his fork to the other hand.

"I guess I'm not used to these places," said Rob with a rueful laugh.

"That's the nicest thing about you," said Lisa, her voice rumbling with the distant thunder of desire.

"You been a model long?" said Mona to Rob.

"No. I'm not really a model. Everyone tells me I'm going to be. I'm doing the Whitney campaign," he said.

"Is it something you need training for?" said Abdul. "Or are your good looks enough?" He managed to insinuate that he believed the latter. Lisa looked at him sharply. Okay, Arabs dealt from both ends of the pack, but watch out, sandy gland. Don't play the Saddam Hussein around my boy or I'll nuke you, trust me.

"That's what worries me. But Christa says it'll be fine. I don't know."

"You gotta be able to move it and shake it about, baby, an' the camera gotta like you, gotta love ya. Can't be too shy. Can't be too mean." Mona laughed to disguise her discouraging words.

Rob started again. "Christa . . ."

Mona cut into his sentence. "Christa was okay in her *day,* honey, but Christa ain't seventeen no more. Guess now she's more of a *business* bitch."

"Don't talk that way about Christa around me," said Rob, his face flushing.

"Uh-oh," said Mona. "Listen, I'm not puttin' her down. That's just the way I talk." She smiled like a miner who'd hit a golden streak. She looked at Lisa. She glanced at Abdul. Did the supermodel know that her toy had the hots for Christa Kenwood? If not before, she did now.

Lisa did, now. She reddened, but said nothing. Her mind raced. It had to be a crush thing. Christa wouldn't have encouraged it. Hell, probably even Rob didn't know what he felt. It was nothing, and the body memories were hers. There was no competition. No sweat. Shit! She felt the beads of perspiration form between her breasts. What had happened in the famous Christa/Rob conversation when they had discussed all the usual fatuous topics like God, right and wrong, and the meaning of life? Had the mind masturbation surfaced from the unconscious? Had it hit subconscious? Had it blasted out into the reality of consciousness? Difficult to say, but it needed monitoring. Christa was hovering on the brink of becoming a Lisa Rodriguez rival, and that would make life very interesting for the fledgling Kenwood agency, the Steve Pitts shoot, and Mary Whitney's campaign.

"Where's the wine, Abdul?" she said absentmindedly. She needed a drink. The evening was happening all over the place, and it had hardly started. Mmmmmm. It felt good. She needed aggravation, competition. Ease was too easy. Difficulty was what she liked to chew on. It made winning so much more satisfactory. Her mood brightened. Mary Whitney, the billionairess fashion guru, wanted to bed her boy. Christa Kenwood, the modeling legend and the megabuck-to-be agency panjandrum, was just possibly in the running for his body. And then there was Steve Pitts, who could single-handedly make him a star. Steve had drooled when his gimlet eyes had settled on Rob Sand. Nor should she forget little Abdul, whose boat would be trimmed with gold and other nastiness: little Abdul, the soundless farter whose nocturnal tricks would certainly bridge the gap from AC to DC; from S to M and back again; from the pleasures of a girl's body to the delights of a boy's. Oh, yes, the Rob Sand stakes were filling up, but she was the one to beat. When the gates opened, it would be Lisa Rodriguez, the thoroughbred, who started first; and when the flag came down, she would finish first, too, and the devil would take the also-rans.

"We could have some more champagne," said Abdul, "and the chardonnay looks good. Then we really ought to have some Jordan as the red. Lots of Perrier."

He looked at Lisa as he spoke, eager to please.

"Whatever," she said.

"You know, this place reminds me of Chelsea in the sixties," said Abdul. "The energy, the self-confidence, the fun. There was a place called Alvaro's, and another called the Arethusa. All Italian, noisy, full of beautiful people." His voice went dreamy as he remembered.

"You were *alive* in the sixties," sneered Mona.

"Somebody had to be," replied Abdul with metaphysical calm. He was rather regretting Mona. His distant expression said so. The Rodriguez/Kenwood milieu appeared far more attractive, coming as it did with the remarkable-looking boy who wore his innocence like a spotless djellaba.

"You know," said Abdul, "I've always very much admired Christa Kenwood. I'd love to meet her. Did someone say she was coming to Miami tonight?"

"Yes, she is," said Rob. "She's driving up from Key West. She'll be in the office tomorrow."

"Rob is our local Christa expert," said Mona cunningly.

"I'd love to see your boat sometime," said Lisa in retaliation. She leaned across the table to Abdul as if seeing him for the very first time. He blossomed like a rose on fast film. Lisa smiled at Mona. "Kiss your Abacos trip good-bye, bitch," said her smile. "I can cut off your cash with a flash of my eyes."

"That would be a great honor," said Abdul. "I can have it down in Miami by morning. Or there's a helicopter that could fly you up. Some people think my paintings are rather good."

"You *paint?*" said Mona, furious at Lisa's flanking movement onto her turf.

"I'm sure that Abdul means paintings he bought," explained Rob with a laugh.

"Well, excuse *me,*" huffed Mona. She looked around the table. The venom bubbled inside. She wanted to hurt all of them now. Lisa first. And the white boy who wouldn't know a gutter if he fell in one. And the slimy moneybags she'd found at Au Bar. They had all tried to patronize her in their fashion, and they would all pay for it. Johnny would see to that. Johnny was her man. He was her number-one guy. Whatever he had planned for Christa and Lisa, there would be enough unpleasantness left to pour over the others. And she, Mona, would be his instrument of retribution. But she must move carefully and not forget the game plan. She had to join the Kenwood agency. That was what Johnny wanted. So she mustn't blow it. She must be fun and light and bright, and that meant a toot. There was some in her bag. She didn't like using her own, but this was an emergency. She pushed back her chair.

"Gotta go to the john," she said. She summoned up a dazzling smile from somewhere, and then she was gone.

"In this place, the line for the john must be like for the lifeboats on the *Titanic,*" said Lisa. Rob hadn't a clue what she meant. Abdul smirked.

"Would you like to hear the specials?" said the waiter. Nobody listened to him. The food at Mezzanotte was great but was not its point. The orders were dragged out of them like secrets in a Spanish Inquisition.

"So this is Miami café society," said Abdul, peering around the room as if searching for its essence.

Lisa summed it up for him.

"Yeah, it's odd. Wilder than New York, less sophisticated, more fun, more energy. The Spanish thing gives it Euro-style, but you're allowed to have American things like muscles and suntans. When you go out with a guy you want to know what boat he's got. Forget his car, or what he thinks, or what he does. Everything's on the surface, and it's still Reagan materialism, and fuck finer feelings and all the sensitive crap that everybody else pretends to be into. This place is on the edge of the Third World. The only thing the players want to do is to stick as much cash between them and it as they can without landing in jail."

"Hah," said Abdul. "I should do well. I have quite a long boat, and lots of the material things, but maybe my feelings are a little too fine."

"I wouldn't bet on it," said Lisa.

Rob sipped at his Coke. His mind was still fuzzy from the champagne at the News Café, and that added to the feeling of unreality. He couldn't work out if he'd won the lottery or lost both legs at the knee. It was impossible to say whether the things that were happening to him were good or bad. All he knew was that he had slipped his moorings in the night, and now he was adrift. His conscience, usually a fiercely accurate compass, was all over the place, and the sharp distinction between right and wrong seemed irretrievably blurred. He didn't know exactly at what point it had all changed. He just knew it had. Was it the day he had answered Mary Whitney's tennis coach ad? Or the moment Christa had stalked into the dive shop? Or was it the evening of the party when Lisa and he had made extraordinary love in the tennis pavilion? Maybe it was all of them, dragging him down into the pit of vast success, or was it pushing him up to the pinnacle of possible fame? He tried so hard to keep God in the forefront of his mind, but God kept fading amid the miasma of opportunity, undreamed-of wealth, and heady sensuality. Christa was safe, good, kind . . . but was she? Perhaps she was the worst of all, misleading him for her own purposes in the guise of a friend. No! Christa was pure. She was God-like in her beauty and self-confidence. He could trust her. More. He could love her. The thought lanced into his mind, letting out a torrent of dammed-up emotion. He could see her face, calm, serene, smiling at him, not mocking him. He could see her long brown body, wrapped tight in the scuba gear, her muscles rippling beneath the brown skin with its soft blond hairs. He could hear the subtle drawl of her upper-class accent, smell the honest smell of her, feel the touch of her fingers on his arm as she emphasized a point, as the lazy smile rested on her lips, and his heart speeded in his chest. Christa. In Key West, but coming back tonight.

But the hand on his thigh wasn't Christa's. It was Lisa's. Christa was dreams, illusion, the romance of the forbidden and unobtainable, but Lisa Rodriguez was flesh and blood, here, now. She was frighteningly, deliciously real, an ego trip and an icon, and a body and a face that had no right to be so perfect when they clothed a soul so naughty. Lisa lusted for him. Her every movement was an invitation to the conspiracy of lovers. She smothered him with the juice of her sexual attraction and everyone could see it. Everyone knew that he was her target, the unknown boy from nowhere who the supermodel wanted, who the superstar had so comprehensively had. It was a different kind of wonderful. He was flattered. Was that so strange? The guys at college wouldn't believe this. The guys at the church wouldn't want to. It was too much to resist. He was a junkie in a landscape of snow. God had given him lust, and placed him at an age when lust was a pain that gnawed and twisted at his body. Then God had shown him Lisa and made her want him, and given her all the tricks of the Serpent in the Garden until the fruit on the tree dripped its juices down on him and drove him mad with its sweet aroma. Already he had fallen far from grace, and now he was in danger of falling once again.

"Are you enjoying yourself?" whispered Lisa, rubbing her leg against his under the table, and sending her fingers rippling across his thigh. He nodded, not knowing if it was true, but lost in the enormity of the process, whatever it was. Her breasts rose and fell inside his eyes. They were sliding on the surface of her dress, brown and firm, braless, full and faultless. He could see the beginnings of the nipple he knew he was supposed to see. He remembered it in the shafts of moonlight. It had reared against his tongue. It had filled his mouth and his mind. Slick with his saliva, it had glistened below him as he had entered her, and now it was promising to do so again. He could hear it calling to him. Oh, God, she was beautiful. He swallowed. He felt the sweat break beneath his arms. He felt the hardness begin. He shifted his bottom on the chair, not knowing where to look. Across the table, Abdul was smiling at him. He heard Lisa laugh, because she knew what she could do, what she had done. Her hand was harder on his thigh. Her leg was plastered tight against his.

"Are you all done," said the waiter, "or are you still working on it?"

"Go away," rasped Lisa. But the moment was gone. It had shattered like crystal beneath the rock of banality.

"Moron," snarled Lisa as the waiter retreated in confusion.

"Actually, he's an oxymoron," said Abdul.

"Huh?"

"An oxymoron. A contradiction in terms. There is no more poignant paradox than the American waiter. Your country is horrified by the notion of servitude and so it has elevated bad service to a fine art form. Waiters are the equivalent of gas-pump attendants. They exist merely to facilitate the human fueling process that is considered not a pleasure, but a time-consuming necessity. Points are awarded for doing it fast, safely, and with minimal mess. You 'work' on your food, and you are to be congratulated when you are 'done,' and then you are rushed onto the carbohydrate which is the only thing Americans are interested in anyway. If you relax for a second and talk or give the digestive process a chance to operate, then your plate is snatched from under your nose as if it's a health hazard."

Abdul gave a superior laugh as he delivered his social comment.

"I guess where you come from the trick is to remember not to guzzle the sheep's eyeballs with the hand you used to wipe your butt," said Lisa.

"Ah," said Abdul enigmatically. The noise he made sounded like someone had stuck him with a pin.

Lisa turned to Rob. Could the moment be salvaged?

But Mona was back, talking machine guns, from the john.

"You won't believe what this mother said to me back there. He said if he laid some bucks on me, could I show him a good time. Shit, this loser, he made me so mad." She plunked herself down and turned around to blast Abdul. "If you were the gentleman you pretend to be, you'd go blast that sonofabitch off the face of the planet. You know what I'm sayin'? You hearin' me? Shit, what is this stinkin' place? These dudes crawled outta the swamps. The mother pulled his wad out . . . some dope-dealin' asshole. There he is. There he is." She jumped up and pointed across the room. A vast man-mountain was sitting down at a table of brittle blondes. He smirked across the room at the top table, happy on his turf.

Abdul was bobbing like a cork. His cosmopolitan composure was falling apart. Mona was beginning to look like a bad mistake.

"He's probably drunk. Forget it, Mona. There are idiots everywhere," he tried hopefully.

"Sounds pretty insulting to me," said Lisa wickedly.

Mona's voluptuous mouth was quite suddenly wide as an orange.

"You fucking asshole," she screamed across the room at the guy she'd met in the john. "You fucking piece of dogshit. Go fuck your mother, you hear!"

She was blue beneath the black, leaning into the insults as if she were throwing javelins.

Conversation stopped. There was silence in Mezzanotte. Abdul was white. Rob was leaning forward in his chair. Lisa was smiling broadly.

The maître d' stood paralyzed at his lectern as he tried to assess the damage. The girl from the Rodriguez table was screaming at the dealer from the Grove who dropped a thousand a week in the restaurant. It was as bad as it could be, but it could only get worse. He swiveled his head to the dealer. A joke, maybe. The guy would take it as a joke. Oh, no, he wouldn't. He was hitched around in his chair. His bimbos were watching him.

"Do it to your mother. You got a mother, asshole?" yelled Mona.

He stood up. Somebody dropped a fork. The noise was deafening.

"Shut up," whispered Abdul. "Shut up."

"Cool it, Mona," said Rob. "The guy was probably joking."

But Mona was not cool. She was hottest. Her mind was racing and her blood was pounding, and she had started something that the others would have to finish.

The guy walked slowly across the room. He was big, so big that he had to squeeze between some of the tables. His arms were out by his side because his triceps were vast pads that held them there. He wore a lightweight suit in an unnatural shade of blue, polished, rather pointed shoes, and an outsize Rolex. His hair was long at the back, but very thin on top. As he walked, he cracked his knuckles in the palm of his other hand.

The Mezzanotte silence had reached epic proportions. You could actually *hear* it. Rob watched him come. Abdul sank deeper and deeper into his chair.

He had arrived. He stood behind Rob, staring at Mona and Abdul.

"What did you just say to me?" he said.

Mona was quiet at last. She turned away from him and looked at the ceiling. Abdul breathed again. Could there be an Arab solution to this . . . one in which cash rather than blows were exchanged? Americans and their John Waynes! His stomach churned in terrible fear. Allah, be merciful. Let the dreadful Mona eat humble pie.

"What she said," said Lisa, "was that if you had a mother you should do it to her."

The guy turned to her, and for a second his face lost its terrible resolve. He knew who Lisa was. He would have liked to have been introduced to her. He would have liked to have been her friend. Even at this moment of honor defense, there was a part of him that wanted to relate to her. But it was impossible, and Lisa had made it so. Behind him were the bimbos he had to live with. They were on his boats to Bimini. They worshiped his balls. It was high noon. The black tramp had called him out in front of the entire town. Blood would have to be spilled, but whose? You weren't allowed to hit a girl in Florida. That was for more sophisticated places. It meant he had to find a surrogate man. The little dark one? Possibly. The kid? Only just. Anyways, a champion for the mouthy black looker would have to be found from somewhere, was all.

"Listen good, you parcel of cunt," he tried. "You take your filthy mouth back north where it belongs, and you take your faggot boyfriends with you. I don't like 'em around while I'm eating."

It happened very fast. Rob was directly beneath the dealer. He didn't just stand up. He rocketed upward. As he did so, he flung the chair on which he sat away to the left. His knees straightened. He was going up on tiptoe. His momentum was furious. The guy was short and built, shorter by six inches than Rob. The top of Rob's head hit him on the point of the jaw that he had stuck out with his insult. It wasn't a mistake. Rob's neck was rigid at the point of contact, his shoulders wedged beneath his head in straight-line support. He was a human battering ram, 170 pounds of muscle and bone. The shock wave rippled up the stranger's chin and turned his brain to shuddering jelly. He went over backward into the lap of the girl who was still perched on the lap of the guy who was ignoring her. He slid across the table and his weight flattened it. The whole mess crashed to the ground and a fine spray of broken glass, shrimp, cutlery, and blood merged with the quivering atmosphere of Mezzanotte. The guy's left leg twitched for about five seconds, then stopped. It was over, as they say, before it had begun.

Rob sat down. Lisa, Mona, and Abdul, mouths wide open, watched him.

"It was the only thing to do," he said. "I think."

Behind them, the restaurant erupted into a cacophony of sound. They had witnessed a Hemingway-esque brawl. It was perfect.

The superstar's superstud had just given his cojones an outing.

A woman's honor had been protected. A man's sexuality had been defended. David had zapped Goliath, in real life, for their amusement, and at no extra charge.

"Rob, that was *unbelievable,*" breathed Lisa. Frank lovelight beamed from her eyes. "Is your head okay? Oh, Rob!"

"Bloody good show!" said Abdul, who'd been to Oxford. He wiped a bead of sweat from his upper lip with a silk handkerchief.

"We're gone," said Mona.

All agreed on that, especially Abdul. He dropped fifteen one-hundred-dollar bills on the table so that nobody would have an excuse to stop them on the way out. Lisa led the way. She was as regal in retreat as she had been in advance. The maître d' made ambiguous gestures with his hands as she swept past, wanting her to leave, not wanting her not to come back. Three women and one man said "bravo" equivalents to Rob on the way out. A drunk in the corner clapped ostentatiously. Then everybody in the restaurant decided they needed another drink. Already the incident was solidifying in the wet cement of South Beach folklore.

28

"Semper," in Latin, means "always," which is an optimistic name for a nightclub. The entrance to the club is guarded by a red rope and by three men who are basically too big for their job, which is to keep undesirables out. "Undesirables" are not necessarily whacked-out dope fiends and filthy street people twitching with paranoia and brandishing knives. They include people in polyester, tourists, the elderly, ugly people, nervous people, and anybody else who does not appeal for whatever reason to the mountains of muscle on the right side of the red rope. These unfortunates are told, with patient politeness, that Sempers is a small private club for members only. This is true. What is not pointed out is that the rule is waived for the "right" people. It is more difficult to categorize the type of person who is semper welcome at Sempers. It is sufficient to say that Lisa Rodriguez is the epitome of such a person. When Louis and Jan Canales started the place, it could well have been with the shining vision of Lisa in mind. Now, as she approached, the incredible hulks fumbled with the rope barrier, their glacial power melted to a glutinous and obsequious subservience.

"Good evening, Ms. Rodriguez," they murmured loudly, heads held low, arms out wide to separate the star from the curious street losers who huddled on the sidewalk.

"Are you members?" said a rude college kid with a few Buds on board. He'd already been refused entrance, and he was bright enough to realize that it was a reflection on his desirability as a human being.

Rob looked around, shrugged, and smiled at the guy who could have been him. Nobody else twitched a muscle in response. They went down the spiral staircase like corkscrews into a bottle. There was a fuss of recognition at the reception desk, and then they were spirited through the tables to an enormously comfortable chintz sofa and satellite armchairs that sat in a cluster in front of the girl who was the cabaret.

Abdul ordered a bottle of XO, some more champagne, and the coffee there hadn't been time for at Mezzanotte.

"Would you like some ice for your head?" he whispered solicitously to Rob.

Rob waved it away. Actually, the points of jaws were surprisingly soft, heads surprisingly hard. He was feeling good, caught up fully now in the spirit of the evening. "Can I get a Coors or something?" he asked, and Abdul added it to his shopping list.

"This place looks like a flea market," said Mona. She was wrong. Sempers looked like an enormously funky Annabel's. It was done up to resemble somebody's drawing room, and the question was "whose?" The answer was a cross between Gertrude Stein's and the sugar plum fairy's. It was dazzlingly original. Pictures like postage stamps dotted the walls in damaged gilt frames. Table lamps with tassels dangled dangerously over small mahogany side tables. The sofas swallowed you, the threadbare Persian rugs netted your toes like shrimps. There were glass ashtrays, and silver salvers, candelabra and flocked wallpaper in shades of burnished orange and primrose yellow, and all was faded in the warm gloom, glowing in a delicious decadence that slipped into your mind like old champagne.

"Berlin," said Abdul definitely, to no one in particular. He was looking at the singer. She would have turned Hitler on. She was a blond, blue-eyed Aryan, and she'd got the twist on a torch song that Dietrich would have envied. Her dress was shiny gray and condom tight. She wiggled about like a worm on a hook and gave off an androgynous sensuality that was designed to appeal to all shades of sexual preference. This was just as well. Most shades were represented in Sempers.

"I get a kick out of you," she sang, aiming the unlikely sentiment at a pony-tailed pianist who smiled up at her through wisps of smoke from his Belmondo cigarette. There was a glass of champagne on the Steinway whose ivories he tickled.

"Someone around here's seen a lot of movies," said Lisa.

Louis Canales, the owner, hovered over the table. He had.

"Is everything all right? I'm sorry we're a little crowded tonight."

"Your people are doing us jolly well," said Abdul, pouring a generous measure of brandy into a wafer-thin balloon.

Lisa smiled sweetly, saying nothing. Words were extra.

The spirit of South Beach drifted away, but his eyes would be on them in the torchlight. Around the room the word was out. Lisa Rodriguez was there. Linda Evangelista was, apparently, in another corner. And Jean-Paul Gaultier had dropped in earlier, or so someone said.

The singer's charisma hosed out over the group. She defined vivacity, wrapping strawberry lips around the phrases and holding the microphone like she was going to love it. She grabbed the eyes of someone in the crowd and vamped him till he was limp. Then she laughed at the wonderful discomfort she had caused, and moved on to another victim. Sometimes she swayed out into the audience and threatened a lap, her fingers plucking at the collars of shirts, twirling through the hair of selected males, caressing the shoulders of carefully chosen women.

"I get no kick from champagne," she breathed. She swept up the glass from the piano and put it to her lips, making a little pout of distaste, puckering up beautifully for the charade.

Abdul shifted to the edge of the sofa. Mona sat back with a smile on her lips. Lisa watched Rob. Rob, too, was staring at the singer. The waiter poured the wine—pink Laurent Perrier, the kind from which everyone but the singer got a kick.

The blonde with the voice, the body, and the personality that tied them together had picked up on the group. She was an expressionist.

Powerful, pretty people were her bag. Danger vibed her up. Tension was what it was all about.

"Mere alcohol doesn't thrill me at all . . ."

She moved in on them, into their space. She was standing by the table, in front of their sofa, her legs in among their legs. A shapely ankle touched Mona's. Neither moved. The singer sang into Mona's eyes. Mona didn't flinch. Abdul's eyes were shining bright in the night forest. Lisa watched carefully. She was always one step ahead. Two steps. Rob was smiling. The singer looked at Lisa, sizing her up. She saw the trouble there, and laughed in the song because she didn't care. It was her room. She could feel its collective heart beating in the palm of her hand. Nobody could touch her while she held the microphone. It was a whip and a club and a weapon that gave her the total control she loved.

Her eyes swiveled toward Rob.

"I get a kick out of *you,*" she sang. The "you" was emphasized and her whole body swung toward her new target as she hit the note. Her arm shot out and her finger pointed. Her blood-red nail was aimed like a gun barrel right between Rob Sand's wide-open eyes.

"Uh-oh," murmured Mona.

Abdul looked at Lisa. Lisa sat stock-still, the smile of the Sphinx inscrutable on her face.

It was the part of the song when the pianist took over. His fingers rolled up and down the keyboard, burying the tune in cunning camouflages of his own invention. He smiled at the ceiling. He smiled to himself. His clever notes bent the air of the smoky room. The singer wasn't on time out. She was in overdrive. She bent at the knees and wiggled her butt. She shimmied in a show that proved sister Kate to be an amateur. She threw back her head, and she laughed and laughed, and she walked in among Rob Sand's stretched-out legs as if she had been invited. He didn't take them away from her. He just sat there, a smile of embarrassment and pleasure all over his face. The pianist was running into some kind of climax. So was the singer. She turned around and showed Rob her backless dress. The beginning of the cleavage of her butt was visible. She shook it from side to side so that he could see she wasn't wearing any panties. A spotlight found her, and showed the rest of the room, too. Then she sat down in his lap.

She turned around and put her lips right into his face, over her shoulder, until the microphone brushed his mouth and hers at the same time.

"I get no kick from cocaine," she breathed.

Lisa Rodriguez didn't say a thing. She was still smiling, but she was no longer still. She reached forward for the open bottle of champagne, and she pulled it out of the ice bucket. A waiter darted forward to help pour her drink, but the waiter had gotten it wrong. Lisa held the bottle in one hand, by its bottom. Then, not hurrying, surprise on her side, she upended it carefully and stuck it like a dagger into the singer's superb cleavage. The spotlight froze the action. Two scintillating mounds of flesh were separated by the frosty green ring of the bottle's bottom. The shape of the champagne bulged from the slinky dress. Its neck bisected her torso. Its opening was at the level of her belly button. It was from this point that the wine now began to spurt like a geyser from some underground spring. It gurgled happily from the sheer, shiny material and it pooled in the singer's lap. From there, constantly replenished, it sank away between her legs onto the part of Rob Sand on which her butt rested. The pianist was still tinkling away, but the song died in the throat of the songstress.

"Oh, fuck!" she wailed.

"I say," said Abdul, who'd had an English nanny.

"Way to go, Lisa," enthused Mona.

"Get the fuck off my guy's lap," hissed Lisa Rodriguez.

"Oh, *shit!*" said Rob Sand.

Once again, there was no coercion, but it seemed that leaving was the polite thing to do. On the sidewalk outside, a warm breeze was blowing. Rob rubbed at his soaked pants.

"Damn it, Lisa, I didn't ask her to sit on me." He was angry.

"Neither did I, Rob," said Lisa. She was through it already. That was the advantage of fearless spontaneity. You got it out. You got it over. The singer had been blitzed. Lisa had won. It made her feel good.

"That baby sure got no kicks from champagne." Mona giggled.

"I'd have liked a little more of that brandy," said Abdul. Wherever they hit next, he was going to drink fast.

"I'm *soaked,*" said Rob.

"You'll dry, honey," said Lisa. She took his arm, holding it tight with both hers and cuddling in to him. "I'm sorry, honey, I got jealous. I get jealous."

"But . . . I mean, it's like a war going out with you," said Rob, trying to get a bead on the whole extraordinary evening.

"But you'll always be on the winning side," said Lisa, giving him a squeeze. He half smiled, then whole smiled.

"Jeez! I don't know, Lisa. You're crazy."

"Crazy for you."

"You're a lucky guy, Mr. Sand," said Abdul enviously.

"So are you, greaseball," said Mona, kicking him on the shin.

"Ha! Ha! Mona," said Abdul through tight teeth.

"Well, where to?" said Mona.

"Might I suggest somewhere not quite so grand?" said Abdul. "Somewhere a little looser to accommodate the mood of the evening." He'd learned his understatement at Harrow.

"Island Club," said Lisa.

"Sounds like some brothers and sisters there," said Mona, hoping for home turf.

"Yeah, nobody'll care that Rob messed his pants." Lisa laughed.

"I didn't mess them. You did."

"But I will mess with them." He moved out of range as she lunged at him, laughing at her over his shoulder as he moved ahead a few paces.

"We love ya, Lisa Rodriguez," shouted a guy from across the road. She waved back. Pretty soon she'd have a street named after her. It felt good. The evening felt good. Little Abdul was free with his wallet. Mona at least had energy. And Rob was a great big target in her sights.

"Come on," she said.

There was no red rope outside the entrance to the Island Club. There was simply a gaping black hole through which emanated noises and smells that could well have come from the devil's bowels.

Abdul looked at it with suspicion. "Are you sure this is the place?" he said. No sign said it was.

"This is my town," said Lisa. They trooped into the darkness. The reggae band was up on a platform in a cloud of smoke. People clung to a long bar as if afraid they would fall off it into some nameless pit. A few tables were scattered along a wall, at which people ate food that might have been "soul." A dance floor was crowded beneath the band. The air was thick with the stench of ganja, sweat, and rum. There was an empty table toward the back of the room. They gravitated toward it, Abdul covering his ears to shut out the music. They sat down. A waitress slouched over. This was no place to order champagne. Abdul was out of his depth. Lisa ordered a bottle of Mount Gay, a jug of o.j., and four glasses.

"This is where we get down," she said.

"Hey, Sheik of Araby, let's dance," said Mona. She stood up and wiggled the bait in front of Abdul's nose. His libido led him off into the gloom. Lisa and Rob were alone.

"Enjoying yourself?" she said.

He turned to her, smiling. "Yeah, it's fun." He paused. "You're fun, Lisa," he added.

"Yeah, I am, aren't I?" She laughed.

"I was never very good at fun," said Rob.

"It's okay to be serious. It's good. I like it. Anybody can do the other."

"Not me. I'm always thinking, always worrying. Always caught up in the bigger picture . . . you know, the future, what things mean, what the point of them is. You can let go. You let your feelings take over."

"You've been known to do that." She reached forward and took his hand in hers, drinking in his beauty, his solemnity, his fascinating angst. She made her voice warm and sexy as she asked him to remember her body and the things he'd done to it.

He swallowed. "Yeah, but we're opposites, Lisa."

"You know what opposites do. They fit into each other."

She captured both his legs beneath the table with hers to emphasize her point. His swallow became a gulp. She watched him, her face serious in sensuality. The reggae music washed over them. She let go of his hand and poured him a drink, her every action heavy with meaning. Drink up, she was saying. Let go. Be mine. Don't fight it. Feel it. Be it. Become it. Join in the celebration, join the joyful nation, banged the rhythm of the band.

"Here," she said. He leaned in toward her, his eyes wide with sudden lust. He swayed out across the table to meet her and she to him. Her lips were parting, his still closed. Closer, they came.

"Rob?" said the voice. "Lisa?"

It was a warm, excited voice, soft and well known. Its owner stood by the table, willowy tall, wreathed in a halo of light from some chance naked bulb.

"Christa!" said Rob Sand.

Lisa looked up. "Well, hi!" she said, unsmiling. She didn't like surprises. So Christa was back from the Keys, and her first stop was the Island Club. Still waters! The irritation bubbled beneath the surface. It had been a neat moment, neatly sabotaged and by an almost-rival. For a second Lisa wondered about conspiracy. No. There was no way. The Island Club had been her production. Yet

South Beach was small, and her party had hardly kept a low profile. It wouldn't have been the cleverest thing in the world to have tracked them down.

"This where you hang out, Christa?" she said.

"Not really. I've been here a couple of times before. Steve wanted to see the soft underbelly of Miami before we crashed. I guess this is it." She laughed, looking at Rob and then looking away from him as a strange intensity loomed up in his eyes.

"Where's Steve?"

"I'm here, dear. With the drinks and the attitude. Are we the party or are there reinforcements somewhere?" He looked at the four glasses on the table. "Hi there, Rob-aroo. *What* a pretty table we're going to be."

"Hi, Steve," said Rob, still looking at Christa.

"You remember Mona from Elle," said Lisa. "The black girl with the tits who used to ball Johnny. She's with us, and some sand man with a boat in Lauderdale."

"Jesus, what's Johnny's girl doing sitting with you?" said Christa, pretending to be alarmed.

"Ex-girl. She blew him out. Left the agency. She was wondering if you wanted her for yours."

Christa sat down. She was interested. Very. Mona worked. She wasn't *Vogue,* but she got booked all over the place.

"Where is she?"

"Vamping the oil well." Lisa stuck out a finger at the dance floor. Mona was swaying over Abdul as if casting a spell on him. Half her size, he seemed to be trying to look up her skirt.

"I used her once," sniffed Steve. "Trouble, I seem to remember. Big fan of the Bolivian marching powder. Used to yack right through the shoot till I told her she had halitosis."

"She did that Estée Lauder commercial, with all the cats. Remember? And Helmut used her in that great spread in *Stern.* She'd be bread and butter in the agency. I can handle her," said Christa.

"She picked a fight with some dealer in Mezzanotte," said Lisa, inclining toward Steve's "trouble" diagnosis. "Poor Rob had to knock the guy cold."

"What?" said Christa. "Rob, you *didn't!*"

"A fight?" said Steve, enormously impressed.

"He did," said Lisa proudly. "He like butted him with his head, and the guy went down all over the place and he didn't get up."

"It was a pretty nasty moment. The guy was about to go crazy. I was lucky to get him a bit before he was ready," said Rob modestly.

"You mean you knocked him out? Rob, that's so unlike you. I can't believe it." Christa was looking at him as if she had never seen him before.

"Thank God he did," said Lisa. "We were all in real trouble. The guy was built and really mean, calling the fellas faggots, and Mona a hooker or whatever."

"Sounds like he was half right," said Steve Pitts.

"Are you feeling okay? You didn't hurt yourself?" said Christa.

"No, I'm fine, but thanks for asking." Rob smiled at her. She put out her hand and ruffled his hair.

"He's fine," said Lisa sharply.

"Here comes the black snowstorm," said Steve. "Rapping like a group."

Mona slithered across the room, a sweaty Abdul in her wake.

"Hi, Mona," said Christa.

"Christa! Baby! What a surprise . . . you back from the Keys?"

"No, she sent her apparition as an advance party," grumbled Steve.

"Hi, Steve . . . haven't seen you since Aruba . . . you sweet, kind man!" Mona turned back to Christa.

"Darlin', you know little Abdul, he's got a boat . . ."

"At Lauderdale with bedrooms," finished Lisa with a theatrical yawn.

Abdul was deeply honored. Christa said she was, too.

"You left Johnny?" said Christa simply to Mona. There was no time like now.

"Sure did. He's crazed. Lisa 'n you put him over the top. It was like livin' with a psycho."

"What are you doing for an agent?"

"I was wonderin' if you'd be interested."

"Sure I'm interested."

"You are? That's great! I got some guys that use me a lot. I was all booked up at Johnny's."

"I know that. You're a great model, Mona. It would be terrific to have you with us. I'd give you whatever you were getting at Elle."

Mona let out a whoop of excitement. She hugged Christa. She tried to hug Lisa. She massaged Rob's shoulders. She ignored Steve Pitts.

"Come on, babes, I feel like gettin' blasted." She reached for the rum. "Book me out for tomorrow, honey."

"Should do wonders for Rossetti's peace of mind," said Steve.

"Don't!" said Christa, hand to her mouth in mock horror. "Maybe I should call him, say sorry, it's nothing personal, only business."

"Business is personal, dear. Sometimes I think it's the only stuff that is."

"Well, the creep had it coming," said Christa, who didn't deal in olive branches.

"Right on, baby," said Mona. She drank the rum like water to quench her thirst. Tonight she would celebrate, but tomorrow *she'd* be the one who called Johnny. Oh, yes, she would. Lunchtime tomorrow, when her headache wore off. "I'm inside, sweetheart," she'd trill. "Now how do you want me to waste 'em?" She looked around her. They were all so pleased with themselves. They were rich and white and soooo superior, but she was the clever one. When they woke up to the fact, it would be way too late.

"How was Key West? Did you find some good locations?"

"Christa found a superb location," said Steve. "Remember the writer at Mary's party. Well, my dear, there's been a rapprochement . . . and remember the English learned their understatement from me!"

"Oh, shut up, Steve." The blush was all over Christa's face. She was red as a beet.

"You're blushing," said Lisa in the fail-safe blush-amplification ploy.

"I'm not blushing," said Christa, passing through vermilion.

"The guy who was diving alone?" said Rob. He sounded incredulous.

"We really ought to give him his name," said Steve. "Peter Stein. Pulitzer man. Nobel laureate to be."

"He explained all that," said Christa to Rob, well aware that she sounded less than convincing. Her face was burning. But the embarrassment was oddly pleasant. The tingling all over her body reminded her of his touch. His name hung in the fetid air of the Island Club, bouncing around on the reggae rhythms. Peter Stein had undone her lock. She was wide open to him, as she had been open wide on the floor of his writing room, his masterpiece beneath her butt, his complex persona stealing into her heart.

She spoke out brightly, to hide the thumping of her heart.

"Anyway, Peter Stein, literary hero, is no slouch at finding locations. He suggested we shoot on the Dry Tortugas, and he was right.

We checked it out on a chopper. It's magic. Total loneliness. Halfway between Key West and Cuba."

"But there's nothing there," said Abdul. "No water, no electricity, no food." What he meant was no nightclubs, no shopping, no champagne.

"Yeah, it's a logistic nightmare, but it's worth it. I don't think anyone's shot it before, which counts for a hell of a lot. It's virgin territory. This time of year there's no one down there, so we can do what we like without tourists getting shocked by Lisa's chest. It's paradise. Believe me. A lovers' dream!"

They were all quiet on that one.

"I imagine Peter Stein will be able to struggle over on his boat," said Steve with a laugh.

"He *did* suggest the place," said Christa, laughing too. Her blush was back.

Rob looked away over his shoulder into the room.

Lisa caught his foot beneath the table. He didn't resist. He didn't push back. *Lovers' dream* was ringing in her ears. Steve Pitts arched his eyebrows. The boy was something. He could picture the celluloid, bending with ambiguity. The good looks were half of Rob Sand, the rest was the conflict. Lust and the Lord would battle it out in his eyes and Steve would get it, on film. The rest would be the stuff of fashion glory. Lisa Rodriguez didn't know how to look bad, and he couldn't remember when he'd last taken a mediocre photograph. It was a wrap. The shoot was going to be perfect, as long as the personal chemistry didn't explode. He saw Rob steal a glance at Christa, saw her catch it, saw Lisa pick up on it, too. The alarm bell rang. Oh, no, surely not! Could Rob be interested in Christa?

It would make sense. She was strong and sensible on top of the beauty. She'd make a divine mother/authority figure for a young kid way out of his depth. And she'd be drawn to his vulnerability. Tough women always liked little boys lost. Okay, she wouldn't reciprocate, but she might be flattered, might unwittingly fan the flames, and then Lisa . . . Steve put his hand over his face. He'd been here before. Location shoots could be poison tours, especially when sex reared its ugly head. And love . . . well, forget it. Thank God, Mary Whitney and her pussy whip were out of the equation. The algebra was looking bad enough as it was.

"Do you want to dance, Rob?" said Lisa.

"Oh, yeah, great," said Rob. He tried to catch Christa's eye as he stood up. She managed to avoid it. Lisa stood up. Even in the throbbing darkness of the Island Club, that was an event.

"You look wonderful, Lisa," said Christa, meaning it.

Lisa put up both hands and wiggled side to side.

"Thanks," she said. She knew the compliment was true, but she was grateful for it nonetheless.

"I never thought I'd see the day when Lisa went overboard for a guy," said Steve, after she'd left.

"Rob's lucky," agreed Christa.

"He doesn't look as if he feels very lucky," said Steve.

Rob looked back over his shoulder at their table on the way to the dance floor.

"In fact, he looks as if he's going to be shot," said Steve.

"Okay, Steve," said Christa. She meant "That's enough."

"I wouldn't have minded a girl like that when I was his age," said Abdul wistfully.

"I think he's got the hots for you, Christa," said Mona.

"Nonsense," said Christa, too fast.

"Yeah, he keeps givin' you those moody ones, you know, that James Dean shit."

Steve's smile was agreeing with Mona.

"He's just confused. This whole world isn't really his speed. I guess I'm the familiar face. That's all."

"Would you like to dance?" said Abdul.

"Not a lot," said Christa.

"*I'd* like to dance," said Steve. "How long's your boat?"

"Ha! Ha!" said Abdul.

"You wanna dance, okay?" said Mona, grabbing Abdul.

Steve and Christa were alone.

"Bitch!" said Christa with a laugh.

"Well, Mona's right for once."

"It's just a crush."

"That you find cute."

"Wouldn't you?"

"Yes. In spades."

"Lisa knows, doesn't she?"

"Oh, yes, Lisa knows. She's cool for now 'cause you're not encouraging it. If he keeps it up, or gets worse, we'll be in trouble on the shoot."

"What do I do? If I'm mean to him, it'll probably rev him up."

"Give him Peter Stein's books to read."

"Steve!"

"They'll depress him so much, he'll forget about puppy love."

"Peter's books aren't depressing."

"They were last week."

"Well, they're not this week." Christa was mock defiant. "Actually, I don't know how I can joke about it. I think I've got it pretty bad."

"You're telling *me* you've got it bad. You look positively luminescent. You're glowing in the dark. He *is* quite good looking."

"Quite?!!!"

"But not my type. Too gloomy. Too deep." Steve looked suitably sad.

"Not like Rob."

"Ah, now you are talking. Although in his way, he's gloomy and deep, too. But the fan club is a little crowded. I think I'll keep my distance."

"You better had. Lisa would roast your balls on the beach."

"After she's through roasting yours."

"Come on, Steve, girls don't have balls."

"Believe that, you'll believe anything."

They laughed together as only old friends could. They knew each other's strengths and weaknesses. As a team, they couldn't miss.

"We're going to be okay on this shoot, aren't we, Steve?"

"Better than okay. We don't even need luck."

He reached for the rum and let it loose on the back of his throat, almost gargling with it.

"This feels like some kind of a celebration," he said. He lifted the glass. "To love," he said. "The bitch."

"To love," she said. "The bastard."

There was an insistent warbling noise.

"What the hell's that?"

"My telephone. Sorry. I know it's bad manners."

Christa fished the cellular out of her bag. She looked at her watch. It was midnight.

"Christa, it's Mary. I haven't woken you, have I? Listen, I can't sleep and I don't want anyone else to. What's that terrible noise in the background?"

"Mary! No way. I'm on the cellular. I'm in some club. How are you? What gives?"

"Nothing 'gives.' That's the problem. What a dreadful expression, Christa. 'What gives,' indeed. Mr. Butler wouldn't have liked that one at all. How was Key West?"

Christa did a "Mary Whitney" with her mouth to Steve.

"It was great. I took Steve over to the Dry Tortugas. He went overboard. Thought they were a dream."

"But there's nothing there."

"That's what he liked about them."

"I went there once on some bore's fishing boat. Quite pretty. There was a fort that Jefferson built, I seem to remember. Can you turn down that terrible noise?"

"No. It's a band. Some reggae guys from the Islands."

"Are they any good?"

"What!"

"The band, stupid. Are they any good?"

"Yeah, actually they are. Better than your lot the other night."

"That's not saying much. Who are you with?"

"There's a crowd. Steve, Lisa, Rob. A model called Mona. Some Arab called Abdul who has a boat."

"Not Abdul ben Azziz?"

"Could be. Small and dark. English accent. Quite sweet."

"Well, they're all like that, aren't they, except the sweet bit. If it's Azziz, he's almost as rich as I am. Not quite. Ask him if his father got his balls shot off by a belly dancer in Oslo."

"In *Oslo?*"

"I think it was Oslo. Somewhere cold where belly dancers aren't supposed to be, anyway. I know that was the point of the story."

"I'll ask him. He's dancing."

"Well, you all seem to be having lots of fun down there." Mary's tone was accusing. Christa had a sudden premonition of what was coming.

"It's a pretty hellish place, actually. I guess we'll have a couple of drinks and split."

"What's the time?" said Mary.

"It's twelve."

"I think I might come down. I could be there in an hour and a bit if I get the chauffeur to hurry. And I can't sleep."

"Are you sure?" said Christa.

"Getting surer. Are you all drinking rum?"

"Yeah, we are."

"Okay, I'm there. Give me an hour and a half. What's the dive called?"

Christa gave her instructions. She pushed the off switch.

"Oh, shit," she said. "Mary Whitney's driving down."

"Rob and Lisa will be ecstatic," said Steve.

"Now we've got to wait till she arrives," said Christa. "And then I guess we have to keep her happy for an hour or two. Mary didn't mind the idea of the Dry Tortugas. That's a relief."

"She's okay. She's enough of a pro to hire the pros and then let them get on with it. It's only when someone doesn't deliver that she hits the fan. She's a bitch, but I like her."

"That's what she says about you, Steve."

"Takes one to know one."

Christa laughed as she poured herself a glass of rum. Abdul and Mona were back.

Abdul sat down, letting his head fall theatrically to his chest in mock exhaustion. Mona reached for the Mount Gay.

"Was your father ever in Oslo?" said Steve, a wicked smile on his face.

Abdul looked wary. "Oslo?" he said.

"An accident in Oslo," said Steve, throwing diplomacy to the wind.

"There was some unpleasantness in Helsinki," said Abdul carefully, a sly smile on his face.

"Ah, so your second name is Azziz," said Steve in the role of irreverent Sherlock Holmes.

"It sure ain't pizazz," grumbled Mona. "He dances like a corpse."

"Mary Whitney's coming down from Palm Beach to join us," said Christa, heading off the unpromising conversation at the pass.

"She's almost as rich as I am," laughed Abdul, thankful for the diversion. "Not quite."

Rob and Lisa were back. Everyone was sweating. The Mount Gay was half empty, or was it half full?

"Mary Whitney's driving down," said Steve.

"Shit, what for?" said Lisa.

"For fun," said Christa, with a hollow laugh. "Everybody had better behave."

"Well, that shouldn't be a problem. Everyone has behaved perfectly so far," said Abdul sarcastically, pissed that the party was about to acquire another multimillionaire.

"Doesn't she like to ball young guys?" said Mona, the rum blurring her words.

In the noise desert of the Island Club, there was a sudden oasis of silence. Everyone looked at Rob Sand.

"It's just gossip," said Christa.

Lisa draped a protective arm over Rob's shoulders. Rob stared into space.

"I'm not hanging around this hellhole all night, waiting for Mary Whitney," said Lisa.

Christa took a deep breath. Juggling balance sheets was one thing. Juggling people was another, especially tricky people, famous people, beautiful people. Mary Whitney was her business future. Like it or not, her whims had to be indulged. If Mary traveled sixty miles to a party, the party had better be there. It didn't take a Freud to work out which particular ingredient in the group was the essential one. Rob was. Even if the party held together for the Whitney arrival, the rest of the night promised to be a mare. Somewhere among the watering holes of South Beach, powerful personalities would clash. It would take a conductor of phenomenal skill to keep the orchestra harmonious. Christa's heart sank. Was she up to it?

"We don't have to stay here. We can go somewhere else," said Christa easily. "Mary can always find me on the portable."

"All we need now is Peter Stein," said Steve suddenly.

Rob looked up. Lisa watched him. Mona closed her eyes. Abdul perked up at the thought of fresh blood. Steve chuckled.

Christa took a deep breath.

"Thanks a *lot,* Steve," she said with a rueful smile.

But even as she dismissed it, a voice in her mind said "Why the hell not?" She wanted to see him more than anyone else on earth. Leaving Key West and saying good-bye to him had been agony. She stole a look at her watch under the table. It was half past midnight.

She stood up. "Excuse me," she said. "I've got to go to the john." But she scooped up the phone as she left.

She squeezed past the loudspeakers at the edge of the dance floor and her chest wall vibrated as the sound waves hit. The ladies' room at the Island Club announced itself by the smell of the adjacent men's room. Christa wrinkled up her nose and plowed down the rickety stairs to the basement, flattening herself against the wall to let a drunk pass. The thought of Peter had fired her up. Of course he wouldn't come, but she would talk to him. She would hear his sleepy voice, and it wouldn't matter if he was cross because she had woken him. She had no idea what she would say. It was deeper than that. To hear him would be to flesh out the memory of him and to give substance to her fevered daydreams. Hell, his answering machine would be enough, if he had such a thing.

Suddenly, business was a million miles away. The perfume campaign didn't matter now. Lisa and Steve, Mona and the Arab could fight it out among themselves. Mary and the others could tear each other's hearts out over poor Rob, and she didn't care. She only cared about one person. And now she was seconds away from his voice. She went in and locked the door. She sat down on the loo, and tried not to read the explicit graffiti. She punched the number. Her mouth was dry. She licked her lips. Was it imagination, or could she still taste him? It rang.

"Hello!"

"Peter?"

"Christa?"

"What are you doing?"

"Where are you?"

"In a club in Miami."

Silence. A Marley song drifted down the stairs. They were miles away from each other. Christa's stomach sank. Oh, dear, this hadn't been a brilliant idea. Peter Stein was not a spur-of-the-moment teenager. Neither, for that matter, was she. Yet, here she was calling him up in the middle of the night from a john in a club. It didn't seem a very grown-up thing to be doing.

"I didn't wake you?"

"No, I was thinking about bed." He laughed. Embarrassment. Something else.

The rush of desire took her. It lifted her up, out of doubt, into courage.

"I want to be in bed with you. I want to do it with you in bed."

"Oh, Christa." His voice had a break in it. Her talk had moved him, half an hour after midnight, way down at the bottom of America.

"I miss you," he said.

"After four hours?"

"After four seconds."

Pause. "I miss you, too." Her voice was low. "How much do you miss me?" she added.

"How much?"

A nervous laugh. "I don't know that I can quantify it."

"Try."

"You're doing it again. Showing me that I don't have words."

"I love you. Oh, God, Christa." Again, his voice broke with a shuddering sigh of resignation. "Where exactly are you?" Once again he tried to get back to firm ground.

"A 'where' question," she said. "I'm in a club on South Beach. I want you to be here, and you're not allowed to ask a 'why' question. Remember?"

He laughed, more relaxed now. She felt strengthened by that.

She went on. "I ran into Lisa and Rob and a whole load of people, and now Mary's coming down from Palm Beach. It's going to be a nightmare, and then I thought of you and how it could end up as the second best evening of my life so far."

"It's a four-hour drive, Christa."

"We could have breakfast together, and lunch and dinner and whatever came *before* breakfast."

"I have to work."

Her heart gave a syncopated beat. I have a wife. I have a lover. Something else is number one.

"You could work on Star Island. I could watch you. I could distract you. I'd be research."

Then, "How would I find you in four hours' time?"

The adrenaline was pumping. Christa felt the rush of excitement. She'd never expected it, but he was weakening. She was winning.

"You call me on my phone and I beam you into me."

Her voice was husky, for him, for her.

"In four hours you'll only want to sleep."

"With you. I want you, Peter."

"You're crazy. Wonderful, but crazy."

"Are you coming?"

"I think I am."

She fought back the war whoop of victory.

"Hurry!"

"I'll call you?"

"Yes, all along the way if you like."

"Christa?"

"Yes."

"It was special, what happened. You know that. You know what I'm saying, don't you?"

"Say it to me when you see me. Show me."

"Later, then. Good-bye."

She touched the END button, as she murmured her own good-bye. And then she wondered just what the hell she was going to do with the longest four hours of her life so far.

29

Christa hurried back toward the table, running on the rich fuel of obsession. It was happening again and she had thought it never would. Everything seemed super real. The love in her heart was exploding, and there was enough for everyone. She loved the sweaty dancers all around her. She loved the Island Club and South Beach, and her wonderful life. Soon she would be back among her dear friends: Steve, and beautiful Lisa, and dear, sweet Rob who had a post-teenage crush on her. There was even enough love for the Arab with the castrated father, and for Mona, her brand-new model. The singer, eyes hooded, swaying dreamily to his music, summed up her feelings. "Don't worry 'bout a thing-boom-bang-bang-boom 'cause every little thing's goin' to be all right." "Right on," murmured Christa to herself, as she headed back to the party.

It had grown. Two young guys had drawn up chairs. Their backs were toward Christa as she approached.

"Hi, darling," said Steve. "We've found these two divine friends of Lisa's, cruising the town. Isn't this fun? Look at this one. Can you believe him?"

Christa looked. He was very good looking. Latin, well-born, and with the insolence of young beauty mixed with strong booze. His friend was more of the same, only less so. Neither boy was listening to Steve. Both were locked onto Lisa like missiles following a sleek black jet. Lisa was enjoying the extra attention, but she was using the boys to wind up Rob. Christa could see that. Each time she made them laugh and long for her, she checked Rob for his reaction. But Rob was standing up to welcome Christa back to the table, like a genuine young gentleman. For a second, the luminous smile on Lisa's face closed down. Then it was back. "Don't worry 'bout a thing," sang the singer, but Christa was suddenly not quite so sure that every little thing was going to be all right.

"This one's called José," said Steve, sticking out a thumb at him, and raising his eyebrows to the ceiling in theatrical appreciation of the boy's visuals.

"José del Portal de Aragon," said José grandly. Then he saw Christa. He stood up. His attitude changed. He knew who she was.

Christa put out a neutral hand. Her brilliant mood was still intact.

"Why do I know your name?" she said pleasantly.

"Perhaps you know my father," said José, pompously. He was trying to be so grown up, but there was sweat on his brow from the drink, and his automatic assumption that his father was the one that people knew fingered him immediately as a professional child.

"You know his name," said Lisa, "because it was his boat that blew up my parents."

There was no answer to that. José's friend tried to snigger. José went white. Everyone else lapsed into silence. Even Mona was quiet. They were all trying to remember the details of the accident.

"How awful!" said Abdul at last.

"My parents would have agreed with you," said Lisa, not missing a beat. Her jaw was set. There was a grim look on her face. There was a part of her that cringed at the memory, the weak part. Nobody must ever know it existed, or they would use it against her.

"It's not funny, Lisa," said Rob.

"I never said it was," said Lisa. "It was an expensive boat."

"Whoa!" said Mona.

"Lisa!" said José. The look in his eye was slavish. He was hypnotized by her. It was impossible to think anything else. Whatever had happened out there on the bay, this boy had not been the prime mover. He had been moved. Christa knew that with a cold and absolute certainty.

"Will Daddy buy you another one, José?" asked Lisa.

He looked down, not answering.

"What kind of a boat was it?" said Abdul, quite unable to resist relating to money.

"Cigarette. Forty-seven foot. Custom," José mumbled.

"Oh," said Abdul. "A little boat."

"For a sweet little boy," said Lisa, softening her insult with a radiant smile and a hand reaching out to stroke the Aragon knee.

He looked at her as if she had just declared undying love. His expression tried to tell her of his. Then he looked at Rob Sand. Hatred blasted from his deep brown eyes.

"What are you boys drinking?" said Steve. They had brought glasses with them to the table.

"Rum and Coke," said the José friend.

"Cuba libres," said Rob pleasantly.

"*What* did you say?" said José.

Rob looked taken aback by the sharpness of José's tone. He hadn't said very much. Had he got it wrong about Cuba libres? He didn't think he had.

"Cuba libres," he said again.

"Take that back!" said José. He pushed out his chin and puffed up his chest, and his furious eyes attacked Rob.

"What back?" said Rob with a laugh, splaying out his hands and looking around the table in bemusement.

"You have insulted the honor of my country," said José. He stood up. "Cuba is not free. Cuba is in chains. Because of the treachery of America and fools like you, my people are slaves."

"Oh, dear," said Steve, smiling broadly.

"Tell it like it is, bro. Right on, baby," said Mona. She hadn't a clue what he was talking about, but it was her affectation to identify with the underdog everywhere and anywhere, despite her Teflon heart and her half a million a year.

"Rob wasn't insulting anyone," said Christa sharply. "And actually, you're sitting in my seat. Can you please get out of it?"

José was standing up, so Christa elbowed him aside and sat down at the table.

José continued to hover, hoping that he looked threatening. His wrath was for Rob only. It had zero to do with Cuba.

"I don't understand what's going on," said Abdul, reaching for his drink. A sixth sense told him this was going to be the third watering hole they would have to leave in a hurry. As a playboy he was congenitally drawn to evenings such as this, but he was beginning to feel that he might have bitten off more than he could chew with Lisa Rodriguez and her speedy friends.

"He's trying to pull a Cuban number," said Lisa. "You know, Bay of Pigs, *la lucha,* the struggle, and all that shit. Actually he's jealous of Rob because he's worked out that Rob and me are together."

"That's not true," shouted José, becoming younger by the second.

" 'Tis too," Steve wanted to say.

"We're not 'together,' Lisa," said Rob. He made the mistake of looking at Christa as he spoke.

"Oh, we're not, are we?" said Lisa ominously. She, too, looked at Christa. Her look was not reassuring.

"Take it back," howled José at Rob.

"Oh, take a hike," said Rob in exasperation.

"Leave us alone, José," said Christa.

"He told you to take a hike, José," said Lisa shrewdly. "Aren't you going to obey him?"

The José friend put a hand on his sleeve. "Come on," he said. José shook it off.

"Do you want me to go, Lisa?" said José. He swayed a little. He was pleading with her.

Lisa sat back in her chair. She smiled and shrugged. "A man has to do what a man has to do," she said. There, that should do it. It did. There was only one thing on this earth that José had ever wanted to be. A man. Now she was inviting him either to prove he was one or to admit that he wasn't.

He darted toward Rob, grabbed him by both shoulders and yanked as hard as he could. Rob went back in his chair. The chair tipped on its legs and hung there for a second. Rob reached out for the edge of the table to steady himself. But the backward momentum prevented him from reaching it. Instead, he caught the edge of the tablecloth between thumb and forefinger. As he fell backward, he didn't let go of the tablecloth. It followed him, with the remains of the bottle of rum and six glasses, onto the floor. There would have been no damage done, but for the falling glass. One of the tumblers flew through the air and landed on Rob's lip, cutting it. As he struggled to regain his balance amid the debris of the table, blood flowed.

Lisa, who had caused the incident, was the first to attempt to repair it. José, who had simply been her instrument, was the second.

Lisa crouched down among the wreckage and cradled the bemused Rob in her arms. "You bastard," she screamed over his head at José, who knelt beside her amid the broken glass.

"I'm sorry. I'm sorry," he mumbled. He was on the edge of tears. His life was falling apart. There had been no glory in his halfhearted assault.

Lisa dabbed at Rob's lip with her finger in a move that did nothing to stop a steady stream of blood. "You little asshole," she shouted at the trembling José.

"Should somebody call a doctor?" said Abdul. All around in the Island Club it was business as usual. The people at the next table had already stopped looking.

"Let me *up*," said Rob.

Christa and Steve looked at each other. Both had reached the bottom line fast. No damage had been done. You could see that. It was nothing more than a scratch, and lips healed fast. Rob wasn't really hurt. Neither were the looks that would be needed for the campaign. It was a laugh-or-cry moment. Lisa Rodriguez was a lethal weapon. And Mona was at least a blunt instrument. The two girls apparently caused havoc wherever they went.

"Come on, José," said Steve. "Let's get you out of here." He stood up and led the devastated José away from the table, his friend taking his other arm. "I'm sorry. I'm so sorry," bleated José over his shoulder as he retreated.

"Oh, go back to Cuba," said Lisa.

José began to weep. Steve wedged the sobbing youth against the end of the bar and ordered him a drink. "No harm done," he said in a kindly tone. "But better stay out of Lisa's way, okay?" José nodded glumly. Steve took a deep breath and wandered back to what was left of the table.

Christa was reaching for a warbling cellular phone.

"Hello!" Her voice was eager.

"Don't worry," said Mary Whitney. "I'm nearly there. Save some fun for me. Hello! Christa! Can you hear me?"

"Hi, Mary. Yes, I hear you. Where are you?"

"Just passing Turnberry Isle. You know the place where poor Gary Hart got hooked by Donna Rice. You still at the Caribbean place?"

"We're just leaving. Some Cuban just zapped Rob."

"Good for the dago. Nothing minor, I hope."

"Oh, come on, Mary! No, he's fine. It's just a scratch. Are you sure you're ready for this evening? I'm not sure I am."

"Nonsense, darling. No evening's any good without a fight. Stimulates the appetite."

"We've had two and a half already, and it's only one fifteen."

"Well, don't have any more till I arrive, okay? Where are you going to now?"

"We're going to play billiards," said Christa.

"Oh, balls," said Mary Whitney.

"Whatever," said Christa. "Check in when you get across the bridge, okay?"

Mary Whitney was gone.

Christa looked at her watch. Mary would be there in forty minutes. She needed to get out. Claustrophobia was biting. She wanted fresh air, even fresh friends.

"Who wants to go play billiards?" she said without too much enthusiasm.

Steve picked up on it. "The trumpet sounds uncertain," he said. "Who shall prepare themselves for the battle?"

"You've got blood on your dress, Lisa," said Mona.

"Oh, shit!" said Lisa, grabbing a napkin and dabbing at the stain. "Why did you have to bleed all over me, Rob?" Her priorities were set in cement. Her appearance came first. Lovers came second. If you looked after the one, the others took care of themselves. "Shit, I've got to go back to my hotel and change."

She stood up. The Cardozo was only a couple of blocks away. The party would wait for her. It always did.

"I'll be back," she threatened, and she was gone.

"I'd like to go play billiards with you, Christa," said Rob.

"Fine," said Christa. "You coming, Steve?"

"I think I'll hang around here," said Steve. His eyes flicked over to José, who seemed to have passed out at the bar. "This is such an energetic place."

Abdul and Mona weren't included in the invitation to billiards.

"I think Mona and I might try another bar, if that plan of action is acceptable to my lady of quality," said Abdul with heavy irony.

"Suits me, dick-head," said Mona pleasantly. "We all goin' to meet up at Warsaw later?"

"Helsinki," said Steve.

"Inevitably," said Christa, thinking about Peter Stein. If he'd left immediately, he would be about three hours away. Mmmmm! The thought of him lit up a halo around her heart.

They left Steve at the table, after they'd discussed where Warsaw was. He waved cheerfully to them on their way out. On the sidewalk outside the club, the soft breeze was pure oxygen. A full moon lit the ocean down the street. The reggae music came from a million miles away. Abdul and Mona said good-bye. They had decided to troll around for, respectively, more peace and more aggravation.

"Where's the billiard place?" said Rob when the others had gone.

"It's that way," said Christa, pointing away from the ocean. "Do you really want to do that, or would you like to walk on the sand for a bit?"

"Is that what you want to do?"

"Yes."

He wanted it, too. Surprise. Surprise.

They didn't talk as they crossed Ocean Drive to the beach. It was deserted. They kicked off their shoes. A lifeguard tower guarded the emptiness. The sea was flat, shimmering in the moonbeams. The damp warmth surrounded them. Behind them, Art Deco land shone in the darkness, muted jazz merging with soft rock. Above, in the desert of stars, God was alive and well in his world. Or so Rob thought, as he watched Christa walking beside him, glowing with the radiance of a good deed in a naughty world.

"What a night," he said.

"It's not over yet." She laughed, throwing back her head and turning to him.

"You're beautiful, Christa," he said.

"You're beautiful, too, Rob." She didn't mean what he meant. Both knew that.

They walked on.

"Where do seagulls sleep?" said Christa, heading toward conversational safety. He shrugged, not wanting to do that.

They were at the edge of the water. Christa waded into the shallows. "I'd like to swim to the Bahamas," she said.

"I'd like to go wherever you go."

"Come on, Rob, lighten up." She smiled at him, telling him that she knew what he was trying to say, and that he mustn't say it.

"I don't love Lisa," he said.

"Neither do I." His face fell as she tried to joke him out of his earnestness.

"Christa, you know what I'm saying."

"You're saying you like me a bit. That's okay. I like you."

"It's not just a bit, Christa. It's more than that."

"Rob, it isn't. It isn't. You're young. Maybe you like me 'cause I've been around, seen it, done it. Really, I'm old and dull, and Lisa's crazy for you. You like her. I can tell. You're just confused."

"Hell, I'm not confused." He raised his voice to her, emphasizing his terrible confusion. "Please don't say I'm confused," he said. He walked into the water toward her.

She moved a few feet along the beach. He followed her, coming closer. The moon had his face in its spotlight. It was the face of a god in trouble. Christa had never seen him look more beautiful. Inside her, molecules moved.

"Rob. Don't. Don't do it to yourself," she said.

"Are you in love with Peter Stein?" he said, hopelessly.

"Yes, I think so."

"When are you seeing him again?"

"He's coming up from Key West tonight."

"Why do you love him?" The "and not me" hung in the night air. The pain was alive on his face as he asked the unanswerable question.

"Oh, Rob. I don't know." She flung out her hands to encapsulate the impossible mystery of love.

"He was such a jerk when we met him that time diving." He couldn't help it, although he knew it was stupid as hell to say something like that.

"We're all jerks sometimes." The rebuke came winging back as he had known it would.

They were quiet, wading the shallows, and allowing the sudden poison to disperse.

"The shoot's going to be hell," said Rob at last. "Maybe I should just get lost."

He felt the pang of guilt as he played a cunning card. He could almost feel Christa stiffen. She was so good, so pure, so very ambitious. And wasn't everything supposed to be fair in love and war, even a little gentle blackmail?

"You're not a quitter, Rob," she said. "You're strong and responsible, and you keep your word. That's what I like about you."

It was a start.

"I know. Don't worry. I won't let you down. It's just that Lisa is like so . . . I mean . . ."

"Lisa's the most beautiful girl on earth, Rob, and deep down she's a good girl, beneath the shark exterior. She had a terrible childhood. She dealt with it. I admire her. She loves you. You'd be crazy not to feel something for her."

"I never met people like Lisa before."

It was Christa's turn to feel guilty. She was responsible for the things that had happened to Rob, if you could ever be responsible for someone else's life.

"I guess we all take some getting used to."

"You're not like Lisa."

"Maybe deep down I am."

"I don't believe that. You won't change what I feel by telling me how awful you are. You'd have to actually *be* awful, Christa, and I know you're not."

"Why do you like me so much?"

Christa wanted to take back the words. They'd slipped out. Why?

Because she hadn't yet tired of flattery? Because Rob Sand was so sweet? Because of the way he looked in the moonlight?

His face softened. It was a tiny opening. She'd asked him to say the things he wanted to say.

"Because you're beautiful, and you don't trade on your beauty. Because you're clever, yet you never put anyone down. Because you're kind and sensitive and caring, and yet you're strong and not weak."

She stopped in the water. It was the nicest thing that anyone had ever said to her. She felt herself tremble. Electric fingers played on her spine. She was suddenly aware of her breathing. Rob Sand had always been two people to her—the charming, complex boy whose dilemma was that he was too good . . . and the supreme physical work of art with the body of Adonis and the face of an angel. Now, in the sea of South Beach, the two Rob Sands had merged into one.

"Oh, Rob," she said, as her defenses melted. She had been keeping him at bay with words, with body language, with her maternal indifference. Now, she was signaling her surrender.

He waded through the warm sea to her side, and he held her hand in the moonlight. He squeezed it, standing in front of her, his face inches from hers. He held his breath as he longed for her. The adoration shone from his eyes into hers. He rested his other hand on her waist, and he felt her shudder beneath his touch.

She closed her eyes and swayed toward him. He cupped her face in his hands and moved his lips to hers. His mouth touched her mouth. He pressed against it, willing her to respond to him. She opened her mouth a fraction, not yet committed to intimacy. He touched her with his tongue, wriggling it gently between her parting lips. Her body was hard against him now. His was harder against hers. He could feel her heart beat. Beneath his fingers he could sense her indecision. He had moistened her mouth, watering the shy flower of her. It hung in the balance. At any second she could be lost to him. Then he felt her tongue. It brushed against his and her mouth opened wider. They were kissing. Both of them. It was a gentle, tender kiss, and her arms reached out to bind him to her and her head moved beneath his hands asking for more closeness as she prepared to sign the contract of lovers.

But suddenly she froze. He felt her body stiffen. Her arms were against his chest, pushing him back. Her lips retreated from his. In their place was her stricken face, her mouth already searching for the words that would shatter his glorious vision of the future.

"No, Rob! I can't. We mustn't," she murmured in desperation.

There were tears in her eyes as she denied herself the passion. There were tears in his as he learned he had lost her.

"Please," he said.

She didn't answer him. She put out her hand and she ruffled his hair, her gesture full of the affection and tenderness that had nearly been so very much more.

"We have to go back," she said.

30

Lisa had hurried back to the hotel. She seldom felt she was missing something, but right now the feeling was strong inside her. It was instinct. The South Beach evening was unfolding, and at every point there were new twists and turns in the drama. Rob was hers, but only just. He had a crush on Christa that infuriated Lisa. But Christa was in love with Peter Stein. That put her out of the running. It was just as well, because any minute now, Mommy Warbucks in the shape of Mary Whitney would turn up with the golden key to any future that Rob cared to dream up. Steve Pitts was hovering like a bald eagle over the canyons. And the dreadful Mona, who would do the hunchback of Notre Dame as long as it involved stealing him from another woman, had her hungry eyes on Rob, too. Lisa looked down at her dress. She could hardly see the bloodstain, but she knew it was there. That was the only thing that mattered. Perfection must remain perfection. It was rule number one.

The Cardozo was on the beach. She stomped into the lobby, not bothering to reply to the "hello" of the girl at the desk. Stairs or elevator? Her suite was on the top floor of eight, but the elevator took forever. She took the stairs, devouring them as if they were a Stairmaster at the gym. What the fuck did Christa and Rob think they were doing playing *billiards?* Okay, it was a fun thing to do at Lisa's age, but Christa was too old for things like that, and Rob was, well, too young. She stuck the key in the lock and plunged into the room. Already she had targeted the replacement dress—a skin-tight Montana that could be guaranteed to crack nuts all over town.

She darted into a closet and fast-changed into the Montana runway-style. She smoothed down the dress over the best body in the world and checked out the result in the mirror. She twirled in front of the looking glass like Maria in *West Side Story.* Pretty woman, yeah, yeah, yeah. She was dressed to assassinate.

The moonlight streamed into the room from the balcony. She wandered over to the French doors. What was the hurry? The world always waited for a star. She flung the doors open. The sultry air rushed across her face. She stepped out onto the balcony and walked to the railing. It was a beautiful night. The moonbeams were painting the water silver. The palm trees were silhouetted against the cloudless sky. Mmmmm. It was a night for lovers. She could feel the romance in the warm night breeze. She stared out over the sand to the water's edge and watched a couple embrace in the shallows. She didn't envy them, because soon she would *be* them, making far cleverer love, to a man far more beautiful than the loser on the beach. Wasn't she Lisa Rodriguez, goddess of the nineties, the girl who set the love standards for the mere mortals to imitate? She laughed. She actually felt sorry for the boy and girl out there. She pitied their insignificance and the banality of their feeble fumblings as they sought silly togetherness in the picture-postcard night. As she watched, the lovers parted from each other's embrace. Then, hand in hand, they walked back along the sand toward the road beneath her hotel. Lisa watched them, her lip curled in supercilious superiority. They made her feel good, these nobodies. The girl walked well, like a model might. There were enough of those on the sands of SoBe. She smiled to herself as she watched them. They were talking hard to each other. He looked a bit like a poor man's Rob. He was certainly well built. And the girl was tall, with very good posture. Her body was not unlike Christa's, but of course the face would be a major-league disappointment.

It was impossible to pinpoint the precise moment when Lisa learned the truth. The awareness shaded in from the edges like a fast cloud obscuring the sun. One moment Lisa's mood was sweetness, light, and pleasing condescension. The next, it was not. They were at the edge of Ocean Drive, still hand in hand, but now revealed in all their sexual splendor by the light of a street lamp. Lisa's heart leaped against her ribs as if wanting out of there, and she caught the breath in the back of her throat, as hormones flowed she never knew existed. She had seen them do it with her own eyes. Fate, luck, the devil, had conspired to produce the ultimate joke. Christa and Rob had kissed each other on the beach for an audience of one. Lisa had stood in her own private box and watched the show. She had even criticized the performance. The desire for vengeance on the sexual traitors was overwhelming. She wanted to fly down from the balcony and obliterate them with the bullets of her hatred, shower them with the napalm of her venom, cruise into their souls with the missiles of her fury. She held on to the balcony, her knuckles whitening, as she fought to control her feelings.

Then, with a superhuman effort, she forced the feelings back inside, like a Ghostbuster canning a room full of demons. She didn't scream out to the lovers from the top floor of the Cardozo. She didn't throw things. She did something else. She stepped back into the room. She closed the doors carefully behind her. Then she stood stock-still in the darkness, and she communed with Lucifer.

"You *bastards!*" she hissed. "Nobody does this to Lisa Rodriguez."

31

The Island Club, like the Rock of Ages, had not changed much in everyone's absence. Lisa stalked in first, looking for the lovers like a sheriff for outlaws in the Last Chance Saloon. They weren't there, but Steve Pitts was. Another bottle of Mount Gay sat on the refurbished table, and José and the friend were sitting at it with the photographer. Steve stood up as Lisa approached, stumbling slightly as he did so.

"Ah, Lisa, darling. Reinforcements. I hope you don't mind, but José is back, chastened, contrite, and more than a little drunk, I am afraid."

"Where's Christa?" said Lisa.

"Isn't she playing with balls somewhere?" Steve laughed.

"You'll never know," said Lisa darkly. José stood up, a silly smile on his face. He tried to say something about being in love with her. She ignored him. Then Christa and Rob walked in.

They headed toward the table.

"Hi," said Christa, color on her cheeks. "Great dress, Lisa."

"Thanks," whispered Lisa, wondering how long she could hold it in, wondering why she was bothering to.

"How was billiards? Fast, apparently."

"We didn't go. We took a walk on the beach instead," said Christa. "It was beautiful out there."

"Sounds romantic," said Lisa, trying to keep her lips straight as she spoke.

Rob looked at the floor.

José staggered over to Rob and put an arm around his shoulder. "I'm sorry, man," he slurred.

"It's okay," muttered Rob, grateful for any diversion.

He was totally confused. He didn't know if he was ashamed, guilty, disappointed, thrilled. Everything had happened so fast. There had been no time to get a perspective on it. Christa had so nearly let him in, then, at the last moment, she had shut him out. As they'd walked back across the sand, both had tried to make sense of what had happened. The trouble was that the sense each had made had been different. Christa had blamed the moonlight for turning her friendly affection into a momentary starburst of fake passion. Rob blamed it on the heart he could no longer control. He was miserable that she had rejected him. Yet he was elated, too, because Christa had allowed herself so close to him. Part of him said he could build on that. The other part warned it was a one-way ticket to heartache.

Christa didn't like the way Lisa had said "Sounds romantic." Her antennae were vibrating. The Cardozo, where Lisa had changed her dress, overlooked the beach. Oh, no! Surely not! The surge of anxiety zipped through her. Damn it to hell. How could she have kissed Rob and allowed him to kiss her? She had been around too long to make a mistake like that. She was a million miles from loving him. She loved Peter Stein, who would be hurtling through the middle Keys at this very minute. Yet she had been so flattered, and he had looked so sweet, and . . . and . . . She tried to turn her thoughts and obliterate the mistake, but it nagged away at her. The deed lived on, not only in her mind, but in Rob's mind, ready to be turned from a molehill to a mountain. And worse, just maybe it lived on in Lisa's mind, where it would be a nuclear bomb poised for detonation—a bomb that would destroy everything, her business, her new love, the happiness that short minutes ago had been wrapped like fairy lights around her heart.

But her telephone was ringing again.

"Watch the door," said the voice of Mary Whitney. As Christa did as she was told, the billionairess walked through it, a cellular clasped to her ear. She bowled up to the table, smiling wickedly. Abdul and Mona sidled along in her wake. She peered around her, taking the pulse of the party and finding it faint. "What is this?" she boomed. "I found Azziz and his 'friend' slinking around on Collins, like refugees from a bad time. Now here you all are looking as if some rich relative has survived major surgery. Obviously, I have arrived not a moment too soon. What is this place? And who are these Hispanic youths? Are they dancing partners? I think I should be told."

She lifted them all up by their bootstraps. Her energy was an infection.

"We need a change of location," she diagnosed in a definite voice. "It's quite clear that familiarity has bred contempt. Come on. Who's the Indian scout around here? Where to?" Her laughing eyes sprayed the scorn of the superrich over the lesser mortals.

"We were going to end up at Warsaw," said Lisa.

"End up? End up?" brayed Mary McGregor Whitney. "Nonsense! This fucking night hasn't started."

32

In the world of Johnny Rossetti, nights were not for sleeping. He sat at the round table in Au Bar, the one that controlled the foot of the stairs, and he slammed into the vast balloon of XO as if it were oasis water in a desert of despair. Sissy, at his side, was nervous.

"Are you okay, Johnny?" she tried.

He didn't answer her. Instead, he stuck out a hand and began to play with her leg. It wasn't a nice feeling. His movements were cruel. His hand roamed rudely over her thigh as if he was testing meat for tenderness in a European butcher shop. She wanted to push him away, but she didn't dare. He didn't look at her as he felt her. It was a demonstration to anyone watching both that he owned this girl and that he didn't care for her. He was telling everyone she was merely a beautiful contraption for getting him off.

"Johnny!" she said.

He didn't stop. He worked harder at her leg, kneading the flesh beneath the material of her jeans. He was pinching her hard. It actually hurt. He gripped her harder, sticking stiff fingers into her quadriceps.

"Ouch!" she said.

"Do you honestly care if I'm okay?" he growled at her, his fingers sinking like arrows into her thigh.

"Please, Johnny. Don't! You're hurting me."

"Yeah," he agreed, letting go at last. His evil mood was global. He wanted to spread his angst like muck in a field. Wasn't that what the girls were for? Sissy was gorgeous, but she was merely a model who worked for him and desired desperately the material things he could give her. In that, she reminded him a bit of Christa and Lisa in the early days, of Lisa anyway, so hurting her was fun. He turned to look at her. Her pixie face was miserable. There were tears in her great big eyes. His face twisted in disgust at her weakness. She hated him, of course. They all did. But she was bound to him by the Krazy Glue of ambition. "You dumb fuck," he snarled at her.

"I'm *not* dumb." The tears thickened in Sissy's eyes. It was true. She wasn't dumb. She'd been accepted by UCLA. Her dad was a teacher. The tear squeezed out of her eye as she thought of him. Why had she deserted her family, ignored all the good things they had taught her, and swapped a life of decency for a deal with the devil in the city of sin? She herself couldn't understand it. She knew money wasn't everything, that fame was a joke, and that however rich and powerful they might be, a jerk was still a jerk. Somewhere along the line she had become a junkie for success, and the addiction had cost her her soul. Where had the character flaw come from? Not from her dad, who taught school with love and for love, and who had never wanted money. Nor from her mother, who'd never asked for anything more than health and the happiness of her family. No, her ambition was her own perversion. So now she stared from the covers of *Elle* and *Allure* and she peddled her beautiful body to the piece of filth who'd put her there, and the world in its wisdom envied her beauty, her bank balance, and the "freedom" she had earned.

"You must be dumb to be with me," sneered Johnny, encouraged by the sight of her tears, and by the fact that she was daring to answer back and not just suffering in silence.

"Do you hate yourself that much?" Sissy wondered where she'd found the courage for her reply. From the thoughts of her family. That was where.

"Ha!" Johnny shot out the exclamation of surprise at the rebellion. His girls weren't allowed to say things like that. When they did, they were punished. If they didn't submit to punishment, they were discarded, and their fledgling careers ruined. It was the cruelest punishment of all for the upwardly mobile models he selected as his "special" girls.

"I didn't mean that you were dumb to be with me because I hate *myself,* darling," he whispered. "I meant you were dumb to be with me because I hate *you.*"

Sissy felt the chill on her spine as his words pounded into her. Her stomach sank. He'd never said anything like that before. He *hated* her? This man who'd made love to her body a hundred times in a hundred days. With cold clarity, she saw herself. She was a girl who lived and slept with a man who loathed her. In exchange, he gave her things she wanted. She was a whore, a more dismal, pathetic prostitute than any street hustler who sold blowjobs at traffic lights in the poor parts of cities. She felt sick. The nausea welled up within her. She should leave. She should walk out this second. Tomorrow she should fly home and exchange the "glamorous" life of a woman who stared from the glossy pages of magazines for the life of a person who could look proudly into a mirror. She knew with a greater certainty than she had ever known anything that that was the right thing to do. She also knew she couldn't do it.

"Blankheart was in the office today," said Rossetti in a matter-of-fact tone. "He was having second thoughts about using you on the Smiley jeans thing. He was worried your butt was too big. But I think I can talk him into keeping you. Oh, and did I mention that new Condé Nast magazine wanted a blonde for their cover? I guess it could be you at a push, unless I persuade them to use Gail . . ." He tailed off nastily, as he dangled the carrot and waved the stick. Then he sat back in his chair, sucked at his cognac, and waited for her reaction.

She sat still. Now she had something more important to worry about than shame. The Smiley campaign was vital to her game plan. And it had been baked in the cake. She hadn't actually signed anything, but it had been verbally agreed. Panic gripped her. Johnny was bluffing. Blankheart himself had wanted her. Her butt *wasn't* too big. It was the best part of her body, bar none. But the uncertainty lingered. Had she put on weight during the Seychelles shoot? Had she been working less hard with the trainer? God, maybe it was a tiny bit bigger. She wanted to rush off to the john to check it out. Shit! What the hell was that booze doing on the table in front of her? She should be on Perrier. She was trying to keep the anxiety off her face, but she knew she was failing.

"It'd be a pity if you lost Smiley," said Johnny, ladling it on, "because of your fat ass."

He smiled as he spoke. Mid-range models were notoriously insecure about their personal appearance. Only at the very top end, where the Lisas and the Christas lived, did you get the super self-confidence that translated into megabucks and superstardom.

"Johnny, I want Smiley. I need Smiley," said Sissy. Her voice was urgent. She reached out and tried to hold the hand that had insulted her thigh a few moments before. He brushed her away. He smiled his triumph.

"Well, honey, you know how it is. Blankheart and I go way back. Like forever. He owes me several. I can call in the IOUs if I want, but that means I've used them up, doesn't it? I get to use up my IOUs so that you get to stuff your outsize rear into poor old Smiley's jeans. Doesn't sound like the greatest deal for me."

"Johnny, please, don't . . . I mean, my butt's not big . . ."

He laughed as he watched her plead. Smiley would be three hundred thousand to her, and she had the job all wrapped up. But she didn't know that. Her picture-perfect derrière would be a work of art draped in Smiley's blue denim, but she was gripped by an insecurity born of wanting too much for too long. People who "needed" were such fun. They could be treated so *very* badly.

"Prove it."

She swallowed. "What do you mean?"

"I mean, prove to me your butt's not too big."

Sissy looked around in desperation. The club was full to bursting. There were half a dozen people she knew, a couple of guys, quite a few models. Her stomach churned. Panic gripped her. Johnny was going to make her do something. He was going to punish her for answering him back. And if she didn't comply, he was going to take away the ad campaign that she needed as much as her fingers and toes. She steeled herself. Whatever it was, she would do it. The passivity flowed within her, and in the total surrender there was even a flicker of pleasure. She wasn't in charge of herself at this moment. He was. Freedom had gone away. If robots could feel, they would feel like this.

"Where?" she said.

"Here," he said. "Now."

"Oh, no, Johnny. Please. Not in front of everybody."

"On the top of the table," he said.

The tears were back in her eyes. "I can't." Her voice caught on the edge of humiliation.

"Do it, and you can have Smiley."

She gulped. "How long?"

"Till I tell you."

The firing-squad look was all over her face. She stood up. She waited at the edge of the table, trembling. She didn't know how to do it, but she was a model. Somehow, she would manage. She looked at Johnny for a stay of execution, but there was only the glint of malice in his eyes, malice licked by lust. He reached down to his crotch, as her heart leaped in panic. Her humiliation was turning him on. Her mouth was dry. Her eyes were wide. Please, God, let it be brief. Let it pass like any mad moment of a crazed evening in a city that called sin sophistication. She closed her eyes and prayed for strength. Then she opened them, and she climbed up onto the table. She was aware of the eyes upon her. They were expecting her to dance. Late at night, after buckets of booze, great-looking chicks sometimes did that. But she didn't dance. She stood like a statue in the middle of the table. Then, as Johnny stared up at her, she forced herself to obey him. She undid the buckle of her belt. She fumbled with the buttons of her fly.

"Oh, boy," said a loud voice from the next table. "The chick's gonna strip."

She wiggled the butt that was supposed to be too big, and she slipped down the jeans to reveal it. Her panties were pure white silk, against the brown of her suntanned flesh. They were tiny, barely more than a rumpled thong of material, buried in the cleft of her pert, firm buttocks. Johnny could see the goose bumps of terror on her soft skin. He could see the tiny, downy hairs at the base of her spine standing rigid with fright. She held herself proudly before all the eyes that raped her. Her head was thrust back in defiance, eyes closed in shame, as she endured the public humiliation. Several people shouted things. Somebody clapped. Not anybody criticized the magnificent bottom that would one day be selling Mr. Smiley's jeans.

Then from somewhere, she found strength. She opened her eyes and stared hard at Johnny. She was in control of herself once more and to prove it she would go one step further than he had asked. She reached down and hooked her finger into the elastic of her panties. Then, suddenly, she pulled them down and showed him the whole thing. Her butt stood there in the dim light. One leg was pushed forward, the other thrown back. The lines of her bottom flowed in secret harmony, up to her long graceful back, down forever to her muscular molded thighs. It wasn't peaches, or the draped lines of luscious fruits, nor was it the childbearing pelvis of an earth mother. It was the pouting, thrusting, round perfection of an athlete's musculature. It was a ballsy, business butt honed to rock hardness on the gym floor, and programmed for supremacy by faultless genes.

In all his miserable life, Johnny Rossetti couldn't remember seeing anything so fine. His voice croaked with desire as he whispered "Get down here." His whole body quivered with lust as the girl he had humiliated swept up her panties and blue jeans and did as she was told.

Sissy knew that somehow she had won. Her face was flushed as she sat down, but so was his. He was leaning forward in his chair. There was a nightstick in his pants. His breath whistled through bared lips in uneven gusts. It had been over so quickly, and the hell of humiliation had been mitigated to some extent by the jaded indifference of the majority of the New York nightclubbers. And she had gotten her way. She would get the campaign now. The thrill of winning unleashed a fountain of feeling within her.

The maître d' was hovering at the table.

"Is everything all right, Mr. Rossetti?" he asked unctuously, eyeing Sissy uncertainly.

Johnny waved him away. The show was over. He was already looking forward to a private encore.

"Did you like my ass, Johnny?" she murmured. "Was it too big for you?"

"It's beautiful," he whispered, his voice strained.

"You want to play with it, don't you?"

He nodded. He couldn't do words anymore.

"You want to play with it in the john," she said.

She stood up slowly. He wiped a bead of sweat from his brow. He watched her walk across the room. When she was out of sight, he stood up, fighting back embarrassment at the visible signs of his arousal. He followed her to the restrooms. Everything had changed. They had switched. He had been the master, she the mistress. Now his desire had him in chains. He was the one who wanted. She was the one who would manipulate *his* need.

One door said MEN. The other said WOMEN. Where was she? His gut knew. He looked around furtively. Then he slipped into the women's restroom. It was empty, but he knew where to go. He tried the door of the first cubicle. It was unlocked. His breath shuddered in his throat. He opened the door. It was empty. The second door was locked. He knocked quietly on it. He licked his lips. The catch of the door was drawn back. He pushed against it. It swung open. What had she prepared for him? What would happen now? The unknown gnawed at his stomach.

She was as she had been on the tabletop. Her back was toward him. Her naked butt was thrust back at him. She faced the wall, and she didn't turn around as she spoke.

"Get down on your knees and kiss it," she said.

There was no part of him that wanted to disobey her.

He knelt. Her legs were astride the cistern, her jeans and panties lowered to her knees. Both her hands were flat on the back wall, steadying herself as she pushed her rump back at him. He couldn't see her face. She couldn't see his.

He reached out to touch her.

"Only your tongue." Her voice was sharp, commanding.

He leaned in toward her, resting his cheek against her silken skin. He could feel her heat. It radiated against his face, musky sweet, warm and sensual. She wriggled aggressively against him, until he was buried in her sweat-soaked cleavage. He leaned forward, thrilled by the coercion, reveling in the alien role of the submissive. He could hardly breathe in the cramped space. His whole being was on hold as he prepared himself to please the woman who had previously existed only for his pleasure.

"Do it," she ordered. He did it. He lapped at her, shyly at first, then hard, hungrily. He was lost in her forbidden place, loving it, and loving more the strange subservience his position signified. She ground against his face. She painted it with her wetness. She sponged his eyes, his nose, his mouth, with the part of her he had dared to criticize. His head was forced back, and now she, too, inched backward in the tiny cubicle, driving him before her as he retreated on his knees. First his back was against the door. Next his head was against it. Then there was no more retreat. He was trapped. The hard door was tight to the back of his head. Her hard butt was crammed against his face. He sank down, fighting for breath in the delicious, dripping jungle. When it seemed he would drown, she permitted him partial escape. She eased herself up higher, letting him move beneath her, and allowing his eager tongue to find her other entrance. Now, she flowed over him, soaking his upturned face with the abundance of her desire. He fought to feast from her. It was his turn to beg. He had to have her.

"Please," he murmured from her damp depths.

She spoke clearly. "I want Smiley, the magazine cover, *and* the bottled-water deal. Okay? Do you hear me?"

"Yes, yes."

"You promise?" She squeezed her legs around his throat. She lowered the whole weight of her body onto his face.

"I promise." His strangled voice was barely audible.

She laughed the laugh of the winner.

"Okay, you dumb fuck," she said. "Go ahead. Help yourself."

33

"Will we all fit in the car?" said Christa.

"The whole beastly club would fit in the car," said Mary. "In a perfect world I'd let the homeless use it."

She shepherded her flock onto the sidewalk. The limo seemed to stretch the length of the block. A chauffeur guarded it against a small group of curious natives. The names "Lisa Rodriguez" and the occasional "Christa Kenwood" rippled among the crowd. They all climbed in.

"This is a very nice limousine," said Abdul, staring around appreciatively. "Where did you have it made?"

"Goodness, I don't know. Wherever one gets one's cars made, I imagine. Where do you get your cars, Rob? Ragtops?"

"I haven't got a car," said Rob with a laugh.

"Dear me, how original. I hadn't thought of that. Well, now that you're going out with the famous Ms. Rodriguez, you'll probably have to get one. Maybe she'll buy you one out of her winnings from my ad campaign."

Mary's tone was chatty, but the daggers were flashing just below the surface. She talked about Lisa without looking at her.

"I think it should be Christa who buys Rob's car," said Lisa. She smiled a nasty smile and stared hard at Christa.

"Oh?" The Whitney eyebrows shot up.

"Listen, if it's okay with everyone, I'll buy my own car when I want to, and not before," said Rob. His smile was growing thin.

"Why," said Mary Whitney into the silence that followed, "would Christa be a starter in the Rob Sand car-purchasing stakes?"

Christa looked away.

It was Lisa who spoke.

"Didn't everyone know," she said, her voice icy calm, "that Rob and Christa are lovers?"

"What?" exploded Mary, her eyes wide with glee and surprise.

"Oh, for God's sake, Lisa!" said Steve.

"I saw them doing it on the beach," said Lisa, "when I went back to the hotel to change. I was standing on the balcony. They were doing it in the sea."

She sat back against the cushions. The cluster bomb she had unleashed exploded in an airburst in the geometric center of the limousine.

Rob closed his eyes. Christa closed hers. A joyous incredulity blanketed Mary's face. Shock/horror scudded across Steve's.

"Surely they were playing billiards," said Abdul diplomatically.

"On the *beach?*" laughed Mona.

"Good *heavens,*" said Mary. "*What* dark horses you are."

"I've had enough of this," said Christa. She started to get out of the car.

"It's not true," said Rob.

They all turned to look at him.

His face was bright red. "I did something very stupid," he said. "It had nothing to do with Christa. She didn't want to know. She's in love with someone else."

He looked at Christa as if it would be an honor to die for her.

"You tried to rape Christa on the goddamn beach?" said Mona.

"Oh, shut the *hell* up, Mona. Of course he didn't try to rape me. Don't be so pathetically thick. Why the hell don't you all mind your own business?" Christa's voice was a snarl.

"I like to think it *is* my business," said Lisa.

"You don't own Rob," snapped Christa. "He's free to do what he damn well likes."

"Yeah, and I'm free to do what the fuck I like, and I don't think I like being on the books of the Christa Kenwood agency."

Christa's face was on fire. It didn't matter now. The bitch had gone too far. Life would go on without her. Not a particularly successful life compared to the one that might have been, but life nonetheless.

"People. People. People!" said Mary Whitney fast. Fun was fun and angst was angst, but megabucks were megabucks. "Tom, dear, drive, will you? Anywhere. Just troll around for a bit, okay?" Nobody would be able to get out of a moving car. Peacekeeping negotiations were best carried out between captive antagonists.

"You know what you are, Lisa," said Christa. "You're a spoiled child. You shouldn't be allowed to play with the grownups."

Lisa sat forward on the edge of her seat. "Well, thank *you,* Grandma. Maybe the grownups around here should try to keep their filthy fingers off the kids." That was a global attack. Mary, Steve, and Abdul were all generously included in the innuendo.

The car stole away from the sidewalk like a supertanker leaving harbor. The row raged in its hold.

"I think we all ought to pray."

"Oh, *can* it, Rob," screamed Lisa. "You fucking hypocrite. All you do is rap on about God while you crawl into everyone's pants."

Mary Whitney couldn't suppress a smile, despite the fact that her precious campaign hung in the balance. Young Rob had had that coming.

"Shouldn't we all try to calm down a bit?" tried Abdul.

"How *dare* you talk to Rob like that!" Christa was shouting. "For the very first time in your miserable life a really decent guy starts to like you, and you have to drag everything into the gutter and make it cheap and disgusting. I don't want people like you in my agency. I don't want people like you in my goddamn life, okay? Go take your cash and your bitchiness back to Rossetti. You deserve each other. You're both slime bags."

"A slime bag? A *slime* bag?" howled Lisa. "Did you just call me a slime bag?"

"You'd better believe I did."

"*Stop* it," yelled Rob at the top of his voice. "Both of you. *Stop* it." They both stopped it. A silence followed that was shaken, not stirred. "Listen. Listen to me." He lowered his voice. They were listening.

"All right. All right. Okay. Look, this is all about me. I don't know why, but it is." He paused . . . not knowing exactly what to say, but sure that he had to say something. "I mean, I really liked both of you . . . really like both of you. I didn't want it that way, but it happened that way. And Lisa liked me back, and Christa didn't. It's my fault what's happened, but don't blow everything because of me. Christa didn't do a thing, Lisa. Not a thing. It was all me. Blame me. Not her. The best thing I can do is get the hell out of everyone's life." There was the mist of tears in his eyes. He held his hands tight together in his lap.

"No!" said Lisa.

"You don't have to go anywhere," said Christa.

"Here, here," agreed Mary Whitney.

"I am sure we should all be friends," said Abdul. There was silence as war waned.

"I'm just not a slime bag," Lisa broke in. "I mean, really, I'm just not one." Her face was still a mask of wounded astonishment.

Steve was the first to laugh. The surreality of the situation was total.

Christa's face softened into the beginnings of a smile. It was Lisa's face that was the catalyst. Christa's child diagnosis had been right on target. Lisa sat there, impossibly lovely, absolutely devastated by the slur on her physical appearance. It was totally childlike.

"Lisa," laughed Mary Whitney, "your face!"

"Ha! Ha!" agreed Abdul.

Even Rob was beginning to smile. He put out his hand and touched Lisa's knee in a gesture of support.

Lisa tossed her head, the last to the joke, and still not quite there.

"I'm not, am I," she said with a charming plaintiveness.

"Of course you're not, Lisa. I'm sorry. I guess I wasn't used to being a grandma," said Christa.

"And a child molester," giggled Mona, as Abdul raised his eyebrows to the ceiling.

"Just a squall, dears," brayed Mary. "Clears the air. Lets off the steam. One should never underestimate the truth of clichés."

"Dancing," mumbled the drunken José. "I wanna go dancing."

"I think our man from Arthur Murray should be indulged," said Mary, gripping the leg of the comatose José and fingering the hard young muscle speculatively.

"Well," sniffed Lisa. "If anybody listens to children around here, I guess we could all go lose it at Warsaw."

"Right on," agreed Steve. Abdul was game. Mona was ready. Rob was resigned.

"Terrific," said Christa. "When my top girl speaks, her wish is my command." It was as well to confront that one as soon as possible.

Lisa smiled her assent. Mary Whitney sighed her relief.

"Advance on Warsaw," said Mary, her tone Napoleonic.

"Let's hope we'll be able to organize a safe retreat," prayed Christa.

* * *

The music at Warsaw wasn't just loud, it was dangerous. You could almost see the sound waves shake in the fetid air. Strobe lights bounced. A thousand dancers worked out on the floor. Sweat flew.

Christa's rib cage was vibrating. It was a weird sensation as her upper body became a sound box for the armoire-sized speakers that were scattered around the cavernous room.

"Great, no?" she mouthed at Steve. In answer, he pointed toward the bar. Conversation looked possible there.

They pushed through the shoulder-to-shoulder crowd, amazed that Miami could be like this. This was formula-one fun, hard-core loss of inhibitions, heavy-duty nightclub action. New York would have been proud of it. The others looked around them in bemused excitement. Only Mona and Lisa had déjà vu. Abdul, with the oldest ears, was on the threshold of pain. Both his hands were clasped over the threatened orifices. His mouth was wide open to equalize the pressure. Mary Whitney actually appeared impressed, the alien emotion playing on her face with the uncertainty of a novice actor on an unfamiliar stage. Both Rob and José looked like they could handle a few more decibels.

They all made it to the bar.

Abdul wrinkled his nose when he learned the champagne was American. He tried to convey the bad news. Nobody cared.

"No wonder young people don't go to health clubs," said Mary. "This is high-impact aerobics."

"You want to try it?" said Rob.

"Good God, are you asking me to dance?"

"Yup."

"Am I allowed to, Lisa?"

"Be my guest."

"Oh, well, I guess so. It doesn't look like cheek to cheek anyway. I ought to be all right."

Mary led the way to the dance floor, Rob following her.

He started to dance. "Why do you make passes at everyone except me?" she said. He pointed to his ears. "Can't hear."

She smiled and moved in close. She danced well and knew it. She gripped his waist and swung her hips, pushing her leg between his, dirty-dancing style. Her lips were against his ear. She repeated her question.

In answer, he shrugged. He didn't push away from her.

"The trouble is," she pouted, "the young have no respect for cash. I'll probably end up with Abdul. At least we can screw each other's bank balances."

He laughed.

"What *really* happened on the beach?"

"Forget it, Mary."

"You nearly blew my whole ad campaign, all on your own."

"You don't seem too upset."

"I don't get upset. I upset other people."

"Don't upset me."

"I'd like to excite you, not upset you."

He tried to push away then, but not too hard. She held on tight.

"Mary, don't. If you keep this up, there's going to be another fight."

He looked over toward the bar. At one time or another, everyone was watching them.

"I rather enjoy fights."

"I don't."

"But you enjoy doing it, don't you. Doing it with models. That really gets you off."

She rubbed against him. Nothing. She looked up into his guileless, beautiful face. Jesus, he was God. It was almost enough to make one a believer. No wonder Christa had fallen from grace in the moonlight. No wonder Lisa was a cat on hot coals. No wonder she was as horny as a sailor on a steamy Saturday night. Could she pull him at this very late stage? Could she scoop the others, and walk away with the Rob Sand exclusive? It was very far from likely, but it could be all kinds of fun trying.

"If you make love to me, I'll give you a million dollars," she said.

"You're joking!" He laughed uncertainly, determined to believe it was a joke.

"I never joke about money. It's the only thing that isn't funny."

She left enough laughter in her voice to keep the question mark hovering over the proceedings. That was always useful in case retreat became necessary.

"I'm not for sale."

"Popular wisdom has it that everyone is."

"I'm not."

"Two million . . . to Save the Children. Babies would live because of it. Hundreds of them wouldn't die. Thousands."

He didn't answer her.

"You'd be an instrument of God. Here on earth, you'd be his agent, giving life, fighting death and suffering and disease. One night. Tonight. And tomorrow, the children will live."

Again silence.

"Am I so disgusting? Isn't the end worth the means?"

She was serious now, because she could feel him weaken.

"You're playing with me," said Rob, his voice reproachful. "You wouldn't do it. You're testing me." There was a question in there somewhere.

"That's because you think two million is real money," she said. "And that's because you think I'm like all the other losers on this silly earth. I'm not. I'm special. When I want things, I get them."

"I'm not a thing. I'm a person."

"What on earth is the difference?"

"I'm going back to the others."

"Three million."

He made no move to leave her.

"You'd give three million to charity to make love with me . . . once. Why, Mary? Why? What's the matter with you?"

"I'm a foolish, middle-aged, deeply capricious woman . . . and I am incredibly, obscenely rich."

His heart was beginning to pound. He hadn't thought she meant it. Now he did. He hadn't thought for a single second in the world that he would ever consider her bizarre offer. Now, to his fascinated horror, he was. Three million dollars of food and trucks, of medicine and transportation would be answered prayers to God's oppressed. He would give his body, and they would receive the gift of life. What possible reason could there be to refuse the madwoman whose legs were locked against his? His pathetic pride? His irrelevant principles? His totally unimportant feelings? Compared to the defeat of death, and the wonder of life for the innocents, he was nobody and nothing.

"You want me that much?" he said. He had to be sure.

"It's not that much."

"Just one night?"

"Tonight."

"Where?"

"In the back of my car."

"Oh, shit!"

"And then you'd have the check. Afterward. After your services had been rendered, so to speak. Then you could go back to Lisa. Yes, that would be very nice. She could have my leftovers."

She pulled herself away from the ear into which she had injected the devil deal. His face was white. Was she the ghost he had seen? Goodness, was she that unattractive? She'd simply have to blank out a month for surgery.

"What do you say? Yes or no?"

"Yes," he said.

"Good," she said. "That's settled, then. Let's go back and find the others. Oh, and Rob, I think we ought to keep our little contract under wraps, don't you, darling? I'm not sure that everyone else would entirely approve."

On the way back to the bar, Rob Sand couldn't keep his eyes off Mary McGregor Whitney's swaying butt, but a voice in his mind kept repeating, "Three million dollars for the children."

"There you are, Lisa, dear. I brought him back . . . untouched by human gland. I think you're going to have to give him some dance lessons, darling, but you can always swap them for tennis sessions, scuba classes, religious instruction. No money need change hands." She laughed at the secret joke. Rob's whiteness was already turning red.

She reached out and squeezed his buttocks. "Now you go on and enjoy yourself, sweetheart. We geriatrics can't monopolize the young, can we? Maybe I'll catch up with you later for another dance of one kind or another. Yes, that would be nice." She turned to Steve. "Come on, Mr. Pitts, kind sir. Come and dance with me and talk some business. I'm getting a bit tired of pleasure, aren't you?"

"Somebody ought to strangle the stupid cow," said Lisa as Mary departed with Steve for the dance floor.

"*After* the shoot is a wrap," said Christa with a laugh. Rob looked at the floor.

"Did she come on to you?" said Lisa, whose sixth sense was a finely developed instinct.

"No, she just flirts, that's all."

"Bitch," agreed Lisa.

"But a rich bitch," said Abdul.

"Yeah," moaned Mona. "Rich bastard doesn't sound so good, does it?" She reached for the Azziz buttocks as she spoke, on the principle that rich bastards felt better than they sounded. "Come on, moneybags, you need exercise."

Together they followed Mary and Steve to the dance floor.

Back at the bar, conversation was sticky.

"What's the matter, Rob?" said Lisa. "Are you feeling okay?"

"Yup, I'm fine."

"Come on, then, let's dance. If you can stomach Mary Whitney, you ought to be able to handle me."

There was no way to refuse her. They were gone.

Christa was alone, unless you counted José, who was draped over the bar like a wet flag. She sighed. God, people were hard work. She looked longingly at the cellular and then at her watch. How soon to Peter Stein? Where was he? What was he thinking as he powered toward her?

Quite suddenly she had had enough of the noise and excitement. She walked out of the club. The silence on the street outside soothed her. All around the ice-cream colors of the Art Deco buildings glowed in the street lamps. A couple of bikers sat languidly in the armchair saddles of their gleaming Harleys, talking quietly. In the laundromat across the street night people thumbed through the magazines from the stall that stood next to the washing machines. A couple of models, arm in arm, meandered across the road. No six o'clock start for them tomorrow morning, thought Christa. South Beach was a scene in the making. Ocean Drive was in a constant state of flux, as bars and hotels opened, and derelict buildings sprouted new façades, but the real action was back a couple of blocks on Washington, and the side streets off it where now she walked.

There were surprises everywhere. She peered through the smoked windows of Club Deuce. It could have been a neighborhood bar anywhere in America, but the girl in the doorway was a French model that Christa recognized from a hundred magazines, her bare breasts pert and pink beneath a knitted see-through top, jet-black bikini briefs clearly visible through tight silk brocade pants. She was draped around a small swarthy man who had to be a photographer. Further on, neon nighteries interdigitated with Cuban delicatessens. Hispanic doctors' offices merged uneasily with private clubs called The Loft and Daisy's and public ones called Dreemz and ESP. There were boarded storefronts, and minimalistic boutiques, photographic studios, and trendy travel agents. A life-size Marilyn Monroe waxwork squatted over a jet of hot air, her skirt permanently fluttering around her waist, a full smile on her luscious lips. Tutti Plein had a six-foot-high sculpture of piled human hands in its window. A few doors up a life-size surfer showed by the outline of his underwear that all men were not created equal. Christa could feel the energy of SoBe radiating up through her feet from the sidewalk. In two years this place would become unrecognizable, as the rest of the world learned what now the cognoscenti knew. And here she was in the middle of it, midwife to the birth of a new Miami. She wanted to shout it from the rooftops, and let the others know that the party was beginning, here in America in the city by the sea. One day, much later, there would be the hangover, but right now America was giving a bash that would turn Europe green with envy. It was at that moment that the thought occurred to her. It surged up into her consciousness on a tide of excitement. She had a name for Mary Whitney's new perfume. *Miami.* That was it. The new Whitney collection should feed from energy of the future's city. Christa breathed in the aroma of the night air—orange blossom, night-flowering jasmine, the hint of gardenia from a hidden garden. Already in her mind's eye she could see the result. Mary Whitney's Miami, the scent of lovers. Mary Whitney's Miami, for all those moments when your skin needs to be kissed. She stopped. Forget the Dry Tortugas. Who needed the hassle when the aquamarine sea was here, minutes away across the caramel sand? The shoot on South Beach would be a logistical dream. Here there were air-conditioned Winnebagos, places to press clothes, hairdressers, makeup artists, an endless supply of film, and photo labs. Everyone was geared to photography. The police were helpful, communications were a cellular phone call away, props and transportation could be hired, and the hotels were cheap and stylish. Costs could be kept to a bare minimum, and all the usual hazards of a location shoot could be avoided. Miami was Lisa's town. The smell of it was the smell of her. Its Hispanic fire flamed in her eyes, its sophisticated Latin rhythms beat in time with her heart. And Rob was the other part of Miami, the WASP all-American, blond and wholesome, sweet and uncomplicated. The chemistry between the two would be the explosive reaction of the melting pot, the hubbling, bubbling caldron of exotic opposites that gave the rich flavor to Miami.

"Miami," said Christa out loud. "Miami," she repeated. It sounded so very good.

She hurried to retrace her steps. There was no time like now. She would float the idea at Mary Whitney while it was still zinging around in her mind. But when she got back to Warsaw, Mary Whitney had gone. Mona and Abdul, lathered like race horses in a cream of sweat, still staggered about on the dance floor. José was asleep in a chair in a corner, despite the rumbling rock. Rob and Lisa, Steve and Mary were nowhere to be seen.

"Where did they go?"

Mona shrugged. "Out," she yelled back.

"Where do you think?"

"What day is it?"

"Friday."

"Maybe Cameo. Maybe the Loft."

"Shit!"

She could find them, but it might take an hour or two.

"Listen, Mona, come into the office first thing, okay, or whenever you wake up. We'll get you signed up and working. Catch you later, Abdul."

Outside again, she made her decision. She was going home. She was going to slip by the office and organize Mona's contract, and then she was going to go to bed on Star Island. When Peter arrived at last she would guide him into her on the cellular. And that thought made her smile in the middle of the South Beach night.

* * *

At the front table of ESP the spotlight kept straying toward the Lisa Rodriguez profile, and away from the far less appetizing face of the girl on the stage who was playing a harp. As always, Lisa was the main attraction. But right now she was thinking. When she had seen Christa split, she had engineered her own splinter group. Now she was wondering what to do with it. Her initial aim had been to separate Rob from Christa, the only serious competition. But now she had achieved her goal, it had paled a bit. Rob seemed strangely subdued. Mary Whitney, however, was clearly having the time of her life. Steve Pitts, too, seemed energized.

"I can't believe this place," said Mary. "Forget the downtown scene in New York. This is wild."

"Pretty neat, huh?" Lisa never lost sight of the bottom line for long, and for the next year or two the bottom line for her would be Mary Whitney. Okay, their relationship had gotten off to a rocky start over Rob, but that was then. This was now. Mary Whitney had to be persuaded that she could become that mythical entity, a Lisa Rodriguez female friend.

"How long has it been like this?"

"Maybe a year. Maybe a year and three months. In ten blocks there's a higher concentration of pretty people than anywhere else in the world. Miami's kinda emptied Europe and America of beauty."

"What do you think, Steve?"

"From the photography point of view, it's got everything. The girls are moving here from New York. Living's cheap. They can fly all over, to Texas, the coast, Europe. They can even fly to New York and work there. The Europeans are flying over and booking girls straight off the beach, saving a fortune on air fares and hotel bills. They've got guaranteed light and sun and sea. It's a photographer's paradise. You can scoot off to the Everglades, the Keys, the Bahamas, and be back in Toni's Sushi for dinner. There's the architecture, the atmosphere, the civilization. It's a natural."

"Mmmmmmm," said Mary Whitney, suddenly lost in thought.

"Do you like it, Rob?" said Lisa.

"Oh, yes, sure," said Rob distractedly.

"Are you feeling okay?" said Lisa.

"Oh, you know Rob," said Mary wickedly. "He's probably dreaming about starving children, or some other worthwhile cause."

Lisa said nothing. She was in diplomatic mode. The old rat-bag had it in for Rob because he didn't want to jump on her billion-dollar bones. Then the thought occurred to her. It was getting late. Very late, and even though Lisa had booked herself out to be totally available for the Whitney shoot, she didn't do late nights on a regular basis. Top models didn't do those until they were ready to trade work for pop stars at the end of their short careers. It would suit her if she could slip away without bursting Mary Whitney's good time. What better way of doing that than to leave Rob behind as a hostage? He wouldn't get into any trouble with Mary. He wouldn't fancy her pickled. And Lisa could always pick up tomorrow where she'd left off. Rob Sand wasn't going anywhere. She had the whole campaign during which to capture him.

"Listen," she said. "It's getting pretty late. I'm bushed. Would anyone mind if I split?"

"Not me," said Steve, well aware that late nights wrecked faces.

"I won't say that the night is young," said Mary Whitney. "I only tell lies to make money."

Rob looked panic-stricken.

"You don't mind, do you, Rob?" said Lisa, making it plain she was leaving him behind.

The battle raged on his face. Part of him wanted to leave with Lisa. The other part kept him rooted to his seat.

"Whatever," he managed.

"So I'll see you all tomorrow afternoon, okay? At two in Christa's office, is that right?"

She stood up, loathe to leave, looking forward to bed.

"Be good," she said with a radiant, magnanimous smile.

"Oh, we'll be very, very good, won't we, Rob," lisped Mary Whitney.

Lisa wondered why he was blushing.

"Maybe catch you later," said Lisa to Rob. She wasn't talking about breakfast.

He smiled wanly at her.

"Bye," said Steve. He looked speculatively at Mary, and then at Rob. It was clear that he was in the gooseberry business. He, too, consulted his bottom line. The name Mary Whitney was written across it. The shrewd move was obvious. He stood up so that there was no room for argument, not that he expected any.

He looked at his watch. "I think I'm going to copy Lisa and call it a night," he said. "I can walk you back to the hotel, darling. You can protect me."

"Goodness," said Mary, pleased as punch. "All the faint hearts are folding like nine pins."

Then they were alone. She looked across the table at Rob. "You know what we're going to do, sweetheart," she said. It was not a question. "We're going to close every club, bar, and bordello on this fun-filled little island, and then I'm going to put you in the back of my car, and I'm going to fuck your brains out."

34

"Is it you?"

Christa tried to wake up faster. It was difficult to speed the process, and she knew she mustn't sound sleepy.

"No, it's a wrong number," said Peter Stein.

"Oh, Peter." Then, "Where are you?"

"I'm crossing McArthur Causeway. Am I warm?"

"You'll get warmer." Already the sex was crackling in her voice. "You're close," she said. "Can you feel it?"

"I'm not sure I can feel anything. After four hours on a narrow road I'm a hypnotized rabbit."

She was wide awake now. She stretched, like a sleepy, well-fed cat.

"Do you know where Star Island is?"

"Yes, I think I do. Isn't it on the left somewhere . . . opposite the cruise liners?"

"Slow down. You must be passing it about now."

"Yup, there it is. Here I am. How did people cope without cellular phones?"

"It was rough on lovers."

"What do I tell the gate guy? It's the middle of the night and I haven't shaved. He'll probably shoot me."

"Tell him you've come to make love to Christa Kenwood."

"Is *that* what I've come to do?" He laughed.

"Oh yes, it is."

She could hear him talking to the security man. Christa had already left instructions with the guard to let Peter through.

"I'm in," said Peter. "He said you were the third house on the left, and then he leered at me. Are you going to be standing in the doorway?"

"The door's open. I'm lying in bed."

"You're so shy, Christa!"

"Sarcasm is the lowest form of wit."

"I'm sure we could argue about that."

"We can argue about anything, but tomorrow . . . not tonight."

She heard his car crunch onto the gravel of the driveway. She heard the engine cut off, the door open and slam shut. Christa clasped her legs tight together. The excitement was building. She felt deliciously wanton. She was naked beneath the single silk sheet. Her lover had driven through the night. Now he was standing in the hall of her house.

"Peter?" Her voice was husky, as she spoke into the phone.

He didn't answer, yet she knew he was still there on the line.

Silence. She had heard the front door open and close. He was inside. But the silence grew.

"Peter?"

Her mouth was dry as she realized he was going to play games with her.

Her bedroom door was ajar. She listened carefully for the sound of footsteps on the stairs. Nothing. She listened to the phone. There was only the mild crackle of static, the spooky sound of no one when you knew somebody was there. It was dark in the room. The blinds were drawn against the moonlight. The ticking of Christa's bedside clock was softer by far than the beating of her heart.

She pulled the sheet around her shoulders. A sudden chill had descended. In the blackness, there was only anticipation. The thrill of the unknown gripped her. She was naked in bed. Her door was open to the world. And down below there was a man in her house, waiting, wanting the body that now shivered on the edge of fear.

She swallowed. She wanted to say his name again, but she didn't want to spoil the game. Doubt grew in the silence. It *was* him, wasn't it? It had to be Peter who had gotten out of the car in the moonlight. She smiled to herself as her mind played tricks. The night could do this. The night could do so much.

Then she heard the sound of feet on the stairs, stealthy feet, feet treading carefully to make no sound as they rose toward her. The adrenaline squirted. Desire was mixed with alarm now. The feet were the feet of a stranger. This was not the Peter Stein she knew. Hell, she hardly knew Peter Stein.

"Peter?" She spoke out loud, both into the phone and through the door of her bedroom. Her voice lanced out into the darkness, surprising her with its loudness. "Don't play anymore, Peter," said the sensible part of her. "Play with me until the end of eternity," said her deepest emotion.

She tried to see in the darkness, but the blinds were black-out blinds. She slept without chinks of light. It was a "thing" of hers. The feet made no sound, but the hinge of the door creaked as it opened. She could sense a presence. He was standing in the doorway. *Somebody* was standing in the doorway. It couldn't be anybody else. Could it? It couldn't be a weird, sick joke by the evil side of a too-brilliant mind. No, silly, it was the game. This was what she was meant to wonder. When the alien hands touched her flesh, she was supposed to shudder in delicious alarm as she gave her body to a stranger in the dark. She had often dreamed of it. She had lain alone and conjured up visions of anonymous lovers, shorn of their personality and meaning. Nameless, faceless bodies had pleased her on many flights of fantasy. But here fantasy and reality were colliding. Whoever had been at the door was walking across the carpet toward her.

She took a deep breath. It was the point of no return. She could play, or she could refuse to play. She could reach for the light and call his bluff. Or she could stay quiet in the blackness and give herself to him. Her rational mind tried one more time. What were the odds of this being terror? A hundred to one? A thousand to one? It was laughable. But the one, the one. In a billion-to-one, there was always the one. She stopped breathing. Her heart thundered on. Her stomach was tensed tight. He was standing by the side of her bed.

She could hear him moving now. He was doing something, barely two feet from her. Oh God! He was getting undressed. She bit her lip so as not to cry out. Fear held her tight, squeezing her. Her pent-up breath wanted out, but her mind screamed for silence. A great shuddering gust of air rushed from her throat. It caught on a ledge of lust, and broke free as a sigh of hopeless passivity. A hand was picking up the edge of the sheet. She felt it peel away from her skin. Her breasts were bared. Now her stomach. And her thighs. She covered herself with her hands in a reflex action. Her lips were too dry for speech. She was rigid with the most wonderful fear.

The hand touched her shoulder.

"Oh!" she moaned, starting back in shock. The hand moved to the side of her neck, gripping it firmly. The fingers buried into her flesh. His touch was commanding, not rough. There was no hesitation about it. It was sure of its right of ownership. There would be no resistance, it promised. There would be only obedience to the will of the stranger.

His other hand was on her knee. He pulled her leg up and to one side, until she was splayed open for him and she quivered with longing and terror at his touch. Christa had never felt more helpless. The drums beat in her stomach. Any second, his hand would be at the heat of her, exploring the damp hairs, slipping inside her to explore her body.

They didn't speak.

The silence was their conspiracy. She knew the precise moment it would end. They would not talk until the time they screamed their climax. Only when his molten passion was spent within her, would she be allowed to see her lover.

He climbed over her, straddling her with his legs. His thighs were tight against hers, his hardness crushed against her wetness. Now, he moved above her. She knew she should do nothing. For these thrilling minutes, she existed only as a joy machine for the pleasure of a man in the night. Then his thighs and his lower stomach lifted away from hers until he was supported only by his arms on either side of her. In the absence of touch there was only the delicious anticipation of touch to come. She licked the perspiration from her upper lip, and tried to force the moment deeper into memory. Then she felt him. The stick of his passion was probing the damp lips of her entrance. It explored her, wetting itself with her moisture, slipping and sliding through the so-soft hairs. It pushed in, then pulled back. It painted her with her own liquid, hot and hard, as it stroked at her silk soft lips of love. She forced her legs farther apart, opening wide to welcome him, and a feeling of the most intense subservience coursed through her, turning the tap of the fountain of desire. She was flowing around the point of him. Her thighs were slick with lust. His tip bathed at her spring, daring, taunting, promising, threatening. Then, he seemed to decide. He was still. He rested against her body, the end of him nestling in the pale pink skin of her opening. She could feel him throb. He was pulsating against her most sensitive place. He was caught captive in the crevice of bliss, and she pushed out at him longingly as her body pleaded for him to make her whole.

He heard her. He swooped down like an eagle from the night skies and he forced her open wide as he rammed home. He sank like a dagger into the dripping depths of her, slamming hard against the back wall of her world.

Christa shook with the force of his assault. She sank back, buried into the bed by the momentum of his invasion. Had he been so big? She was full of him. There was nothing else in her body but the hard hotness at her core. For long seconds he stayed there, his buttocks taut with the strain as he crammed himself inside her. At last, they relaxed. He slid back, surfing on the foaming sea of her lust, to the place it had all begun. She reached out with both hands to his hips. She wanted to guide him home again. She wanted to draw him back, to feel with feeble fingers the engine of wonder that rampaged in her body. She lifted up her butt from the already wrecked sheets, and held herself ready. He dived down at her once more, hammering in and out, and round, and down as her legs and thighs slapped against his in noisy celebration of the making of their love. She ground her hips to his, screwing them tight to him, moving from side to side as he moved forward and back. All the time the juice of her passion flowed like a champagne river, anointing him with its awesome abundance.

"Oh . . ." she moaned, lost in the moment. She wanted to say his name. She wanted to say "Peter." Then, as suddenly as it had gone, the doubt was back. He hadn't spoken to her. Dear God, he had said nothing. Her hands fell from his body, as his furious pace quickened. It was the size of him. He hadn't been this vast. She stopped breathing. She tried to think in the middle of the storm of bodies. But her mind wouldn't work. She was too far gone. This act ruled her. There was nothing else. No other thing mattered, but the blissful sweet conclusion. She could feel the beginning of her orgasm. It came from far away, like a voice on an uncertain wind, and she knew she would experience a pleasure more complete than she had ever known. The fear had done it. The astounding, mind-numbing fear that gripped her was growing as her passion grew. Now it soared, a piercing descant, over the thunderous music of desire. Before it had been Peter. Now it was only possibly Peter. Doubt surged around the edge of the moment, as the velvet walls of her sex slid tight round the tense skin of her lover. He moved faster to a furious rhythm, his legs and stomach banging against hers, fearsome, ferocious, as he headed toward his own moment. She rode him, matching his every motion with a counterattack of her own, and they hurried together toward the inevitable destination. It seemed impossible to speed the slapping, tearing union of bodies, but as each second passed their motion accelerated. Now, there was only the threshing of limbs, the magic sounds of liquid love, and the thick scent of musk that wrapped them both in a mist of lust.

He didn't pause as he came. An animal growl exploded in the depths of his throat. It was the signal Christa needed. She clamped down over him, and the jets of passion that exploded deep within her soaked her mind as they played into her body. She threw back her head, as her body exploded, and she yelled her ecstasy into the unseen face of the stranger. They splashed into each other, and the impatient purpose of their motion collapsed into chaos. Her legs thrashed at the air, her heels descended on his bottom, her fingers clawed desperately at the arms that straddled her. Her muscles milked him of his gift, and he pulsed within her, giving to her, baptizing her, making her his. On, on it went until at last the flowing tide was ebbing at the end of the dream. Peace descended. Their spent bodies luxuriated in the steambath that was now the bed. It was the moment for tenderness, for reassurance at the end of the little death that had been their orgasm.

"Oh, Peter," murmured Christa into the liquid silence.

"Peter?" said the growling voice in her ear.

35

"Where's Christa?" said Mona. She hovered over the secretary in the office of the Christa Kenwood agency like a black depression.

"And you are . . . ?" said the secretary.

"I'm Mona. I'm supposed to come in this morning and sign a contract with the agency. Obviously nobody's expecting me." She raised her eyebrows to the ceiling. Shit, *she* was usually the breakfast flake. She'd always imagined Christa would be totally gripped.

"Oh, yeah, Mona Applegate. Christa left a note about you. Late last night, I guess, when she got back from the Keys." The girl foraged around on the desk, found it, and held it up. "Says there's a signed contract in the filing cabinet, and all you have to do is countersign it and the deal's done."

"Oh," said Mona, smiling through her hangover. "Great. That's fine." She picked up the contract. It didn't matter what was in it. It only mattered that Christa had signed it. Jeez, the girl was a mover after all. She must have dropped by the office in the middle of the night to do the paperwork. That was pretty busy. She collapsed into a chair and pretended to read the contract for the benefit of the hired help.

"Got any water?"

"There's a Coke in the fridge."

"That'll do. So, where's Christa?"

"I don't know. I was expecting her this morning. I called the house a few times, but the answering machine's on. I guess she had a pretty late night. She has a really important meeting at two o'clock. She'll definitely be here for that."

Mona made a noncommittal noise. Christa could sleep till hell froze as far as she was concerned. The bottom line was the Kenwood signature on the bottom line . . . and there it was.

"Got a pen?"

The girl came over with one. Mona scrawled her signature next to the *X* that Christa had marked for her.

"You have to initial each of the pages. Then I witness your signature."

"Whatever," said Mona, scribbling her initials.

"Welcome to the agency," said the secretary brightly.

"Yeah," said Mona. "You the booker?" It paid models to be nice to bookers.

"No, that's someone else. She's having lunch."

"Listen, make me a copy of this when you're done, okay?"

"Sure," said the girl. "And I'll go get that Coke."

Mona was alone. Despite the heavy-duty hangover, she was elated. She had achieved her objective at record speed. Johnny would be proud of her. She could hardly wait to tell him. The second she was through here, and the contract was in her needy palm, she would split and call the main man. The News Café was on the next block. She could phone Johnny from there.

She looked around the room. Model agencies never looked like much compared to the cargoes they handled. Christa's was no exception. Head sheets were pinned to the wall; Rolodexes, containing the models' names and work schedules, fought for desk space with numerous telephones; piles of magazines lay around the room on coffee tables. There were three desks, a couple of faxes, some filing cabinets, and a sitting area with an old stuffed sofa and three armchairs. The best part of the room by far was the view. Mona stood up and walked over to the window.

There was a haze of heat across the sand. Two separate crews were shooting on the beach by the lifeguard tower. Mona smiled in contempt. Had to be a catalogue operation. The sun was too high for decent photographs, and the photographers were hardly creative geniuses to have chosen that particular section of featureless beachscape. Jesus, the rival teams were so close they would end up as background in each other's shots. Mona's professional eye checked off the details that others wouldn't notice. The photographers were both using thirty-five-millimeter Nikons rather than the Hasselblad view cameras that would give that extra quality that high-fashion photography demanded. They were trying to improve on the harsh light by using reflector boards, but it was hopeless. The overhead sun would cast dark shadows from the models' cheekbones. They would end up looking as soft and appealing as Dracula's sisters. The only reason for choosing the location would be the closeness to the Ocean Drive hotels. It meant that an endless stream of girls could quick-change through a long list of clothes, each of which would rate no more than a single motor-driven roll of film. On a *Vogue* shoot, in contrast, they might spend an entire morning on a single garment.

"Great day, isn't it?" said the secretary as she returned with the photocopy of the contract and the Coke.

"You'll never know," said Mona, turning back from the window and taking them from her.

Outside, she hurried along Ocean Drive to the News Café. The contract was neatly folded in the pocket of her cut-off blue jeans. A model girl and a model boy skated past on pink roller blades. Mona stepped over wires to a boom microphone from a sidewalk commercial shoot, and threaded through the crowded tables of South Beach's most durable meeting point. She was a regular there. Borrowing the phone was no problem. She knew just where Johnny would be. It was one o'clock. He would be sitting in Le Bilboquet. She had the number in her head, and she put the call through collect to Jacques. Despite being French, he wouldn't turn down a call from Johnny's girl.

He didn't.

"Jacques, it's Mona. Johnny's Mona."

"I know, darling. You wanna speak to Johnny?"

"Is he there?"

"Yeah, he's here. Hang on."

Mona waited. She could feel the powder-puff softness of cloud nine beneath her sneakers.

"Yeah, Mona. What's up, honey?"

"I'm in, Johnny," she bubbled. "I got in. I joined Christa's agency."

"You did? You signed on it?"

"I got it here, baby. I got it right here. Didn't I do good? Didn't I do like you said?"

He let out a sigh of satisfaction that was far more eloquent than words.

"You're my girl, baby. Sweetheart, you're a star."

"What you want me to do, baby? I'll do just what you say."

"Listen, Mona. I owe you. I owe you big, but I want you to hang on in there for a day or two till I get a few things straightened out, okay? You read me? Just do nothing. Just make like you're the new girl at the agency. That's what you are. Take the stuff they give you. Shake butt. Earn bucks. Do whatever, okay? An' I'll be in touch. In a day or two, okay, honey? And listen, Mona. You're the one. I'm missing you. When you get back we're going to *party,* and you're going to sign deals that'll be like Christmas, baby. Oh yes, you are. You trust Johnny. Sweetheart, you're going to be shitting money . . ."

She shivered with pleasure.

"I love you," she whispered.

"Me too, baby," said Johnny, unaware of the ambiguity. "Okay, gotta go now, honey. Got a client to feed. Just hang in there, baby. 'Bye-bye."

He was gone. And Mona had arrived. If you stuck close to Johnny it was silver dollars. If you crossed him you were dirty dimes.

She put down the phone. With her right hand she made a fist and she stuck it in the air.

"Yessss," she hissed.

36

Johnny was nervous. These guys made him nervous. It was what they did, of course. If they couldn't make people nervous, they were nothing. He was behind the big desk, but he wasn't taking the meeting. He was doing the talking, but it was the listeners who were calling the shots.

"I know we have a fair deal. The fairest. We have an agreement and you don't ask for things and I don't ask for things. With us, it's always been equal. Right? The time to worry is when the cabby says thanks for the tip. Ha. Ha."

He paused to see where the attempted joke had landed. It hadn't. It sank without comment.

The three men stared back at him, impassive, impermeable, unimpressed. One studied polished nails. One adjusted the crease of immaculate Gotti-style pin-striped pants. The other looked through Rossetti rather than at him.

Johnny cleared his throat. Hold the funnies, okay? He stumbled on.

"But I have a problem. I have big problems. Now I know you guys shouldn't have to worry about my problems. Maybe you have problems of your own . . . The thing is, I'm hurting. My top girl, Christa Kenwood, she quit on me. But she didn't just quit, did she? The bitch takes off to Miami and opens an agency in competition with mine. Next, she takes my other mega-girl. That's Lisa Rodriguez. You all know these girls. Shit, they're the biggest. They earn the bread. They're the prestige. They're what made Elle number one. I've got a fucking great hole in my bottom line and I'm bleeding bucks through it. That's what my problem is. That's what it is."

He'd worked himself up into a lather as he spoke. But he was angry and frightened. Something had to be done. Whatever IOUs had to be called in or taken out, vengeance was as vital as air to breathe.

"And it impacts on our deal . . . how?" said the finger gazer, still finger-gazing.

Johnny swallowed. This mustn't sound like a threat. Carrots were the things with these guys, never sticks.

"Well, we've had a great deal going. It's worked for both of us . . ."

"You just said all that."

"I know. I'm sorry. I'm worked up. I'm pissed. I'm deeply, deeply pissed." He swallowed hard. Hold on, Johnny. Get the words right. It's what you do.

"I mean, we washed a lot of money together over the years. It's been smooth as velvet. You put it in one end, and it comes out the other smelling of roses. My business is international. The stuff goes all round the houses and comes back to you clean as a whistle, less my cut. We've never fallen out. I like to think I've helped you out, and got well paid for it. But the whole thing is at risk now. That's what I'm trying to say. Without Christa Kenwood and Lisa Rodriguez's earning power, my turnover is off maybe seventy percent. That's going to light up my books like a Christmas tree. When they were pulling it in, there was cash all over the place. It could come and go, get lost, get found, and who cared and who knew? Now it's like low tide on the beach. All the creepy crawlies are scurrying about on the sand for everyone to see. When the banks get the message, they'll want to check everything out. You know how it starts. When you're doing gangbusters, everyone loves you. When you start to go down, everyone lines up to dump on you. Any minute now I'll have regulators all over me, not to mention the IRS. Jesus, it isn't going to do any good for any of us."

Silence.

"So you're saying that your problem is like . . . our problem," said the striped pants.

"I guess so. Okay, we could put a hold on the cash recycling. But I'm worried about what investigators might find last year and the year before if my business reversal gets the wrong people interested. I'm bringing you guys in now in the hope that you can help me sort this thing out."

"Getting your two girls back?"

Johnny held his breath. That was nearly it.

"Kenwood is the problem. She's already taken Rodriguez. She's landed a megabuck perfume deal with Whitney Enterprises. If she takes any more of my people, and she may do that, I'm gone. I need her out of business, bust, fucked, on her back, and not just 'cause I owe her one. If Christa Kenwood was history, I know I could get Rodriguez back. I invented the girl. We got a relationship going. The day she walks back through my door, my troubles are over. It's as simple as that."

"And just what do you have planned for Christa Kenwood? The girl's got a pretty high profile. This isn't Marla Hanson time, Johnny. We got a class reputation to protect."

It was the first time the boss man had spoken.

"I know that. If I don't know that, nobody knows that. Working with you has always been a deep pleasure, an honor. I trust you like I would my mother. I just wanted you to suggest something, because I'm losing it here. I'm looking at losing everything here, and when I lose, you lose, and that's upsetting me as much as anything else. Believe me when I say that."

"I believe you, Johnny," said the guy with the x-ray eyes. It was the most frightening line Johnny Rossetti had ever heard, because of the sinister smile that came with it.

"There *is* one thing I've done that could be a help. I have this girl . . . she's nuts about me, do anything for me . . . an' I got her to join the Kenwood agency. So there's someone on the inside. I thought it might be a help."

"How's about we frame the Kenwood chick in some drug deal?" said finger beautiful.

"Ah," said Johnny.

"Your girl runs some drugs, a big load, somehow gets busted, points it at Kenwood, cops a plea. How fond is she, Johnny? That fond?" said smart pants.

Johnny's mind was racing. How fond was Mona? Not very fond. But Mona was buyable. It would cost him, but worthwhile things always cost cash. It was how you knew they were worthwhile.

"I think she'd go for it." He was on the edge of his chair. The hot sweat beneath his shirt was cooling. "I could arrange for her to be booked somewhere . . . maybe somewhere not too obviously druggy. Have her pick up a package for Christa. Have her bring it back through Miami airport. Maybe we could even arrange it so Christa meets her. Takes physical possession while the DEA watches. We'd need some heroin, a key, maybe more. Nobody would get it back."

Johnny looked around the room uncertainly. He was talking serious money. If they did this for him, he'd be in hock to hit men for the rest of his life. He wouldn't own himself anymore. The title to his soul would be in somebody else's safe. But in broad brush strokes it was a neat scheme. It would do the job with nobs on. Christa Kenwood's agency would be obliterated. Christa would do time in the state pen. Lots and lots of time. And the bodybuilding dykes would line up to take a shot at her. He smiled. Christa had never played his games. But if things worked out, she might end up playing them against her will for the better part of ten years. Yes, that would be better than a short sharp death, or even a face slashing that top-money plastic surgeons could always repair. A drug conviction would tear down Christa's pride. It would rip her apart in the only area no one had ever been able to touch. It would be the rape of her soul.

"We'd probably be able to find some drugs from somewhere," said the boss man with a short laugh. "Of course you'd have to pay for them, Johnny. You'd be in for over a million to make it a worthwhile bust. And if we set this one up for you, it's outside our deal. It's on top. You'd owe us."

Johnny took a deep breath. These things didn't need to be said, but now they had been said, and before witnesses. One day there would be a call for a godfather favor. It worked like the movies. Maybe it had even been copied from the movies.

"I know that. You'd have my gratitude forever. You'd be saving my business. I know how it works."

If he had signed a page in blood on a parchment made of his own skin, Johnny couldn't have entered a more binding contract.

They all stood up. Nobody was going to remark on the weather.

"I'm gonna think a bit more about this, Johnny. Run it through my mind. Then I'm gonna get back to you. Tomorrow. Get your girl booked for a trip to Mexico. Yeah, fix that up right now. We can fill in the details later."

He leaned over the desk and put out his hand to shake Johnny's. His grip was firm, too firm. It was a handshake that meant something terminal. His eyes bored into Johnny's as the flesh was pressed, and, as it was meant to, Johnny's flesh crept.

"We'll be in touch." The others nodded their agreement. Never had the word *touch* sounded so ambiguous.

When the door of his office closed behind them, Rossetti was trembling. But it wasn't all bad trembling. There was excitement trembling, too. Although he had just done a deal with the devil, there were supremely good things to look forward to. He reached for his

Filofax and picked up the phone. He direct-dialed the Mexico City number. He didn't want to go through the switchboard.

"Buena Vista," said the secretary.

"John Rossetti calling for Jorge Jimenez."

In seconds he was through.

"Jorge. How are ya? Johnny. Yeah. Good. Good. Listen, Jorge, I want you to do something for me, okay? Can't get into too much detail on the phone. Yeah, that's right. Yeah. Ha. Ha. I want you to block-book a girl named Mona for a week in Mexico City. Line up some go-sees for her. I don't care if she gets any work or not. I just want you to hire her for a couple of weeks from the sixteenth on. Put her up, be nice to her, keep her happy, no questions asked. You understand? She works out of the Christa Kenwood agency in South Beach, Miami. Get the number from Directory. Tell them you've got a magazine fashion spread lined up. Tell them anything, but book her and pay whatever her going rate is. Bill me for everything, okay? I'm paying. And listen, Jorge, you do this for me and I'll send you your next Elle girl as a freebie. Got it? You get a middle-of-the-roader for nothing. Yeah. That makes you happy, okay? Call me when it's fixed, will you? You're a good guy, Jorge. You're my number-one guy. Next time you're over here, I'll get you fucked. You'd better believe it. You'll never want to do it again. Ha. Ha. You bastard."

He put the telephone down thoughtfully. Mona was next. He punched the number of the Park Central. There was no reply from Mona's room. He left a message.

"Tell her she's block-booked on the sixteenth for two weeks by the Buena Vista agency in Mexico City. Johnny says to take the booking, and he'll be in touch."

The girl read the message back to him. She'd gotten it.

He sat back at his desk.

Christa Kenwood had made a mistake when she'd crossed Johnny Rossetti. Now she was going to pay for it with the rest of her life.

37

Christa opened her eyes. The room was black as pitch, but she knew it had to be midmorning, perhaps later. For a second or two she lay still, allowing her mind to digest the night. Then she stretched and licked still salty lips. She put out her hand to see if he was still there, knowing that he would be. She smiled in the dark. Dear Lord, it had been beautiful. She had lost count of the times they had made love. After that first wild, weird encounter, when he had whipped her into a lather of lust by persuading her that he was a stranger, it had changed. It had, unbelievably, gotten better. After fear, there had been hunger and they had torn impatiently at each other's bodies. Later, as they had filled each other up with passion, there had been the love of connoisseurs, gentle, time-consuming, each kiss a lifetime, each touch a lingering journey of discovery. Then, toward what must have been the early morning, refreshed by sleep, they had loved each other as experts wise in the ways of ecstasy. They had learned each other's secrets by then, the tricks of the subtle trade of sensations, and their knowing tongues and clever fingers had squeezed sensuality from feelings all but exhausted by the excess of their lovemaking.

She touched his shoulder. He stirred.

"Peter! Are you awake?"

His grunt was her answer. A lazy hand surfaced to capture hers.

"I might have died and gone to heaven," he said.

He held her hand tight in his. With his other hand, he reached out and touched her stomach, sending shudders through her body.

"Mmmmmmmm," she murmured. His hand moved lower, until it lay in the darkness against her warmth. His fingers dipped down gently and touched her dry lips of love. He parted them, waiting for the damp welcome. Again she moaned. The feelings were starting again. She moved imperceptibly against his hand and the moisture was there again, first as a sheen of dew on the petal pink, then as a cover of wetness sealing one lip to the other. The tiniest noise signaled their separation beneath his careful fingers, a little liquid sound of mock protest. Then the rain began. It was a drizzle of desire at first, soft but insistent. His fingers luxuriated in the quiet shower, slipping deeper into her, increasing its intensity. Now, beneath his touch the heavens opened. The mist of droplets became a torrent, a tropical storm unleashed on a suddenly dripping jungle. Her legs splayed open as his hand sank down into the flood she had become.

"Peter! Peter! No!" she murmured hopelessly through the instant crescendo of lust. He stopped. Like an undammed river, her body raged on. She was split in two. Her mind cried "back" as her soul cried "forward." Her brain was shouting at her. What time was it?

Hell, she'd forgotten the two o'clock meeting. But, God, she wanted him one more time. She needed another half hour of Paradise. She thrust out at his quieted hand, willing it to play with her some more. At the same time she clamped her legs together around it, forbidding him to excite her, as she drowned his flesh in the wetness he had created.

"What's the matter?" he whispered. His voice was thick with longing.

"I have to get up. I have to get out of this bed," she said. Her voice broke into a laugh of helplessness. Christa lived by the will. Her life was about control . . . of herself, of others. But here she lay in wrecked sheets, stuck to them by the glue of sex. Part of her believed she would stay there forever.

"I have a meeting," she added. "I've no idea what time it is. Shit, I hope I haven't missed it."

"It's one o'clock," said Peter.

"You can see in the dark? God, what else can you do?"

"I eat lots of carrots."

"You eat lots of me."

She rolled on top of him, crushing his body with hers. She found his face, and kissed him with the desperation of the love addict. In the future, she would have to do without him for hours at a time, for mornings, afternoons, for whole days. . . .

He lay still beneath her, except for one part of him. It heaved against her damp, primed flesh. It was one o'clock. She had to bathe, and dress, put on makeup. She should eat. She had to get to the office before two to make sure things were okay. Was there time? His tongue snaked into her mouth. His erection pushed shamelessly against her, raking her slick stomach, combing her slippery pubic hairs with its hot head. Where did he find the strength? Where did she? Where did it all come from—the lust and the longing? How had God dreamed up this cruel triumph of desire over feeble flesh? There seemed to be an inexhaustible stream of wanting. The moment passion was spent, it had to be spent again.

"Peter, there's no time."

"No," he agreed, "there's no time."

He reared up beneath her. His pelvis slipped down below hers. Then he thrust upward. He took her by surprise. One minute he was throbbing against her stomach, her thighs, her soaked hairs . . . the next he was deep inside her.

She rose up on the force of him, but her lips clung to his.

"No time." The words echoed in her mind, shorn of meaning. They were two pathetic words, nothing more than two silly sounds, unheard and uncared for in a deserted forest. What was a meeting to this? *This* was the ultimate meeting. This was a union of souls, the only true contact between people doomed forever to be islands in the cruel stream of life. For these moments the pain of existence and loneliness could be forgotten and forgiven. It was a joining with the universe, the oneness that humans found only in the womb and the grave. It could be surrendered for nothing. And then Christa knew something else. She knew with the certainty of the seer what would happen now. His seed would flow into her. It would meet with hers. All night long they had been making love. Now, in the middle of the next day, they were making a baby.

The knowledge opened her heart. If there had been any doubt, there was none now. This was not selfish love, the demeaning search for gratification, for partnership, for the qualities in another that filled the void in oneself. This was giving. Her love beamed out at this man beneath her. She asked for nothing in return, but she was about to receive the ultimate gift of life.

He seemed to know, too. Their union transcended mere pleasure. No longer was it about joy. He moved inside her with the reverence of the faithful. She held him carefully in her body. Something holy was happening. They were coming together, and the result would be their future. She looked down at him tenderly, unseeing, and unseen in the darkness, but knowing him as she had never known another human. He stared up at her, tears of love in his eyes, as she moved so gently over him. He was between her legs, inside her body, but on a deeper level he was touching the part of her that would never die with the piece of himself that would always live.

Christa stilled herself for the moment. Her passages were open for him, twin aisles of entrance to the altar of her heart. There was no resistance at the edge of creation. Yes, she would come as he came, but her orgasm was incidental, as his was. The peaceful, easy feeling was in her. She could feel him tighten at her core. She had never felt such tenderness. Her mouth was soft against his, but she pulled back because she wanted to tell him what was happening at the moment it happened.

He hardly moved as he came. He shuddered beneath her. She felt him expand, contract, expand again. Then her own orgasm broke across his, and the precious ribbons of life streamed into her, warm and wondrous as the tide of her welcome that rushed out to meet them. He swam into her. She floated toward him. Now, now, their child was transformed from nothing to being and their hearts stood still in awe of the moment.

"You're making me pregnant," she whispered to him in wonder.

"I know," he murmured.

38

They were there. All of them. Christa walked in, bounced in, flounced in, whatever. Everyone in the room knew at once that something wonderful had happened to her.

Mary Whitney had a sour speech about the virtues of punctuality ready to play. She never got to press the button. Christa's mood, merry as Christmas, simply preempted it.

"Hello, darling," said Steve. "For some reason you look more than usually beautiful."

She smiled at him. Was it so obvious? She was glad it showed. It had to. She was reborn. She had been wrecked and recreated in a night and half a day by the man she loved. She hurried to her desk and sat down.

"Hi, everyone. Sorry to be a little late."

"Don't you worry about it," said Mary Whitney. "We none of us have anything else to do, and you must be *so* busy, darling."

"I guess it was a long night," said Lisa. She lounged on the sofa, taking up all of it. She looked, if it were possible, like a kitten in a foul mood.

She stared at Rob as she spoke. He studied the carpet. Mary Whitney glanced at him, then at Christa, then at Lisa. Clearly the previous night had been better for some than for others. Mary Whitney appeared to have been one of its winners.

"We lost you early, Christa," said Steve. "Wise virgins get their sleep."

"At least in theory," said Christa with a laugh. She squeezed her legs together. She felt divine. Nothing could touch her. She felt like a wife and a mother, and the most beautiful, sexy, glamorous young girl in the whole wide world. Having it all felt like this.

"Rob isn't a 'wise virgin,' " said Lisa. "He didn't get in till eight o'clock."

"That was my fault," said Mary Whitney. "We got into this discussion about starving children and how they could be kept alive, and it just went on and on and on . . ."

Rob was blushing. Through her joy, Christa noticed it. Why?

"Why are you blushing, Rob?" said Lisa.

"I'm not blushing," said Rob.

"It's hot in here," said Mary Whitney. "It was hot last night. Shit, this is Florida. It's supposed to be fucking hot."

"Could you turn up the air-conditioning?" said Christa to the secretary. "Oh, did Mona show up to sign that contract?"

"Yes, she did. And then half an hour later I got a call from Buena Vista in Mexico City, wanting to block-book her for two weeks. Pretty quick, ha?"

"Great! Wonderful!" Christa clapped her hands together. Could today get any better?

"Why on earth would anyone want to pay good money for Mona?" rasped Mary.

"Some people have more money than sense," said Lisa, an all-purpose insult.

"If you've got money, you don't need sense," said Mary Whitney.

"How did the Mexicans know she was with your agency if she only signed this morning?" said Lisa.

"Mona must have told them," said Christa. "You know how it is. Often models have closer relationships with clients than their agency does. Maybe she was saving the booking to impress us. It worked. I'm impressed."

"Yeah, and I bet Johnny'll be pretty impressed," said Lisa.

"Johnny won't know until someone tells him," said Christa curtly. "I can't imagine that Mona's going to let him in on the secret."

She looked at Lisa pointedly. Nobody was going to wreck her good mood.

"So what did everyone think about Miami nights?" said Christa. It had been one hell of an evening. She looked at Mary. When would be the right moment to broach her idea of the Miami perfume? It would have been better to get her alone.

"It was splendid," said Mary Whitney. " 'Very fun,' as the young would say. Or rather the 'slightly younger.' In *fact* . . ." She sat up in her chair in a gesture that said she was about to say something important. "In fact, in what was left of the night after my long conversation with Rob, I had one of my 'ideas.' "

They were all listening. Mary Whitney had a way of communicating her rare seriousness.

"I was impressed with Miami. I *am* impressed by Miami. This is a very happening town. The rest of America hasn't realized it yet. They're still thinking tourists, polyester suits, and sleazy low life. But that was last year. The future is going to be something else, I sense. And sensing is, after all, what I do best."

Christa was smiling. Surely not. Was Mary going to do the job for her? God bless coincidence. But, no, *coincidence* was the wrong word. It had connotations of luck. What was happening here was the ancient phenomenon of great minds thinking alike. Mary Whitney's mind and Christa's had coincided, not by chance, but because of Miami and what was going down there.

There was a strange light in Mary's eyes as she continued. "*We* see what's happening here. The Europeans seem to know about it. But Americans are always the last to recognize their own glories. They must be taught to see them. We can teach them. We could call the scent Mary Whitney's Miami and shoot the whole campaign right here on the beach outside the window and in all those wonderful, crazy clubs we were thrown out of last night. We could join the party. We could *be* the party. Above all, we could bottle the essence of the party and all the wild, exciting things that it has to offer. The scent will capture the smell of the place, night-flowering jasmine, gardenias . . . sensual, exotic, and at the end of the day, *American.* You can drive to get here. You don't have to get blown up in an airplane. You're in Spain, but you're *home.* You're a pathfinder, but you don't need a passport. You can go topless on the beach; you can skate down the street; you can be brown as a berry; you can drown in my scent, and every single man in America is going to want to love you."

She was on the edge of her seat, the words spewing out of her mouth like a sermon by a preacher on speed. You could feel her enthusiasm. It swept around the room like a contagious disease. Christa was flooded by the adrenaline. Lisa was smiling. Steve's mouth was wide open. Rob was sitting at attention. Of course it made sense. But why hadn't anyone else thought of it?

Steve said it. "Miami means different things to different people," he said. "Up North a lot of people think it's where you go to die."

"You can die here. Nothing to stop you. You can die of rum, of sunshine, of too much zipping around on boats. You can die of too much fantastic Cuban food, of staying up too late in clubs whose music is too dangerously good. You can drown in the surf, and wipe out on your Harley, and, if you wear my scent, you can die from making too much love. Listen, Steve, I'm not talking yesterday. I'm talking tomorrow. That's where the money is. People are going to think of Miami differently. They can't not. Look out of the window. Go down to the bar. Spend a morning at the News Café. Believe your own eyes. That's all I'm doing. It's started, but it hasn't started. Five years from now this place is going to define America. In a few short years the sophisticated world and his wife are going to want to live and die in Miami. Shit, I want to now. In fact, I'm going to buy one of these hotels this afternoon. Maybe this one. What do they want for it? Four million? More? Nothing!"

"She's right," said Christa.

"I know," said Steve. "I was playing devil's advocate."

"Ah," said Mary Whitney.

"Fabulous," said Lisa.

"It's great," agreed Rob.

"So we have youth on our side," said Mary.

"You have youth in agreement," corrected Lisa.

"But the perfume must be made up already. Does India smell like Miami? Surely not. Can you just change the name?" Steve sounded doubtful.

"The scent can be altered in a long weekend. It costs money and a bit of time, but nothing that matters. The important thing is the concept, the dream. If you get that right, everything else fits into place. I'm excited. God, I haven't been so excited since . . ." Mary paused. She looked at Rob. "Well, never mind . . . but what I'm saying is, the magic comes out of the excitement. That's what creation is about. You care and you believe, and your juices flow and . . ." She snapped her fingers in the air. ". . . You have a winner. It's as simple as that."

There was a faraway expression on her face. "Miami is rich and fierce with the fragrance of flowers. It takes over your head, until you can only feel sensual feelings and only think sultry, steamy thoughts. You are wrapped tight in the heat and the warm breeze of dusk, and the moon is painting silver ripples on the water and casting shadows on the beach where you will meet your lover. Behind you are the fun and the lights of the Art Deco buildings. In front of you is the ocean.

Above you are the stars. You reach up for the container that hangs around your neck on a pink string. You undo the stopper of the glass bottle that is shaped like the seashells beneath your feet. The perfume slides into your mind. You smooth it on skin browned by the sun, and your man moves closer, drawn to you by it, and by the moment. He, too, breathes in deep, the scent of you, the scent of Miami, and he makes love to you, and all the happiness in the world is yours . . ."

"Mary? Is that you?" said Christa.

"God, I'm not sure. Is it? Am I? Heavens, I haven't felt like this since my summer collection that creamed Paris in the late seventies. Some people reckon I made my billion on the basis of that one."

"So we shoot right here, all around Miami, and the theme is love," said Steve, cutting through to the heart of the matter.

"Oh yes, we do," said Mary. "And, oh yes, it is."

Everyone looked at Rob and Lisa. It was where they came in.

39

"Things are getting pretty exciting," said Steve. The others had gone. Christa and he were alone.

"More for some than for others."

"Meaning?"

"I'm gone, Steve. I'm not just *in* love, I'm all around it, over it, under it, every which ways."

"Absence makes the heart grow fonder?"

"Don't you believe it. He came up last night from Key West. He cooked me lunch."

"He must be a superb cook."

She laughed.

"Actually, he is. He can do anything."

"I'm jealous. How long is he staying?"

"Forever, if I have anything to do with it."

"That bad, huh?"

"Worse."

"What does he think about it all? I imagine he's long on thoughts. Writers usually are."

"How does one ever know what people are thinking?"

"You watch what they do, and never listen to what they say."

"So far, then, he's staying."

"Sounds like you're in for a long one."

"The rest of my life."

"What? Surely not discussed yet."

"Felt."

"Well, I imagine he'll have his own best man, but I've always wanted to be a maid of honor."

"And a more honorable old maid it would be hard to find."

"Thanks for nothing, sweetheart. I hope he snores."

"He sleeps like a baby."

"It's too early in the day for the *b* word," said Steve, wrinkling his nose in distaste.

"You might have to get used to it," said Christa, smiling broadly.

Steve put up his hands in mock horror. "This is all too fast for me, darling. Give me a break. Can't we change the subject and talk about something less threatening . . . like a nuclear winter?"

"We can talk about this shoot."

He laughed. "You mean the sideshow to your love affair with Mr. Books!"

"It's important to get one's priorities right."

"Well, the shoot's easy, isn't it? I mean, we just call up Carrie Simon at ACT and she handles the permits, locations, the Winnebago side of things. We could be 'go' for tomorrow. My stuff's coming down with the assistants this afternoon. We could catch the early sun and blaze away. Mary's apparently got a couple of rooms full of swimsuits on the floor below, and a couple of stylists to handle them. The only things left to worry about are our supermodel leading lady, and our unknown principal boy, and the chemistry between them."

"I wish I could say that would be no problem," said Christa. "But what the hell was he doing with Mary until eight o'clock this morning?"

"Talking about hungry children?" tried Steve.

"Yeah!" Christa wasn't buying it.

"It's unlike Lisa to let him out of her sight."

"From her remarks at the meeting, it seems she regretted it," said Christa.

"Mary's such a bitch." Steve laughed. He had always had a weak spot for those.

"But surely Rob wouldn't go for her jazz, when he's got Lisa Rodriguez," he added.

"I can't believe he would," said Christa.

"You don't sound totally convinced."

"Yeah, I know. Mary's always got an angle, and she's no fool. She's ruthless when she wants something."

"Or someone."

"Precisely."

"I for sure wouldn't want to separate Mary and Lisa if it came to a cat fight," said Steve.

"It couldn't be done," said Christa, looking out of the window and wondering why, at that precise moment, a fluffy cloud had obscured the sun.

40

Rob Sand angled his face against the sun. He breathed in the smell of coffee, fresh-baked bread, and the ozone of the Ocean Drive morning. Around him, South Beach was stirring. He appeared to be in the French section of the News Café, out on the sidewalk, submerged in Gauloise smoke, and surly, good-looking Gallics flicking petulantly through the pages of the *Herald Tribune.* He scooped a wedge of creamy salted butter onto a piece of crisp baguette, and drank deep on the strong coffee. Mmmmmm! He almost felt good. His life was running at double speed, and it was difficult to focus on the blurred images and to make sense of it. One particular scene recurred relentlessly. He and Mary McGregor Whitney had consummated their bizarre deal. Now he wondered if he would ever be able to wipe the memories from his mind. Together they had closed South Beach. Each café, each club, each hole-in-the-wall had been visited and done to death until the glow of the sun had painted the horizon. Then Mary Whitney had walked with him to the limo, told the driver to get lost, and parked it herself in a back alley among the cats and the trash. There hadn't been much pomp and circumstance about what had followed. She had stripped him of clothes as if peeling a banana, and she had devoured him as if he were the same fruit. Never before, in his sheltered life, had he experienced such a shameless, voracious appetite for sex. He had endured it, and worse, an hour later, he had gotten to the edges of enjoying it, but all the time he had concentrated on the bottom line . . . the extraordinary check for the children that he was trading for his body.

Of course it had been prostitution. There was no other word for it.

But the price so very nearly made it right. Did the end justify the means? In all his wrestling with religion, Rob had never experienced such an acute moral dilemma. Now, he sighed in the sunshine, and popped a piece of bread into his mouth, biting down on the chunky jam and the delicious, crunchy bread. Last night was history, but history had a way of bending the future. The players in the drama hadn't gone away. How would Mary behave? Would she let the cat out of the bag? And what effect would that have on Lisa Rodriguez, whose phenomenal attraction was only equaled by her terrible temper? And then there was Christa, whom he had embarrassed and whom he respected so much. Would she get to know the whole story, or just the ugly half? Would he have to endure the reproach in her eyes, and the delighted scorn curling the lips of Steve Pitts? Hell! He tried not to think about it. The girl at the next table helped him. A tawny model, she had locked onto his looks. She smiled at him as she bent down low over her magazine, allowing her shirt to fall away and showing him perfect, dangling, naked breasts. He smiled back at her.

"Beautiful day," she said, acknowledging his interest. Her accent was thick and husky.

"Sure is," he agreed, hesitantly. He didn't want any more complications, but he was incapable of being impolite.

"Are you a model?" she asked. Her smile broadened. Her tits were still there. Rob tried not to look at them.

"I've just started," he said. "I'm doing a perfume campaign."

"Which one?"

"For Whitney Enterprises, with Steve Pitts."

"Oh, Steve Pitts," said the girl, deeply impressed. "And you just started? You're lucky."

"I guess I am," said Rob. "And you?"

"I'm doing catalogue," she said. "This time," she added quickly. "Which agency are you with?"

"Christa Kenwood."

"I thought she was a model."

"She just opened an agency."

"Is she looking for girls?"

"I think so."

"She's only looking for beautiful girls," said Lisa Rodriguez.

She hovered over the table, eclipsing the sun. The French girl shrugged, and she laughed a short, sharp, French laugh. She put up her hands in mock surrender and turned back to her magazine.

"Hi, Lisa," said Rob. "Wanna sit down?"

Lisa sat. She shot a look of withering scorn at the French model. "Do you talk to just *anybody?*" she said in a loud voice.

"Yes, don't you?"

She didn't answer. She didn't like her days to start badly, and this was the second false start in a row. How on earth could a boy like Rob be so deeply difficult? Apart from the mind-altering looks, his total lack of affectation was his main attraction. But if he was so straightforward, how come he was so efficient at winding her up?

"There are more second-rate . . . third-rate . . . models in this fucking town than grains of sand on that beach," she fumed. "I can't think why they don't all shove off back to San Pellegrino, or wherever it is the ugly hookers come from."

"Cool it, Lisa," said Rob. The French girl was still listening. The red spots on her cheeks said so.

"Don't give me orders," snapped Lisa. "You're just a new kid in this game. I'm the star."

"The old, old star," said the French girl, sotto voce.

"What did you say?" snapped Lisa.

"Huh?" said the French girl, looking up. The French liked to do their sniping from the sidelines. Head-on confrontation wasn't their bag.

"That's enough," said Rob, raising his voice. "If you want to wreck someone's breakfast, go do it somewhere else."

"Oh! Oh, I'm wrecking your breakfast, am I?" said Lisa. Her expression said she was in shock. Every straight man in the world would be honored to share his breakfast with Lisa Rodriguez. Yet here she was, sitting at the table of the one man who was, apparently, the exception to the rule. The ways of the world were strange.

"Will you please order me some coffee?" She changed tack suddenly. It was almost an apology.

Rob waved to the pretty waitress, praying that *she* wouldn't come on to him. Maybe he should pay some plastic surgeon to wreck his nose.

"We start shooting tomorrow," said Lisa as Rob ordered the coffee. It was both a threat and a request for a truce.

"I know," said Rob. "Are you looking forward to it?"

"I've done it once or twice before."

"I know that, Lisa." There was exasperation in his voice. He caught the waitress's eye and ordered the coffee. Lisa watched him. He wasn't weak. All the humility, the desire to make people happy, the lack of ambition might have pointed in that direction, but there was a deep inner strength to him. He could be pushed just so far and no farther. Then he became an immovable rock and a hard place rolled into one. *He* knew where his limits lay, and he didn't wear them on his sleeve. People who thought he was a pushover thought wrong. Maybe that was the American hero, a Shane, a Jimmy Stewart, the nice guy slow to anger, but terrifying when the time came at last for war. The Latins did it differently. Lisa and her blood relatives kept the swagger for the outside. The world saw their balls from dawn to dusk. They passed for tough guys, but on day ninety-nine, when push came to shove, the Latinos were macho no longer. They moved aside when the battle started, and they left it to the Rob Sands of this world to do the bleeding.

"Yes, actually, I am looking forward to it. Very much. You want to know why?"

"Why?"

"Because I'll be doing it with you."

"Thank you."

"Because I'm falling in love with you." She deliberately raised the ante. The sunlight fell on his face. He was lit by God.

"No, you're not, Lisa. You just . . . you play games with people. You play games with yourself."

"I *don't* play games. People like Mary play games. I feel. I feel deeply. I'm emotional. I'm not afraid of emotions. Are you?"

He laughed, embarrassed, not knowing what to say.

"I don't know, Lisa. People like you are foreign to me. I'm not used to you. I can't keep up with the . . . intensity of it all. The mood swings, the drama you all deal in."

"I know it's difficult," she said. "I *am* a bit crazy. We all are, I guess. But deep down I'm a good person. I believe in God. I try to do decent things."

She assumed what she hoped would be a pious, contrite expression. It was a pity she hadn't a headscarf handy as a prop.

"Oh, Lisa, I know you are. I can sense that." He put out his hand to her and held hers, touched by the confession that she had finer feelings. "I'm not criticizing you. I'm just saying we're opposites, that's all. I really like you. I really do."

"You find me attractive?" said Lisa, cutting through to the bottom line.

"Wouldn't anybody?" It wasn't the answer she wanted.

"Do *you?*" she insisted.

"Yes, I do." It was true. He did. Her beauty was out of this world. She was frighteningly beautiful. When he had made love to her, it had terrified him. Lisa could be addictive. He had already tasted her forbidden fruit. There was a part of him that now possessed the knowledge of her. If you bit more than once into the Lisa Rodriguez apple, you might never escape the habit.

"Well, then," she murmured, squeezing his hand in hers.

"You probably just use that for the shoot," he said with a shy laugh. "You know, leading ladies and leading men liking each other for the duration of the movie. It makes the acting easier, and then it's 'good-bye and good luck.' "

"Is that what you think?"

"I don't know what to think."

Lisa Rodriguez surprised herself. She knew suddenly what she was going to say, and she couldn't stop herself.

"I think I want to marry you," she said.

"Marry me?" spluttered Rob.

She didn't answer. She burned him with her eyes. There was mist in them. Dear God, she meant it. What could he possibly say to her? Had she really fallen in love with him?

"Are you serious?" he said.

"Do I look serious?" Oh, yes, she did. To emphasize it, a perfect tear squeezed from a perfect eye.

"Maybe we should go walk on the beach," he said. He threw some money on the table and stood up. This conversation didn't need an audience.

She followed meekly by his side, in her brand-new role as humble, spurned lover. They crossed the road and walked to a bench beneath the palm trees. The sun shimmered through the fronds, dappling them with light. There was a haze over the ocean. It was going to be a hot day.

"Should we be doing anything about tomorrow? Like practicing or something?" said Rob suddenly. Changing the subject seemed a good idea. The "marry" word was still reverberating in his mind. It was shocking, but already it was something else. It was flattering. Lisa Rodriquez, walking by his side, wanted to marry him. Lisa Rodriguez, the most beautiful girl in the whole wide world.

"We *could* practice," said Lisa. She was smiling now, the tear a shiny memory on her high cheeks.

"How?" said Rob.

"We could kiss. There's going to be lots of that."

"Here, in public?" It certainly wasn't a refusal.

"Models have to do everything in public."

She leaned in to show him what models had to do, and all at once Rob tired of the resistance business. Her face was so close. Her lips were so lovely. The early morning smell of her alone was enough to make him want her. He closed his eyes, letting her do it. She knew all these things. She knew so much more than he.

In the darkness, in the sunlight, he felt her mouth breathe its way into his. She held him tight while she kissed him, as if she didn't want to lose him, as if her arms were chains that would hold him forever. She was incredibly gentle. It wasn't Lisa. It was another person, a gorgeous child holding him like a teddy bear in the frightened night. Her mouth at his was pleading. Forget who I am. Forget what I represent. Believe my body. Believe that I love you. It was the right way to him. His defenses melted. His mouth sank hungrily into hers. Still she squeezed him. He was wrapped in her arms, all crunched into her, and the curves of her body tuned into his innocence in a secret harmony of clever passion. Now he leaned against her, still her captive, and he tasted once more her sweet, dangerous taste. She was inside his mind, as her tongue crept into his mouth. He opened his eyes to look at her. Her eyes were wide open, frank at last, playing no games, honest pathways into her soul. He could see the love there. It lay in a shining, shimmering pool, and around it was the high foliage of her vulnerability. This girl knew so much about the making of love, but so little about love itself. The paradox was there in her eyes. She was scared. She was in a foreign land, and she didn't know its language. She wanted, but she didn't know how to ask.

Rob felt the tenderness well up inside him. It sprang from the same fountain that had fathered desire. Suddenly nothing was impossible. He could learn to love this girl. He could protect her against herself, against the brittle, self-destroying strength of her. He could teach her God, and she would learn from him the ways of heaven as he would learn from her the ways of the world. They were equals in youth. They had had different experiences, but the same quantity of experience. They would offset each other, and shore each other up in the war against loneliness that went by the name of living. And now, at this Epiphany, marriage was no longer so strange, so distant, so crazily bizarre. So he reached out and held her hard to him, and their kiss deepened as it acquired meaning, and their bodies throbbed together in the brand-new awakening.

"Oh, Rob," she whispered in the wetness, sending her warm breath into the back of his throat. She nuzzled at his lips, biting them gently with her teeth. She ran her tongue across them, painting them with her saliva. Her hands were clasped tight in the small of his back, but her mouth was soft against his. She was telling him that she knew how to be tender, and that her hunger was for his soul as much as for his body. Her eyes searched his for reassurance. In answer, he tried to tell her that she was closer to him now than she had ever been, even at the moment when they had screamed their joy in the twilight at the dance when it had all begun. That had been ecstasy, the overwhelming passion of two young bodies. This was something else. It was the moment when physical intimacy became so much more. Both knew it. Against all the odds, they were standing in the shadow of love.

Suddenly she withdrew from him. She looked puzzled.

"Rob, will you tell me something?" she said. "Promise you'll tell me whatever I ask."

It was a moment for bravery.

"I promise."

He didn't think. He just said it. He had only one thing to hide.

But of course it was the one thing she wanted to know.

"Rob, what exactly happened last night between you and Mary Whitney?" she said.

41

"Soldiers can fight after two nights without sleep," said Peter Stein. "After three, they fall apart."

"I wonder what they do after a sleepless month," said Christa with a laugh. "I have a feeling we're going to find out!"

He laughed, too. His life was changing. It was a rebirth. The sky looked new. The world smelled different. Food tasted better. If Freud was right, and love was neurosis, then neurosis and happiness were the very same thing. Across the breakfast table, poolside on Star Island, sat Christa Kenwood. She was the one who had made it happen. She was wrapped in a toweling robe, without makeup. He had never seen her look more beautiful.

"More melon?" she said. The table groaned with fruit. Papaya, mango, grapefruit, all growing on trees not fifty feet from where they sat.

"No, I'm full."

"So am I. Full up with you."

"Fed up?"

"Full up."

Her voice was husky.

He laughed. "Christa, don't do it to me. At least we should finish breakfast."

"If you reward a rat that rings a bell by stimulating the pleasure center in its brain, it rings the bell till it dies. It doesn't take time off to eat. It just bell rings!"

"I never thought I'd feel like a rat," said Peter.

She laughed, letting him off the sensual hook. Pointless as it seemed, life had to go on despite love.

"Are you going to write today?"

He covered his eyes with his hands. "Don't even talk to me about it. I didn't bring my typewriter. I'm not in my room. God, everything's different. Maybe I'll never write again."

It was a daily feeling, but it was nice to have genuine excuses for it.

"Now that you're with me, you're going to write better than you've ever written before. I promise you."

"I've always maintained that loneliness and anxiety are the best parents for words. If you're contented, what possible point can there be in scribbling?"

"You think too much."

"That's a silly thing to say. Everyone thinks exactly the same amount. It's just that some people deal in profound thoughts and others in clichés." A professorial tone was creeping into his words.

"That's pretty stupid. Clichés are the most profound remarks of all. They've stood the test of time. It's their profundity that keeps them around. A thought isn't always profound just because it's new."

"Try writing in clichés and see if it sells."

"That's like saying 'Try writing the truth and see if it sells.' "

Peter put down his napkin. There was a flush on his cheeks.

"You know, it's the most extraordinary thing. Everyone fancies himself a writer. Everyone. Each time I go out into the world, there's some brazen idiot telling me he could write a book because of all the fascinating things he's seen and done. There's a little bit more to writing, I like to think, than trolling around the world and capturing experiences. I realize you've written a book of sorts but that sort of thing comes under the heading of promotional literature, not the real kind."

"I don't believe you said that, Peter. I can't believe what you just said."

"Well, don't tell me how to write, or what to write, or when to write. It makes me mad."

"Oh, it does, does it? Well, I'm so very sorry for making you mad. I must be much more careful what I say in the future, mustn't I? I'm good enough to fuck, but not good enough to think. Is *that* the deal? In that case I'd better get up and get on, and shovel some shit, and make some cash." She stood up and threw her napkin onto the table. "And you can churn out some more 'profundities,' though why you bother I don't know, because nobody pays you anything for them. The amounts you pick up for all your clever thoughts wouldn't pay my telephone bills."

"Don't talk to me like that," he shouted, jumping up too. "How dare you suggest I don't handle my business affairs properly. How could you possibly know anything about my private life?"

"I know that you roll your eyes to the ceiling when you come. Is that your personal life? Maybe you should go see a neurologist about it. At your age you can't be too careful."

His mouth was working, but there was no sound coming out of it. She'd taken away his words again. There was a red mist in front of his eyes. He'd never been more angry. The squall of fury had burst from the middle of a perfect morning. The *bitch!*

"Do you honestly think you know anything at all about business?" he spluttered, sidestepping the totally unconfrontable bit about what his eyes did in bed. "You might be able to scratch a living around a whole lot of stupid models, and you might have conned some idiot into paying a fortune for your frivolous beauty book, but I hardly think you'd cut much of a dash in the publishing world trying to sell something serious. They know a dumb girl when they see one."

"Pah, you idiot!" Christa snapped her fingers. "I could get you triple what you get with a couple of phone calls. Double the first print run, twice the advertising. You're a business asshole, Peter Stein. Maybe that's what ivory tower 'artistes' think it's grand to be. Whatever. You hacked it. You're *it,* baby. Jesus, those publishers of yours must be weeping with laughter all the way to their bank."

"You . . . you . . . you are just so . . ."

"There speaks literate man. Don't waste the words, Peter. Save them, and write them down somewhere, and then sell them for peanuts like all the others."

"I don't have to stand here and listen to this," he managed.

"Neither do I."

It was a battle to see who could leave the table first. Christa won. She left him. To avoid colliding with her, he had to allow himself to be left. He stood there, shaking with fury, as her proud back disappeared through the French doors into the house.

But already, as she disappeared, the fury was fading. Something else was climbing into the vacuum vacated by anger. The little thing called love was stealing back into his heart. That he knew. What he couldn't know was that, so soon, it was creeping back into Christa's.

42

Christa sat back on the sofa and looked out of the picture window over Central Park. She'd forgotten how much she missed New York. Even in decline, it was magnificent. One day it would come again, as it always did. The exiles would flock back, the cockiness would return, and once more it would become the center of the universe.

"I can't tell you how pleased I was to hear from you, Christa. I haven't seen you since the Miami Book Fair. I thought you'd vanished from my life."

Lewis Heller looked pleased, really pleased. He sat on the corner of a desk that could have been a helicopter pad, and wondered just how the hell he could spin this unexpected meeting into a Four Seasons lunch. That would be one in the eye for the publishing honchos in their commissary. Lewis Heller's lunching of Christa Kenwood would get the tongues wagging and the juices moving all right. She was something of a legend in the industry since her book had sold for a cool million. It was due next year, and everyone would imagine that Heller was discussing a sequel. But, as he table-hopped his way out and made the introductions, Christa would be described as his "old and dear friend" and Lewis Heller's personal stock would rise to the margin on the spot. He adjusted an immaculately tied tie and waited for Christa to reveal her hand.

"Lewis, we're friends. I'll never vanish from your life. It's just that

I've been so busy with my new agency. You know how it is. Work, work, work."

Lewis had known what work was like until he had become god at Twentieth Century Books. Now, work was what the others did while he cracked the whip and dreamed up "strategy," the think-tank jive that consisted mainly of finding ordered explanations for business chaos.

"I know, I know," he muttered urbanely, trying to look as if he remembered what it felt like to be harassed. "We scurry about turning bucks, and all the worthwhile things in life—friendships, children, marriages—get put on the back burner until they get burned." He laughed. Had he managed to insinuate that marriage to Rhonda was rocky? He rather hoped so. One never knew what was on a beautiful girl's mind. Freud had been right about that, if about nothing else.

"What I really wanted, Lewis, was your advice."

"For what it's worth, it's yours." He held out his arms to show how open he was.

"I wanted to talk to you about Peter Stein."

"Peter Stein. What about him? He was with you, wasn't he, at the book fair? I haven't seen him since. I think I told you he was rude to me once. Prickly bastard, didn't you think?"

"I know precisely what you mean," said Christa with feeling. "What I really meant was, what do you know about his publishing profile? I mean his sales, how well he does, whether he's with the right publisher."

Lewis looked quizzical. "Do you mind my asking why you want to know?" he said.

Christa looked him straight in the eye. "I'm in love with the prickly bastard," she said.

"Oh, goodness. Heavens, I didn't mean to pry into your personal life. In love with Peter Stein. Well, well, well!"

It wasn't entirely clear whether Lewis Heller was pleased, impressed, or disappointed. Perhaps all of the above.

"So the two of you are an . . . item, as the gossip columnists say?" So much for a disinclination toward personal prying. What Lewis meant was "Does Stein love you back?"

"I guess so," said Christa with what she hoped was an embarrassed laugh. "But the thing is this, Lewis. Peter's absolutely brilliant, but business-wise, he's completely hopeless. You know he hasn't got an agent."

"Yes, I knew that. He doesn't take an advance. He's been with World forever. He has a really good relationship with his editor there. Of course, World's a good house. Very old-fashioned. Very correct. Not an *exciting* house, you might say. Hardly cutting edge in terms of squeezing the last drop out of the orange . . . to put it mildly."

Lewis was already slipping into dealing mode. He had an inkling of what was coming. It might be a business lunch at the Four Seasons after all.

"Would you like some coffee, Christa? How rude of me. I am so bowled over by your beauty that I've forgotten my manners."

"Yes, that would be great. Thanks, Lewis." He organized it on the intercom.

"I suppose what I'm really saying is that Peter might be ready for a move."

"Is that what *he's* saying?" said Lewis carefully, trying not to show his excitement.

Christa looked him straight in the eye.

"Yes," she lied.

"And he hasn't got an agent, but you're a pretty shrewd business-person, and you said 'Why don't I go and see my old friend Lewis?' "

Christa just smiled. Her smile was taken as a yes, as it was meant to be.

Lewis walked to the window, shooting the cuffs of his coat. He turned to face Christa. The first thing to do was to put in the boot on the opposition.

"Actually, it is no secret in the publishing business that the people at World aren't doing the very best for Peter Stein. You know, they play on the old rubbish of artists and gentlemen not wanting to get bogged down in the sordid details of money. The bottom line is that to any publishing house in this town Peter Stein is worth a hefty premium over his royalty payments, and he's not getting it at World. That's one side of it. Then there's the marketing. World isn't an aggressive house. They don't have their own sales force. They use Falcon's. They don't advertise much. They don't build excitement on a book, because (a) they don't know how to, and (b) because they think it's common. Frankly, they could double their first print run and sell one helluva lot more Stein books than they do. We could. I know that. The editing relationship is something else. Peter has a very good relationship with the guy there . . . I forget his name. Obviously, they trust each other and they work well together. That's an intangible. I don't know how much Peter relies on his editor. That relationship may be so important to him that nothing else matters."

He watched Christa carefully. So far, it had been a soft sell. It could get harder.

"That's exactly what I thought," said Christa. "They're getting him cheap. They're not pushing him. They're coasting on him. They sit back and say, 'We sold x copies of the last book and the book before, so let's print x again because that's how many copies Stein sells.' Minimal returns. Minimal hassle. Predictable contribution to the bottom line."

"You put it well. It happens all the time. He's bread and butter to them. To a company like ours he'd be caviar and champagne."

"Would Twentieth be interested in Peter?"

"Well, publishing is a small business. We don't like to step on toes. We don't like to poach authors . . . but yes . . . very."

Lewis Heller was bursting. It was almost impossible to keep the lid on his excitement. Twentieth were the bullies on the publishing block, as far from World in terms of style as the devil from grace. To them, books were commodities to be peddled as aggressively as soap. In popular fiction they were numero uno because they paid top money to the top sellers and then hyped them remorselessly, without shame or pride. Because of this, there were few "quality" writers in their stable. The literary giants gave them a wide berth, and it was beginning to hurt. They desperately needed to increase the prestige of their list. It had been the chief topic at the board meeting that very morning. Now obviously, Peter Stein was aware that Christa Kenwood was seeing Lewis right now. That meant that in principle he had no serious objection to Twentieth if he ever decided to untie the knot with World. It was hard to believe, but then a lot of things were. Maybe the proud Pulitzer winner needed some cash to finance his new girlfriend. Christa didn't look cheap. Lewis had never seen a more expensive-looking woman. She wouldn't be the type to spend the rest of her life prancing around in Key West. She'd want to travel. The best hotels. First class. And it wouldn't be Victoria's Secret and Gap for the clothes. One thing was certain, though. If Peter Stein was to be persuaded to peddle his principles, it would be for a very large sum of money indeed.

How large? was looking to be the question.

"Can you give me the vaguest idea, some ball-park guesstimate, of what a company like yours might be able to do for Peter?" said Christa.

Lewis's eyes narrowed as he smiled.

"Difficult to say, isn't it, without the sales figures? But . . . I don't know . . . imagining he does, say, one hundred and fifty thousand in hard, and well, seven hundred in paper with World. Put it this way, I'm pretty sure Twentieth could push him to three hundred thousand hardcover, and I'd be disappointed if he didn't do one and a half million domestic in mass market. Of course, all that would be on the back of a major, major campaign."

"So you think you could double his sales?"

"I'd hope to. That's what I'd be looking to do."

"So if he's earning around eight hundred thousand per book at World, you could double that to one-point-six million, and guarantee it to him up front."

Lewis laughed. "It doesn't work *quite* like that, Christa. You see, the increase in sales is a rough estimate. That's what we'd *hope* to do. We couldn't guarantee it. Yes, we could improve on eight hundred thousand, if that's what he's earning, and we could guarantee an advance, of course. But I don't think it could be anywhere near the figure you mention. Unfortunately, we don't have any crystal balls in terms of sales. We just have educated guesses."

"But Twentieth doesn't have a lot of Pulitzer winners on its list, does it?" said Christa. "How many, actually?"

Lewis swallowed. Why was it that beautiful girls had the reputation of being dumb? The ones he knew were as sharp as razor blades. Christa, apparently, was sharper.

"Actually, none," he said, fingering his tie.

"Well, if you had Peter Stein, you'd have one. And once you had him, you might find a whole lot more coming along once the ice had been broken, so to speak."

"Yes, that would be nice."

"And nice things are worth money, aren't they?"

"Yes, you're right. Twentieth would be very happy to have someone like Peter Stein." Lewis smiled a sickly smile.

"In fact, he'd probably be worth that one-point-six million up front, wouldn't he? Maybe more."

"Listen, Christa, we're talking hypothetically here. I mean, I'm the head man at Twentieth, but I have colleagues. I'd have to discuss. . . ."

"Balls, Lewis," said Christa. "I remember when we had dinner once, you told me you didn't have employees, you had doormats."

"I'm sure I never said that." Lewis smiled awkwardly. After the third martini, he was always saying it. It was one of his favorite remarks.

"I'm sure you did," said Christa. She didn't smile. It was time to be tough. "Anyway, Lewis, I was just kite-flying here. Twentieth isn't really Peter's bag, as you can imagine. There are other houses that are somewhere in between World and Twentieth in terms of their literary reputation. If you think you can't make a serious commitment to him, then we'll look around."

"How many books are we talking here?" said Lewis quickly.

"Maybe three books," said Christa, watching him weaken.

"Around four and a half?" said Lewis.

"Around five million dollars," said Christa.

"Are you doing anything for lunch?" said Lewis suddenly. "I usually go to the Four Seasons around this time."

"I'll join you," said Christa.

43

Lisa Rodriguez banged on the door of the penthouse suite at the Park Central as if she were knocking at the gates of hell. A maid opened it.

Lisa Rodriguez put one hand on the chest of the servant and pushed as hard as she could. The maid went stumbling back into the room, mouth and eyes wide open. Lisa followed hard behind.

Mary Whitney was sitting at a table by the window. She was having her breakfast. She raised her eyebrows at the sight of the intruder. Otherwise, she continued to sip at her coffee.

"You fucking bitch!" screamed Lisa. "You fucking bitch!"

She rushed to the table, fists clenched. For some reason she stopped at the border of the Whitney personal space.

"It's a little early," said Mary Whitney, "for loudness."

"But it's never too early for a little fucking, is it? *Is* it?" yelled Lisa, cranking up the decibels.

"I presume you are referring to the . . . uh, 'encounter' Rob and I enjoyed at the end of a wonderful evening," said Mary Whitney, allowing a smile to play infuriatingly at the edges of her mouth. "It *was* a little cramped in the back of the limo, but I think that in the circumstances we each acquitted ourselves with honor. It may well be that I shall have to have it stretched a little farther. The limo, I mean."

"You bought him, you bitch. You bought him with your stinking money."

"I did, dear. You're right. It's what the money's for. Buying things."

Lisa was in awe at her own anger. She had never felt like this before. It was a whole new world of fury, red mists, adrenaline hurricanes, bubbling, boiling caldrons of venomous hatred. The sight of it alone would reduce most people to rubble. Mary Whitney, however, was totally intact.

"You paid . . . you actually paid millions of dollars to fuck my boyfriend." Her words defined incredulity. Somehow, spoken out loud, they made the dreadful deed seem worse.

"Not very *many* millions," said Mary with a wicked smile, "and it *was* for a good cause, whichever way you look at it."

"But he's mine," howled Lisa.

"I'm sure he is, darling. I just borrowed him for a bit, like Christa did on the beach. Anyway, I did find him first. You know how it is: finders, keepers; losers, weepers."

"I'll kill you for this," hissed Lisa, her teeth grinding in her twisted mouth. Her eyes were narrow with hatred.

"I've always wanted to go with a bang," said Mary, unfazed.

Lisa stared wild-eyed around the room. How could the ante be raised? Should she go to the ground war now? Or should she employ a little more aerial bombardment? Mary looked pretty well bunkered down. It would be a question of scoring a direct hit.

"Poor Rob," snarled Lisa. "He was sick to the pit of his stomach. I don't know what you did to him, but taking your clothes off must have been mind-boggling gross."

A spot of color high on the Whitney cheek registered the hit.

"Really, Lisa, I haven't the time or the inclination to sit here all day and listen to your stream of consciousness. Is there anything you want to *do* about it?"

Lisa stopped in her tracks. Apart from blood, what did she want?

"I want out of your contract, and out of this job," she hissed. "Go find some other girl to sell your scent."

"So it's 'good-bye millions,' is it, and 'hello lawsuits,' and in the meantime I find some other hot chick to get sexy with young Rob on the beach?"

Yeah, well, okay, let's slow down here. Lisa swallowed. She didn't mind losing the millions. Or did she? There were so many of them. But lawsuits? That was something else. Did she have grounds for reneging on the contract? Probably not. Lawsuits were always won by those with the deepest pockets, and the Whitney pockets were bottomless. A dragged-out legal mess would ruin her financially, while the adverse publicity unzipped her reputation. She was already known as something of a loose cannon. A Whitney suit would confirm that impression. And the facts of the matter were hardly for public consumption. She wanted out of the contract because the client had screwed the male model that Lisa wanted to screw. It would not play well in Liz Smith. It wouldn't play well anywhere. Then there was the new girl who would be hired. She might not be Lisa Rodriguez, but she would be no dog. And she would end up with her tongue in Rob's mouth in the sunset. It was not the raw material for happy dreams.

Lisa made up her mind fast. For some extraordinary reason, the anger began to fade.

"You must understand," she said in a more reasonable tone of voice, "how upset I am by what has happened."

"Darling, I never understand anything at all about other people or their feelings. I have my hands full trying to work out my own."

"Are you really going to give all that money to charity?" Lisa's tone was fast becoming downright conciliatory. Could she learn to see it Rob's way one day, as a decent deed for a decent cause at the whim of some bizarre, but original, eccentric?

"Of course I am, sweetheart. I said I would. I will."

"I don't know what to do," said Lisa.

"Well, you can start by sitting down and having a piece of toast. You're giving me indigestion, standing there and trying to be rude. Being rude, you know, is a very fine art. I'll give you a lesson. Rule one is never lose your temper. Rule two is to zero in on a person's weakness."

Lisa sat down.

"What's your weakness, Mary?"

"I don't have one," said Mary McGregor Whitney.

"I wonder," said Lisa Rodriguez.

44

Christa's Star Island bedroom was the biggest room in the big house. She liked it like that. Bedrooms were where you spent your time. She could do telephone work in bed. She could relax on the outsize sofa and catch a movie. She could wash and smarten up in the cavernous marble bathroom. And now, the bedroom was where the memories were. She couldn't stop thinking about Peter. Already she bitterly regretted the row about nothing. In the whole wonderful mixture that was him, there was only one bad taste. His intellectual patronization of her. Twice it had brought them to the edge of blows. Would it go on doing so until their relationship was a heap of rubble? Shit! What relationship? Since the moment she had stormed out on him, he had disappeared from her life. When she'd gotten back to the house, he was long gone, presumably back to Key West and the cold comfort of his work. He hadn't called. Hadn't left a bitter literary last word. Nothing.

For a day she had seethed and longed for him, and hated him, and conjured up ways to hurt him. But she hadn't called him. Pride had sabotaged that little idea whenever it had raised its pathetic head, despite her strange premonition that she was carrying his child. His words had gone round and round in her mind, lying heavy across the steamy memories, crushing them, camouflaging them. "I hardly think you'd cut much of a dash in the publishing world trying to sell something serious. They know a dumb girl when they see one."

A dumb girl! Who couldn't sell things. That was what hurt. He could have called her ugly, mean, weak, dull, but dumb . . . dumb! And a business nerd! Christa, who had never dealt a deal that didn't suit her. It was intolerable. It was worse than that. It was untrue. And it had to be avenged. It hadn't taken her long to work out how. Her Filofax held the numbers of a string of admirers accumulated over the years—captains of industry, stars, artists, politicians, bureaucrats. Every one of them had wanted her. Every one had promised to lay their personal piece of the earth at her feet. She hadn't given them what they had wanted, but she had given all of them the time of day, keeping them in play until some future moment when they might be needed. They got Christmas cards, drop-dead photographs of Christa Kenwood signed with friendly hellos that kept the recipients on their toes throughout the years as they basked in the reflected glory of the supermodel's endorsement shining into their living rooms from pride of place on the grand piano. Such a man was Lewis Heller, the power panjandrum behind Twentieth Century Books. He had lunched her a couple of times, dined her once, bedded her never, but she had listened to his confessions of undying love and how he would leave the wife if she said the word. The moment Heller's name had flashed in her mental computer, she had known what she would do.

She would prove to Peter Stein once and for all who was business bright and who was a business basket case. The millions she would make for him would be the trump that clinched the argument. It would be a double whammy, as she both proved her point and made him rich. He would be made to look a fool, and, at the same time, he would be forced to get grateful. On his knees he would thank her, the dumb business broad who had scored him megabucks in the time it took most women to get their feet tired at Tiffany's. She had jumped on a plane, showed up at Heller's office, and drunk Perrier at The Four Seasons while he tried to ply her with Pol Roger. By the end of lunch she had done the deal. She had gotten Stein a five-million-dollar hard/soft guarantee for his next three books, and a commitment to print runs and advertising budgets unlike any he had ever before experienced. She had doubled his money in two short hou... And the poor love didn't even know about it. Yet!

That was next. She would call him. She would be nice. She would be conciliatory. A return match would be fixed up. Then, when they had made up, she would hit him with both the good news and the bad news. The bad news would be that he was a business schmuck. The good news would be that because of her he was a rich one. She giggled to herself as she combed her hair in the mirror, and wondered when exactly she would allow herself the pleasure of the call.

The telephone rang.

She started. It was him. He had jumped her gun and now he was ready with his very own apology. She stood up. Okay, even better. Her heart was jumping a bit. Whoa! Slow down, Christa. The cards are in your hand. You've got the drop on the literary lion . . . the cash drop, the one that counts. She sauntered across the room and scooped up the telephone. Why was she so sure it was him?

"Hello," she drawled.

"Christa?" It wasn't his voice. It was vaguely familiar, but for sure it wasn't Peter.

"Who is this?"

"Bill Braddock. Christa?"

"Bill, how are you?" Damn! Christa tried to keep the disappointment out of her voice. Braddock was a very good expatriate Brit photographer, who did a lot of work for the top magazines. As such, he was an important person to Christa. She wanted to represent more photographers, and Braddock was right up there at the top end of the market. If she played her cards right, she might get to sign him. If not, at least he might book some of her girls.

She wondered how he had gotten her home phone number.

"Yes, Bill, sorry, it's me. How are you? I haven't seen you since Antigua."

"Yeah, it's been a long time. Too long. I heard about your agency, and Steve joining up, and Lisa, and the Whitney campaign. You're off and running. I want to say how pleased I am. You were always a lot more than the hottest body in the business and the greatest face."

"Thanks, Bill. You haven't forgotten how to lay it on!"

"Yeah. Yeah. Listen, we ought to get together sometime. My agent drinks too much. Doesn't put himself about enough. I got more than enough work, but I could do with some more bucks for it."

Christa saw the carrot.

"Sure, we should talk, Bill. Steve always speaks highly of your work. And I've always been a big fan."

"You sure beat up on that rat Rossetti. Last I heard of him, he was foaming at the mouth with fury 'bout you taking Rodriguez, and then getting the Whitney thing. Are you signing a lot of girls, taking a lot of bookings?"

"It's literally just started. I signed Mona yesterday. You remember her, the black girl from Elle, did the Estée Lauder ads. Signed her in the morning, and that afternoon she got block-booked for two weeks in Mexico City with Buena Vista. How's that for instant action?"

"Mexico. She's going to Mexico? When?"

"She flew out this morning. Why?"

"Oh, that's just perfect. Listen, Christa, you couldn't help me out, could you? Or get Mona to. I was down in Mexico City for *Cosmo* a few months back, and I got a couple of Hasselblads stuck in customs. You know, the usual crapola about bad paperwork, when all they really wanted was a backhander. I was out of travelers' checks, and I had to leave the cameras there. I'm so pissed about it. Would there be any chance of you faxing Mona in Mexico City, and getting her to spring my cameras and bring them back? I could send my assistant, but I'm booked solid and I can't spare him. And I can't ask Buena Vista 'cause they stiffed me on a deal and I'm trying to sue them. I'd be really grateful. I mean, I'd really owe you one."

"I don't see why not. Fill in some details."

"Oh, just fax her saying could she bring back the two cameras. I can get the weasel from customs to pack them up and drop them off wherever she's staying. If she could give him three hundred bucks, I'll give her six when she comes back. And on top, I'd book her for *Bravo.* I've got pretty much carte blanche there."

"No sweat, Bill. I'll do it now. I just tell her to give three hundred to some guy who will contact her, mention you, and hand over a couple of Hasselblads. And you'll give her six for her trouble, and hire her for a *Bravo* shoot. Sounds great. She'll jump at it."

"That's it, Christa. God, I'm grateful. It was really getting to me. I don't like to lose cameras. You get attached to them. Oh, and Christa, this customs guy . . . he's a shitty little bureaucrat on the take. It's best if you just say in the fax he's expecting three . . . don't mention bucks . . . and that she'll get six for her trouble. She'll know what you mean, and if not, the Mexican can explain it when he drops off the cameras."

"Sounds reasonable. Bill, have you thought seriously about changing agents? I know I could up your price. Things are going like gangbusters around here. The Whitney job is panning out like a dream. There'll be lots more work there. Have you ever worked with Mary?"

"No, and I'd like to. Look, let's lunch. I'm down on South Beach next month for *Elle.* Let's break bread and discuss it. I really appreciate this camera thing, Christa. I get stuff on my mind and I can't get it off. Obsessional. Know what I mean? And I hate the idea of some dago getting one over on me. Anyway, gotta go, darling. You got the idea on the fax to Mona?"

"Don't worry about a thing, Bill. You'll have your cameras in a couple of weeks. And I'll look forward to next month. I'd like to have you on board, Bill. You're a star. Take care."

He was gone. As she put down the phone, Christa wondered if she'd handled Braddock correctly. Signing him would be a coup for the agency. Damn! She'd been expecting Peter. Had her disappointment showed? Whatever. The trick to entering Braddock's good books would be to get his stupid cameras back.

She walked over to the word processor and sat down. Typing was another of her skills. She flicked open her address book and found the fax number of the Mexico City Hilton. She worked fast.

> For Mona Applegate, Hilton Hotel, Mexico City. From Christa Kenwood.
>
> Dear Mona,
> Can you do me a big favor? A man will contact you and deliver two Hasselblad cameras. They belong to Bill Braddock. He had to leave them in customs and I said you'd help him out and bring them back for him. Please give three to the man who brings them. When you get back, Bill will give you six for helping out. The man will explain. I hope this isn't too much hassle. Bill has promised to book you for *Bravo* when you get back. So it will be a double pay-off! I hope you are getting lots of work. See ya soon.
> Lots of love,
> Your friend,
> Christa.

She scrawled her signature over the typed Christa, and stuck the single sheet in the fax. She dialed the number of the Hilton. The machine ate the paper. Good. That was done. What next?

Peter Stein. *He* was next.

The number was in her head. He answered fast.

"Yes?" He would be "working," sitting at the desk, staring out morosely over the pool. Christa could smell the room. She could see it as if she were standing in it.

"Are you working? Did I disturb you?"

"Hello, Christa."

His voice was flat. Was he trying to make it sound like that? Or was it coming naturally?

"How are you?"

"I'm well. How are you?"

"I'm sorry," said Christa.

There was a long pause.

"Sorry about what?" said Peter.

"I'm sorry that the destruction of the Amazonian rain forest will cause an insufficiency of ozone in the earth's atmosphere, which will produce the effect of a greenhouse being erected over the planet, with a resultant global warming and rise in the tides which will threaten coastal areas such as Miami and Key West."

She strained to hear him smile.

"Ah, so *that's* what you're sorry about." There *was* a smile in his words. "Anything else?"

"I'm sorry I upset you, and I'm sorry you left in a huff, and I'm sorry you're not here right now."

Her voice was deepening. The apology was turning into an invitation.

"You were very rude, you know."

"I was angry. When I get angry, I get mean."

"I'm sorry if I made you angry and mean."

"You are forgiven."

"So we're friends again?"

"We're lovers again." Her voice caught on the words.

He laughed softly.

"How do you suppose I'm going to sit here for the rest of the morning and churn out my quota of literary depression if you are going to turn me on with telephone sex."

"Telephone sex?" said Christa. "Mmmmmm. Isn't that a great idea? It's pretty big these days, isn't it? Maybe we should try it."

"Christa!"

"What do you like, Peter? S or M? Do you like California schoolgirls, overweight women, girls who have girlfriends? Say the word, sir. I am your mistress's voice. Just give me your credit card number and I'll start the clock."

He laughed, but he didn't change the subject.

Neither did she. She didn't know what effect she was having on him, but she knew what was happening to her. She was warming up. She could feel the flush on her face, the prickly sensation beneath her arms, the funny vacuum in the pit of her stomach. She walked over to the bed and sat down. She fell back against the pillows. Blood rushed to her head.

"If you don't know what you want, then I'll have to tell you," she whispered.

"What do I want?"

"You want me."

The silence stretched out after her words.

"You're right," he said at last. His voice was strangled. "I've got to see you."

"Oh yes, my darling, you have," she murmured into the telephone.

45

"Nervous?"

Rob nodded. He smiled, saying nothing.

Lisa threaded her hand into his. "Don't be. I'll help. Forget everyone else, and concentrate on me."

"Shouldn't be hard." Rob squeezed back on her hand. He was beginning to understand this girl. Gentleness had blossomed from her like a flower in the desert, as she gave herself over to the alien process of love. All her life she had learned the dangers of depending on people because all her life she had been surrounded by the wicked. Now, damaged, her petals crushed by cruelty, she was opening up at last in the sun of his kindness and his faith. It filled Rob's heart with happiness to see her grow as a person before his eyes. She had hovered on the brink of the evil abyss, but she had stepped back because deep down she was good. But she still equated goodness with weakness. He would have to teach her how to trust. In the meantime, she would have to teach him how to model.

Inside the air-conditioned Winnebago, there was an atmosphere of controlled panic. They had staggered out of bed that morning at 5:30, pulled on some jeans, and struggled down to the motor home in the darkness. They were still trying to wake up on Thermoses of coffee as they pulled away from the hotel and headed to the location site.

The makeup artist hovered over Lisa, sizing her up as the Winnebago powered through the dark streets. The hairdresser, whose turn would be next, sat back on the sofa, flicking through *Vogue.*

"Have you ever used Preparation H for bags under the eyes after a late night?" said the makeup girl.

"I never have bags," said Lisa. "And when I'm working I don't stay up late."

The girl was unfazed by the haughty tones of the supermodel.

"A lot of the girls do. Swear by it. Never tried it myself."

"You should try some Ben Gay on your cellulite," said Lisa, irritated that she hadn't managed to upset the makeup girl.

"What, you just rub it in?" she said.

"You rub it in before you go to bed and then wrap your legs in cellophane. I had an aunt who tried it. She said it worked like a charm." Lisa was warming to the girl. She admired people who could withstand her insults.

"It's amazing what some girls do to look better. There was a Ford girl in New York who had all her eyeteeth out to give her cheekbones some definition."

"She *did?*" said Rob.

"Oh, yeah," said Lisa. "The dogs do anything. Atropine to dilate their pupils; laxatives and coke to lose weight; lips pumped full of collagen to look like they give good head. Luckily, I don't have to bother with all that shit."

"Come on, Lisa. Everyone has a trick to use to look better, even someone as great looking as you."

This girl could go far, thought Lisa. Actually, come to think of it, she *had* gone far. Steve Pitts/Lisa Rodriguez shoots were the moon to makeup girls.

"Okay, I have one, maybe two things I do."

"Come on, spill."

"I've got Hemingway eyebrows. I make them stand up by putting hairspray on a mascara brush and touching them up with that. It lasts for most of the day."

"Cool. Anything else?"

"Well, now it's matte lips, not high-gloss, I sometimes put a dab of white lipstick in the middle of my lower lip. It gives a highlight effect. Quite subtle."

"Yeah, I heard about that. Never tried it. Might do that today."

"You want to get started?"

The girl went to work, standing legs astride as the Winnebago swayed beneath her. The makeup would have to be in place before they got to the location. Steve would need time to set up his equipment, and that time would be taken up by the hairdresser. The morning magic-hour light would be gone by eight-fifteen, maybe earlier, and Pitts would have a fit if everybody wasn't ready to take advantage of it.

"Do I get made up?" said Rob.

"You get some powder on your nose if you get too steamy in the clinches," said Lisa, laughing at him in the mirror. "Otherwise, fellas are thought to look good enough as they are. It's seldom the case . . . but it is with you . . ."

"Ah," said the makeup artist, with a knowing smile. "You two have worked together before."

"Sort of," said Lisa.

"Lisa, what do I do? I mean, when the shoot starts, what do I actually do?"

"Don't *worry*, darling. Steve will tell you. I'll show you." She had a sudden thought. "Did Steve's van leave much before us?"

" 'Bout ten minutes. He's got Mary Whitney with him. I'd never met her before. I said good morning, and she said 'How on earth do you know yet?' Is she a bit weird or something? I'd always imagined her to be incredibly laid-back, but here she is, up at the crack of dawn with all her makeup on, going out on a shoot with all of us."

"Are you sure it was Mary?" Lisa looked incredulous.

"Yes, I recognized her. She was dressed to kill in some amazing outfit, sort of over-the-top Gaultier. She looked neat."

"She's a rat bag," hissed Lisa. "Shit, that's the last thing I need, the fucking client bossing everyone around."

"What's she like?"

"Ask Rob," said Lisa, her good mood gone. "He's the Mary Whitney expert around here."

Somehow the makeup girl knew not to ask.

"Where are we going?" said Rob, aware that a change of subject was required.

"Somewhere called Key Biscayne. There's a park there with a lighthouse. It's supposed to be very beautiful," said the makeup girl.

"Not with Attila the Hen around," snarled Lisa. "What the hell is she up to? She must have a billion hangers-on who could handle this thing better than she can."

But of course she knew. It wasn't over. Maybe it had hardly started. Mary Whitney hadn't finished with Rob. Mary and Lisa were rivals. *That* was what the rich bitch was doing in the dawn. She was keeping tabs on the boy she wanted. Hah! Lisa had been right. Mighty Mary did have a weakness. And the name of her weakness was "Rob." Lisa smiled. Okay, that was fine. She was up to the challenge. She was more than up to it. The Rodriguez beauty and sexual charm would be matched against the Whitney power and the Whitney billions, and the prize would be, not life, but the body and soul of the boy who sat so close to her.

"I hope Christa's coming," said Rob.

"Oh, yes, Christa will be there," said Lisa. "All your fan club will be present and correct. Come to think of it, maybe you *should* be nervous."

"Don't, Lisa," said Rob.

Immediately she softened. It wasn't his fault that everyone adored him. And if she was going to walk away victorious, she would have to step carefully.

"I was joking," she said quickly. "Just don't go soliciting any more megachecks, okay? Believe me, you've done more than your fair share for charity. You crammed a lifetime of good works into a single evening."

"Lisa, we've been through all that."

"I know. I know. I'm sorry."

"There, that does it. You look wonderful, Lisa. Do you like it?" The makeup girl stood back, hoping for a compliment.

"It'll do, I guess," was all she got.

The Winnebago had arrived.

It had parked next door to an identical motor home, near some fir trees.

Christa was waiting as they disembarked.

"Hi, Lisa. Hi, Rob. Hi, everyone," she said. Her cheerfulness sounded genuine. Rob's spirits rose.

"Steve's gone up the beach with his guys, and Mary. Did I tell you Mary was coming?" she added.

"You kept that little nugget of information to yourself," said Lisa as she dismounted.

"You look wonderful," said Christa. "Great makeup. I'd get right on with the hair. The sun's coming up and Steve sets up fast. You okay, Rob? Not too nervous?"

"Not now you're here," said Lisa, unable to avoid the sarcasm.

"The first shot is water's edge, catching the reflection with the boards. Two lovers kissing tenderly. Both under the influence of Miami. Shouldn't be so hard for you two."

"And if we have any problems, you and Mary will be able to jump in and set us straight. After all, you're the ones with the most recent experience of seaside sex."

"Hair," said Christa definitely. She took a deep breath. This was day one, shot one, and already the sniping had started. She prayed it wouldn't end in disaster.

Lisa climbed back on board. Rob dismounted. Christa winked at him. He smiled back.

"Come on, I'll show you the way," said Christa. They threaded through the fir trees in silence. The path ended. The beach opened up wide before them. Steve was down by the water, peering through the lens of a tripod-mounted Hasselblad. A couple of assistants were in the shallows, directing light with reflector boards at a third. The horizon was ablaze with deep reds and oranges. The sun was coming up. Steve looked at his watch as they approached. Mary Whitney was standing by his side.

"How's it going?" said Steve. "I want to start in about quarter of an hour."

"On target. Lisa'll be done by then. Rob is blue jeans and bare feet for this first one, isn't he?" said Christa.

"And bare torso," said Mary Whitney. "Good *morning,* Rob. You look good enough to eat, but then I haven't had any breakfast."

Steve and Christa exchanged looks. Rob said nothing.

Mary pulled a small shell-shaped bottle from her bag. She held it up.

"Scent, not brandy, dears," she said. "I thought we should have this around in case anyone forgets why we are all here. We might sprinkle a little over Lisa to remind her she's a woman, and make her more appetizing for young Rob. Don't worry about getting close to Lisa in the clinches, Rob. She only turns into a vampire after sunset."

Steve sent his eyes toward heaven. Mary was in evil form.

"What do you think of my outfit, Rob?" said Mary. She pirouetted on the sand.

"Looks great," tried Rob.

"How gall*ant* of you to say so. Great. You'll be the couture critic for '*W*' yet."

"Here comes Lisa," said Christa. "God, that was quick with the hair."

"We're going for the wet look for this shot. The story line is that she's been swimming. He's met her at the water's edge, and she *still* smells of Miami," said Steve.

"I don't remember designing that bikini," said Mary Whitney. "That's not string, that's dental floss."

"Hi, Mary," said Lisa with a dazzling smile. "Great bikini, no? Shows off my butt beautifully. What do you think, Rob? Pretty cute, huh?" She obliterated the memory of Mary's awkward pirouette with a fabulous one of her own. Everyone looked at the Rodriguez bottom. "Pretty cute" was the understatement of the millennium.

Mary Whitney glowered, as she was supposed to. Rob gulped. Steve wondered if he had ever seen a better backside on a boy. The three assistants tried to look cool. Christa's heart sank as she watched the conflict escalate.

"Into the sea with the two of you. To the knees, please. Backs to the sun as it rises. Lisa straight on to the camera. Rob angled in profile. We'll warm up with a few smiley ones. Sexy lips, Lisa. Sex smile, not happy smile, okay? Unless they're the same thing to you, dear. Rob, just look strong and handsome, like you always do."

"But not too *dumb,* love," said Mary Whitney. It wasn't clear whether she was talking to Lisa, Rob, or to both of them.

"Mary, can you leave the directions to me?" said Steve. "By all means say what you think, but to me, not to the models, if that's okay . . ."

"Anything you say . . . *sir.* I'm only the poor client."

They all let it go.

"There! That's it. That's good. Very warm, very friendly. Lean a bit closer to her, Rob. Put your face closer to hers, but from the side. Like you're going to nibble her ear. That's it. Perfect. You're cooking, Lisa. You look like a dream. Now nuzzle her ear, Rob. Imagine you're going to bite her lobe. And smile . . . like she's just cracked a sexy joke. You really love her. She's your girl. Got it? That's good. Fine. Okay. Okay."

Mary Whitney shifted from one foot to the other.

"When do we get to kiss?" said Lisa with a laugh.

"Patience is a virtue," said Steve.

"Nonsense," muttered Mary.

"Am I doing it right?" said Rob.

"You deserve a medal, dear," said Mary.

Lisa's smile deepened. She was winning. Mary Whitney was beginning to lose it before her eyes. Her hands fidgeted with one another. Her feet wouldn't stay still. There was an expression on her face that was not far from pain.

"Okay, let's try a kiss now," said Steve, crouched low over his camera. "Boys, focus the light on their faces. I'm in close-up now, heads and upper bodies. Let's do a kiss and a Polaroid for the light. Looks about 5.6 at 125 to me. Ready, Lisa? Give me as much open face as you can, while you do the deed. Nice open mouths, as if you're doing it for real. Just relax into it, boys and girls."

They did. Lisa led, acutely aware of the camera angle, but aware too of the lips of the boy she loved. Just before she leaned into the kiss, she managed to catch the Whitney eye . . . and she winked.

"That's it," said Steve. "Oh, boy, that's it, isn't it, folks?"

It *was* it. The kiss roared on, and everything was in it . . . teeth, tongues, hearts, souls. The only sound was the muted rumble of the surf and the manic clicking of the Hasselblad shutter.

"Okay. Relax. New magazine."

But they didn't stop. They looked as if they had hardly started. Steve laughed. So did Christa. An assistant moved forward to load a full magazine onto the Hasselblad. Mary Whitney, however, did not join in the muted mirth. Her face was twisted in a terrible rage. Christa could have sworn she had actually gone green. Her fists were clenched by her side, her knuckles white.

"That's *enough!*" she said suddenly, quite loudly. But the kiss thundered on. Mary Whitney opened her mouth, big and round. "Stop it!" she yelled at the top of her voice.

The make-believe lovers unwound. They turned to stare at her. So did everyone else. There was silence apart from the surf.

"It's all right, Mary," said Christa quickly, not quite knowing what she meant.

"What on earth is the matter?" said Lisa, who knew precisely what the matter was.

"Okay, everyone, let's stay calm. It's going to be a long morning," said Steve.

Mary was shaking with rage. Her face was gray-green now, a sickly off-white creeping in from the edges to make her look like a member of the Addams family.

"How dare you . . . how dare you make a mockery of my shoot!" she spluttered.

"It's not your shoot. It might be your campaign, but it's Steve's shoot. And I don't think Steve has any problems if we want to practice kissing," said Lisa, tossing her head back in defiance. "After all, it's what you're paying us to do."

"You tart, you harlot, you, you . . . whore. How do you have the nerve to stand there and answer me back? You're corrupting that boy. You've corrupted that boy . . ."

The smile of triumph on the face of Lisa Rodriguez came up like dawn on the Mandalay road.

"Ah," she purred, like the cat who had finally caught the mouse. "So that's what it's all about. You're jealous, Mary, aren't you? *That's* what it is. You want to be where I am, doing the kissing, don't you? But the trouble is, you haven't got the face for it. You've got the cash, but not the face, or the body, or anything else. And then there's Rob to think about, isn't there? Got to think of his stomach, haven't we? We could hardly have him kissing you, and then puking his guts out all the way through the shoot."

"Lisa!" said Rob.

"Shut up, Lisa," shouted Christa.

"Oh, shit," said Steve.

One of the assistants giggled.

Mary Whitney was in shock. The unthinkable had happened. Public humiliations didn't come any larger. She opened her mouth, but the words weren't there. Her vast armory of insults was bare when she needed it most.

"I . . . I think . . ." But thoughts had gone. There weren't any around. The phrase that kept coming into her mind was "I think, therefore I am." But Descartes' 'Cogito ergo,' while profound, wouldn't cut the cake in this context.

Christa hurried to the aid of the mortally wounded billionaire. She walked up to her, put her arms around the sagging Whitney shoulders, and led her firmly away from the scene. Mary followed, like the little lamb she had so suddenly become.

They walked in silence through the firs, until everyone was out of sight. The Winnebagos were empty, the drivers smoking cigarettes outside in the sun. Christa led Mary up the steps of the nearest, and sat her down on a sofa.

"Are you all right?" she said at last.

Mary Whitney's answer was one large tear from each eye. Then another, then others. At first her tears were soundless. Now they acquired a soundtrack. It started as a shower of sobs, then the sounds deepened and the torrent of liquid intensified, until a full-blown sorrow storm was under way.

Christa held her hands and tried not to look. It was never easy to watch a tough guy cry. She racked her brain to find the right words. The trouble was that Lisa had been right on target. The facts spoke for themselves. Mary had fallen for Rob. Lisa had fallen for Rob. Rob appeared to be falling for Lisa. It might not be the most original situation in the world, but it was always the hardest to handle.

"Oh, Christa," sobbed Mary. "I'm just no good at this. I've never . . . I've never been . . . in love."

"Nonsense, Mary," said Christa. "You're not 'in love.' It's a crush. They happen. It's difficult, but time passes. One day you'll be able to laugh about this like you do about everything else."

"But I don't *care* about everything else. That's why I can laugh about it," spluttered Mary.

"Listen, Mary. Listen to me. Rob is a fantasy. He's sweet and he's innocent, and he's good. And he's young. God, he's young. Can't you see why we all love him? He's all the things we're not. He's like a child, and we're world-weary adults, longing to be children again. He's naïve, and we're bored to death with our sophistication. He's an optimist and we're worn out by our pessimism. He has no ambition except to be happy and to be kind, and we have agendas as long as your arm, and deep down we're not too proud of them. We think he can give us back our youth. We think he can turn the clock back to a time when everything was simple and straightforward and . . . fun. But he can't, Mary. He can't do anything. He doesn't know how, and we're knee deep in illusion. It's not reality, Mary. It's make-believe. We've just got to wake up and stop dreaming."

The gale of the Whitney sorrow was blowing over.

"Are you saying you're in love with Rob, too?" she said. Her cunning had not deserted her.

Christa laughed nervously. "Of *course* I'm not. I'm in love with . . ." She chopped off the words. "But I know how you feel. I can see Rob's attraction. Anyone could. I know it's a dreadful thing to say, Mary, but at our age it's not uncommon to make a fool of oneself with a kid like Rob."

"I'm not making a fool of myself," said Mary, fishing out a handkerchief and blowing her nose. She smiled a wintery smile. "Well, maybe a little fool." She dabbed at her cheeks. A chip of her old humor had reappeared. Christa breathed a sigh of relief. The day could yet be saved.

"But what in God's name does he see in a cheap hustler like Rodriguez?"

"Oh, Mary, come on! Are you serious? I mean, you hired Lisa for your perfume because she's probably the best-looking animal in the universe. More important than that . . . she's Rob's age. Shit, they probably smoke dope together, and watch MTV and like to *dance* and things. You know, red Corvettes, rap music, and talking till three in the morning, imagining what they're saying is *original.* Don't you remember what it was like to be young? Hell, *I* remember what it was like when you were young. Remember that cop you screwed under the Jeep outside 264 for a bet? Jeez, *that* was young."

"It was a Volkswagen."

"Whatever." Christa laughed.

"No, it was important. Volkswagens have less room underneath than Jeeps. It was more of an achievement!"

She was smiling properly now. "You're right, Christa, I guess. No fool like an old one. But it's just that I haven't met anyone like Rob, and it seems so unfair that I can't have him, when I've always had whatever I wanted. My whole *life* has been having what I wanted. I'm absolutely *addicted* to it. I wish I could explain to you the absolute *horror* of not having one's own way."

"You don't have to explain it to me," said Christa grimly.

"Yes, you are a bit like me in that respect, aren't you? But you're less direct, more cunning, and you have more charm. But that's it, isn't it . . . wanting and getting, getting and wanting. Being and enjoying and having simply aren't in the equation. It's silly, isn't it? You don't know how silly it is until you meet someone like Rob."

"Yes, but think of all the things we'd have to give up if we were like him. Power, the cash that buys the freedom, success, fame. You say he's got all the answers, but he's a pawn in all this. He's simply not in control of events. How would you like that? How *do* you like it, being in love with him and seeing him fall for Lisa? It isn't making you happy to be in the passenger seat for a change. I've never seen you look so damned miserable."

"I'd give half my business to have him love me," said Mary Whitney, her eyes misting over once more.

"Half?"

"Well, a quarter . . . maybe ten percent. An awful lot of money, anyway."

"Poor Rob. He's just gone from half a billion to a few million bucks in a second, and you haven't started dealing yet."

"What should I do?" said Mary.

"Not a thing. Go back to Palm Beach and throw yourself into your business. Hire a guy to work on your backhand. It's crazy to hang around here and drive yourself and everyone else nuts."

"I was thinking of canceling the whole thing."

Christa steeled herself. Thank God Mary had used the past tense.

"Why, Mary? What for? Why hurt your business, and Rob, and me, and Steve? *And* make Lisa's day. That's what you'd be doing, and it wouldn't solve a thing. You know that."

"Yes," said Mary. "I know that."

"For the first time in your life the right thing to do is to walk away," said Christa.

"Mmmmmmmm," agreed Mary McGregor Whitney . . . but she didn't mean it.

Nobody really understood her. She liked it like that. Oh, they knew she was a tough cookie, a brilliant bottom-liner who ran one of the most successful businesses in America with an iron hand. But her sense of humor hid the real truth. She joked about being addicted to getting her own way, and the smiles and the laughter camouflaged the fact that in her soul she was genuinely ruthless. She could not remember a time in her life she had been seriously thwarted. But such a time was now. Okay, so Rob wasn't a business deal, but he was a desire, a desire of *hers,* and her desires, by definition, had to be fulfilled. For whatever complex reason she had decided to want him, and now a far more important process had been set in motion . . . the satisfaction of the Mary McGregor Whitney needs. Logic might dictate a retreat to Palm Beach, as Christa had suggested, but logic paled before the awesome necessity of fulfilling each and every one of the Whitney dreams. Call it an obsession, call it a madness, call it whatever you liked, the fact remained. She wanted Rob Sand, and not a soul nor a thing was going to stand in her way.

46

Christa looked at her watch. He would be here soon. She had left the front door open. When he arrived, she wanted him to let himself in, look for her, wander out to the pool and discover her there. She was dressed for assassination. The bikini was a state-of-the-tart imagination relaxer. It did all the hard work for the viewer. She lay back on the sun bed and stretched like a leopard. For two days now, he would have been wanting her. Soon he would get her. The feeling was inside her, priming her body for his. But where was he? Damn! He wouldn't be late, would he? Had some godforsaken motorist run out of gas on the Seven Mile Bridge? Would she have to stay looking as good as this for the whole afternoon? How much waiting could a superheated body do?

The klaxon ripped through her mind. She turned to the waterway. A boat was edging toward the island. Damn! Some tourist was trying to dock. She prepared to repel boarders. Then she saw him at the wheel. It was Peter. He'd come by sea. She jumped up, yelling out to him. So much for leopard cool. She was hopping about like a teenager in love. She tried to calm down.

"Do you want to throw me a rope?" she yelled.

"No, I can handle it." He could. The boat turned on its own length, roared into reverse, steadied, and came to rest half an inch from the dock.

"Pretty neat," said Christa, smiling at him. "Not bad docking, either."

Holding a rope, he jumped out and tied up quickly.

Then he was in her arms.

"Oh, Peter," she whispered, lost in his embrace.

"Christa, you witch," he murmured into her neck. Then, "I should tie the boat up properly."

"Tie me up properly."

"With rope?"

"With a marriage certificate."

"You want to spend the rest of your life with a business bimbo like me?" he said.

Christa smiled against his chest.

"Oh, I'll soon take care of that little deficiency," she said.

She leaned back and looked at him. Yes, he was the same. He was deliciously, wonderfully similar to the man she loved.

"You look like a dream," he said.

"The kind that reality destroys?" She smiled as she spoke.

He laughed. She didn't forget a thing. "The kind that reality enhances. I might have to throw away my book."

She laughed. "You can throw away all my rivals. Can I climb on board your boat, and be given the guided tour?"

"Which part do you want to see first?"

"The bedroom."

"It's called the stateroom."

"Whatever. The place where you make love."

She felt him shudder against her. Mmmmmmm! It was nice. She had his switch. She could flick it whenever she liked. Like now. Like always.

They clambered on board. He walked into the main cabin. She followed. He turned to face her. He was dark brown from the sun on the long journey from Key West. The khaki T-shirt and khaki shorts emphasized his color. He looked lean, hard, and hungry. His eyes roamed over her exposed body. She smiled as he watched her, seeing her effect mirrored in his eyes.

"Do you like it?" she said.

He nodded. His throat leaped as he swallowed. She could see him harden. She stepped toward him. Her hands reached out for the belt of his shorts, but he signaled for her to stop.

"No," he said. His voice rasped with desire.

She stopped. She shuddered. He was taking control.

"Take off the bottom of your bikini," he said.

With trembling fingers, she did so. It dropped on the teak floor of the cabin. She stared deep into his eyes, filling them with love. He looked down to the place she had revealed. The blond triangle gleamed in the cabin's muted light. She had thrown one leg forward, one leg back, and the pink of her love lips shone in the downy hair like jewels in a box. They were already parted, already glistening, already ready for him. Her mouth opened as she breathed faster. She stood still.

"Do you want to go to the bedroom?" she whispered.

"No, here," he said.

He stepped toward her. His face was close to hers. He reached down and laid the flat of his hand against her heat. He ran his forefinger along the length of her, sliding it in the groove, lingering at the top at the soft center of her lust. He pressed down on it, gentle, tender. He moved his finger from side to side, and she copied him, with her head, turning it from side to side in the sympathy of passion.

"Ohhhhh!" she moaned. His finger quickened its pace. She thrust herself out at his hand and she willed him to invade her, with his fingers, with his body, with his love. He heard her. One minute his mouth was close against hers. The next it was not. He sank to his knees. His head rested against her thigh. His mouth hovered at the brink of her triangle of need.

"Peter!" she murmured.

He moved closer. She felt his breath against her heat. She braced herself, legs apart, for his touch. Her hands rested lightly on his head, stroking his hair. Then he put out his tongue, and he licked her. It was like being painted with joy. One glorious stroke of pleasure pealed into Christa's brain. He started at the bottom, plunging his wet tongue into her soft pink crevice. Then he drew it slowly upward, parting her love lips as he tasted them, wetting them with saliva as, in turn, his tongue was moistened by the juice of her passion. Upward, ever upward, his tongue moved, until it nestled against the tiny baton that controlled the orchestra of her joy. There it rested, probing gently, swaying over the small knot of ecstasy, slipping and sliding in the steam heat as he loved her. She tensed her legs and bore down on him.

Now, he did it again. His tongue moved lower, pushing deeper, then rose once more, splaying back the pink, up to the top and down again in delicious repetition. He was lapping at her with long hard strokes. His tongue had stiffened, and his head was bent back, his eyes closed, as he gave himself over to her pleasure.

"Yes, darling," she murmured. "Lick me like that. Don't stop. Don't ever stop." Her hands moved on his head to emphasize her words. They swayed in his rhythm, following it at first, then gradually controlling it, until he was the captive on her ride of passion. She pushed out at his tongue, inching her legs apart to open herself wider to him. The waves of pleasure flowed through her. The flood gates below parted further, ready to unleash the dammed rivers of her desire onto his lips.

He reached behind her to steady himself. His hands cupped her tensed buttocks. He drew her in to him, plastering her soft wetness against his face, rubbing himself in her, as she ground herself against him. His tongue was a dagger inside her, lapping, licking no longer. It thrust into her musky depths, luxuriating in the damp, forbidden taste of the girl he loved. His whole face was crammed tight to her. He could hardly breathe in the abundant moisture, the silken lips, the velvet core of Christa. He moved from side to side, burying himself in her lust, desperate to join with her in the union of bodies that was the ceaseless goal of love. He moaned in the wetness, frustrated that his body could not merge with hers. He wanted to climb forever into the warm, liquid bath she had become. He thrust up on his knees, pressing upward with all his strength and, in answer, she bore down with all of hers. Still, he managed to move in the slippery pressure zone, battling for breath but fighting, too, to inhale the scented essence of her so that she could enter his soul, where he longed for her to be.

It couldn't last forever. Both needed the release from a pleasure that had become too intense. Her hands twisted in his hair. Her stomach, covered in sweat, slapped anxiously against his forehead. Her thighs, dripping with desire, clasped tight against his cheeks.

"Peter," she moaned. "Oh, Peter, I'm going to come."

He couldn't answer her, but his lips said "yes." They were poised like the cupped hands of a communicant to receive her. She steeled herself. How could she stay standing? What muscles would be left in the helter-skelter joy ride of her orgasm? She didn't care. She could only feel the awesome power in her body as she moved toward the moment.

Her center of gravity had shifted. She was no longer a brain controlling legs, arms, muscles, bones. She had become instead a tight parcel of longing thrust against a tongue. Soon, the gift would be unwrapped, and the precious present it contained would fly free and join with the spirit of the man who had made it. The rush of pleasure intensified. Her heart stood still. The breath sat caged in her lungs. She tensed into a hard ball of longing, poised above his head. And then she stopped. There was one single moment of beautiful clarity amid all the confusion of passion. For a millisecond she savored it, and then there was only the descent into chaos.

"Ooooooooh," she screamed, her head thrown back in ecstasy. She was coming undone. Everything loosened. Everything was free. Her legs shook in the storm, buckling at the knees. Her hands jerked at the head of her lover. Her lips against his were the floodgates to the creamy river of her longing. She flowed out to him, squirting her passion, hosing him with the liquid of her joy. It was endless. It would never stop. This would go on until she was dry . . . until there was no blood, no moisture, no dampness remaining in the body that was emptying itself into him. He was still before the onslaught. His mouth feasted from her. He was swallowing her. She was entering him in the only way that a woman could. Her love was inside him, as, so soon, his would be inside her.

And then she was spent. She had nothing more to give. He knew it was over, but he didn't leave her. He nuzzled into her in the aftermath of the storm. He nibbled at her, kissing her, reassuring her in the vacuum of passing passion. She fell away from him. Her legs were still parted lasciviously, her core dripping wet, her pinkness shining bright for him to see. He turned toward her, still kneeling, his face awash with her.

"I love you, Christa," he said. "Oh, my God, if only you knew how much I love you."

"I know," she murmured. "You just showed me."

He struggled to his feet and moved toward her, collapsing beside her. He cradled her in his arms, and she smiled up at him.

"Can we go on doing this forever?" she said.

"Forever is a long time."

"Not long enough."

He put his hand on her stomach. She put hers over it. He wanted more. Now.

"Wait, darling. Wait a little while. I want to talk to you. I want you to talk to me."

"I know. I'm sorry. I've never felt like this." He smiled his apology. How could anyone be so beautiful? She was naked beside him, wet with leftover love. She smelled of need, of desire, of passion. He swallowed hard. He had to control himself. Somehow.

"I'd put my bottoms on if I thought it would help." She laughed.

She sat up, gazing into his eyes.

"What am I going to do about you, Peter Stein?"

"You're going to marry me, and we're going to have babies until you break."

"I can all but guarantee I'm pregnant already. It's crazy, but I feel it really strongly." Tenderly, he stroked her stomach. Love shone from his eyes.

Was this the magic moment to reveal what she had done for him? Wives and babies seemed like a good lead into cash talk. Whatever deficiencies she might demonstrate in the marital stakes, screwing up the family finances would not be among them. A man would have to be grateful for that. Especially so, when his face was still slick with her lust.

"We're really going to get married?" she said.

"Oh, yes, we are."

"Then I've got something to tell you," she said. A fleeting expression of uncertainty crossed her face. Peter was so unpredictable in the area of his work. The anxiety passed quickly. The hell with it! Millions of bucks were good news in anybody's language.

"Something wonderful?" he said.

"Something pretty wonderful."

She sat up.

"Well, you remember that time we had the fight, and you said I couldn't sell things, and that the publishing world would think I was a dumb blonde . . ."

"Darling, surely we don't have to go through that . . ."

"No, wait, Peter. You have to listen to me."

"I'm listening, but I thought you'd forgiven me for all that."

"I have. I did. But at the time I was mad, and so I did something about it."

"What did you do?"

There was a smile on his lips. It was a what-sweet-little-thing-did-you-do? expression.

"I went up to New York and saw a friend of mine, Lewis Heller, at Twentieth. Remember, he was at that book fair party the night we met? I told him you might be wanting to move from World, and he offered five million dollars for your next three books. Double the print runs. Double the advertising. There! How about *that* for a business bimbo?"

"*What!*" said Peter. His face was twisted in a look of total, unconditional astonishment.

"I made you two and a half million bucks," said Christa, smiling broadly.

"You told Heller you were dealing for me?" said Peter.

Oh, dear! The smile faded from Christa's face. He had zeroed in on the lie, not the bucks.

"Yes, and it worked. The offer's firm. You just have to say yes."

"No," said Peter Stein. "NO!" he yelled.

"Oh, Peter, for God's sake, what are you talking about? Listen to what I'm saying. Are you following me? You know Twentieth. We're talking an up-front guarantee here. Five million bucks, and they make you a major best seller. That's two and a half million more than you were getting before. It's a dream deal. And I did it for you."

"You betrayed me," said Peter with a venomous quietness.

Christa's eyes widened. Who was this man with her come on his face? She didn't know him. She was talking of marriage and babies, and yet he was a total stranger to her.

"Peter, don't be so competitive. You're a brilliant writer. I do the best deals in the world. You can't be everything."

"You don't understand, do you? You simply don't understand anything about me," he said, his voice thick with bitterness.

"I don't understand why anybody would want to get paid half what he's worth. Is that such a strange thing not to understand?"

He stood up.

"You *dare* . . . " he spat through clenched teeth, "to go up to New York to a sewer rat like Heller in an immoral company like Twentieth, and you dare . . . you dare . . . to tell him that I would be seen dead in a ditch with him for a few million miserable dollars. You don't understand anything but money, Christa. It's a perversion. It's a low, stinking, disgusting perversion, and you should get help for it. I care about my work. I care about my art. I don't do it to make money. I do it because I have to do it. That sounds strange to you, doesn't it, but other artists understand. Heller and Twentieth are literary prostitutes . . . worse than that, because they don't give anyone any pleasure. All they do, day in, day out, is shovel cash around like shit. If I had to be published by Heller, I would chop my fingers off one by one and I'd enjoy doing it. And yet you, behind my back, have gone cap in hand to the publishing Antichrist and offered me up for a mess of pottage. Never, as long as I live, will I forgive you for that."

Christa stood up. There were all sorts of things to say, and many more to regret, but right now was right now.

She bent down in silence and she picked up the bottom of her bikini. In silence, she stepped into it. At the door, she turned to face him.

"I suggest," she said, "that before you get back to Key West, you wipe my come off your face, you egocentric, pompous, self-opinionated bastard."

47

The call came through on his private line. He picked it up quickly. He knew who had the number.

"Johnny."

"Yes."

"You know who this is?"

"Yes."

"Good. Listen. Your girl has the package. We want you to bring her back now. Call her. Tell her to get the American Airlines flight 515 on Wednesday from Mexico City to Miami. Please repeat that."

Johnny Rossetti swallowed nervously. He licked his lips to moisten them.

"She has the package. American 515. Mexico City/Miami. Wednesday."

"Okay. The other thing is this. Get your girl to make sure the target meets that flight. How you handle that is up to you."

"I can fix it," said Johnny.

"Good. That's all you have to do. The trap's set. When the two girls meet in Miami, your problems will be over."

"Thank you, thank . . ."

But the line was dead. Johnny sat back in his seat. The fear and the excitement collided on his face. There was no going back now. It was the end game. All that was left was vengeance, and the terrible price he'd paid for it.

He stood up and walked over to the drinks cabinet. He picked up a decanter and poured four fingers of scotch into a glass. He drank it quickly, exhaling as the warm alcohol hit the lining of his empty stomach. Then he walked back to his desk and dialed the number of the Mexico City Hilton. He looked at his watch. It was six o'clock. There was a good chance he'd catch her in her room.

"Mona? Johnny."

"Hi, Johnny. Hi, baby. How are you? Great to hear your voice."

"Yeah. How's it going, sweetheart?"

"It's going lousy, honey. There ain't no work here. We think *we* got a recession. I seen a whole lotta people, but there's nothing."

"That's fine. No sweat. You get paid anyways. That was the deal. Listen, Mona, I'm missing you. I want you to come home."

"You *are*, Johnny?"

"Yeah. Got a pencil handy? I want you to catch the American Airlines 515 to Miami out of Mexico City on Wednesday. You got that? That's the flight I want you to be on, okay? No other flight, no other day, no other time, you read me?"

"Oh, great, baby! That's the day after tomorrow. You gonna *meet* me or something?"

"No, I can't. I'm stuck up here like forever. But that's another thing. I want you to get Christa to meet you. Send her a fax saying it's vital that she meets you on that flight. Say you've got something really important to discuss with her, and that it can't be talked about on the phone."

"What's going down, Johnny?"

Mona was dumb, but she wasn't stupid. Now she was suspicious.

"Darling, you have to trust me on this. I can't spell it out right now. I want you to tell Christa, when you see her at the airport, that you've changed your mind about working for her. You want to come back to me and Elle. I called you up while you were away, right, and I made you an offer you couldn't refuse. That's why you want her to meet you. That's what you're going to say to her when she does."

"Oh, Johnny, that's wonderful. So I get to come back to New York and everything's like before."

"Only better, sweetheart. Millions better."

"You gonna put me about the town?"

"I'm gonna plaster you over it, Mona. You betcha. Your pretty face is gonna bore the world to death."

"Oh, Johnny!" She giggled into the phone as the wonderful vision filled her mind.

"So somehow me joining Christa's agency and then walking out on her helps you out in some big way."

"You'd better believe it, sweetheart. Hey, anything else happening down there?"

"Not around the Hilton pool."

"Seen anybody while you been down there, apart from business?"

"Nah. Oh, yeah, there was a guy who dropped off a couple of cameras that belong to Ben Braddock. They'd gotten impounded by customs and Christa faxed through to ask if I'd bring them back. He's going to use me for *Bravo.* Now I'm coming back to you, you'll get ten percent!"

"Better not put them through with the baggage. Wouldn't do to lose Braddock's cameras. He's a hot photographer. Anyway, the x-ray machine would probably think they're a bomb."

"No sweat. I'll carry them hand luggage."

"Yeah, and drop them off with Christa at Miami. No point you wasting your time getting them back to Braddock. Fuck him."

"Johnny, I'm so excited."

"You're gonna be more excited when you try the new stuff I got for you in my closet."

"What have you got for me in bed, Johnny?"

"Let's just say it didn't go away since it saw you last."

She laughed. He laughed. But they weren't laughing about the same things.

"Can I come right on up to New York from Miami?"

"Just as soon as you've seen Christa and given her Braddock's cameras and the 'dear Jill.' I'll be sitting right here, waiting."

"I love you, Johnny."

"Ditto," he said. He'd seen *Ghost.*

She hung up.

There were a couple of other calls to make.

The first was easy. American Airlines confirmed that flight 515, Wednesday, Mexico City/Miami, was wide open. There were a ton of free seats. The next was only a little more complicated.

"Braddock?"

"Yeah."

"Rossetti."

"Hi, man."

"Only one thing, Ben. On Wednesday you're gonna get a call from the DEA in Miami, or from a lawyer, or from our mutual friend, the model. Maybe from all three. And you're gonna say . . . ?"

"That I haven't talked to Christa in two years."

"Never left any Hasselblads in Mexico. Never asked anyone to bring parcels from anywhere to anywhere else."

"Right on, Johnny. I know the line. We went through it. I got a memory."

"Okay, an' you remember what you'll be getting for your help in this?"

"I never forget a number, especially big numbers."

"Don't do it wrong, Ben. There are people involved, if you know what I mean. People who make good enemies. You screw up, we all screw up."

"Relax, Johnny. I'm a big boy."

"Okay, Ben. I know that, baby. See ya."

He put down the phone. He ran through it in his mind as he had a million times before. Had he overlooked anything? Had he covered the angles? There were things that could go wrong. There always were. Flights could be late. Tires could have blowouts. People could screw up. But the chances were that it would work.

And on Wednesday morning at Miami airport at around twelve noon, Christa Kenwood would be arrested as she took physical possession of a parcel of heroin addressed to her, with a street value of approximately one and a half million dollars.

48

The fax sat on Christa's dressing table as she combed her hair. Like Mona, it spelled trouble.

> I'm coming back early. I have to speak to you right away. Essential you meet me at Miami tomorrow, Wednesday, American Airlines Flight 515 from Mexico City arriving twelve noon. Very important. Please be there. Mona.

Christa had called her the moment she'd received the message, but Mona was not taking calls. It was maddening, but it meant she had to go to the airport, despite the unfolding drama of the vitally important Whitney shoot. Mona was a big model. Christa's agency was small. There was no alternative. What the hell did Mona want? Why had she walked out on the Mexico City deal? It was pointless to speculate. She would find out at lunchtime. It had occurred to Christa that Mona might want to get out of the contract she had so recently signed. If that was what she wanted, fine. Christa wouldn't hold her to it and get rough legally. You could take a girl like Mona to a camera, but you couldn't make her think. If she was unhappy for whatever reason, it was best to let her go.

She sighed and sipped at her coffee. Actually, Mona was the least of her problems. Peter Stein wasn't. He loomed large over Christa's life. Once again, he had demonstrated his unique capacity to charm and infuriate her at the same time, and she was enough of a realist to know that she did precisely the same thing to him. It wasn't hard to work out why. They were opposites in every single way except one. They both shared an overwhelming certainty that they were right. The trouble was they disagreed on what "right" was. Christa was strong as steel. Peter was diamond man. Each were irresistible forces and immovable mountains. One was a rock. The other was a very hard place. But if their form was identical, their substance was diametrically opposed. He thought black. She thought white. He dealt in fantasy. Her currency was reality. He was a head-in-the-clouds idealist. She could have written the book on pragmatism. Their last struggle was a microcosm of all the battles they had fought, and would fight, if they ever had a future together. Peter didn't care about money, or winning in a deal, or about selling lots more books. He cared not a jot for fame, success, and material reward. What turned him on was the music in his words, the struggle to communicate subtle meanings, the daily war to produce work that pleased his own merciless critical judgment. Christa understood that was a vital part of his life. What she would never comprehend was how it could become the only part. He had to do the work anyway. The blood, toil, sweat, and tears were a constant. Why, in heaven's name, when the heavy lifting was over, would anyone neglect to ensure they were paid the going rate for the job? To do otherwise was negligence. To be negligent was to shortchange oneself. And oneself was the most important commodity on earth.

Time and again she had tried to understand his violent reaction. Each time she had ended up explaining it in terms of arrogance, artistic snobbery, and the inability to admit failure. Peter, she was certain, had been so angry because she had been so successful in an area in which he had no natural expertise. To that extent he was exhibiting a weakness, the small-minded refusal to admit to a mistake. But at the same time she was bright enough to realize that all explanations were filtered through the distorting spectacles of one's own version of reality. Could it be that Peter *really* didn't care about material things; that he had a genuinely deep disinterest, maybe even a dislike, of monetary success, of best-seller lists, of fame, fortune, and of the people who sought such things? Such animals were *supposed* to exist out there, although Christa had never come across a genuine example.

Damn! Damn him, and his fierce pride, and his fierce body, and the things it did to her. She shuddered at the memories, and the void yawned its pain inside her. Oh, God, was this the end of him? Surely there could be no comeback from this one. If he was even *beginning* to be as pure as he pretended, then she had done a dreadful thing indeed. She had lied. She had besmirched his good name by insinuating that he would willingly join a commercial house like Twentieth. And she had jeopardized his standing with his own publisher and long-term editor and friend, because in the gossipy world of publishing, secrets did not stay secret for long.

But shit, she had scored him two and a half million *bucks!* He should have fallen to the floor and kissed her feet, rather than the other bit of her. How could anybody behave like that? It wasn't looking a gift horse in the mouth, it was kicking the bloody thing in the teeth. Hell, he was lucky she hadn't charged him a two-hundred-and-fifty-thousand-dollar commission on the deal. She was getting angry again, milliseconds after she had been getting sorry. One minute she had been wondering about her apology. Now she was dreaming up his.

Then there was the shoot. Mary hadn't gotten up for the dawn chorus that morning. Christa had been ready for the "off," but hadn't gone to the location when she'd found the billionairess was staying in bed. That, at least, was good news. But Mary had failed to return to Palm Beach as Christa had suggested. That was the bad news. Until she was long gone, the potential for disaster remained high.

The telephone rang, cutting into the worrying thoughts.

"Christa, it's Mary. I'm in my car outside your house. Can I come up? I need to talk to you."

"Of course, Mary. I'm having some coffee. The door's open. Come on up to my bedroom."

Christa took a deep breath. Boy, did agents earn their money!

Mary came in fast. She was smiling. She looked her old self.

"God, what an enormous bedroom. You could screw a battalion in here."

"Hi, Mary, what's up?"

"Not a lot. Not a lot. I skipped the torture chamber this morning. I think my masochism must be in remission."

"But you're still here."

"Yes, I'm finding Miami a little difficult to leave."

"It's seductive, isn't it?"

"Yes, I'm buying that hotel where your office is. That'll make me your landlady, dear. I'll be able to hound you for the rent."

"Goodness, I didn't know it was for sale."

"It wasn't, but it still got sold."

"Goodness," said Christa. "Isn't life exciting." Sometimes the sheer weight of Mary Whitney's money was overpowering.

"Talking of excitement, how's Peter?"

Christa sighed.

"He split. We had the father and mother of a fight."

"Great! Both of you must have had a wonderful time."

"What on earth do you mean?"

"Well, it's obvious that Peter and you are absolutely *made* to have wonderful fights, followed by earth-moving reconciliations. It's called the highs and the lows, dear. Not for the faint-hearted, but then neither of you have faint hearts. . . ."

"Oh, Mary, that's not true. I hate fights. Peter hates them. I'm really upset." She was. She really was. The mist in her eyes said so.

"What was it about? Whether or not Hemingway deserved the Nobel Prize for literature, or something really fundamental like how best to cook vegetables?"

Christa had to laugh despite herself.

"I went up to New York and got a friend of mine to offer a fortune for some books of his . . ."

"Without telling him?"

" 'Fraid so."

"Good Lord! Even I wouldn't have dared to do that. And he found out?"

"I told him."

"Christa, this is wonderful. You're worse at relationships than I am."

"I am not."

"Are, too. Listen, I've decided what to do about Rob. I'm going to talk to him. I'm going to apologize. I'm going to tell him what I feel about him and that I realize that it's not mutual. Then I'm going to wish him luck with Lisa or whomever. And then I'm going to fade away into the sunset in the role of old friend on whom he can always rely."

"You are?" It didn't sound one little bit like Mary.

"Yes. Incredibly grown-up, don't you think?"

"Incredibly. Unbelievably."

"I *did* want to ask you for a favor."

"Ah."

"Could you see your way to arranging a sort of a secret meet between me and Rob so that I can make my little speech? They're back at the hotel having breakfast right now. I saw them on my way over to Star Island. Give him a call and ask him over here around lunchtime. Steve won't want him during the midday sun, and I can get all the bits and pieces off my chest without Lisa sniping from the sidelines."

"But I won't be here at lunchtime. I've got to go do something."

"That's all right, darling. Maybe you could lend me your house for a couple of hours. I promise I won't steal the silver, if that's what you're worried about."

But that wasn't what Christa was worried about. She was worried about something, but she wasn't sure what it was.

"So you want me to call Rob now, and ask him to come over here to see me at lunchtime, and then when he gets here, he sees you instead. Is that it?"

"That's sort of it. Shouldn't be a problem for the girl who peddled Peter Stein's books behind his back. I mean, we're talking *white* lies here."

"Why can't you call him?"

"I can call him, darling. But he might be a little skittish about a tête-à-tête with me right now. The lovely Lisa might have objections. I'm not looking to have a chaperone when I make my pitch."

"Your pitch?"

"My speech, pitch, whatever."

"It *is* a good-bye meeting, isn't it?"

"It's not a hello one." Mary laughed, but she didn't look at Christa as she did so.

"I guess I don't have any problem about that."

"No time like the present," trilled Mary. She was acting uncharacteristically girlish, thought Christa.

Christa picked up the telephone. Within the minute, Rob was on the line.

"How did it go this morning? Great! Oh, that's wonderful! Yes, Steve's brilliant at that. He's the best in the world. Good. Good. Listen, Rob, there's something I need to discuss with you. Could you be an angel and run out here around twelve noon today? The afternoon session won't start till four at the earliest. You know where Star Island is. Just ask at the gate, and they'll direct you to my house. I'll leave word with the guard. Thanks a lot, Rob. It won't take long. See you later. 'Bye."

Christa put down the phone. She felt guilty. But it would be the best thing in the long run. Mary Whitney had to be removed from the chemical mix before she caused it to explode. Christa's breach of faith with Rob might provide for her withdrawal.

"Well, listen, Mary, I've got to get on with my day. I hope it goes well with Rob."

"Darling, nothing *ever* goes well with affairs of the heart."

"Don't I know it," said Christa.

She stood up. So did Mary.

"So, darling. Kiss, kiss. Have fun at the airport."

As Mary Whitney strode out of her bedroom, Christa had the strangest premonition. Somehow she knew that the meeting she had just arranged between Rob and Mary would create far more problems than it would solve.

49

Peter Stein cast his rod over the aquamarine water, but his heart was not in it. Usually he worried about his work, and fishing was an antidote to that anxiety. Now he was thinking about Christa, and fishing didn't help.

"What do you know about women, Ryan?"

Van der Kamp was the nearest Peter had to a friend, but usually they didn't do conversations. Today Peter wanted one.

"I know that no two are the same."

"I agree. People often make that mistake. You can't generalize about people. There you are, you see. I just did it."

"What did you do?"

"Generalized about people."

"Oh."

"What I don't understand," said Peter, determined not to give up, "is how two people can be attracted to one another if they stand for different things, believe in different things, and have totally different values."

"That's you and the girl you just fought with up in Miami."

"I suppose so," said Peter, mildly irritated that Ryan wasn't a dealer in abstractions.

"Maybe it's a physical thing."

Peter laughed. Simple minds understood simple things better than complex minds.

"It has a physical *element* . . . of course, but love is more than that. It seems to me that you love people for two reasons . . . because they have things you haven't got, or because they have all the things you have got. It boils down to a question of self-esteem. If you like yourself, you tend to love people who have the same qualities as you. If you don't like yourself, you love people who have the qualities you don't have."

"So this girl in Miami," said Ryan slowly, "she's not like you, yet you like her. Does that mean you don't like yourself?"

"Mmmmm. It may." Peter frowned. Life was intolerable most of the time, but he did like himself. At least he respected himself, if that was the same thing. "Or, if my theory holds, I suppose the other possibility is that the girl in Miami, as you insist on calling her, is actually more like me than I thought."

"Sounds like she's tricky. That sounds like you."

"Well, she says what she thinks. And she isn't afraid of life. She knows what she wants and she goes out and gets it, and she flattens anyone who stands in her way. She's bright . . . very bright, and you can't tell her anything . . ."

Ryan laughed. "Where did you dig up the idea you were opposites?"

Peter laughed, too. "I guess we're the same computer, but running different programs. We say different things, but we say them the same way."

"Like that book, *The Prophet* . . . same cup, different drinks."

"*Exactly* like *The Prophet,* actually."

Peter was quiet for a bit, absentmindedly reeling in his line. He was glad the fish weren't biting. He needed to think about Christa.

"So you call her and say sorry, and then you start over . . . until the next time," said Ryan.

"*I* say sorry? For*get* it. *She* says sorry."

"Sounds like the kind of thing she'd say, from what you say."

Yes, that was it. That was the Catch-22. What he liked about Christa was the fact that she wouldn't say sorry to him. What drew her to him was the fact that he wouldn't say sorry to her. Their future looked as rosy as hell.

"Uh-oh! I think we got company," said Ryan, standing up.

Peter looked up. The roar of powerful engines came winging across the surface of the sea. A huge catamaran powerboat was speeding toward them. It was painted battleship gray. There was some sort of a crest on its side.

"Cops," said Peter.

"Monroe County Sheriff. Drug patrol," amplified Ryan.

"Shit!" said Peter. "The tag's expired."

Ryan laughed. "You won't do much time for that."

"No, but I'll have to listen to their crap for twenty minutes till they satisfy themselves I'm not a smuggler." Peter Stein groaned. Male authority figures gave him hives. The only way to handle them was to be obsequious, and that turned his stomach.

The police boat slowed down, sending a burst of wake across the Tiara. There were two men on board, dressed in black from head to toe. Both wore identical Ray-Ban aviator glasses, and what looked like .38's on their hips. The cop in the passenger seat held a loudspeaker to his lips.

"Mornin' capn'." The voice that boomed out over the water was deceptively friendly.

Neither Ryan nor Peter replied.

"Looks to me like your tag's expired," boomed the voice. "Turn off your engines and prepare to be boarded."

Peter Stein bubbled with fury. God, in *hell!* They needed probable cause to board and he had provided it. First would come the safety check. "How many life jackets?" "Show me your flares." "Test the horn for me." "Can I see the boat's registration?" If humble pie was not consumed in sufficiently large quantities, the safety check would merge into a full-scale search for drugs. They could be there for a couple of hours, bobbing on the swell. And there was always the nerve-racking possibility that they might have been unlucky enough to have drawn a couple of bent cops not averse to a little evidence manufacturing.

The policemen tied their powerboat onto the Tiara. Next, their legs were swinging over the side.

"Your name, captain?"

"Peter Stein."

The nearest cop eyed him closely. "Do a radio check on the boat I.D., Fritz," he said to his subordinate.

"You're not the writer guy," added the cop.

"Yes, I am," said Peter. In America one should never underestimate the value of fame.

The policeman didn't seem convinced. Suspicious by nature, he also suffered the nearly universal disinclination to believe that he would ever actually meet a celebrity "in real life."

"Didn't you write that book about kids? My wife read that . . ."

"Child's Play." Peter helped him out.

"Well, I'm . . ." The cop let out a short laugh to cover the fact that he wasn't sure what he was. He slapped his thigh. "Yes, that's it, *Child's Play*—that was the book my wife read. By you. Peter Stein. And you won some fancy prize. She said so."

"I did. The Pulitzer."

"Jeez! And here I am, on patrol, an' I stop a boat, and it's Peter Stein. I can't believe it. You got any books on board?"

"I think there are some in the cabin . . ."

Ryan had already vibed into the small print of the conversation. "I'll get one," he said to Peter and the cop. Proof was needed. Then the expired tag and the hundred-buck fine would be history and they could get right on with the fishing. In seconds he was back. *Child's Play* was in his hand.

"That's it. That was the book my wife read. It was on the table next to my bed for a week. Jesus, it's a small world." He called over his shoulder. "Hey, Fritz, can that I.D. check, okay? This is Mr. Peter Stein, the writer." Fritz nodded, a vacant expression on his face. His wife didn't read.

"Looking for drugs?" said Peter Stein. It was the best he could manage in terms of small talk.

"That's what we do all day." The cop laughed, wondering how he could turn this brief encounter into something more substantial. His wife would be hanging on his every word for a month. She was always going on about how poorly educated he was, how he only cared about Bud and football. Well, this would put things straight. He'd get an autograph at least. Maybe a couple of books. Would Stein sign it "To Tracey"? You bet he would, when his tag had expired.

"You writin' anything right now?"

"Yes, I am. I always am . . . writing something." Shit, surely he wouldn't have to endure a conversation about his work with this philistine.

"What you writin'?"

"It's called *The Dream I Dreamed.*" Peter prayed that would be enough.

"What's it about?"

Oh no. There was no way to explain that to this thick hick. Then the thought suddenly occurred to him. He'd been working on a subplot for *Dream.* The hero, his dreams shipwrecked on the rocks of reality, had turned to drugs as a surrogate method of putting them back together again. Drugs were an alien world to Peter Stein, even though he lived in Key West, whose economy was built on them. He'd needed to do some research, but he hadn't gone very far with it. Now here he was with a drug cop on his boat, and the guy was clearly desperate to make friends.

"Well actually," said Peter Stein with uncharacteristic cunning. "Quite a bit of it is about drugs."

"You don't say," said the cop. "Jeez, I could write a book about drugs. The things I seen would make your hair stand on end."

"Would you like a beer?" said Peter Stein.

"We're not allowed to drink on duty . . ." said the cop, in a reflex response. Then he ran over in his mind this evening's conversation with Tracey. "Yeah, a regular guy. We had a few beers, talked about his new book. I gave him a few tips." "What? *You?* You talked to Peter Stein? About his *books?*" It would play well, oh God, it would play well. He'd be left alone to watch TV for at least a month.

"But I could do with a Bud. Why the hell not?" There was a twelve-pack in the ice-box. Ryan shipped them up on deck. The four men sat down.

"What I'd like to know," said Peter, "is what's *new* in the drug business. The latest trends. The up-to-date stuff. It seems to me that it's a world that changes almost from day to day. I guess you have to keep right on top of it."

The cop sucked back on the Bud. "Oh, boy . . ." he began, "did you hit on the right guy for all that stuff."

Peter milked him of his information with superb skill. He leaned forward head on hands in rapt attention, and scattered words of praise and encouragement at judicious intervals throughout the policeman's monologue. He learned that the Medellín guys were back in the saddle after a deal with the Colombian government and that cocaine-wise it was business as usual despite the evidence of a slowdown in demand. He learned where the drugs got hidden on the boats . . . in the guardrails, in the holding tanks that held the shit, on one occasion in a hollowed-out anchor chain. He learned the new hot destinations for boat drops . . . the relatively unpoliced coasts of Georgia and the Carolinas. And he heard the very best, and the very worst, last of all.

The cop was on his third Bud.

"They never stop dreaming up ways to keep us on our toes. I mean this bust I heard about last night . . ." He paused, looking at his watch, "going on right now at MIA, this chick . . . an ex-model, runs her own agency over on South Beach, just opened it up, an' she has her girls ferry the stuff in from their photographic assignments. Neat, no? The DEA boys get a tip-off and when the model flies in from Mexico she'll get cuffed handing over the gear to the boss girl."

Peter Stein's face was a mask. His heart had stopped beating. In the ninety-degree heat he was suddenly ice cold.

"Of course you can't say her name," he said in a voice that seemed to come from a distant planet.

"No way, José . . . but she's a looker all right. Made a movie once. How the hell does a chick like that get into shit like this? You have to wonder. It's a crazy world."

He was right . . . and in Peter Stein's mind the crazy world was spinning round and round.

50

"Excuse me. Excuse me. Hell, get out of my way," Peter shouted as he pushed past the line of disembarking passengers. He looked at his watch as he forced his way through the protesting people. It was twelve thirty. The flight from Mexico City, the only flight from Mexico to Miami this morning, would have landed. At this very moment whomever Christa was meeting would be going through immigration, or worse, customs and, somewhere out there at the arrival gate, Christa would be waiting.

From the moment the cop had spoken, Peter had known that he was talking about Christa. How many ex-models were there who'd both been in a movie and recently opened an agency on South Beach? He'd come right out with it and asked them if they were talking about Christa Kenwood. They hadn't confirmed it openly, but the look they had exchanged had been confirmation enough. They had realized they had said too much, and a few minutes later they had left. That had suited Peter. From that moment on his life had been a blur of action, anxiety, and dread. The cop had said the bust was going on at Miami airport "right now." But when Peter had gotten on the radio and checked on the flights from Mexico via the marine operator, he had learned that the first flight from there was due to land at twelve fifteen. Next, he had tried to reach Christa at her office, but her office had no idea where she was. She was out somewhere and she hadn't taken her cellular phone with her. They were expecting her back after lunch, and they would gladly give her a message. Then, at least, he had known the timetable of the countdown to disaster. There had been a plane out of Key West that would get him to MIA soon after twelve. The Tiara had clocked the forty miles per hour it was supposed to and he had driven on devil's wings to the airport. With minutes to spare, he had made it.

On the bumpy flight in the tiny plane, locked in a womb of forced inactivity, Peter had tried to make sense of what had happened.

There was only one conclusion. Christa was about to be framed. And the punishment for the crime she hadn't committed would wreck her life. Someone had decided to kill her in all but deed. There was even a suspect. He knew about Rossetti. It sounded exactly like the kind of stunt he would pull. But that was unimportant. The only question now was how to avert the tragedy. If he could find Christa before she made the fateful meeting, there would be a chance. He had to stop her from receiving the drug-filled briefcase, or whatever it was, that the courier would be bringing her. If Christa, in ignorance of its contents, accepted the case in front of the DEA witnesses who would be secretly watching her, the door of the jail cell would be as good as locked on her life.

He started to run. The long corridor stretched ahead of him, an obstacle course of children, wheelchairs, and dawdling tourists. He leaped and twisted from side to side as he hurtled along, the air whistling in his lungs. He knew vaguely where he was. He had to get to the basement where international arrivals were regurgitated through glass doors down a narrow, barricaded alleyway toward the street exit. Christa would be there, under surveillance in the milling crowd, oblivious to the terrible danger she was in. He turned right on the main concourse, sweating now from the exertion and the panic as he powered toward his objective. He realized suddenly that he must look like an Identikit terrorist on the run from a bomb plant. So he slowed his pace to a trot, sacrificing speed to decrease the likelihood of being stopped.

Which concourse was American? Was it lumped in with all the other airlines? God, he'd forgotten, but he thought it was. He was nearly at the elevator. There. He jumped onto it. It was stiff with fat foreigners. Nobody was walking. Everybody was taking the ride. He debated whether to try to climb through them. No, it was pointless. So he stood stock-still, seconds from the most frightening moment of his life, shaking with anxiety, on the slowest elevator in the whole of the Western Hemisphere.

51

Christa hated waiting for people. Actually, she hated waiting for anything. She paced the crowded area, cooped up behind the barricades, and endured the glances of the cheap crowd. She looked at her watch. The Mexico City flight had landed on time. Thank God for that. Right now, Mona would be on schedule to cream through the doors, all sassy and sensual and wreathed in fake smiles. It was funny. Some people were trouble, even when they were asleep. Mona was one of them.

Christa caught the eye of a sinister-looking Hispanic, who seemed to be watching her with interest. God, men could be irritating with their eyes. For some reason, just because it wasn't illegal, they felt they were allowed to violate you with that portion of their anatomy. She flicked about like a high-spirited colt in the restricting confines of the starting gate. She didn't like being caged in. She didn't like having to rub shoulders with the crowd. She didn't like wasting her time on the whim of some model she disapproved of. The thought hit her. Rob and Mary would be closeted right now in the drawing room of her house on Star Island. How was *that* little meeting going? Well, she hoped. Otherwise, Christa would get it in the neck from Lisa for so sneakily setting it up.

Shit, where was Mona? Wait a minute, wasn't that her now, on the other side of the glass doors, in the dark glasses and the ridiculous hat?

* * *

Mona was all strung out. She had spent a long, sleepless night snorting the remains of some coke she was wise enough not to risk smuggling through Miami airport. She had done her best to retreat from the world behind the glasses and the hat, but she still felt paranoid, on edge, and with the uncomfortable feeling that something awful was going to happen.

She still couldn't work out why Johnny had been so adamant that she should get Christa to meet her in person, but then Johnny dealt in mysteries. It was part of his charm, if he could be said to have any at all. Anyway, it would be a relief to get rid of Braddock's fucking cameras. They were addressed to Christa, not to Braddock, so the moment they were handed over, Mona wouldn't have to think about them again . . . just about the bucks and the *Bravo* job she would get for her trouble. Yeah, that was a good deal. She tucked the heavy parcel up underneath her arm, and tried to ignore a thin jock with a thinner mustache who had obviously taken a shine to her and was now sticking to her like glue. The asshole would be trying to dream up come-on lines that would close her up like a clam. Jeez! It must be tough being a fella . . . shaving, nasty little socks, and all those horrible choices for underwear.

She rehearsed what she was going to say to Christa. It would be best to keep it simple. Christa wasn't the amateur-dramatics type. She would just hand over the parcel and say she had decided to go back to Johnny and Elle and no hard feelings and good-bye. Yeah, that should handle it. God, she could do with a noseful of blow.

Where was Christa? She'd better be there. That was what Johnny wanted, and Johnny had to be kept sweet. She stared through the glass doors into the crowd. There, that looked like Christa at the back, on the right. Not many people on this earth did.

* * *

Peter Stein put one trembling hand on Christa's shoulder and spun her around. Her eyes opened wide as she saw him.

"Kiss me," he hissed.

"I don't want . . ."

He jammed his lips onto hers before she could finish her sentence. It was a savage kiss. His lips rasped against hers, and his eyes spun in his head like tank turrets as he forced her head back. The crowd stared back at him, some smiling, some impressed, others unseeing. He wrapped his arms tight around her, so that there could be no retreat, and his mind raced in his head as he tried to work out what to say in the seconds he had left.

He moved back from her, his mouth centimeters from hers.

"Well . . . !"

"Christa, Christa. Don't ask any questions. Trust me. Trust me. Promise. You're in danger. We're being watched."

"What do you . . ."

"Who are you meeting?"

"Mona."

"You haven't met her yet?"

"No, she's just coming. I can see her . . ."

"What does she look like? Quick! Describe her."

"She's black, in a silly hat."

"Is she bringing a parcel for you, a suitcase, anything?"

"Yes. She's bringing Bill Braddock's cameras. Why? What's this all about?"

Peter twirled her around so that his body was between Christa and the glass doors.

"Christa. I love you. Do whatever I say. Promise me that."

"Peter, you can't just walk into my life and . . ." She laughed in her confusion. Danger? Being watched? Shit, she was only meeting a model at an airport, and now she had bumped into Peter Stein, the man she couldn't stop thinking about. She'd been wondering if she'd ever see him again and now, here he was saying he loved her and kissing her in front of most of Miami.

"It's a drug frame," he rasped. "Go right out into the street now. Do you hear? Don't talk to Mona. Don't look at her. Go straight to your lawyer's office and wait. Sit in his waiting room all afternoon till you hear from me. Keep in contact with your office. Let them know where you are. Do it now, okay? Walk, Christa. Walk." He thrust her from him.

He looked over his shoulder. A black beauty in a floppy hat was coming through the doors. That had to be Mona. There was a guy walking right beside her. Then Peter caught sight of the other one, ten feet away from him against the barricade. He had seen Mona, and his eyes kept switching from Mona to Christa, from Christa to Mona.

"*Move* it, Christa," said Peter.

At last she obeyed him. She saw it in his eyes, the concern, the fear, the demand to be obeyed. She turned around and she walked quickly, not looking back. The door to the street closed behind her, and he saw her hail a passing yellow cab. The indecision was all over the face of the guy against the barricade. He moved toward Christa. He moved toward Mona. He made a halfhearted move toward Peter.

Peter's mind was in overdrive. He saw it all with the clarity of supervision. Mona was searching the crowd. So was the thin man by her side.

Peter walked right up to her.

"Mona!"

"Yes? Where's Christa? She with you?"

The guy beside her had stopped. He was listening.

"Have you got Braddock's cameras?" said Peter loudly.

"Yeah, right here. I have to give them to Christa. Where is she? Who are you?"

"She said you're to Fed Ex them to Braddock, right away, from the airport." Peter's voice was quivering. He was all but shouting.

"Hey, cool it, baby. I'm not deaf, honey. Listen, I was told . . ."

"Christa says you're to Fed Ex them to Braddock from the airport," shouted Peter. His face was white. His knuckles were clenched. The brown parcel was in Mona's hand.

Which was when it happened. The gun barrel arrived from nowhere at Peter's back. He felt it burrowing in between his shoulder blades. A hand snaked over from behind him and fingers closed around his neck in the vicinity of his left carotid artery. A badge hovered in the air inches from his eyes.

"Freeze. Police. Don't move."

Peter froze. In front of him, around the edges of the embossed badge, he saw the rest of the action. The man next to Mona had also acquired a gun. It was up against her rib cage. And the brown paper parcel was already halfway between Mona and the Drug Enforcement Agency officer.

"You are under arrest," he was gabbling. "You have the right to remain silent . . ."

52

"Where's Christa?" said Rob.

"Christa couldn't be here," said Mary.

"Was that how it was planned?"

"That's how it happened, dear."

Rob didn't look happy about the way it had happened. He had come out to see Christa because she had asked him to. Now he was stuck in a one-on-one with Mary Whitney, and he didn't see how anything good could come out of it.

"Shall we go out and sit by the pool? It's such a beautiful day," said Mary. She moved toward the French doors on the principle that her wishes were also her commands.

Rob stood his ground for a second longer. He had to decide now. He could walk out. Just. But it would be very insulting. And he hadn't heard what she had to say. Maybe it was going to be some sort of apology, best carried out by the proud Mary Whitney at a secret meeting arranged by Christa. Yes, that might easily be it. Christa wouldn't have acted in such a Machiavellian way for anything but the purest motive.

"Okay," he said without enthusiasm, and he sauntered out behind her into the sunlight.

"I haven't seen you," said Mary, turning to watch him over her shoulder as she walked, "since the unfortunate little episode at the beach when I overreacted . . . yes, I think that's the right word . . . to you and Lisa."

So far, so good. Rob said nothing. They reached the Santa Barbara umbrella. Mary sat down in a chair. Rob perched on the edge of a sun bed.

"It may be . . . that I owe you some sort of apology for that."

He smiled. It was not the most generous apology in the world, but for Mary Whitney it must have been like pulling teeth.

"It's all right . . ." he started to say.

"No. No, it's not all right," said Mary. "It's not all right at all. Actually . . . it's all wrong."

"I'm not quite sure what you mean." Rob was puzzled.

"What I mean," said Mary Whitney, "is that you are with the wrong woman."

She smiled, but it was not a nice smile.

Rob's mouth wanted to drop open. This couldn't be happening.

"Which woman am I 'with'? Which one should I be 'with'?"

He had to get this straight.

"Why, in life, must everything be spelled out? You are 'with' Lisa Rodriguez. You *should* be 'with' me," said Mary in mock exasperation.

He laughed at her brazen self-confidence. Who *was* this woman? Was she from another planet?

"Mary, I mean . . . we've done all this, haven't we? It's history. We did a crazy deal, a silly thing, and that was it. I mean, really *it.* It's not that I don't like you and respect you and admire your talent and what you've achieved, it's just . . ."

"That you don't like fucking me," said Mary. Her voice was loud, too loud. Her mouth was small, too small.

Rob stood up, splaying out his hands. He laughed a hopeless laugh.

"Sit down, Rob," said Mary Whitney. There was tremendous power in her voice. The bitterness of her last remark was already history. Alarm bells rang in Rob's mind. For the first time ever, he was beginning to wonder about Mary Whitney's mental stability.

"I want you to hear me out," she said, a calm, glacial smile on her face.

"There is an ancient cliché," she said, "about everybody having their price. I believe in it. Sometimes I think it's the only thing in the world I do believe in. Even you, Rob . . . even you can be bought."

He closed his eyes, wishing this whole scene would go away. It could only get worse. The problems starting right this minute would send shock waves through his life, Lisa's life, Christa's, everyone's.

"Yes, close your eyes, Rob, but keep listening. That's the important part. And keep thinking. I bought you the other night, didn't I? You fucked me to save lives, and the fuck is over, just a greasy memory, but the children live on. Somewhere, out there, they're laughing and crying and living, not dying, because you lent me your dick in the back of my limo. Now that's something, isn't it, Rob? How many gigolos have saved children's lives? It's quite an achievement. You should be very proud of yourself."

"Be careful, Mary," said Rob. Anger was rising up to replace embarrassment that anybody, any woman, could behave like this.

"I'm always careful, even when I'm careless, dearest. It's why I always get my own way."

He looked into her eyes, trying to understand what was happening behind them. This was a new Mary Whitney. He had seen the irreverent, world-weary Mary Whitney, ever-ready to deflate the pomposity of the world. And he had seen the wounded Mary Whitney, unable to deal publicly with feelings that she couldn't control. Both at times had been uncomfortable, but he had excused them as the behavior of a genuine eccentric who, deep down, however spoiled she may be, meant no genuine harm. Now he was far from sure that his and the world's analysis of Mary had been correct. Something nasty was swimming up from her depths. Something very nasty indeed.

"You can't buy people, Mary. I can't understand why anyone would want to try."

The anger crept up her face like a sun rising. Red sky in the morning, the sailor's warning.

"You bastard," she shouted suddenly. "Can't you see I love you? I, Mary McGregor Whitney, love you, you cheap little hustler, and what I want I get. Do you hear?"

"You're sick, Mary," said Rob gently. "I really think you are. I think you need help. What are you talking about? Can *you* understand what you're saying? You're calling me a hustler, and yet you're saying you love me . . . what does that *mean,* Mary? It's garbage. You're just talking garbage."

Mary looked away. There was no explaining this. She didn't know why she wanted him. It was a perversion. It was worse than weird, it was a positive tragedy. He was almost young enough to be her son. Nothing that he ever thought, said, or did resembled any idea, word, or deed of her own. And yet, she could think of nothing but him. She thought of his body in the morning, and the smell of him at night. She remembered the magnificence of his nakedness. She dreamed of the beauty of his soul. In her nightmares she lost him, in her glorious fantasies she owned him.

Her rival, Lisa Rodriguez, stalked in the undergrowth of Mary Whitney's darkest thoughts, filling them with blood, venom, and the music of evil. It was called an obsession. They happened sometimes. They made the sane mad, the good bad, and the happy sad, and they turned the joke that was life into the tragedy of the damned.

She tried to keep her voice from shaking as she spoke. "I have to have you, Rob. What you want is unimportant. It's nothing compared to the strength of my will."

He just looked at her. She was past him now. He looked at her like he might at a serpent, fascinated by the dance of desperation that she was performing.

"Here is what I will do," she said. "I will set up a foundation to be called the Robert Sand Foundation with a capital of one hundred million dollars. You will head that foundation. It will be yours to disburse as you see fit. Any charity, any religion, any worthy cause you care to name will be its beneficiary. In return, you will marry me and you will live with me for one calendar year, and we will be lovers, whenever I say, whenever I like. You will never see or speak to Lisa Rodriguez again. For every year you stay with me after that first year, I will donate twenty million dollars to your foundation. It will be a sacrifice," she said, her eyes burning with a strange light. "It will be a sacrifice, like our Lord's sacrifice on the cross. You will die emotionally, so that others may live, and prosper and thrive. And maybe, in the years to come, you will learn to love me, as I love you . . . and out of sorrow will come a good that will shine so brightly it will blot out the sun."

She sat back in the chair, her hands clasped tightly together like a nun at a shrine. She was smiling with joy, because she knew she had just said the magic words that would give her Rob's soul on a silver salver. She had just bought the body of the boy she loved, not for a Salome dance but for the megabucks of the billionairess.

Rob stood up. There was pity on his face, and contempt, and a terrible sorrow that there was so much ugliness in the world.

"I want to know," he said, "before I leave, and I'm leaving now, if Christa knew you were going to do this?"

Mary Whitney's head jerked back as if she had been hit. This was not the script. There should at least be a negotiation. There should be talk. There should be something. But instead there was Christa.

"Christa? Christa? What's Christa got to do with what I just offered?" she hissed.

"I just wanted to hear you say that Christa had nothing to do with this whole . . . this . . . this pathetic business," said Rob.

Mary's mouth twisted. "So it's Christa, is it? Deep down, it's Christa. Do you know, I thought that. In my gut, I knew that. Christa! On the beach. It wasn't so innocent, was it, Rob? And it was Lisa that was the decoy, and poor old Peter Stein, too. Yes. Yes. Somewhere inside, I always knew that."

She laughed, a horrible, cackling laugh.

"Well, you don't need to worry any more about Christa. We none of us do. I made a little contingency plan, and your precious Christa has gone to the airport, Rob, and let me tell you something else . . .

"SHE WON'T BE COMING BACK!"

53

In the back of the taxi, Christa was in turmoil. She had to work out what had happened from a patchwork quilt of expressions, disjointed sentences, and mysterious actions, and all against a background of high drama that had her heart banging against the wall of her chest.

Two words were ringing in her mind. "Drug frame," Peter had said. That was the central part of it all. Everything else he had talked of . . . the danger, being watched, the talk of briefcases, made some sort of sense in its context. Peter had wanted her out of there. He hadn't wanted her to meet Mona. And yet Mona had badly wanted Christa to meet her at the airport. There had been the strange fax message, and the "important thing" Mona had to discuss, something that apparently could neither be discussed on the telephone nor at the end of a taxi drive from the airport to her South Beach office or Star Island home. It all made chilling sense, because the other element in the equation was the Braddock cameras. There never were any Braddock Hasselblads. The parcel Mona would have handed Christa in front of the watching eyes would have been full of drugs. Shit! Christa sank her head into her hands. How could she have been so stupid? Rossetti was not the kind of man to miss out on attempted revenge. A parcel from the Third World with her name on it! A cryptic fax sent by her, *signed* by her, to Mona asking her to bring the parcel through customs at Miami airport! There was even the business about Mona getting "six" for her trouble, and giving "three" to the stranger who delivered the "cameras." In the clear vision of 20/20 hindsight, might the jury not think that the figures related to sixty thousand bucks as the pay-off, not six hundred? Or, depending on the value of drugs in the parcel, six *hundred thousand* dollars.

Christa went cold at the thought. Would the authorities have a copy of that fax? If so, despite not accepting the parcel physically, she was still very much at risk. Was that why Peter had told her to go straight to her lawyer's office and to wait there all day? Maybe that was the shrewd thing to do, but she had to go home first. She had to make some calls, get her mind straight, and to continue to try to make sense of the threat that had turned her world upside down.

The taxi was traveling over the causeway now. She would be on Star

Island in a few minutes. There were so many loose ends. How the hell had Peter Stein learned about the plot? There was absolutely no answer to that. And was Mona involved? Had she been planted in Christa's agency by Rossetti? It seemed highly likely. After all, she had been Johnny's girl. The apparent bad vibrations between them could well have been a ruse to throw everyone off track. Yes, that had to be it. Johnny had orchestrated the whole thing . . . Mona infiltrating her agency, the Mexican booking, Braddock and his phony cameras. God, it was clever. She hadn't suspected a thing. But she should have. Parcels from places like Mexico were as innocent as genocide. She should have smelled a rat. But she had been concentrating on other things. Her whole life had been taken up with Peter Stein, and with the Miami shoot and the mercurial relationships among Lisa, Rob, and Mary Whitney.

God, she'd almost forgotten. Mary and Rob would be on Star Island right now, in the middle of the tête-à-tête she had arranged. That was okay. Mary would be a tremendous help. She would know what to do. In a situation like this, her experience and common sense would be invaluable.

Bang! The thought lanced into the center of Christa's brain, and lodged there, vibrating from side to side like an arrow in the center of its target.

Mary Whitney's last words were ringing in Christa's ears.

"Have fun at the airport," she had said.

But Christa had never told Mary McGregor Whitney that she was going to the airport.

54

Christa rushed into the house, full of foreboding and the beginnings of a remarkable anger. Sinister monsters were building in her mind, and already one of them looked a lot like Mary Whitney. How had Mary known she'd been going to the airport? Christa was certain she hadn't mentioned it. She remembered that the very moment she had told Mary she had "something to do" and couldn't make the meeting with Rob, she had felt guilty about being "tight" with information. Christa considered that a failing, despite the fact that, business-wise, it made sense to keep people in the dark. So how the hell had Mary known? Christa certainly hadn't mentioned it to her secretary, nor to anyone else. She hated being treated like a chauffeur by Mona, and she hadn't wanted to advertise the fact that the famous Christa Kenwood could be summoned to an airport pickup like the driver of a battered yellow cab.

So Mary had to have gotten her information from the conspirators, whoever they were. From Johnny, from Braddock, possibly from Mona. The bottom line was as clear. Mary Whitney had been part of the plot to destroy her. But, as Christa put her key in the front door, she realized that there was a huge chasm between knowing it and proving it.

Worse, there was a gaping abyss between proving it and knowing what to do about it. One thing was vital. She must keep cool. Her emotions must be kept in tight check. She tried to slow her heart, and take control of the feelings bubbling inside her, as she opened the door and stepped into the hall.

Mary Whitney was walking toward her, head down. Over Mary's shoulder, Christa could see Rob standing by the French doors to the pool. Mary Whitney looked up, and her eyes collided with Christa's. She stopped as if she had walked into an invisible glass door. Her whole body twisted with the effort of ceasing to move forward. In her confusion, she all but fell backward. Her arms shot out in a futile attempt to steady herself on the thin air against which she pushed. Her face read shock, disbelief, panic. If Christa had wanted a confession signed in the Whitney blood, it would not have had greater force and meaning than the expression on her face.

"Christa!"

"Mary?" Christa's voice was quizzical, giving nothing away. "Why are you so amazed to see me walk through the front door of my own house?" was the thrust of her tone.

Mary laughed a high-pitched, forced laugh to camouflage her surprise.

"I didn't expect you back so soon," said Mary, smiling a gruesome smile.

Rob called out from the window.

"You didn't expect her back at all," he said. "You said she wasn't coming back."

"You misunderstood," said Mary quickly, not turning to look at him as she spoke.

"What's happening?" said Christa. "What did you mean, Mary, that you weren't expecting me back?"

Mary waved her hand in a gesture that implied this was a boring conversation.

"Rob and I have had an unfruitful talk. Your name got lumped with Lisa's. I meant you weren't coming back into his life."

Her eyes slunk away from Christa's, exposing the lie.

"You know I was never in his life," said Christa, banging the door shut on the excuse.

"Perhaps in his mind you were." Mary was still avoiding Christa's eyes.

Christa thought fast. Was this the time to ask how Mary had known she had been going to the airport? No. Mary Whitney was far too cunning and too strong to be caught out by mere words. She would deny it. And Christa would be letting Mary know that she knew her secret.

But there were other ways to keep the conversational pressure on Mary. If Christa could unsettle her enough, Mary might be coaxed into providing incriminating evidence of one kind or another.

"How can you and Rob have had an unfruitful talk if all you wanted to do was apologize and to say good-bye?"

Rob walked slowly toward them.

"Was *that* what she said she was going to do?" His tone was equal parts relief and disbelief. It meant Christa had been ignorant of Mary's bizarre offer.

"Yes, it was," said Christa. "Mary? What's been happening here?"

"I don't have to answer to you. I don't have to answer to anyone." Mary Whitney's jaw was up . . . defiant, threatening. Her confusion was gone. She was already slipping into aggressive mode, her instinctual method of defense.

"She offered me millions to marry her," said Rob. "I think she's crazy. I really think she's flipped. She's been ranting and raving and threatening me, Lisa, you, everyone."

Now Mary did turn toward him.

"Shut up!" she hissed. She turned back toward Christa. She was pulsing with hatred. She was tomato red in the middle, milk white at the edges, and she shook like a small tree in a large wind.

"I didn't threaten," she roared. "I never threaten. I just say what is going to happen. And *this* is what is going to happen. Miami is history. The campaign is in the garbage. You're all fired, and you don't get a red cent out of me. And worse, you're all sued . . . for this, for that, and for everything else my legal department can dream up. You'll never work again, any of you, in any country in the world. I personally guarantee it. And you'll lose every single penny of the bird droppings you call your assets, Christa. You'll have to go back to modeling. Only you won't find anyone to hire you. Shit, you'll have to go back on your back, darling. Whoring will be how you pay your bills after my attorneys have stopped picking over your flesh."

Rob Sand moved fast. He walked up to her and picked her up around the waist as if she were a tiny sack of very new potatoes. He strode to the door with her. Christa, smiling defiantly, opened it. He put her down hard on the doorstep, and she staggered as she tried to regain her balance.

"Now get the hell out of our lives," shouted Rob, his voice quivering with fury.

"You wish! You *wish!*" screamed Mary Whitney. "You idiot. You'll never sleep again because of me. I promise. I promise."

"The man you wanted to *marry!*" sneered Rob.

"The man you tried to buy. Oh, Mary! Poor Mary!" said Christa.

"Don't pity me. Don't dare pity me. Pity yourselves. You'll be the ones who are sorry."

"Go!" said Rob. He took a step toward her.

Mary saw the look in his eye. It was an ultimate male/female moment. It was the time when the cunning, the guile, and the general superiority of the female species collided with its most formidable weakness, male physical strength.

Mary teetered toward her car. There was no driver. She said nothing as she climbed inside, but the whole of her world was painted the color of blood. She slammed the door behind her, not minding that her skirt was caught in it. She had to get away from the scene of her total humiliation and she had to find out what had gone wrong.

The gravel streamed from beneath her tires as she took off. She didn't look back. As she turned the corner, she was already reaching for the cellular phone. She punched the numbers as she drove.

"Rossetti? Mary Whitney. What the fuck went wrong?"

"Don't take that tone with me," said Johnny. He was not pleased. His plot had blown up in his face and now one of the bit players wanted to give him lip.

"I'll take that tone with whomever I like," snarled Mary. "I gave you one and a half million to pay for the drugs."

"That's history," said Johnny calmly. He meant that the untraceable notes were already in his safety deposit box, and that they could never be reclaimed.

Mary took a deep breath. The piece of slime was right. She wasn't in a strong dealing position. She couldn't expose the plot without exposing her own part in it. Whatever happened, her money was gone.

"I'm sorry. I was upset. I am upset."

"Listen, baby, we're all upset. I have better reason to be upset than anyone." He did. He really did. His guts were knotted.

"What went wrong?"

"Some guy was what went wrong. A guy called Stein showed up seconds before the handover and warned Christa. He told Mona that Christa had instructed that the parcel be sent to Braddock direct from the airport, and he said it in the hearing of the DEA guys . . . *before* the arrest. That's what I've been able to find out from my guy on the inside. So the case against Christa is iffy now. The finger points at Braddock, but he denies it, and there's no real case against him. Stein is apparently a heavy hitter, with a whiter-than-snow character who writes the kind of books your kids read in school. It's a mess. There's almost a case against everyone, but actually there's a real case against nobody. That's the DEA view. They're going to let Stein go, and when they've seen Christa there'll be no charges there either."

"Who told Stein?" said Mary, her voice quivering.

"I was going to ask you the same question."

"I sure as hell didn't tell anyone. I wanted Christa to go down. I paid a million and a half to buy the drugs that were supposed to be planted on her."

"You're not blaming me, are you?" said Johnny. His voice was threatening. There were other people in this, people who would not be pleased that outsiders like Stein seemed to know the inner workings of their plot. And those people made the cantankerous billionairess about as threatening as a little old lady waving an umbrella.

"I funded this operation," said Mary.

"Do you want me to be quite frank with you, lady?" said Johnny, his voice patronizing. "When you telephoned me and asked me how you could help me put problems Christa's and Lisa's way, this whole business had already been planned. I let you believe you were a prime mover in all this, because, at the time, it suited me. But I had this whole show wrapped up. Me and some friends had it organized. And when I say 'friends,' I use the word loosely. These are people that don't have friends, if you know what I mean. They have enemies . . . and their enemies fear them, fear them greatly, Mary. I do. You should. Okay? Okay?"

"But I paid the money."

"I was going to pay the money myself. Everything was baked in the cake. Then, right at the very last moment, you came along waving your checkbook. I merely allowed you the privilege of financing me. I laid off the risk a bit. Laid off some revenge, you might say. If you'd never called me, the frame would have happened anyway. I'm telling you this so that you realize your whole part in this is peripheral. So now that things have gone wrong, don't go sounding off at me. Shit, it was you that hired Christa and Lisa. It was you that gave them a sniff at the megabucks. You wanted to pay them publicly and have me and my friends take them down privately. The English call that hunting with the hounds and running with the hare. It's not good, Mary. The more I think about it, the less good it is. Especially now that this whole thing has blown sky high."

"They're not working for me anymore. I pulled the plug on the whole deal, and now I'm going to bury them in writs."

"Good. Good. That's more like it. And, in return, I'll keep quiet about our little deal. But your money's gone, isn't it. You'll have to cut back on the housekeeping. Sack the fourth footman. Ha! Ha! Gotta keep one's sense of humor."

Mary pressed down the END button, obliterating Rossetti from her life. She could see it all now, and it wasn't nice . . . any of it. The problem was that no one had ever understood how she worked. From the moment she had first set eyes on Rob Sand, she had known she would own him, simply because she wanted him. She had joked about it. She had even allowed others to laugh about it, and that had suited her because it had been a smokescreen behind which she could operate. There had been dead ends, and setbacks along the way, and mostly they had taken the shape of two people . . . Christa and Lisa. Life for Mary had always been incredibly simple. She got what she wanted. Of course, she had had other aims besides Rob. She had wanted Miami to be the most successful scent in America, which had meant hiring Lisa for the ads. In retrospect, that had been one disaster. And she had misjudged Rob. She had hoped to take him out of obscurity and push him into the spotlight of fame, and to reap the reward of his gratitude. But it had backfired. His honesty and decency, the qualities that obsessed her, had inoculated him against the heady fever of success. He hadn't been grateful to her. He hadn't wanted the money she had floated at him in a desperate attempt to gain his body as a prelude to his love. Everything had backfired, leaving only the deadly end-game. She had called Rossetti, knowing that the enemies of your enemies made the best friends. They had agreed that their interests coincided. They had met secretly in New York, and he had told her of a 'vague' plan of his to frame Christa for a drug bust. He had lied to her and told her that he was having problems organizing it, and that he couldn't find the money to buy the incriminating drugs. In fact, it now transpired, the whole plan had been on schedule, but Mary had leaped at the opportunity to finance it. Money was always so easy. So she had given him the cash, and she had sat back and waited for Christa to be snatched from the world. The disappearance and discrediting of Rob's mentor/heroine/fantasy would leave a vacuum in his Svengali department, and it was a void that Mary intended to fill herself. Without Christa to hold things together, the Miami campaign and the ambitious Lisa Rodriguez would fade away. And Rob could never blame Mary for canceling a campaign that would have been basically derailed by Christa's criminal behavior.

But Christa was safe, and Rob had turned down her phenomenal financial offer, and she had been humiliated . . . and worse, far worse, she had not gotten what she wanted. So now she would pull the whole building down around her. Christa, and Lisa, and, yes, Rob would be destroyed. She had already canceled their present, and from this moment on, she and her mighty fortune would work to cancel their future. Mary was wounded, but she was safe. Her role in the Rossetti conspiracy would remain a secret. Whatever else Johnny was, he wasn't stupid. He wouldn't advertise his own part in the failed plot, and by the same token, he would go to his grave with the secret of hers.

So she drove on, turning right on the causeway toward the mainland, away from Miami Beach. It was time to get back to New York, to the headquarters of her empire. There she would plan the financial and personal revenge. It was all that remained of her dream to own the body and mind of a boy.

There were tears in her eyes as she thought of him.

"Oh, Rob," she murmured. "Why didn't you want to be rich like everyone else?"

55

"Liz, can you be a sweetheart and run down to the News Café and get us some breakfast? Make it for six. Rob and Lisa should be here anytime. Lots of French bread and butter. Thanks."

The secretary hurried to obey. Her haste wasn't just to fulfill orders. Being the third person in a room full of two lovers was a pain.

Peter threaded his hand into Christa's. He did not look good. A day of interrogation at Miami airport had been one thing. A glorious, sleepless night in Christa's Star Island bedroom had been the other. He was soaked in sex. His whole body was awash with it. His mind was a cotton ball of mushy, soft sentiment, and his tired body ached and tingled in the aftermath of ceaseless lovemaking. They had made up. Again. And already Peter Stein was beginning to understand that roller-coaster riding through life might be the way to go after all.

"I'm exhausted," said Christa. But she didn't look exhausted. She looked like a full moon in a cloudless sky; a good deed in a naughty world; the welcoming angel that would show you heaven after a blameless existence. She squeezed Peter's hand. "I think our whole life is going to be exhausting, don't you?"

"I agree," said Peter with a laugh. "I'm always going to agree. I think it'll be simpler."

"Don't you dare patronize me," said Christa, giggling to show she wasn't serious. They could laugh about it now, but there would be a thousand arguments, as they sharpened themselves on each other. They would grow together through a million magical moments of making up, and neither would ever be bored, never not alive, always full to the brim with the life and liveliness that lesser mortals dreamed of. Theirs would be a life of bravery and daring, out there at the edge. They would never know mundanity or drudgery, because they were strong enough to take up arms and to struggle against difficulty. They would be wounded, but the healing of those wounds would make the gaining of them worthwhile. Like now. Like forever.

"I can't believe the luck," said Peter. "I can't believe that I got there in time. It was so close. It was this close to disaster." He held up his fingers, millimeters apart, to show how near they had come to tragedy.

"I know." Christa shuddered. "Don't let's even think about it." But she could hear the slamming of the door. She could picture the tiny cell, the surly roommates, the mind-numbing tedium of a freedom-free life. It would rot her soul. She, more than anyone else, could not survive prison. So many people in the land of the free spent their lives in secret revolt against freedom. They built their own prisons . . . mortgages, wives they no longer loved, children they wished they hadn't had, jobs they loathed, as the minutes ticked away and the sands ran out and the grave, that would be their only experience of liberty, beckoned. She had never been like that. She had always chosen her actions, her opinions, her words. The world might not like them, but it lumped them. When her final trump sounded, at least she would be alert enough to hear it. Hers was a living life, not a living death, but it would not have survived prison. She looked at Peter, at her future, at the father of the child that she somehow knew was growing within her, and she saw at that moment her savior. He had saved her as surely as Christ had died to save humanity. The look in her eyes said so.

"I'll never be able to thank you. It would have been worse than dying, to go to prison for something I didn't do. All those angry, stupid people, all those meaningless days, all the rage and the fury and the tedium . . . I don't know . . . I just . . ."

"It hasn't happened, darling. It never will."

"It *is* over, isn't it? I mean *really* over?"

"The lawyers are absolutely certain. There's been a formal decision not to press charges. At the highest level, they say. You're off the hook. I'm off the hook. The evidence just wasn't there, quite apart from the fact that I think they believed us."

"Not even against Mona."

"She was a pawn. She admitted that Rossetti had asked her to infiltrate your agency. Apart from that, she knew nothing. She was ranting and raving, major histrionics. Imagine Mona in a situation like that. I could even get to feel sorry for the DEA guys."

"But if they believed us, that means that Rossetti and Braddock are guilty as hell. Won't they go after them?"

"It wouldn't hold in court. Braddock hasn't been in Mexico for five years. Swears black and blue he had nothing to do with it. Rossetti, the same. There's zero evidence against him. No witnesses. Nothing."

"So he gets away with it. Shit! The *bastard!*"

"And Mary gets off, too." Peter sighed. "That's the unbelievable part for me. I always say one never knows people, but I guess I always believed *I* had the inside track on them. It's like finding out that the babysitter is a serial killer. I mean, Mary . . . funny, wicked, harmless Mary with her sharp tongue and her pessimism! I could have sworn her hard exterior hid a soft center. It turned out she was totally evil."

"Yes, Mary was the double whammy. I don't hate her. I feel sorry for her. She must be sick. She has to be mentally ill."

"Nonsense. Whatever happened to sin? Psychiatry hijacked it. She's wicked, Christa. Only a genuinely bad person could have done what she did. There aren't any excuses. She deserves punishment, not treatment. Power is the only thing she'll ever understand."

Christa nodded. "Maybe you're right. Well, she's still got power and she says she's going to use it against us. All of us. She won't go away. She'll fire legal missiles at us till she's boxed or bored. It'll be pretty difficult to stay afloat."

"She can't touch you when you're my wife."

"Darling, I can't *just* be your wife. I have to be me, too. And I'm a dealer, remember? You should."

Peter smiled ruefully. He remembered. Twentieth and Lewis Heller! Jesus! But two and a half million bucks! That *was* a lot of money. He could buy a sixty-three-foot Little Harbor. Christa and he could park off deserted islands and make love till all thought ceased. He was becoming a bit like her already. Was she becoming a bit like him?

"Maybe I should go and confront Mary. Tell her what we know. Threaten her," he said.

"Forget it. She'd laugh in your face. She knows we can't prove anything. She'd just be more determined to destroy us, if that's possible."

"Can you believe that someone would risk everything for an obsession?" said Peter.

"There's a sense in which you do it every day of your life at your typewriter," said Christa. "And you took a huge risk for me. Meeting a girl with a parcel of heroin in front of a couple of cops is taking a pretty big risk. Was that for an obsession?"

"It was for love."

"Any difference?"

"We could probably get into an argument about it."

"Mmmmmmm! Let's. Then we can spend another night like last night making up."

He moved toward her. The secretary would be gone another ten minutes.

The sound of the doorbell stopped him.

"Saved by the bell," said Christa with a husky laugh. There would be so much time for them now. They had years to make love. But it would have been nice to start now, this second, standing up in her office . . .

She forced back the steamy thoughts and opened the door.

Lisa and Rob stood in the doorway, mirror-image lovers to the ones they faced.

"Hi, you two! God, you both look absolutely fantastic. Aren't there laws against couples like you?"

They drifted into the room, giving off the heady, dreamy air of young lovers. They plucked absentmindedly at each other, picking carelessly at clothes, rubbing skin, a head nuzzling into a shoulder, their hips touching lightly. They walked in and sank to the sofa. Lying there, not actually intertwined, they seemed somehow to be one person, not two.

"There's some breakfast coming," said Christa.

"Great," said Rob. "I'm soooo hungry."

Lisa smiled at him proudly, like a mother at a brilliant child. Wasn't he clever to be hungry? Wasn't it neat the way he said "great"? Wasn't he just the *best?*

"Hi, Peter," said Lisa. "What an amazing thing you did yesterday. You saved us all, not just Christa. Rob and I will never forget what you did."

"No, we won't. It was . . ." said Rob.

"I am afraid that business-wise, we're in a bit of a mess," said Christa quickly. It was better to confront this now. She had already explained to Lisa the details of what had happened, including Mary Whitney's role in the conspiracy. What she hadn't mentioned were Mary's threats to destroy them all financially. Christa didn't know how much Rob had told her.

"What do you mean, a mess?" said Lisa quickly.

"Well, maybe Rob mentioned it, but Mary said she would do everything in her power to block everything we ever try to do. The Miami campaign is obviously history, but she's going to sue each and every one of us for breach of contract and anything else she can dream up. There's going to be a lot of blackening of reputations. It could be quite nasty."

Lisa paused for a moment, deep in thought, then, quite suddenly, she sat up straight.

She turned to Rob. Her tone had changed. There was accusation in it.

"You said she just made a whole lot of empty threats."

"She did," said Rob.

"That doesn't sound empty to me," said Lisa. "It sounds the opposite of empty, whatever that is."

"Full," said Peter Stein helpfully.

"I just don't think we ought to fool ourselves," said Christa. "Mary has shown how low she'll go to get what she wants. A barrage of writs and some well-organized character assassination will be the very least she'll try. But if we all stick together, we can ride out the storm. We all have each other."

" 'Ride out the storm'?" said Lisa. "Ride out a fucking storm of writs and bad-mouthing? I don't need that kind of aggravation. I've got a career here. I came to your agency because I wanted to do better, not get fucking buried."

"Cool it, Lisa," said Rob.

"I am cool. I'm fucking cool," steamed Lisa. "I'm just pointing out that I'm not a loser. I'm the best model in the whole goddamn world, and I don't need a bad time."

Christa took a deep breath. This wasn't going as planned. Lisa was supposed to be deeply in love with Rob. Rob was still onboard. That meant Lisa was supposed to stay onboard, too.

"Listen, Lisa, I understand all that, but we none of us planned this, and we're all responsible for what happened. You left Rossetti because of the Miami contract, and then Mary fell in love with Rob and he wanted you, and she and Rossetti ganged up to sabotage everything."

"Are you trying to say *I'm* responsible for this crock of shit?" Lisa's tone was incredulous.

Peter tried the unaccustomed role of peacemaker. "Nobody is pointing fingers, Lisa. But you *are* part of the reason Rossetti tried to frame Christa. And you *are* part of the reason Mary Whitney is behaving the way she is. We're just saying you are *part* of the problem. You're in the equation, that's all."

"Yeah," sneered Lisa. "You know, that's my problem. That's been my problem all along. That I was part of the equation. I never should have left Johnny. That was where I blew it. Everything I ever worked for, everything I ever wanted or dreamed of is on the line, because I listened to Christa and joined her half-dead agency with some incompetent hick from hicksville and some fairy photographer. Jesus! I must have been crazy. I wanted to do everyone a big favor, and you all turned around and pissed on me. Just like my fucking mother . . . like my fucking mother . . ."

She jumped up. Rob stood up, too.

He couldn't believe what he was hearing. This wasn't the Lisa he loved. This was a vicious, cruel, self-centered Lisa. Okay, she could be willful and unkind, and determined, but here she was distorting facts, insulting him, and blaming everyone when nobody was to blame. He reached out to touch her, to get through to the heartland where the good Lisa lived. But she brushed his hand away.

Her face was red. Her eyes were wide with rage.

"Well, people," she hissed. "I'll tell you what *I'm* going to do. I'm not going to hang around down here and get blown away by the billionairess bit by bit. Oh, no, not me. You can all go fucking sink, but I'm going to swim. I always have. That's what I do. Nobody gets to destroy me. I *do* the destroying."

"What are you going to do, Lisa?" said Christa. But she knew. She just wanted it spelled out.

"I'm gonna go back to Elle to work for Johnny," said Lisa. "And I don't care what I have to eat to make him have me."

56

"I've never been to your new house, Johnny." On purpose Lisa didn't use the word *home.* It wasn't one. It was a *Penthouse/ Playboy* bachelor pad of mythic proportions, and the kind of people who used the word *home* simply wouldn't have been welcome in it. Right now, Lisa Rodriguez needed to be welcome.

Johnny watched her across the room, as he poured champagne into a flute glass.

"You look better than you ever looked, Lisa," he said. "No joke, I mean it."

"I feel okay." She pirouetted with a laugh. It was going well. When she'd called him, he'd been as skittish as a snake around a mongoose, but he'd been curious too. Curious as hell.

"I want to come back," she'd said simply. "I shouldn't have left, and I'm sorry, and I want you to give me another chance."

He hadn't said much on the phone. She had felt the suspicion winging down the line. After all, he planted Mona in Christa's agency. Might Christa be returning the compliment?

"It never hurts to discuss things," he'd said. And they'd made the meet. Seven that evening. His place. The brownstone on 63rd and Madison, just across from the Lowell Hotel.

"So why the change of heart?" said Johnny with a careful smile.

"Can I be totally honest?"

"Is there any other way?"

"Self-interest."

"Ah," said Johnny. "Now you're talking a language I understand."

"It's the language we both speak."

"Maybe. Maybe." He poured the wine, wary as hell.

"Mary Whitney canceled the Miami thing. She's going to sink Christa. She's going to drown her with money and lawyers and litigation. The best Christa can do is go marry her tame writer, and drop out of life. That's not what I want. I want more."

"I heard there was some trouble for Christa down in Miami."

"She thinks you arranged it."

"I didn't. I had nothing to do with it. There's no proof. If she so much as hints that I had anything to do with it, then she'll get another writ."

He spoke carefully, as if he suspected that Lisa was wired for sound.

"I don't care one way or the other," said Lisa. "I just care about me."

"And about some boy, I hear."

"He was neat. But when push comes to shove, *I'm* all I got. It's always been that way with me, Johnny. You should know that."

He advanced on her with the champagne. His expression was softening. They were alike. They always had been. From that time, so long ago, when she had been so young and so willing, and he had enjoyed her so *very* much.

"But Lisa, you walked out on me. You walked out on Johnny, who invented you. Okay, you had the beauty. You've still got it. But it's more than that, isn't it, girl? It's packaging it, selling it, and making people believers. I did all that for you, and you walked out on me and went with a rival and you put my business at risk. You know how much business means to me. It's all I have. *I'm* all *I* have, but that was your line, wasn't it, sweetheart?"

"I'm valuable, Johnny. You know how much I'm worth."

"I know how much you *were* worth, darling. I wrote the book on the subject, remember? But things happened. Your parents got moved along, didn't they? And now Mary Whitney's on the warpath, saying you're trouble and canceling a vast campaign like the Miami thing. It may be that she's right and that you *are* trouble. The advertisers won't like that, or the photographers . . . or even the agents."

"Johnny . . . please."

Lisa's eyes were wide open. She didn't know how to play this. Johnny didn't like beggars. He liked choosers.

"But on the other hand, it may be that I can talk to Mary Whitney. Talking's what I do, isn't it? Maybe I can get her to call off her hounds, at least as far as you're concerned. Who knows what's possible? But it's going to be hard. I'd have to work overtime to clean up the mess you've made for yourself. I'd have to rebuild your reputation from scratch. I'd have to lie to everyone, and tell them you're not a tricky bitch who ought to be punished and not rewarded."

There was a strange gleam in his eye. Lisa had seen it before. His eyes sparkled like that when he thought of sex. And not of just any sex. He looked like that when he thought of his own peculiar brand of sex . . . sex that hurt. Lisa swallowed nervously. This was the way. She had always known it in her gut. If she was to get what she wanted, she would have to pay the price.

Her voice was soft, almost a whisper, when she answered him.

"If you took me back, Johnny, I'd let you punish me."

"You would?" he said. "Punish you properly?"

"Whatever it took to make you take me back."

"You did a terrible thing, leaving me," he said, his voice low. "It was a wicked thing. In all your life you've probably never done anything as bad as that. And when you do horrible things, you deserve horrible punishments, don't you?"

Lisa took a deep breath. "I do," she murmured. She dropped her head down low.

"Maybe punishment would purge you of your sin," said Johnny. She could see beads of sweat on his upper lip. His fists were clenching and unclenching. She had him. Almost. It was so near.

"You'd have to hurt me," she said through dry lips.

He walked quickly to her side.

He took her earlobe between his thumb and forefinger, and he began to squeeze.

"Oh!" She cried out from the sharp pain, but she didn't resist.

"I'd have to hurt you badly, but I'd have to keep your face beautiful, wouldn't I, so that you could make me money? But then you could always take some time off, couldn't you? I could damage your face just a bit, couldn't I, Lisa, to make you pay for the wicked thing you did?"

Lisa swallowed. Her heart banged in her chest. Was this worth it? Could anything be worth the pain? She bit her lip. Her face, oh, God, her face!

His thumb dug deep into her ear.

"What did you say?"

"Yes," she murmured.

He hit her hard with the back of his hand, and she reeled back with the force of the blow. Her lip split open. She could taste the salty blood. But lips healed. She stood her ground.

"That feels good, doesn't it? Getting what you deserve feels good."

She didn't answer, but she nodded. Up. Down. And she steeled herself to receive his violence. Slap! He hit her with his open hand, a stunning blow across her cheek, splattering blood from her lip in a fine spray across the room.

"Do you like it?" he screamed at her.

Again she nodded through the red mist that had sprung up before her eyes, through the ringing noise in her head. She felt sick. Her knees were weak. She sank to the floor in front of him.

"Then say so. Thank me for it, you bitch," howled Johnny.

"Thank you. Thank you for punishing me." Her lip was already a football. Her left eye was closing. And there was so much more to come. She tried to focus on her objective. To achieve it would make everything worthwhile, any pain, any humiliation, any torture that his warped mind could dream up.

"Do you know what I'm going to do?" said Johnny Rossetti.

His voice quivered with excitement. "I'm going to beat you, and burn you, and I'm going to tie you up, and baby, when you pass out with the pain I'm going to screw you like you've never been screwed before. And then, only then, can you come back and work for me, and it'll be like a brand-new morning."

A big tear rolled down her cheek. She knew so badly what she wanted. She just had to be strong.

"Do I have permission to punish you?" snarled Johnny.

Lisa swallowed.

"Yes, Johnny," she murmured.

She closed her eyes. The tearing noise was her dress, as he ripped it from her. And there were other noises out there in the dark beyond her eyelids, as her tormentor prepared himself for the horrors to come.

57

Lisa Rodriguez came up slowly from the deep. She didn't want to. It was so peaceful down there in the cool and the quiet. The surface would be a bubbling caldron of hideous things, but still she rose toward it. And then she was conscious. The solid wall of pain smacked into her. It broke on impact, disintegrating into a thousand individual bricks of torture. The agony lanced into her brain, sharp and burning, dull and aching. It was everywhere, reverberating through her soul. She opened her eyes. The ceiling swam in and out of focus. She tried to turn her head, but her neck hurt. Oh, God, she was going to puke. She turned to her side and the vomit fountained out of her, her stomach contracting and relaxing, as it squeezed the sickness from her insides. She was cold and clammy with sweat . . . and naked, totally naked. Her torn dress and her ripped panties lay on the carpet beside the pool of puke.

Bit by bit the terror crept back. She tried to push the ghastly memories from her mind. She put a trembling hand to her face. The rope had been cut from her, but its marks remained on her wrists, livid welts of red, sore and inflamed from her struggle with the torturer.

She raised her head from the carpet. Where was he? She tried to say his name, but she couldn't say it. Her tongue was twice its normal size. Her lips were three times as thick. Her mouth was dry with caked blood. She managed to sit up. Ohhhh! The pain was alive between the cleavage of her buttocks where he had burned her. It danced across her beaten shoulders, and cavorted along her swollen arms. It hovered in her head behind her bloodshot eyes. There was only one thing she needed to know. Had he violated her? She reached down to the bruised lips of her vagina, sore and raw from his assault. Oh, yes, he had. Oh, God, he had. She put a finger inside herself. Yes, it was there. He'd done it. Johnny Rossetti had done what he loved more than anything else to do. He had made love to her unconscious body. It was the nearest he could get to doing it to a corpse.

Somehow she managed to stand up. She staggered to the mirror, and she held her breath as she looked at her once beautiful face. It was beaten badly, but apart from the lip there were no breaks in her skin. She felt her nose. It was straight, not broken. She pulled back her swollen lips. Her perfect teeth, caked with blood, were not chipped. She wiggled them one by one. They weren't loose. She felt the trickle down her inner thigh, and her stomach churned, but she didn't wipe it away. Tears of pain ran down her bruised cheeks. She pulled on the tattered panties and climbed into the savaged frock. She had to peer closely at her watch to make out the time. Her eyes wouldn't focus properly. She was dizzy, but she had to hold it together. She half fell down the stairs, holding on to the handrail, dragging her legs after her as if she was crippled. She made it across the marble hall toward the front door, walking with the exaggerated care of a person crossing a frozen lake. She laid her hand on the catch of the door. A wave of faintness welled up inside her. No! She mustn't faint now. Dear God, let her stay conscious. She asked nothing else. She took a deep breath, summoning up every ounce of her willpower. Then she pulled on the catch. The door swung open, and she stumbled through it onto 63rd Street. The street was deserted, but she knew where she was going.

The green awning of Le Bilboquet was only a few yards in front of her. She set her eyes on it, and she reached it. She could see the diners in there. It wasn't the fashionable, frivolous lunch crowd. It was the serious people, who came there in the evening. It didn't matter who they were. It only mattered that they *were* there.

She pushed hard on the door, and it swung open. She stood in the entrance for what seemed like an age. Slowly the hum of conversation faded. She saw a face here, a face there, of people interrupted in the middle of pleasure by a vision from the depths of hell.

She waited until the silence was total, the shock complete.

Then, slowly, she sank down to her knees. She held open her arms to the horrified restaurant, and she said in a still, small voice, "Help me, please help me . . . I've been raped."

58

The interview room of Rikers Island was a palace compared to the filthy cell that Johnny had just left, but still it wasn't much larger than the cubicles in which his models changed. He took a deep breath as he sat down at the metal table. Across from him was his attorney. Usually Johnny looked at the pencil pusher with all the enthusiasm he reserved for messes on carpets. Now he looked at him like he might at a rope if he were drowning.

"We can prove the bitch set me up . . ." he started.

But the lawyer held up his hand. He wanted to go first. Johnny petered out.

"Listen, Johnny, and listen good. You're going away. You're going down. I promise you're looking at twenty without parole. I went to Lenox Hill and talked to the trauma guy there, and the shrink. I've never seen doctors furious before. Cold fish, I always thought. But they were angry, Johnny. They were very, very angry. When they take the stand, they'll be spitting fire and brimstone. And the tabloids are going crazy. New York's big on Hispanics. I don't have to tell you that. And they don't have too many heroes, and they have less heroines. Lisa Rodriguez is one of them. Believe me when I say this, Johnny. You'll be safer in the can. On the streets, you'd be filleted. They keep you away from the other cons on a rape conviction, and you have cash to hire protection. You should get through without too many serious breakages."

Johnny swallowed. But even as he heard the discouraging words, he had the feeling that his lawyer was setting him up for something.

"But she had the motive. She was working for a rival agency. She . . ."

"Johnny, don't even think about it. No jury would believe a girl willingly consented to a beating like that. No sane person would. It was over the top. I mean, the burns on her butt! Jesus! DNA typing will say your semen was inside her. There's her blood in your bedroom. Frankly, I think you'll be lucky to get twenty." He paused. "But there *is* something going down, and I'm not sure what it is. I don't quite understand it."

"What's going down?"

Johnny grabbed with both hands at the lifeline. Twenty years minimum on Rikers Island among the people God forgot. Hell would be a luxury spa by comparison.

"I talked to the Rodriguez lawyer. He said he didn't really understand it either. Anyway, the bottom line is this. Rodriguez wanted to get a message to you."

"She did?" Johnny's heart was on hold.

"She said if you tell the whole truth on the Christa / Mona thing, and if you fully implicate Mary Whitney, Lisa may change her story. I don't know what she's talking about. Do you? Is that *the* Mary Whitney?"

Johnny's mind raced. The math was frighteningly simple. On one side stood twenty plus years. On the other stood . . . what?

"How much time would a man get for trying to frame someone on a drug-smuggling operation?"

The lawyer looked at him carefully. "I can't say. It would depend on the amount of drugs being smuggled . . ."

"One and a half million bucks!" Johnny barked the information.

"It would depend on the person's record. I mean, if it was a first offense, if he was an upright citizen . . ."

"Fuck it!" shouted Johnny. "Give me a ball-park figure."

"Maybe five, maybe seven, if . . ."

Johnny didn't think twice. He remembered Lisa Rodriguez's broken, beaten body on his carpet. He could visualize the "before" and "after" pictures in the crowded courtroom, see the joy in the eyes of the gutter press, the hatred in the eyes of the Hispanic spectators. Rikers was full of swarthy Spanish speakers with knives up their asses and time on their hands. They would sell his testicles for megabucks a few months before they cut the rest off. He'd end up pissing like a girl for the remainder of his life. There was no doubt in his mind about it.

"What do I have to do if I want to confess to a felony?" he said quickly.

Lisa's message was on constant replay in his mind. The whole truth on the Christa frame . . . and the full implication of Mary Whitney. Thank the Lord in his heaven he had secretly videotaped the billionaire bitch as she'd handed over the cash.

59

In the boardroom of her New York office, Mary Whitney stalked backward and forward across the carpet. The room was thick with attorneys.

"Listen, boys," she thundered. "I don't want questions. I want action. You all go away to wherever it is you do the things you do, and you dream up litigation that will drown Rodriguez and Kenwood and . . . and . . . Sand in a sea of paper, okay? Breach of contract. Conspiracy to induce others to break contractual obligations. Vast damages flowing from said breaches. Slander. I don't know. You name it."

She twirled around to the publicity people. "And you people put the word out to anybody that will listen that Rodriguez was scandalous, unprofessional, a drug abuser, a nymphomaniac, and that Kenwood was devious, incompetent, crooked, lazy . . . and that Sand was . . . Well, forget about him. Nobody knows him. Save your bile for the others, okay?"

They nodded collectively. They had learned from the attorneys that questions were not what Mary Whitney wanted.

The knock on the door was insistent.

"Come *in,*" Mary shouted.

The assistant hovered nervously in the doorway.

"I told you I wasn't to be disturbed," barked Mary.

"I know, Ms. Whitney, but there are two policemen downstairs."

"What on earth do they want? Have we had a robbery or something? I do think I ought to be told when somebody steals things."

The assistant was pale.

"They say they have a warrant for your arrest."

Mary Whitney smiled. But it wasn't a smile of amusement. It was a terrible, sickly, Cheshire cat event, a smile of total horror, plastered like yellow custard all over her face.

Her voice, when she spoke, was tiny.

"Oh, dear!" she said.

60

The sun lanced down through the fronds of the palm trees, casting deep shadows on the shimmering asphalt of Lummis Park as Peter and Christa walked hand in hand. To their right, the bright colors of the Art Deco buildings were bleached out in the heat haze. To their left, sand and sea melted together in a steamy mist of caramel blue.

"How is she?" said Peter.

"I spoke to Rob again this morning. He says she's going to be fine."

"No permanent damage."

"No permanent *physical* damage."

"She'll pull through psychologically. Lisa's as tough as you."

Peter smiled as he watched her and he squeezed Christa's hand to show it was a compliment.

" 'Fate worse than death' always sounded like a joke," said Christa. "Not now."

"And she did it on purpose. That's the amazing thing. It was planned. All that stuff in your office the other day—all faked so that if Johnny checked up, everybody would be saying she walked out in a fury. Can you believe that somebody would suffer so much for vengeance?"

"I sort of can . . . with Lisa. Do you remember her parents?"

"I'd rather not think about them!"

"Rob said Lisa did it to get at Mary. The whole thing was aimed at her. She hated Johnny, but he was incidental. She was furious about what Mary did to Rob, and what she tried to do. Of course, it gets me off the hook, too. And Lisa, I guess."

"Yes, Mary won't be bothering anyone ever again," said Peter grimly. "All the money in the world can't argue with a videotape. Can you imagine her in prison?"

"No, and I wonder if she'll ever go."

"Meaning? Suicide?"

"It wouldn't surprise me."

"Me neither."

"Oh, and guess what? Rob and Lisa are going to get married."

"I hope he's got life insurance."

"Oh, Peter, what a terrible thing to say!"

"I was just being pragmatic and businesslike!" He laughed. "From now on, I've got to learn to do that, haven't I?"

"Not unless you want me to turn into a head-in-the-clouds dreamer. And that would be a disaster. Did I tell you I signed another four Elle girls this morning? That's nearly sixteen in the last week. We're going to make a fortune. And you can relax at World, and go on in your own sweet, wonderful, brilliant way."

"Mmmmmm! I was going to talk to you about that. Is Heller really as awful as I think he is?"

Christa laughed, wagging a finger at him. "Oh, no you don't! No selling out. That's what I do."

"It would be rather nice to have a *mammoth* best seller . . . and all that money!"

"Let's talk about it when you've finished the book."

"Ah, finishing the book!" Peter winced in pain. *The Dream I Dreamed* was about the failure of life to live up to expectations. Before he had met Christa, that had seemed a terrific idea for a novel. It didn't now.

"I might have to scrap it," he said suddenly.

"Oh, Peter! Scrap it? You can't be serious."

"I might have to write a happy book."

"Why? You never write happy books."

"That's because I've never been happy until now."

"Oh, darling, what a wonderful thing to say."

"It's nice to experience, too."

"Hold me close and feel my tummy. Feel our baby."

He took her in his arms, looking down lovingly at her.

"Camille can hardly wait. She's decided on a brother."

"You know she calls me her number-two mommy."

"You don't mind that?"

"No way. Number two tried harder."

"I love you," he said, his voice lower, husky.

"Then kiss me, and prove it."

And so he did, and he always would, and, high in the sky, the Miami sun beat down on the backs of the lovers as they merged in the total joy of their moment.